Johnny Ringo

UNKNOWN DESTINY

Johnny Ringo

UNKNOWN DESTINY

Jason McCord

Cimarron Publishing Company

Published by
Cimarron Publishing Company
P.O. Box 4385
Topeka, Kansas 66604

www.ringobook.com

•

10 9 8 7 6 5 4 3 2 1

PRINTED IN THE UNITED STATES OF AMERICA

DEDICATION

This book is dedicated to my father.
I pray he is allowed to read in Heaven.

PREFACE

John Peters Ringo was born in Indiana on May 3, 1850, to Martin and Mary Ringo. Mary's maiden name was Peters. They moved to Liberty, Missouri and John lived there from age six to fourteen. He grew up in a time of violence and bloodshed. He was eleven years old when the Civil War broke out in 1861. The state of Missouri was aligned with the Confederacy of the South, and Kansas with the Union of the North. Liberty, Missouri was only a few miles from the Kansas border. In addition to regular troops there were the bloody guerilla warfare of Quantrell's Raiders from Missouri and the Jayhawkers from Kansas. Ringo's cousin, Cole Younger, rode with Quantrell and later with the Jesse James Gang.

In 1864 the Ringo family moved westward. Martin, his father, died on the way West. Mary Ringo and the five children settled in San Jose, California. Six years later in 1870 at the age of twenty, Johnny Ringo is believed to have ridden back to Liberty, Missouri. What exactly he did for the next several years is not well known. Johnson stated in his book there was a persistent tale that Ringo attended William Jewel College in Liberty, Missouri. He was known to have carried classical books in his saddlebags and was reported by many to be well educated. It is known that an E.V. Ringo was in a list of only twenty alumni that attended William Jewel prior to 1861.

It is believed that Ringo took part in several cattle drives from Texas to Kansas. In late 1874 he moved to Llano County, Texas where he bought a ranch. Llano County was adjacent to Mason County and the border between them became the focal point of the most famous range war in Texas. This part of Ringo's life was well chronicled, and that important part of Texas' history is summarized on the following pages. It was in this range war that Ringo's reputation with a gun first gained widespread notoriety.

The Mason County War: A Brief History

There had always been an abundance of cattle in Texas, but during the Civil War they multiplied and roamed at will. Because there were so many cattle and no market for them, they were nearly worthless. That changed when the railroad moved west and someone got the idea of driving cattle through Oklahoma to the Kansas railheads. Oklahoma was Indian Territory, but there was so much money to be made that cattlemen were willing to take the risk.

By the mid 1870s, cattle prices had risen substantially as a result of the drives. There was now a good market for cattle, and they had become an important possession. Texas grazing land was considered open range, which meant that any rancher could put cattle on the land. The use of different brands was intended to reflect ownership, but brands could be altered or simply ignored. In addition brand laws at the time were local, which meant that brands were unique only within a particular county. Problems also arose over who had first rights to the grazing land and waterholes. Some ranchers used fences to keep other men's cattle out. It was illegal, but the law at the time was often determined by the violent use of a gun. Small cattle ranchers were pitted against the big ranchers, and cattlemen in general against the sheepherders. Range Wars became common in Texas. The bitterest was the Mason County War, also known as the Hoo-Doo War.

With the cattle drives to Kansas greatly increasing the value of cattle, the citizens of Mason County decided to post notices that only local residents were allowed to herd cattle in Mason County. Since there were few fences and cattle didn't know where one county ended and another began, problems quickly developed. Cattle from neighboring counties strayed across the line. The posted notices, if followed, prevented residents of other counties from retrieving their own livestock. Predictably, ranchers from neighboring counties ignored the signs.

The problems escalated when Sheriff John Clark of Mason County got into a dispute with a rancher named Tim Williamson.

After the sheriff had insulted the rancher's wife, Williamson rode into town and challenged the sheriff to a gunfight. The sheriff refused, but was so humiliated by the challenge that he arranged to have his deputy and several other men arrest Williamson. The rancher was taken into custody, and was killed on the way back to town when he supposedly attempted to escape. The deed might have gone unchallenged, except that one of the men who participated made the mistake of telling someone about the murder of Williamson. The story was repeated to another, and then others. It was considered such an intolerable act that the story soon spread across the state.

A former Texas Ranger by the name of Scott Cooley was a close friend of Williamson's. When Cooley heard the story of Tim's murder, he went to Mason County. Scott Cooley, even though an ex-lawman, was a man who lived by the feud. He killed the deputy sheriff and another man, Carl Bader, who were directly involved in the murder of his friend Williamson. The sheriff of Mason County gathered up a posse and chased after Cooley. The Mason County War had begun.

Several months later the sheriff and several citizens of Mason County made what proved to be their biggest mistake. They killed a well-liked rancher named Moses Baird. The man who had been with Baird was wounded, but managed to escape and tell others about the shooting. Baird's death was significant because he was highly respected by many people, and they became so outraged at his murder that they joined the fray. One of the men in Llano County who had been good friends with Baird was known locally as John R. The name wasn't well known at the time, but the sheriff of Mason County had unwittingly brought into the battle one of the fastest men with a gun who ever lived.

Scott Cooley soon learned of Ringo's abilities with a six-shooter and befriended him. A war of revenge developed. Because of his speed and accuracy with a revolver, the name Ringo soon became known throughout Texas. Ringo was arrested by the Texas Rangers on a trumped-up charge that he threatened the sheriff. The accusation was false, but it effectively removed him from the range war and he spent several months in jail in Austin, Texas.

Eventually the war in Mason County ended. Scott Cooley had been killed, but Ringo survived. He was released from jail and the charges against him were dropped. Ringo made an effort to return to a normal life. In addition to owning a ranch, he ran for office as a lawman and was elected. Garnering two thirds of the vote was evidence of his popularity. Seemingly a magnet for trouble, a few months later Ringo was put into a quandary when the sheriff of another county illegally jailed two of the Olney brothers. A third brother, Joe Olney, was Ringo's best friend and had left Texas earlier in fear of reprisal from the sheriff. Arresting the two brothers was an apparent attempt to lure Joe back. Ringo had always been true to his friends and knew the incarceration of the two brothers was wrong. He decided he had little choice but to help. In December 1879, Johnny Ringo and Joe Olney broke the two brothers out of jail and, leaving Texas, headed west to Arizona. Little did Ringo know that even more trouble waited for him.

ONE

In the stillness of the flat and dry West Texas plains, a solitary rider headed east. A small cloud of dust drifted ahead each time a hoof struck the ground. The man on the horse was known across the country as the fastest pistolero since Wild Bill Hickock. Wild Bill died five years ago from a gunshot to the back of the head in Deadwood, South Dakota, while he was playing poker. The two pairs of Aces and Eights he was holding had become known as the "dead man's hand." Johnny Ringo read everything he could about Hickock's death. He didn't want to meet a similar fate.

Now in early April 1881, Ringo was thirty years old. He owned a ranch in Arizona, but was returning to Missouri to sell land he inherited when his father died. On the way he planned to visit an old friend near Austin, Texas. John Franklin was a wise man with vast experience. Years earlier, before Ringo had ever been to Texas, Franklin made him a proposition. He invited Ringo to go to the Lone Star State with him and make a fortune rounding up cattle and driving them north to Kansas. It took a lot of money to put together a cattle drive, but Franklin told Ringo he had the advantage of a wealthy father who would fund the undertaking. They had taken cattle to Kansas three times.

As Ringo came within a two-day ride of Franklin's ranch, he stopped his horse, took off his hat and wiped the sweat from his brow with his shirtsleeve. He turned and looked back at dark clouds over the western horizon. The scene reminded him of a dream he had three weeks earlier. In the dream he saw a dark figure walking in the shadows of the trees behind his cabin. Ringo dreamt that he was looking out the back window in the middle of the night. Suddenly, the figure stopped and turned toward him. At first Ringo was afraid and drew back from the window. When he looked again it was still there; it was a man wearing a long black coat. The gun at his hip could be seen in the moonlight. The man in the coat began walking toward the cabin. Ringo strained to see who it was, but it was dark and the man's hat shadowed his face. Just as the man's head moved into the light Ringo awoke in a cold sweat. He got out of bed and walked to the window but saw nothing in the trees.

The dream had haunted him for several days. Unsure of its meaning he had trouble sleeping. Believing it might have been a premonition he began to wonder if fate held a cruel ending for him. Four nights later, the dream returned. He woke drenched in sweat. This time it seemed he had seen the man's face, but no matter how hard he tried he couldn't remember who it was. Ringo wasn't sure why, but he took the dream as a sign that death awaited him if he ignored the warning. The next morning he decided to get away from Tombstone for awhile. A trip to Missouri to sell the land and a visit to Franklin on the way seemed like a good way to leave the problems behind. He arranged for his neighbor to look after his ranch while he was gone.

Ringo's horse stepped into a creek and cold water came halfway up his boots, bringing his thoughts to the present. Even though it was growing dark he recognized the surrounding area. San Angelo was only a few miles ahead. As he drew close to the outskirts of town he reined in his horse and wondered whether to proceed. He knew it might be wiser to move on and camp beneath a secluded tree. San Angelo was within a hundred miles of Mason County, and there was always the possibility one of his old enemies could be in town. Finally, he decided there wasn't much likelihood of trouble and nudged his horse down the main street of town. A few buildings were freshly painted; otherwise the place was as he remembered. He and

Scott Cooley had come here several times when men from Mason County were after them.

As Ringo pulled up to the hitching rail, he heard voices inside the saloon. Two men came out just as he dismounted. They walked by and seemed not to notice him. When Ringo stepped inside, a man who was talking glanced his way. The man suddenly became silent and stared at him. Before long others were also staring. In moments the saloon was quiet.

Ringo looked for a familiar face, but saw none. He walked up to the end of the bar near the door and nodded at the two men standing there. One was tall and skinny; he wore a brown sweat-stained hat. His skin was dark from too much sun and at the moment his face seemed frozen. He appeared ill at ease and did not respond to Ringo's nod. The other man was heavyset and balding. He had bushy eyebrows and a mustache tinged with gray. His face broke into a smile revealing a gold front tooth.

"Yur John Ringo, aintcha?" the heavyset man asked.

"Yeah, that's right. How you fellows doing?"

"Just fine."

"Yeah, just…real good…Mr. Ringo," added the skinny one nervously.

The bartender approached Ringo. "What can I get you?"

"Good whiskey." Turning to the two men he asked, "Can I buy you gentlemen a drink?"

"Well sure…you betcha," said the skinny man.

"Count me in," said the heavyset one, smiling. He couldn't wait to tell his folks that Ringo had bought him a drink.

The skinny man's name was Elijah; the heavyset one was called Clay. After they finished the first drink, Clay insisted on buying the next round. He and Elijah relished standing next to the legend with a gun. Others had heard of Ringo's arrival and wanted to see the man who had become famous during the Mason County War. Before long the saloon was packed. On the end where Ringo stood the bar was curved. Looking up he could see all the way to the other end. On a few occasions he glanced up. If someone made eye contact he made it a point to give him a slight nod. When he did it brought a quick nod in return, usually accompanied with a smile. Ringo found the conversation with the two men pleasurable and didn't notice the young cowboy trying to find a place at the bar.

The young man, named Jack Gibbon, had envisioned earlier in his mind how this would play out. He would stand at one end of the bar and Ringo at the other, and then he would turn and challenge him. But so many men had come in that they were shoulder to shoulder at the bar. When the young cowboy tried to ease between two men, they had turned and glared at him. Finally, he stood behind the men and turned toward the gunman. He said in a loud voice, "So you're Ringo."

The saloon fell silent. Ringo peered around Clay's head at the young cowboy. He had short, curly light brown hair and a round boyish face. He appeared to be no more than twenty and wore a single holster, which hung low on his hip. His stance, with feet apart and right hand near the holster, made it apparent that he intended to challenge the gunman.

"You know him?" Ringo quietly asked Clay and Elijah.

"Nope...sure don't," Elijah replied. Clay shook his head as they moved away. Others had already started moving aside. The bartender retreated to the other end. Soon Ringo was the lone man standing at the bar. He sipped his drink slowly, then put it down.

"I guess that's me alright."

"I've been looking for you," the young cowboy said more loudly than necessary.

Ringo took it as a clear sign the cowboy was nervous and probably hadn't done this before. Still standing at the bar he used his left hand to take another sip of whiskey. He cleared his throat. "What's your name?"

"Jack Gibbon," he replied loudly, trying to sound sure of himself. His eyes twitched rapidly back and forth, settling on no one in particular.

Ringo set the glass down and poured another drink. He took a sip. "What do you want with me, Jack Gibbon?"

A long period of silence followed. Someone coughed. The room was frozen.

"I want you to face me like a man," Gibbon blurted.

Ringo had hoped the cowboy would reconsider. He wanted him to say anything else, but now he had issued the challenge. Ringo couldn't help but think what John Franklin would say if he killed this boy almost as soon as he returned to Texas. He also wondered if he would be locked up for the night, a good possibility even if this were a fair fight. Because of his past reputation, the Texas Rangers might be called in and order him out of the Lone Star State. These thoughts rushed through Ringo's mind. He tried to think what he could say to discourage him. It was possible the young man was deadly fast with a gun. Just because he hadn't heard of him didn't mean he wasn't the next John Wesley Hardin. Not knowing the opponent made this type of confrontation dangerous. Ringo needed to size him up quickly. He turned from the bar and walked over in front of the young cowboy.

"Have you ever been in a gunfight, Jack?" Ringo asked in a normal tone of voice.

Several seconds passed. The young cowboy's eyes twitched. He glanced quickly toward the men watching. "No, but that don't mean nuthin."

At least his voice had calmed down, thought Ringo. "Then you haven't seen the look on a man's face when he sees blood spurting out of his own heart, and knows he only has a few seconds left to live," Ringo said gravely. He took a small step while he spoke, and now another as he continued. "You haven't seen his body crumble to the floor and watched as his piss mixes with his blood after he dies." He stepped closer. "You haven't seen the far off gaze in his eyes or the fear of death plastered on his face." Another step. "You haven't seen any of those things…have you, Jack?" Ringo now stood in front of the young cowboy, only a few feet away.

The young cowboy looked into blue eyes that seemed to peer right through him. Ringo stood three inches taller and his face showed no fear. The young cowboy wanted to turn and walk away, and probably would have if he were sober. Jack's thoughts went back to all the time he had spent practicing his draw, nearly every day for the last two months. He was far faster than anyone else at the ranch, and would never get another chance like this. Jack tried to swallow, but when he did it hurt because his mouth and throat were dry. There was a slight tremor in his right hand.

"Why don't you walk out while you're still breathing?" Ringo asked in an even voice.

The young cowboy's eyes blinked rapidly again as he considered leaving. Everyone would think him a coward. The other cowboys at the ranch would make fun of him, especially Kruger the foreman. The young cowboy made his decision; his hand moved quickly to his gun. When he felt the gun handle in his palm, his hand clasped around it. He felt the click of the hammer as his thumb brought it back to the cocked position. Jack's gun moved an inch and then stopped. In the flick of an eye he saw the barrel of Ringo's gun pointed at his heart, the tip of the barrel nearly touching his chest. Jack waited, his body frozen, expecting to see blood spurt from his heart just as the gunman had described. Seconds passed, and Jack's forehead developed beads of sweat as he stood looking at Ringo's gun, waiting for the explosion that didn't come. Finally, he looked up at Ringo. The eyes that had pierced him earlier seemed softer. Jack could see Ringo's lips move and knew he had said something. He had been waiting for death and his senses had shut down. Ringo spoke again in a sterner voice.

"I said holster the iron, boy."

It was only then that Jack realized he wasn't going to die. He looked at Ringo's gun, then at the gunman's face and finally at his own pistol. He nodded and let his gun fall back in the holster. His hands were shaking.

Ringo reached slowly with his left hand and took the young cowboy's gun, then turned toward the other men in the saloon. "Anybody here a friend of Jack's?"

There was no reaction at first, but finally a cowboy moved quietly from the back of the saloon. He was taller and a little older than Jack. When he stopped still ten feet away, Ringo motioned him closer with his revolver. Jack's friend gulped, and his Adam's apple moved noticeably up and then down his throat.

Ringo handed him Jack's gun and said, "It might be best if you fellows head on out of town."

The man nodded and put the gun in his belt. He looked at his friend and said, "Let's go."

Jack acted as though he hadn't heard. He was still looking at Ringo, his face white. Ringo met Jack's gaze and motioned with his head for him to follow his friend. Jack tried to form a smile to show his appreciation for what Ringo was doing, but the smile faltered.

Moments after Jack walked out the saloon door, the sound of someone vomiting could be heard by those inside.

Ringo wanted to leave, but thought it best to give Jack and his friend time to ride away. The gunman walked back to the bar and picked up the drink he had poured earlier. Ringo positioned himself so he could watch the door. He didn't think Jack would come back in, but there was always the possibility he might grab a gun and return. Shame a man before a crowd and he becomes unpredictable and dangerous.

The other men in the saloon started talking quietly. Clay and Elijah spoke with one another, trying to decide whether they should rejoin Ringo. As they conversed, they saw a man walk toward him. He wore a black shirt and black pants. They noticed his boots, holster, hat and even the handles of his guns were black. Others watched as he approached Ringo. Clay and Elijah wondered who he was and what he meant to do.

"How you doing, Ringo?"

"Bart! Damn...haven't seen you for a passel of years."

"About four. I see trouble still follows you around."

"Were you here earlier? I didn't see you."

"No, came in just after the boy called you out."

Not wanting to talk about it, Ringo asked, "You live around here?"

"No, mostly stay around San Antone, but go wherever the work is."

Bart Sanders was twenty-four years old. He stood just under six feet tall with dark hair and eyes. Most women thought him to be a good-looking man. He had a deep distinctive voice and spoke slowly. Bart had joined Ringo and Franklin on their second cattle drive to Kansas. On the way he and Ringo had practiced their draw together. The other drovers would watch them shoot at cans, bottles, rocks or whatever was handy. Sanders was fast. Ringo always beat him, but it was close. He had heard that Bart had since become a gun for hire. Ringo refused to do this; he had always thought of such gunmen as whores who lived on the blood of others. There were a few seconds of silence. Bart used the pause to tell the bartender to bring him a glass.

"What are you doing back in Texas?" Bart asked.

"Going to visit Franklin. You remember him?"

"Sure. Guess I haven't seen him for four years, either." After pouring himself a drink Bart added, "I was kinda surprised to see you take a chance like that, letting the boy live. He might back shoot ya later."

"Oh…maybe…but I don't think he'll do anything. To tell you the truth I'm getting tired of the killing."

"Know what ya mean."

"Do you?"

"What's that supposed to mean?" Bart asked.

"Heard you've been doing your share lately."

Sanders didn't like what Ringo said, but had no desire to confront this man. Bart had developed a reputation as the fastest gun in Texas, with the possible exception of Josh Steel, a Texas Ranger. Most thought he was faster than Steel, but Bart thought going against another fast gun was stupid. The odds both would be killed were too great, and this man with him at the bar was said to be the fastest of all. Bart changed the subject.

"You still around Tombstone? I heard that Dodge City lawman went down there, him and his buddy Holliday."

"Yeah, they're there alright."

"Have you had any trouble with Holliday?"

"We had a little set-to a while back. That damn Ike."

"Ike?"

"Ike Clanton, a friend of mine. One night when we were in Tombstone, Ike got into an argument with Doc. When Holliday started getting nasty, Ike says, 'Wayall, if ya wan some gunplay Doc, wah doncha talk to mah frien Ringo here.'" Ringo slurred the words the way his drunken friend had that night. He concluded, "I told Ike later if he ever pulled a stunt like that again I'd shoot him myself."

"So what did Doc do?"

"Oh, we just had a few words. Wyatt was there and said something funny, I guess to ease the tensions. Can't remember what it was he said. Anyway, everybody laughed and that was pretty much it."

"You and Holliday in the same town. That could be trouble."

"Suppose so. I don't go to Tombstone much. Bunch of my friends do. It's far enough from the ranch that I'd just as soon go to one of the small towns nearby. Doc can be a real wise ass. I don't like him much, or Wyatt either for that matter."

"I've never met 'em."

They talked for half an hour, discussing old times on the cattle drive. Once Bart brought up Scott Cooley and the Mason County War, but it was clear that Ringo didn't want to talk about it, and they moved on to other things. Finally, Ringo said goodbye. Sanders had kept the conversation going as long as he could. He already had a reputation, but he thought standing at the bar talking with Ringo like they were old friends would enhance it. Bart considered offering to walk out with Ringo just in case the young cowboy, Jack, was waiting somewhere to bushwhack him, but decided against it. He knew Ringo's reputation overshadowed his. If Ringo were killed, it would make the name Bart Sanders even better known.

Ringo rode in the dark several miles from town. He didn't want anyone to find him. Gunfights, even when no one was wounded, could result in hard feelings and retaliation. He camped near a stream in a grove of trees well off the trail. As he fixed something to eat on the open fire, he heard the call of a coyote in the distance. Otherwise it was quiet, and pitch dark beyond the glow around his fire. There was no moon overhead, just the stars above. He lay down and pulled a blanket over him. Soon he was asleep.

TWO

When Ringo woke the next morning, the first few rays of the sun were just beginning to illuminate the sky to the east. The crisp, cool air blew softly across his exposed face, his body reluctant to leave the warmth of the bedroll. Finally he got up, stretched and started a campfire for breakfast. As he saddled his horse he was thankful that soon his sore butt would have a respite. A few days of rest sounded pretty good to him.

Late in the afternoon two days later, Ringo rode up the lane to John Franklin's home. It was a large, expensive looking house with a covered porch on three sides. There was an attractive flower garden on the right. He tied his horse to the hitching rail, and swatted dust off his clothes with his hat as he walked up on the large porch. An attractive, petite young lady with long brown hair and grayish green eyes came to the door. There was a sprinkling of small freckles around her nose. She spoke to the visitor through the screen door as he drew close.

"May I help you?" she asked cautiously with a slight smile.

Ringo was surprised, not expecting to see such a lovely woman. Her hair seemed to shine even though not in the sun. The perfect shape of her nose and the curve of her full lips were intriguing. Ringo took off his hat and held it in both hands.

"Good afternoon, ma'am."

"Good afternoon. May I help you?" she repeated.

"Uh…yes…name is John Ringo, ma'am. I'm here to see John Franklin. He and I used to work together. We made some cattle drives to Kansas."

"Yes, I recognize the name. John has spoken of you often," she said, smiling warmly. She opened the screen door and came out on the porch. "I'm Lucy Franklin. John and I were married last year."

"Pleased to meet you, Mrs. Franklin." Ringo shook the proffered hand.

She motioned toward a bench on the porch. "Please have a seat and I'll get you some lemonade."

"Thank you, ma'am." Ringo sat down and while waiting looked out at the large barn and many outbuildings on the Franklin ranch.

"Here you are, Mr. Ringo," she said when she returned and handed him the glass.

"Thank you." After a drink of the cool refreshing liquid he remarked, "It appears your husband has done well."

"How's that?"

"He has a lovely home here, a nice ranch, and…well, he has a gracious and beautiful wife."

"Well, thank you. John said you were a charmer." She took a drink and then looked at her glass. The comment about her looks had made her uncomfortable. She wasn't quite sure what to say next and there was an awkward silence. Finally, she smiled and asked, "What brings you here, Mr. Ringo? Is it for business or pleasure?"

He sensed she was uncomfortable. "Actually I'm on my way to Missouri and thought I'd drop by. Haven't seen John for several years. I guess the answer to your question is it's just for pleasure."

"I'm sure he will be delighted to see you, but he won't be back until late tonight. You're welcome to take a look at the ranch until he gets here."

Ringo felt the uneasiness in her offer, possibly because her husband wasn't home or perhaps because she knew of his reputation with a gun. "I think I'll wait and let John show me the ranch. There are some things I need to take care of in Austin. Why don't I come back tomorrow?"

"Perhaps you could join us for lunch?"

11

"Sounds good. What time?"

"Noon."

"Until tomorrow then."

Ringo got back on his horse. He was taken with Franklin's wife, but remembered as he rode away that she was the wife of his friend.

He found a room in Austin and headed for the saloon across the street. When he stepped up on the sidewalk he could hear the piano inside. As he walked closer he picked up the strong scent of cigar and cigarette smoke. Ringo peered over the swinging doors and saw card games underway at two separate tables. The piano was to the far right and the bar to the left. A picture of a nude woman hung conspicuously over the bar. Ringo could see a number of men engaged in various conversations. He strode toward the bar. The saloon became less noisy, and then there was whispering as many heads turned. He didn't let it slow his walk across the room. Several of the men nodded and one said hello as they made a place for him at the bar.

"What'll you have, Mr. Ringo?" The bartender asked.

"Whiskey," Ringo said and looked around for someone he might know. An older man with long gray hair in the far corner looked familiar, but he couldn't remember who he was. As Ringo finished his first drink one of the four saloon girls walked up.

"My but aren't you a handsome feller! Do you wanna buy me a drink, cowboy?"

Ringo noticed she was the youngest of the four women, with long curls of red hair gathered at the back and reaching all the way to her shoulders. "Sure! What'll you have?" Ringo smiled.

She turned to the barkeep as he filled Ringo's glass. "Give me the usual, Fred." She turned and looked into the blue eyes of a man who stood a little over six feet tall. "So you're Johnny Ringo. I've heard you're really fast with those big guns of yours. But you know, nobody told me you were so good looking." She looked him up and down and then added, "Impressive!" The bartender left her drink on the bar. As she turned to get the glass she brushed her knee against Ringo's and gave him a coquettish smile.

After they had been talking for several minutes, she bent forward to put her drink on the bar near his. The top of her dress was cut low showing much of her bosom. As she reached forward she scrunched her shoulders together in such a way that the top of her dress gaped open, revealing to Ringo the entire right breast. She looked up to see his eyes studying the exposed flesh and asked invitingly, "Is there anything in particular you wanted to do while you're in town tonight?"

Ringo's pulse had increased upon seeing the hardened pink nipple on her soft white breast. She was facing directly toward him and moved closer briefly, letting the back of her left hand momentarily rest against the swelling flesh in his trousers. Her dress blocked the view of any curious eyes.

"Well, it has been a long, lonely ride."

"Bet I could help take care of your loneliness."

"Reckon you could at that."

She reached for her drink again using the same motion and allowing him to have another look at her breast. This time when she put the glass back on the bar she moved even closer and the palm of her left hand squeezed the now hardened appendage between his legs.

Fifteen minutes and several drinks later they were still conversing at the bar. While Ringo talked to the redhead, his mind occasionally flashed back to Lucy Franklin. He remembered her pretty face and long brown hair. Then he recalled seeing the redhead's breast and remembered the way she had touched him. The more he drank the more desirable she became, and the more he imagined the other woman, Lucy. After the redhead squeezed his throbbing flesh one more time, he invited her to his room across the street.

As soon as they were behind closed doors he started kissing her. She responded immediately, quite taken with his fame. He unbuttoned her dress and she took off his shirt. When they were both naked he picked her up, put her on the bed and made passionate love to her. Afterwards he lay on top of her breathing heavily. Both were drenched in sweat.

Ringo got up and poured himself a drink, and shortly thereafter poured yet another. As he drank he tried to forget about the face he visualized as he made love to the saloon girl. That woman was not his and never would be. Thinking of her in such a manner made him feel he had betrayed his friend. He vowed never to think about Franklin's wife that way again. After several more drinks his head seemed to spin. He lay back on the bed next to the redhead and before long the bed seemed to rotate. The girl rose up on one elbow and tried to kiss him on the lips. He turned his head away. Within minutes he dropped into a deep sleep, still naked.

Several hours later, loud laughter woke Ringo and he noticed the door to his room was slightly ajar. Sitting up in bed he realized the girl was gone. When he checked his pants he discovered his money was missing. Hearing voices in the hall and the word "dollars" mentioned, he got out of bed. Angered by the disappearance of his money, he grabbed his gun and headed for the door. Stepping into the hall with pistol in hand he saw three men standing nearby. One of the men was about to give some money to his friend. When the three turned, one of them recognized him from the saloon and said in a shocked voice, "Ringo." The three stood there wide-eyed. They had no idea he was staying in the same hotel.

Ringo's thoughts were blurred from liquor. "Which one of ya bastards has ma muny?" he asked, slurring his words. Several seconds passed as they stood with a look of fear and disbelief on their faces. "Well?" Ringo blurted out louder than before.

All three men were dressed in suits and didn't have the appearance of needing any money from a drunken stranger. Finally, the youngest of the three managed to say, "Mr. Ringo, sir, we didn't take your money. We've only been here a few minutes."

Even in a drunken state, Ringo could tell that the young man was speaking the truth. Again slurring his words he asked, "Did ya see a redhead leev here?"

They shook their heads, not saying another word. Just then a middle-aged couple turned the corner of the hallway. The woman was overweight and wore an excessive amount of makeup with bright red lipstick. The man accompanying her was thin and had a long protruding chin. Her eyes opened wide as she looked at Ringo. She didn't know who he was, but was shocked at the sight. Ringo was so drunk that all the while he stood in the hallway, he hadn't realized he was still naked. The man with her gave him a dirty look as they walked past. It finally dawned on Ringo that the woman had stared at his crotch nearly the entire time. Looking down he realized why and said, embarrassed, "Well, excuse me fellas, I...seem tuv fagotten ma pants."

He went back into his room and got dressed, planning to go after the redhead, but was soon lying on the bed fast asleep. An hour later Ringo didn't hear the constable knock on the door. The sound of the door being kicked in did wake him, but he couldn't recall being hauled off to jail. The next morning after he woke Ringo had a terrible headache. He recalled the night with the redhead and confronting the three men in the hallway, but had no recollection of how he came to be in jail. Ringo began to worry what else he might have done while he was drunk before they locked him up. Hopefully he hadn't shot anyone nor done anything that was a serious offense.

Before long the jailer brought him food, and when asked informed him that the three men had complained he threatened them at gunpoint. Ringo was relieved he hadn't done anything worse, but began to worry about not getting out in time to make it to the Franklins' for lunch. He thought of possible explanations, none of them truthful, to cover his absence. Ringo drank what remained of his coffee and rubbed his forehead. The jailer woke the man in the next cell and gave him a plate of food. His red hair looked as though it hadn't been combed in a week and his body odor attested to his dislike for bathing. The man looked to be well over six feet tall, and Ringo guessed his weight at over two hundred and fifty pounds. As Ringo glanced his way the man cleared his throat by forcing flem into his mouth, which he then spat on the floor.

"Damn you, Johnson!" yelled the jailer. "You do that again and I'll make you lick it up."

"You go to hell, mister. I'll spit wherever I damn well please, and if you don't like it you can just let me outta this pisshole."

"If you want anything else to eat today, you best mind your manners, Johnson. Any more trouble out of you and I'll get Big John."

"Aw, to hell with you. We don't need him back here."

"You give me any more trouble and that's who you'll be seeing."

With that Johnson became quiet, the conversation ended and the jailer walked away. Ringo wondered who Big John was, and why it calmed the man named Johnson down so quickly. Whoever this Big John was, Ringo decided he didn't want to make him mad.

With the jailer gone and the prisoners eating, it became quiet. Ringo's thoughts drifted back to the last time he was in this jail. He couldn't see the cell he was in then, but knew it was down the hall to the left and around the corner. He was locked up during the Mason County War for supposedly threatening a sheriff. The sheriff had asked for the help of the Texas Rangers, and they had brought him to Austin for fear his friends would break him out if he were jailed anywhere near his home county.

Ringo recalled when he met John Wesley Hardin who was also incarcerated at the jail. The two had a friendly conversation. He was well aware of Hardin's reputation as a gunslinger and killer. Later, Ringo realized he felt uncomfortable being associated with a man like Hardin. They both had reputations as gunmen, but Ringo had always thought of himself as a man others wanted to be around. Hardin seemed to enjoy killing. He was reported to have killed more than forty men. People were afraid of him. Ringo admitted to himself that when he was younger he might have wanted men to fear him. Now he knew he wanted people to both respect and like him. Meeting Hardin helped him realize the difference.

Spending those long months in jail, wondering what would become of him, was something Ringo did not want to repeat. It meant giving control of his life to other men. He particularly didn't like being locked up this time for something as stupid as getting drunk and causing a scene. What a scene he must have been. The jailer told him he had confronted the three men buck-naked. A smile broke out on his face as he remembered the fat woman walking by and staring at his jewels.

Suddenly it occurred to Ringo that he no longer had any money with him. He would have to send a telegram to his bank in Tombstone. It would be needed to pay the fine for last night's difficulty and for the rest of the trip to Missouri. Earlier in the morning he had hoped he could get out of jail before noon. It was now nearly eleven, and he figured there was little chance he would be having lunch at the Franklin ranch today. Even worse, he was fearful the judge would want to keep him locked up for several days. While he was staring at the floor, a familiar voice reached his ears.

"Well, Ringo I heard you were in town; in fact I guess the whole town has heard," said John Franklin, looking through the iron bars at his friend.

The jailer opened his cell. When Ringo looked at the jailer, surprised, he just motioned toward Franklin with his head. Ringo was embarrassed at having to be bailed out by the friend he came to visit. "Reckon I drank a little too much," remarked Ringo apologetically. Then he added, "A little redheaded hussy took all my money."

"Yes, I know," replied Franklin. "When I got here the sheriff already had it. It seems the saloon owner heard the story and found out what the girl did. He was so concerned you'd come back and shoot up the place that he went to her room, took the money from her and brought it to the sheriff. Here's two hundred and ninety dollars. The saloon owner said she claimed the rest was hers…for services rendered."

Ringo took the wad of money. He couldn't prevent the grin that erupted as he put the money in his pocket, remembering that part of the night. "Yep, she rendered service alright…gotta give her that."

John Franklin shook his head slowly, unsure how happy he should be that his friend had returned to see him. Ringo had many good qualities, but over the years it seemed as though he was often in trouble. Franklin was well aware of Ringo's reputation for being unpredictable when he drank too much. Finally he said with a chuckle, "Come on, let's get out of here."

On their way out they stopped at a door while the jailer unlocked it. In an office adjacent to the hall was the biggest man Ringo had ever seen. He was black and dressed in jailer's clothes. His shoulders looked like they belonged to an ox, and his arms were as big around as Ringo's legs.

"I've never seen so much muscle on two men put together, let alone all of it on one man," Ringo said quietly to Franklin.

"Me neither," Franklin replied.

Both men stood there and stared for several seconds. The jailer escorting them noticed their gaze and smiled at the two men's reactions.

17

"That's Big John," the jailer said.

The big man heard his name and it caused him to look up. He walked around the table and headed toward them. Big John had to bend down to walk through the open doorway. Looking at Ringo he asked, "Ya be John Ringo?"

It was the deepest voice Ringo had ever heard. There was no expression on the man's face. Ringo wasn't normally afraid of any man, but he was unarmed and didn't think he had a prayer with bare fists against this huge person. He felt a tremendous urge to turn around and run, but didn't.

"Uh…yeah," Ringo managed to utter.

"Wal sir, I wants to tell ya a story and see if ya member it."

"Okay," Ringo replied. His voice masked the apprehension he felt inside, wondering what this huge man was about to tell him.

"A black man named Samuel was gatherin wood for the fire. Three white men rode up an gave him trouble. Dey beat poor Samuel an likely would a kilt him, but another white man rode up an tol 'em to stop. When dey asked who be tellin 'em to stop, he tol 'em his name. He said…" The big man paused for a few seconds.

"John Ringo," added the gunman. "That was in Oklahoma, several years ago. John Franklin here and I were on a cattle drive. I was looking for strays."

"An ya gave Samuel a ride to his cabin on ya horse, whilst ya walked."

Ringo nodded. "He was busted up pretty bad."

"Samuel mussa tol me dat story a hunred times. He never knew iffin it was really John Ringo. We thought maybe it was jest someone usin ya name to scare dem fellas. I sho be proud to shake ya hand, Mr. Ringo."

Ringo held out his hand and watched as a huge black hand engulfed it. As the hand started to squeeze, he became concerned some bones might snap should the man decide to grip firmly. But it was a gentle handshake that Big John gave him, along with a genuine smile.

"Thanks ya, Mr. Ringo. Next time I see Samuel up in Oklahoma, I gonna tell him it sho nuff was ya, and dat I met ya and shook ya hand."

"I'm pleased to meet you, Big John. I didn't know his name, but I do recall Samuel. I'm glad I was there to help."

Big John nodded and smiled, and then turned and walked down the hall. After they were out of the building Franklin turned to Ringo and said, "That would be a good friend to have."

"Yeah, I reckon he would be. I'm just glad he's not my enemy; there for awhile I wasn't sure."

Franklin had already gotten Ringo's bay from the sheriff. The horse was saddled and ready to ride. As they headed out of town Ringo noticed that several men and a few women waved or called out to John Franklin. He could see in their faces that they respected this man.

While they rode toward the ranch, Franklin reflected on his friendship with Johnny Ringo. They had attended college together in Liberty, Missouri. There were few men of the time that went to college. Franklin was about to graduate at the end of Ringo's first year. He had heard from mutual friends that Ringo was restless and would not return in the fall. This didn't surprise Franklin because most of the students only went to college one year. He and Ringo had not been close friends, but Franklin had seen him demonstrating how fast and accurate he was with a gun. It was because of his capabilities with a six-shooter that Franklin had asked him to join his cattle venture. Over the next several years he grew quite fond of the now famous gunman.

After lunch, Franklin took him on a ride around his ranch. Ringo was impressed; it was a large and beautiful place with rolling green hills and ample water. That evening the three sat down to a meal of pot roast and carrots prepared by Lucy. After Ringo finished his second plate, he sat back in his chair and put both hands on his stomach.

"Ma'am, I haven't eaten anything quite so tasty in a long time."

"Can I get you some more roast or are you ready for dessert?"

"Oh I'm ready for dessert, ma'am. I don't want to make a pig out of myself."

"Too late for that," her husband replied.

"Yeah, well I don't get this kind of delicious food all the time like you do."

"Guess you need to find yourself a woman then. This one is taken, just in case you didn't know," Franklin said smiling as his wife left the table. He had noticed the visitor's admiration for her.

"Don't suppose she has a sister?" asked Ringo.

"Yes," Franklin chuckled and then said more softly while his wife was in the kitchen, "but she's bigger than a cow."

"John, you be nice!" Lucy overheard and shouted back.

Franklin grimaced, knowing he would pay for that comment many times over.

Laughing quietly to herself Lucy cut the apple pie she had baked earlier in the day. She had been afraid of Johnny Ringo at first, but had since found him to be a very affable man. It was easy for her to understand why her husband had befriended him. It was amazing to her that the man so many others feared was educated like her husband. He had told her Ringo was considered one of the brighter students.

As they ate dessert, Lucy looked at Ringo and asked, "Mr. Ringo, everyone has heard about your abilities with a pistol. Have you ever thought how odd it seems that a man of your reputation with a gun is a scholar?"

Ringo smiled, and thought about how to answer. He was sure his uncle, Edward Ringo, was disappointed in him. The businessman from St. Louis had studied law at William Jewel. Back when the family lived in Liberty, Edward had taken a liking to the then young John Ringo. He had promised the lad that if he wanted to go to college later he would help him. When Ringo was twenty he returned to Missouri and took his uncle up on the offer. These thoughts flashed through Ringo's mind in just a few seconds, and then he came up with an answer to Lucy's question. He had recalled another gunman who was educated.

"I guess it does seem a little strange, but I'm not the only one. You've heard of Doc Holliday; he has a better education than I do."

Ringo went on to tell Franklin and his wife about the confrontation he had with Holliday in the gambling house owned by the Earps in Tombstone. It was the time when Ike Clanton had gotten into an argument with Doc and then drawn Ringo into it. The two gunmen didn't know each other well, having met only one other time.

20

While they were sparring verbally, Ringo had been surprised when Doc had spoken a phrase in Latin. Ringo's amazement was nothing compared to the shock on Holliday's face when Ringo had answered in the same language. The Latin duel they had that day was the first time Holliday realized Ringo was an educated man.

Ringo continued, "Curly Bill Brocius was there and he told me later, 'You should have seen the look on those cowboys' faces when you and Doc started speaking some foreign tongue.' Hell...excuse the language, ma'am...most of those cowboys never made it past the fourth grade, and they're listening to us argue back and forth in Latin. Curly Bill said it was the funniest thing he had ever seen." Ringo explained to the Franklins that many of the ranchers tended to band together when problems arose, believing in the adage of strength in numbers. The group of ranchers that included Curly Bill, the Clantons, the McLaurys, himself and about fifty others were known in Arizona as the "Cowboys."

The gunman's laughter, his sparkling blue eyes and the picture he painted of the encounter with Doc Holliday intrigued Lucy. It amazed her that the two men with the reputation as the fastest guns in the territory were both educated. Lucy had brought up the fact Ringo was a gunman and a scholar in hopes of guiding him into a different line of endeavor. The story of Doc Holliday had taken the conversation in an unexpected direction. Lucy decided she would try again later to steer this man toward something less violent. It seemed to her that Ringo was too likeable and easy going to warrant the reputation that surrounded him.

That evening, after Lucy had gone to bed, Ringo told Franklin what had been happening recently in Arizona. He told him about the attempted robbery of a stage carrying a huge amount of money. It happened only a month ago and many in Tombstone believed Doc Holliday took part in the holdup. One of the robbers shot and killed the driver. As the driver's body fell it struck two of the horses pulling the stage, and the team bolted into a dead run. The shotgun guard managed to empty both barrels toward the robbers. A few miles down the road the stage came upon five cowboys headed for town, and the robbers broke off their chase.

Ringo finished up the story: "Because there were so many rumors Holliday was involved, a lot of people believe Wyatt might have planned it."

Franklin nodded. "The part about Wyatt seems to make sense. I heard about that attempted robbery and they say there was a large amount of money on the stage. With the Earps being lawmen, Wyatt had inside knowledge of when the stage was carrying that payload. Whoever decided to put all that loot on board didn't think any outlaws would come to know about it."

Ringo was surprised the news had traveled so far. He didn't know if Holliday was involved or not, but thought it a possibility. Ringo was quiet for awhile, and then shook his head and replied, "I have my doubts on Wyatt doing the planning. If it's true, how can you win? They've got everything in their favor."

"Maybe you need to think real seriously about going somewhere else, getting out of Arizona."

"I already had to leave Texas," Ringo replied dejectedly, remembering when he had to depart from the Lone Star State that he dearly loved. "Maybe you're right though; maybe it would be better to move on."

Franklin leaned forward to emphasize what he was about to say. "I would if I were you. In the meantime, stay out of any trouble with the Earps. They're lawmen, and you can't win going against the law."

Ringo nodded, recalling his long stay in the Austin jail.

"Hang on just a second, Ringo, I want to get us something."

John Franklin went into another room and came back holding a couple of cigars. He invited Ringo to join him out on the porch. Franklin explained that his wife didn't like for him to smoke in the house. They sat in chairs enjoying the cool night air. It was a peaceful night, and off in the distance they could hear a calf calling its mother. One of the horses in the corral whinnied and stomped its hoof several times. Franklin decided to use the break in conversation to ask Ringo something. Before Lucy retired for the evening, she had made a suggestion to her husband. She wanted to plant an idea solidly in Ringo's head.

"Have you found a woman you're interested in at all? You know, someone you might marry, have kids with and all that."

22

"Heck, I guess I haven't even thought about trying to settle down with a woman." Ringo was surprised by the question. He thought about it for a few seconds and added, "Here in Austin, things might seem pretty calm, but in Arizona it's a whole different story. We've got rustlers, Apache raids, and the Earps and Holliday in Tombstone. No man in his right mind would take a woman he loved into that mess."

Franklin nodded his head and smiled. He remained quiet, allowing time for the idea to sink in. Ringo enjoyed the flavor of the cigar and thought it must be expensive because he had never had one quite so good. He enjoyed the tranquility of the evening as they sat on the porch. A little later Franklin went into the house and retrieved two glasses of bourbon.

Ringo sipped his drink and smoked the expensive cigar, enjoying the quiet time with his old friend. The investments Franklin made with the money he earned on the cattle drives had allowed him to prosper. Ringo could tell the people of Austin respected Franklin for his accomplishments, but he knew there was more to it than that. He could see it in the way they spoke to Franklin. They, like he, admired him because he was an honest and honorable man. Ringo wished he could trade lives with Franklin.

"You've done very well," Ringo said suddenly, breaking the silence of the past several minutes. "You have a wonderful ranch, a lovely wife and the best cigars I ever did smoke."

Franklin smiled, pleased. "You could do the same, you know. A man just has to do some planning, saving, hard work...and then stick to it. What you need is a reason. That's why I asked about a woman earlier, and I don't mean some redheaded saloon girl."

Ringo couldn't help but chuckle. What Franklin had here seemed far removed from what he currently possessed or was likely to acquire anytime in the near future. "Maybe I do need to find a different spot to settle. Things happen around Tombstone that shouldn't, and then my friends expect me to be the one to do something about it."

"Because of your gun," replied Franklin. He realized the burden others placed on Ringo due to his reputation. Years earlier during the cattle drives he had seen other cowboys rely on Ringo to get them out

23

of messes they got themselves into, all because of his speed with a gun.

"I guess that's right. They do expect me to carry the lance, to be the one to settle things."

They sat on the porch for another half-hour, finishing their cigars and drinking bourbon. Ringo's head felt like it was spinning slightly from the liquor.

"I'd say it's about time to turn in," Franklin said.

Suddenly Ringo became very serious. "In case I never told you, you've always been a good friend."

"So have you," the rancher smiled.

"Even if it doesn't always seem like it, when you give me advice I hear it."

Franklin nodded and squeezed Ringo's shoulder slightly as they walked in the house. Ringo slept soundly that night.

Ringo said his good-byes two days later. When he left their house he rode the bay up to the highest hill overlooking the Franklin spread. From there he could see the whole place. To the right was a large herd of cattle, and behind them horses grazing in the pasture. It was a ranch to be proud of, and he couldn't help but envy his friend. As he sat on his horse he wondered if Franklin ever came up here just to admire what he had. "If it was mine I would," he thought out loud. Finally, he patted his bay on the neck, turned and headed toward Liberty, Missouri.

As he rode north he thought back to when Franklin asked him about finding a woman and settling down. Even Franklin's wife, Lucy, brought the subject up on the last day, stating that any man as good looking as he was ought to have a wife. Ringo was flattered by her remark, particularly because she was such a pretty woman and one any good man would want to marry. He had never considered getting married before, and still didn't think the time was right. First, he needed to get away from Tombstone where there was too much death and dying.

That night as he lay on his bedroll, his mind repeated the words they spoke. Deep within Ringo a void had been opened. He didn't quite understand it, but somehow his life now seemed incomplete.

Ringo's trip to Missouri was uneventful. The land sold for a fair price and he used part of the money to buy the finest horse he had ever seen, a big black stallion with a shiny coat and no marks of any other color. The muscles on his chest rippled when he walked. The owner and several others in Liberty claimed it was the fastest horse in the territory. Ringo raced against him on his bay and was amazed at the speed with which the black pulled away. The sound he remembered most was the thunder of the black horse's hooves as he stretched his lead to fifty yards in an incredibly short time. He decided to name him Thunder, a stallion to father many fine colts.

As Ringo rode back toward Tombstone on the bay, leading the black stallion, he realized he might have to move on to find what he sought. He recalled the beauty of the scene as he looked down at Franklin's place from atop the hill, and remembered Lucy's smile. Somewhere there was another ranch, and hopefully another woman like her for him.

THREE

In July 1881 Ringo arrived back at his ranch late in the afternoon. As he rode up to the house he could hear hammering. His neighbor, Jeff, was on the roof of the shed where the feed was stored. Jeff had his back to the house and hadn't realized the owner had returned. Ringo climbed off his horse and walked out to the shed.

"What are you doing up there, Jeff?"

Jeff looked down over the edge of the roof. "Fixing the roof. You just get back?"

"Yep. Had some wind, huh?"

"Yeah, three nights ago it blew something awful, tore a few boards off. A couple of sacks of grain got wet on top, but I think they'll be okay. I'm just nailing the old boards back down. Some of them are cracked; reckon it'll leak in a good rain."

"Well, I'll put on a new roof. It's been needing one anyway."

"The horses got out too. Near as I can tell lightning hit that old oak tree at the back. Must have spooked them, cause they busted out. I rounded them up and fixed the fence enough to keep them in. It don't look very good though."

"Much obliged. Sorry you had to go to so much trouble."

"Oh I don't mind. That's a hell of a horse you got there. Is he yours?"

"Yes sir. I'm right proud to say he is. Name is Thunder. He can sure run."

"I've got one more board to nail down, then I'll come take a look."

Jeff explained that until the rainstorm there hadn't been any problems. No livestock had been taken from any of the nearby ranches. After filling Ringo in on the other local news, Jeff offered to help put on the new roof. Ringo declined the offer knowing his neighbor had plenty to do at his own place. After Jeff left, Ringo went out and took a look at the roof of the shed and then the corral. The roof was a simple design. The boards were laid horizontally, with the board above lapping over the one beneath it. The fence around the corral would also have to be repaired. Where the horses broke out Jeff had put up a makeshift barrier of broken rails and fence posts at various angles. It was solid, but Ringo thought it made the place look like it belonged to a poor man. The following day he bought new lumber and spent two days putting on the new roof. He worked for the rest of the week mending the corral and making other needed repairs around the ranch.

The following Saturday night Ringo decided he deserved a little relaxation for all of his hard work. He went to the saloon in Galeyville, and joined three men playing poker. Two of the men were local ranchers. He knew them, although not well. The third was a businessman named Stacy Cullen. He sold leather goods and traveled a great deal. Cullen was short in stature, being under five and a half feet tall. The stranger was good at his business and equally talented at cards. His pile of winnings was the largest of the three.

Ringo sat down with a bottle and glass. He was good at cards and started winning initially, but he began to drink more than he should. Before long he started losing money, and within an hour he had lost everything he had gained. As the night wore on he continued to drink and lose money.

Ringo knew he should quit playing, but was determined to win back what he had lost. He drank even more and was soon too inebriated to think straight. After losing most of his cash he finally had a good hand, a full house with Queens high, and a chance to win much of his money back. Apparently the stranger also had a fair set of

27

cards because he continued to raise Ringo's bid. They went back and forth, each raising the other. If Ringo had been sober he would have called rather than raising, but he continued to raise. Cullen raised the bid higher than Ringo had money to cover.

"Thas more than I got here. I'll sign a note and call yur hand," Ringo said, slurring his words.

"Rules are table stakes. If you can't come up with the money you have to fold," the stranger replied.

The other two men were shocked at the response of the businessman. "John R is good for the money. I'll vouch for him," said Bob. He had heard Ringo was easy enough to get along with and was good for his word, but he was not a man to rile when he was drinking.

"Yeah, me too. Nothing wrong with John R's note," said Fred, emphasizing the name John R. He looked at the stranger with raised eyebrows and a facial expression that suggested he should reconsider.

The stranger would have none of it. "Well, that's not the way we play where I come from and we said up front it was table stakes. So if you don't have the money you're out of the game, mister."

"But John R wasn't here when we agreed to table stakes. He joined us later," Bob countered, almost in disbelief the stranger would treat Ringo this way.

"Doesn't matter," said the businessman, "it's still the rules."

Fred shook his head and said, "Well, it doesn't seem fair to me."

"Who asked you?" retorted the stranger impatiently. "Well, what's it gonna be, mister? Have you got the money or not?"

Ringo knew the stranger had him. It didn't matter that his cards might be better, if he didn't have the money to call the hand, the stranger had technically won the pot. Ringo fumed. No man had ever pulled this on him. Everybody knew he was good for the money. The stranger was using a rule to win that nobody ever observed in Galeyville. The blood vessels on Ringo's temple swelled noticeably, and the frown on his face would have caused most men to change their mind. He waited for one of the other two men to intervene in his behalf, but both sat silently. Ringo scowled at the short businessman, and thought about picking the little fellow up and throwing him out the door.

"So thas how it's gonna be, huh?" Ringo asked in an angry voice, slurring his words.

"Yep!" replied the stranger.

Seething with anger, Ringo threw his cards on the table and headed toward the door. When he walked by the table nearest the door he kicked the chair in his path and sent it flying to the corner, breaking one of the legs.

Bob spoke first after Ringo left. "You're a brave man, Mr. Cullen. I sure wouldn't have done that to John R."

"Why not? You guys keep calling him John R. Who the hell is he anyway?" the stranger asked as he pulled in the pile of money.

"You mean you don't know?" Fred asked, shaking his head and laughing a little.

"I guess not," Cullen replied.

Both of the other men looked at each other and started laughing. Finally, Fred said, "Bob, tell him that story about the mules so he'll know."

Bob nodded, and then waited a few seconds while the two men from the bar walked closer to better hear the story. "John R there, he was selling a couple of mules to Bill Hanks up north of here about thirty miles. When he signed the bill of sale, he just signed John R cause that's how everybody knows him." Bob stopped to laugh for a few seconds and then continued. "Well, that fellar is kind of a hermit, and he didn't know who John R was. Bill Hanks looks at the paper and asks, 'John R what?'"

At this point both Bob and Fred were laughing, having told and heard the story several times before. "So John R takes the paper, he was really pissed, and signs a last name. When ole Bill Hanks looks at it next time, it reads John R Godalmighty."

Bob and Fred laughed for nearly half a minute. The two men at the bar were laughing as well. The stranger sat perplexed, still not understanding what was so funny about it or who John R was. Finally, Bob explained to the stranger, anxious to see the reaction of the businessman. "Well, you see John R figures everybody in Arizona ought to know that John R stands for John Ringo."

Cullen's eyes went wide. "Holy shit! Do you mean *the* Johnny Ringo?"

"Yep!" Bob replied. He and Fred laughed all the more.

"Oh Lordy, why didn't somebody tell me that was Ringo?"

Bob and Fred were soon making loud guffaws. Bob laughed and slapped his leg and Fred finally fell out of his chair and onto the floor. Fred was saying as he fell, "Did you see his face when he heard the name Ringo?" It was difficult to make out some of the words Fred was saying because he was laughing so hard. The other two men in the saloon were laughing along with them. The stranger's face was pale as he sat and watched them laugh at his expense.

Twenty minutes later, Bob and Fred had long since laughed themselves out and were sitting back at the table. They were still talking to the stranger when Ringo, gun in hand, walked back in with a friend of his named Dave Estes. Ringo looked even drunker than before.

"This is the fella, Dave, the one I was a tellin ya bout." Ringo's breath reeked of alcohol. "Hands up, ya butt faced little shithead," Ringo said to the stranger. The words were slurred, but understandable. The fact that he was so drunk scared them all the more. "Ya asshole! Ya think I'm gonna let ya get away with wat ya did?" Ringo stuck the barrel of his gun right under Cullen's nose. "Now wat ya got to say, half pint?"

The stranger sat in his chair petrified; his eyes were cross-eyed looking at the gun barrel. He couldn't speak. After a few seconds a small puddle of yellow liquid began forming near the heel of his boot, and his pant leg was wet. Ringo gathered up the money he had lost, nearly five hundred dollars. He looked at the other two men, and was mad at both of them for not getting the stranger to take his note. Ringo cocked his pistol, aiming it at Bob's right ear, as though he was going to try and nick it with a bullet. Bob's eyes were open so wide they looked like they might pop out. Then he aimed the gun at Fred's boot. "Say goodbye to yur toe, Fred."

Fred's leg started twitching as he waited for the bullet, hoping it wouldn't leave him a cripple.

Ringo holstered his gun unfired, and then spoke, still slurring his words: "Ya boys let me down. Thought I cud count on ya. If I see any of ya agin tonight I'll put a bullet rite up yur asshole." He staggered to the door and left, followed by his friend Dave. After they were outside Dave winked at Ringo and said in a loud serious tone, "Let's put some rock salt in the shotguns and teach those boys a real lesson."

The stranger sat motionless in his chair, too frightened to move. Bob and Fred were afraid because they had heard Ringo was dangerous when he was drunk. They had no idea whether the shotguns were on the horses or they had to go somewhere and get them. When they heard Ringo and Dave ride away, all three men hurried out the back door and ran into the nearby woods. They ran through the trees until they came to an old shack. Cullen was in front and ran inside. Bob and Fred followed him. All three men were breathing heavily and trying to catch their breath. Still panting, Fred told them the little old cabin hadn't been used in years and not very many people knew about it. They decided to stay hidden in the little shack, not wanting to risk being found by Ringo and Dave.

After a sleepless night, Cullen talked Bob and Fred into signing a complaint with him. He insisted that Ringo would realize he was in the wrong after he sobered up. Bob and Fred were reluctant because of his reputation as a gunman, but didn't want to let him get away with threatening to shoot them the way he had. At first light, all three snuck back into town and went to the sheriff's office.

After Ringo and Dave had left the saloon the night before, they had ridden back to Ringo's ranch. They were so drunk they went to sleep within minutes after getting there. It was late the next morning when Ringo woke up with a terrible hangover. Seeing the money on the table he recalled what he and Dave had done. He tried unsuccessfully to wake Dave. Not wanting to get into any more trouble, he decided the best plan was to have Jeff return the money for him. He considered taking it back himself, but was embarrassed. He tried once more to wake Dave and then headed over to Jeff's place.

"Damn, he's not here," Ringo said out loud as he stood on Jeff's porch. No one answered the door and a quick check in the barn revealed Jeff's horse was gone. It was a little over ten miles to Joe Hill's place, but Ringo decided that was better than taking the money into Galeyville himself. After Joe listened to Ringo's story about the card game, he agreed to take the money to the stranger.

"Tell him I never intended to keep the money," Ringo told Joe. "Tell him I was just trying to teach him a lesson for not taking my damn note."

"I'll return it alright, but I ain't saying nothing about no lesson. That'll just piss him off." Joe shook his head as he turned his horse to leave.

"Whatever you think best," Ringo said. As Joe rode away Ringo yelled to him, "You woulda done the same thing if that little shit talked to you that way."

When Ringo got back to his ranch Dave was gone. The cabin was a mess. Dave had puked just inside the back door, and the smell was putrid. Because they had eaten beans last night, the vomit looked more like diarrhea. Seeing chunks of beans within the foul smelling liquid made Ringo nauseated, and nearly caused him to add his own dinner to the mess. He was still cleaning up the cabin when he heard a rider approach.

"John R, you at home?" someone asked outside the cabin. Ringo recognized the voice and looked out the window to see the sheriff. His name was Buster Woodruff and he was forty-six years old. Buster had a gut that hung well over his belt. He normally wore a gun but had none on today. The sheriff had decided earlier that if Ringo refused to come in right away, that was fine with him. He'd just ask him to come in sometime in the next couple of days.

Ringo walked out on the porch, still feeling the effects of the earlier hangover. "Afternoon, sheriff. What can I do for you?"

Buster stroked his chin with his right hand. He had two days growth of beard. "Well, John R, I'm sorry to say I got some complaints filed against you. Three men said you robbed them last night."

Ringo grimaced. "Oh shit. I didn't think they'd turn me in. I had Joe take the money back to them this morning. He's probably already given it to them."

Buster shook his head. "Well, I don't doubt you none, but you still have to come in. You can post bail and be out right away."

Ringo was mad, but only at himself. "Okay, let me get some clean clothes on. How much you think bail will be?"

"Oh, I reckon fifty dollars will do."

The sheriff took him in, and Ringo posted his bail and was back out the same day. The trial would come later unless the men dropped the charges. Ringo discovered later that all three were pretty mad about the matter. They had become the laughing stock of the area for hiding in the old shack all night. The other men at the saloon saw the puddle of urine under the table. When the story was told around town, people were saying that all three "peed" their pants and hid in the trees until morning. The stranger went on his way, but Bob and Fred were the butt of many jokes around Galeyville. At least for the time being they weren't very forgiving of the man that had caused them such shame.

After the problems associated with the card game in Galeyville, first Joe Hill and then later Jeff confided to Ringo that he could get real ugly when he was drunk. Joe had been his best friend for several years and reminded Ringo that he never drank that way when they were in Texas. Joe blamed Dave Estes, Curly Bill and Ike Clanton, all of whom drank too much, for the unwelcome change in his friend. Now Ringo had the weight of a trial to think about in addition to the other problems he was facing. His attorney told him there was a good chance Bob and Fred would drop the charges over time, and advised him to use a number of stalling tactics.

Ringo wondered whether John Franklin or his wife Lucy would hear about this latest escapade. He wasn't sure why it bothered him so much this time, but he truly wished it hadn't happened. Several nights later as he was eating supper at the table, he imagined the disappointment on Lucy's face if she were to hear of it. He felt a sense of shame for his actions and hoped the Franklins would never know. Later that evening, as he thought of his friend, and of Lucy, Ringo vowed to quit drinking to excess.

A few weeks later Jeff rode up to Ringo's cabin. He knocked on the door but there was no answer. Looking toward the corral he saw Ringo's new black horse, and then heard a gunshot coming from behind the barn. As he started walking in that direction he heard another shot. He knew from the sound that Ringo was practicing his draw. Having seen him practice only one other time, Jeff walked to the edge of the shed where he could watch.

There was an old wooden barrel behind the barn, and three small boards varying from four to six inches in height sitting atop the barrel. Jeff saw Ringo draw and shoot one of the boards. Even though he had seen him practice before, Jeff couldn't help but be amazed. He watched once again, trying to see Ringo's hand move, but the gun was suddenly out of the holster and exploded. Another board flew off the barrel. This time the board split down the middle and both pieces struck the back of the barn. A few seconds later he drew and shot the last board. Jeff's face reflected the awe he held for this man. Ringo began reloading his gun as he walked toward the visitor.

"Have you heard about Old Man Clanton?" Jeff asked.

Ringo shook his head and waited to hear.

"A bunch of Mexicans killed five men; Old Man Clanton was one of 'em," the young man said.

"Damn. How about Ike?"

"He wasn't with 'em."

"How'd it happen?"

Jeff told him that Old Man Clanton and five other men were helping Billy Lang drive a herd of cattle from his ranch to Tombstone. The seven men were just getting up. A large group of Mexicans opened fire without warning and killed five of the seven men. The other two managed to run and hide in the trees. Later they made their way to Henry Berry's place and told him about the killings. Henry spread the word and asked Jeff to come over to tell Ringo. Jeff concluded, "Johnny, we ought to go down there and make it right. Can't let them Mexicans get away with this."

Old Man Clanton and Billy Lang were friends of Ringo. He had bought land earlier with Old Man Clanton's son Ike. The plan had been to buy cattle in Mexico where they were cheap, fatten them on the tall grass in the San Simon Valley and then sell them to the Indian Agency and Fort Hood. It had worked well and they had earned a fair amount of money, but there had been a feud brewing between the ranchers and outlaws of the two countries.

Rustling and legitimate cattle buying were occurring on both sides of the border by both countries. The Mexicans rustled cattle in the United States, and the Americans in turn took some back from them. They were both in the right and the wrong. If it weren't for the

Mexican bandit, Brigido Reyes, rustling so many cattle north of the border, it was likely the ranchers would get along better with their neighbors to the south. Ringo knew they could put together fifty or sixty men and get retribution for the killing of the five men, but he also knew that if they did the United States Army would be waiting on them when they got back.

"Jeff, you know what'll happen if we do that. There'll be so many blue coats around here we won't be able to take a piss in the ditch without asking permission."

"You mean we're just going to let them get away with it?"

Ringo thought hard about how to answer, knowing Jeff would repeat it to others. "I guess what I'm saying is that sending a whole bunch of men down there isn't an option. The Army won't let us get away with it." After a pause he asked, "Do you know if they were Lang's cattle? He might have stolen the cattle from those Mexicans, you know."

Jeff shrugged his shoulders, but said nothing for the moment. He didn't know if the cattle were stolen; it didn't matter to him. The Mexicans had stolen their cattle too; if Lang stole them, he was just getting some back to replace the ones he had lost. Jeff was surprised and disappointed in Ringo. This was the man all his friends considered the leader of the "Cowboys." Ringo had always seemed fearless, but now he was hesitant. Jeff looked away and took a deep breath. He had hoped Ringo would come with him, and they would ride down with a large group of "Cowboys" and get even.

On the other hand, Jeff thought, Ringo was right about the Army. They had given a stern warning to all the ranchers on the border after the last group of men had gone down and shot up a Mexican town. The President of Mexico had complained to the President of the United States. That was the problem with living so near the border. Brigido Reyes could steal their cattle and disappear back into Mexico in a matter of minutes. If they went into Mexico after him, they would get in trouble with the Army.

Finally, Jeff replied, "It just isn't right to let them get away with killing our friends."

Ringo never got involved in stealing cattle back from a Mexican ranch, but he had gone down with the men on one occasion well over a year ago just to put a scare into Brigido Reyes. The Mexican bandit had heard of Johnny Ringo's reputation, and had sent a messenger a short time later letting Ringo know they would never take any livestock from his ranch. Ringo had never mentioned that to anyone and didn't plan to now.

"I agree, Jeff, but the Army is a problem. If we go down there, they'll be all over us."

"Yeah, I guess you're right. "

"You know it as well as I do. These killings were probably a payback for the Mexicans that were shot a while back."

"Still doesn't seem right to just let them get away with it."

"I reckon they felt the same way about us when a bunch of their people were killed," Ringo said. He shook his head and looked off toward the south.

"I was headed over to the Clantons. Are you coming?" the youngster asked. He felt dejected, but still respected Ringo tremendously.

"I'll be over a little later. Ike will take his father's death hard. Try to keep him from going down to Mexico until I can get there."

After Jeff rode off, Ringo reflected on the look that the youngster gave him when he said they shouldn't go to Mexico. The killing of Old Man Clanton saddened Ringo. He had liked the man, but wanted no part of having problems with the Army. Ringo decided that in the near future he needed to sell some of his cattle, and even some of the horses, so there would be less to steal. Even though Reyes had assured him he wouldn't take any of his livestock, there were other bandits. Ringo thought back to the advice of Franklin about leaving Arizona, and realized it no longer made sense to stay in ranching so close to the border. But to Ringo, leaving meant the abandonment of his friends.

Later he rode to the Clantons and spent time with Ike and the family. A lot of ranchers were there and more came; some of them were ready to head south on a killing spree. Others were concerned about what the Army would do and Ringo added his weight to their argument. The cooler heads prevailed and further bloodshed was avoided. Several weeks of quiet went by.

In the very next month trouble reemerged. It was September 1881; Ike Clanton rode up to Ringo's cabin. He was sitting on the porch replacing a bridle strap.

"There's been a stage robbery," Ike told Ringo.

"Another one? Do they know who did it?"

"The Earps have arrested Frank Stilwell and Pete Spence."

"For robbing a stage? Hell, they wouldn't do that," Ringo said, looking puzzled.

"I guess it was attempted robbery. Whoever it was didn't get the money. The Earps took in Stilwell and Spence. They're in jail right now," Ike replied.

Ringo was furious. The last thing he wanted to do was to get involved in a confrontation with the Earps. Up to now he hadn't, but the arrest of Stilwell could change that. Frank Stilwell was a deputy sheriff and a good friend of his. Tombstone had both a city marshal and a county sheriff. The sheriff, John Behan, was Democrat, and the city marshal was Republican. Rather than working together, the sheriff and city marshal were often at odds with each other. They were also aligned with opposing cultures. The city marshal and the Earps tended to side with the mine owners and businesses, and the sheriff with the ranchers. Frank Stilwell, whom the Earps had arrested, worked for Sheriff Behan.

"That's hard to believe," Ringo responded.

"They claim somebody told them Stilwell did it," Ike said, shaking his head, anger evident on his face.

"Oh hell, that's just bullshit!"

"That's what I said. What are we gonna do about it?"

Ringo was trying to figure out why they arrested Stilwell when he suddenly remembered that the election was coming up. If the Earps could defeat Behan in the election for sheriff, they would control both the city marshal and the sheriff's office. Ringo believed that would give the Earps too much control of Tombstone.

"They're just grandstanding," Ringo replied. "My guess is they're trying to embarrass Behan before election time. There will be a trial. If they don't have any proof they'll have to let him go. I'm with you, though; I don't like it much. Let's go to town and see if we can hurry up the legal process."

"We can pick up Curly Bill on the way," Ike added, glad that his friend was coming through for them. He knew the Earps were afraid of Ringo's ability with a gun. Even Holliday was careful when Ringo was in town.

By the time they got to Tombstone things were heating up between the Earps and Behan, and citizens were choosing sides. When Ringo, Curly Bill and Ike walked into the saloon, about a dozen men were arguing. Five of the men were part of the group of ranchers known as the "Cowboys." When the men who were arguing with the five "Cowboys" saw Ringo walk in they grew quiet. A man wearing a business suit appeared to be their spokesman. His name was Orville Finan and he owned the general store down the street. He looked up at Curly Bill and then Ringo, and nodded to each of them. He said something quietly to the other six men with him, and they all headed toward the door. A couple of the men nodded to Ringo as they left.

"How you doing, Johnny?" Tom McClaury asked.

"I'm doing okay," Ringo replied in a serious tone. "Where's Stilwell?"

"He's still in jail," Tom answered.

"Damn Earps don't have no business arresting him," Tom's brother Frank added.

"Well, I think they're doing it cause the election is coming up," Ike Clanton remarked as though he had come up with the idea.

Several of the ranchers nodded and Tom said, "Hell, I never thought about that."

Ike smiled confidently. "Well, I'll bet that's why Stilwell is in jail. The Earps want to embarrass Behan. Damned assholes can't win fair. They're trying to fix the election just like they fix their damn roulette wheel."

Tom McClaury turned to the bartender. "Give our man Ike here a drink on me." Turning back to Ike he said, "So that's what this is all about."

Orville Finan was a good friend of Wyatt Earp. After leaving the saloon he went to the city marshal's office to let Wyatt know Ringo was in town. Wyatt asked his brother Virgil to get the judge to let Stilwell out on bail. The jailed man was back on the street thirty minutes after Ringo rode in, and headed over to the saloon where his friends had gathered. Ringo was both pleased and relieved when Stilwell joined them. His release eased the stress for the moment, but the hard feelings the ranchers had toward the Earps had been re-ignited.

FOUR

The month of October 1881 brought more than its share of difficulties for the "Cowboys." There were still problems with Mexicans to the south and the Earps in Tombstone, but in October the Apaches came down from the reservation to raid in force. The Army had confined the Apaches to a small desolate reservation called San Carlos. It was an inhospitable location and little food could be grown on the land. The Indians on the reservation were starving. Many citizens claimed the Indian Agent at San Carlos, a political appointee, was shortchanging the Indians and pocketing the money.

During the next two weeks there were many raids by the Apaches, and a lot of nearby ranchers lost livestock. Ringo had been lucky, but some of his friends and neighbors weren't so fortunate. He stayed on his ranch and kept the cattle, and particularly the horses, close to the cabin. He knew it wouldn't be long before the Army rounded up the Indians and took them back to the reservation. In the meantime he kept a watchful eye.

The very next week the McLaury brothers lost nearly thirty horses to the Apaches. The two brothers were the sons of a respected lawyer back east. They had decided to go into ranching and had bought a place adjacent to the Clantons. Being neighbors and friends, the Clantons were helping the McLaurys gather their remaining livestock. Because of all the problems with the Mexican bandits and now this big loss to the Indians, the McLaurys decided to sell out and leave Arizona. Before heading for Tombstone to join their brothers, Billy Clanton and Frank McLaury rode over to Ringo's ranch. It was the twenty-fifth of October, 1881.

"Still got your horses, I see," Frank said as they rode up.

"Yeah, I heard about yours and decided to bring them up near the house," Ringo replied. "Jeff told me you're gonna sell out and head elsewhere."

"Just makes good sense to me, Johnny. We're going broke losin so many horses."

"The Army is saying they'll have the Apaches back on the reservation soon," remarked Ringo.

"What they say and what they do can be two different things," Frank fired back.

"Seems that way sometimes."

"We came by to see if you wanted to take yours in too."

"That might be the smart play alright, but I reckon I'll wait a couple of weeks," said Ringo. "The prices are down right now with so many ranchers selling. I think the Army will have the Apaches back at San Carlos before long."

"I already tried to tell Frank and Tom that, but they won't listen," Billy Clanton interjected.

"We've had it, Johnny. We're tired of the Mexicans and the Apaches stealin our stock. To hell with 'em, we're getting out. Sure you don't want to come with us?" Frank asked.

"No, I might regret it later, but I'll stay put for a couple of weeks. If the Army doesn't do something by then, I'll be right behind you. Why don't you come in and eat?" offered Ringo.

"Thanks, but we told Ike and Tom we'd meet them in Tombstone tomorrow," Frank said. "We need to get goin. Good luck to you, Johnny." Frank McLaury and Billy Clanton left Ringo's place and headed for Tombstone. They wouldn't get there until the next day.

Tom McLaury and Ike Clanton were already in Tombstone and had finalized the sale of the McLaury livestock. They were tired from rounding up the cattle and horses, and then driving them in. They were also angry, with the Indians, the Army, the Mexicans and the

Earps. Like the rest of the "Cowboys," the McLaurys and Clantons were good friends with Frank Stilwell.

Ike Clanton in particular was thoroughly fed up with the Earps and Holliday. Ike had a tendency to drink a lot and talk too much when he did drink. Both Ike Clanton and Tom McLaury drank more than they should that night. By late evening Ike was drunk and started bragging that he was going to kill Wyatt Earp and Doc Holliday.

The next morning, one of the men that overheard Ike's death threats told Wyatt and Doc about it. They each went separately looking for Ike. Doc Holliday found him thirty minutes later in the dining area of the Occidental Hotel. Several men were eating at a nearby table. Ike was eating alone and had almost finished his breakfast. Holliday walked slowly into the room and moved within ten feet of Ike.

"Well, if it isn't Mr. Ike Clanton. You know it really hurt my feelings, Ike, when I heard you've been telling people you were going to kill me. That makes me think you don't like me. It isn't true is it, Ike?" As Holliday spoke he moved the front edge of his jacket back behind his gun, and a smile revealed his teeth.

Ike wasn't armed, and at the moment was relieved because he was no match for Holliday. He said while looking at his plate, "Aw, I was drunk, Doc. I didn't mean any of that."

"Is that so? Well I'm glad, because if it wasn't I'd have to tell you what a low life cow kickin dumb ass I think you are." Doc's smile was gone, and his hand rested on the gun handle.

Ike couldn't help but glance at the other men in the saloon. Several were looking at him and a few had smirks on their faces. "I'm not carrying a gun, Doc."

"And if you were, Ike, what would you do if you had a gun?" Doc's voice was pleasant but mocking when he asked the question. Now his voice turned ugly: "You dumb son of a bitch cowboy. You're not brave enough to draw on a man who's facing you."

Ike's anger was evident as he got up from the table and walked to pay the cashier. A man standing nearby had a rifle in his hands and Ike thought for a second about grabbing for it. As he came close to the man with the rifle, he looked back at Holliday. Doc smiled and winked at him, then moved his hand away from his gun and shook it in feigned nervousness. Ike and everyone in the room knew Doc was tempting him to make a move for the weapon. A slight tremor developed in Ike's body because of his anger from the embarrassment, but he knew a grab for the rifle would be suicide. He paid the cashier and without another word headed for the door.

"Better be wearing a gun next time I see you," Doc said as Ike went through the door.

Ike could hear the laughter of the men inside. He looked down to see his hands shaking and decided he would kill Holliday at the first opportunity. No man was going to humiliate him like that and live.

Ike found Tom McLaury and told him what Doc had done. Tom listened, but he and his brother were about to leave Tombstone. The last thing he wanted was to be in a shootout with a gunslinger like Doc Holliday. He tried to cool Ike down, but didn't succeed. By late morning Ike had strapped on a gun and went out on the street alone. Virgil and Morgan Earp saw Ike carrying a weapon in violation of the city ordinance. Less than a minute later, they walked up behind Ike and hit him over the head with a pistol. Confiscating his weapon, they took him to the judge. The judge fined him and set him free, but before Ike was out of the courtroom Wyatt Earp walked in. He stood in the doorway blocking Ike's path. Wyatt's face showed anger and contempt.

Wyatt said quietly to Ike so the judge couldn't hear, "It's a good thing for you that it was my brothers and not me or Doc that caught up with you. You put on another gun today and you'll be a dead man. If I hear you been talkin about killin Doc or me again, you'll be a dead man. Do you get the drift?"

Ike had already been humiliated twice today, and was in no mood to be embarrassed by anyone else. He pointed his finger in Wyatt's face. "You best keep your friends close by, Earp."

Ike pushed past Wyatt, knowing the lawman couldn't do anything about it in the courtroom with the judge present. Wyatt was angered even further by the veiled threat, and followed Ike outside. There on the sidewalk he found Tom McLaury waiting for Ike.

Tom noticed the look on Wyatt's face and sneered at him. "You upset because you weren't the one that hit Ike over the head?"

Wyatt didn't say a word. He walked up to Tom, drew his gun and hit McLaury across the face with the barrel. The blow knocked him to the ground. Ike could hardly believe his eyes and took a step toward the lawman, but halted when Wyatt pointed the pistol at him and cocked the weapon.

"Best keep your friends close by," Wyatt said mockingly to Ike.

Ike helped Tom up and they walked away. Two men standing nearby hadn't heard what McLaury said to Wyatt, but knew what the lawman did wasn't legal. They reported the incident to Sheriff Behan. Minutes later Behan confronted Wyatt outside the city marshal's office.

"Got a complaint you hit Tom McLaury with your revolver," Behan said.

Wyatt shrugged his shoulders. "He was armed and refused to give up his gun."

"Tom and Ike said neither one of them had a weapon. There were two other witnesses there. Both of them said Tom and Ike weren't armed. They said you just up and hit Tom for smartin off to you."

Wyatt was looking across the street and nodded at someone. Finally he replied to Behan, "Well…they lied."

"If Tom was wearing a gun why didn't you arrest him?" Behan pursued. "Your brothers arrested Ike for wearing a gun. Why didn't you arrest Tom?"

Wyatt looked right at Behan. "Haven't you got something else to do, sheriff? Why don't you go catch some stage robbers?"

Behan knew Wyatt's comment was an attempt to provoke him. Suddenly, he heard footsteps from behind.

"Well, if it isn't our esteemed sheriff," said Doc Holliday. "What seems to be the problem?"

When Behan turned around and looked at Doc, he saw Virgil and Morgan Earp crossing the street toward them. The sheriff knew this situation could get ugly fast. He was unsure what Wyatt might do, but was particularly afraid of Holliday. Behan turned and walked away.

Later that day, approximately 2:00 PM on October 26, Billy Clanton and Frank McLaury rode into town. They had been on horseback since early morning, having left Ringo's ranch the day before. Orville Finan, the owner of the general store, looked through the store window and saw Billy and Frank. He watched as they met up with Ike and Tom at the vacant lot near the OK Corral. It was clear to Finan that the two pairs of brothers were angry about something. Ike was talking nonstop to the new arrivals. Finan couldn't hear what they were saying so he walked to the doorway of his store. He strained to pick up the nature of their conversation, but heard only the names Earp and Holliday. Finan decided to tell Wyatt about the four men. When he got to the city marshal's office, Wyatt and Doc were drinking coffee.

"I just saw Billy Clanton and Frank McLaury ride into town. They're talking to Ike and Tom down by the OK Corral," Orville told them.

"Did you hear what they were saying?" Wyatt asked.

"I heard Ike say your name and Doc's. Thought I should say something to you, Wyatt. Sam told me a little while ago that when Ike was eating he said he was gonna kill you and Doc."

"Today?" asked Holliday.

"Yeah, just a couple of hours ago."

"That's after you warned Ike at the courthouse," Doc said to Wyatt.

"Were Billy and Frank wearing guns?" Wyatt asked.

"Yeah, they just rode in."

"How about Ike and Tom?"

"No, at least I don't think so."

"Have you seen Ringo?" Doc asked Orville.

"Nope, don't think he's in town."

Wyatt started to say something, but thought better of it. "Thanks, Orville. Appreciate it."

He waited until after the businessman left, and then told Doc, "Go get Virgil and Morgan. We need to get down there while they're still wearing guns."

"You planning on taking their guns or shooting them?"

"I'm planning on trying to arrest them. If they go for their guns...well...then we won't have much choice."

Ike Clanton continued to tell Frank and Billy what happened. All four of them were mad about what Holliday and the Earps had done that morning to Ike and Tom. Ike said, "I say we round up a bunch of 'Cowboys' and kill the Earps and Holliday."

"We can't do that, Ike, they're the law," his brother Billy said.

"You should file a complaint against Wyatt," Frank McLaury told his brother, Tom.

"A lot of good that'll do," interjected Ike.

"We aren't gonna be here Frank. We're leaving...remember?" Tom McLaury reminded his brother.

"Yeah...I remember," Frank replied, "but what they did ain't right. They ought to be in jail."

"Jail, hell, I'm gonna kill both those assholes," Ike said.

Morgan, Virgil and Wyatt Earp, along with Doc Holliday, approached the vacant lot where the four men were talking. Their path would take them right in front of Bauer's Butcher Shop. Inside the butcher store, Martha King had just bought a roast. As she stepped to the door she noticed it was a sunny day and there was a stiff breeze from the west. She was about to step through the door when she saw four men approach rapidly on the sidewalk. As she looked at them the wind blew one of the men's coats open, and she saw that he carried a shotgun beneath the coat. Mrs. King recognized Doc Holliday. He quickly put his coat back over it. She waited in the doorway while they walked past. Mrs. King heard Holliday ask something but couldn't make out what he said. She did hear one of the men answer, "Let them have it," and then heard Holliday reply, "All right."

The Clantons and McLaurys were in the back of the lot and had not seen them coming. The three Earps and Doc Holliday came around the corner of the building next to the lot, seeing the two sets of brothers.

"You men are under arrest for carrying weapons," Virgil Earp said. "Now get your hands up."

The lawmen caught them completely by surprise. Ike looked at them in shock and disbelief. The four lawmen looked angry and had their hands on their weapons. Ike held the palms of both hands forward as the lawmen walked closer.

"We don't want no trouble," Ike said as he stepped in front of Wyatt.

"Time for talk is over," Wyatt replied. "He said get your hands up."

"But I don't have a gun," Ike said.

Wyatt drew his revolver and made a move to pistol whip Ike. Clanton saw what Wyatt was about to do and grabbed the lawman's arm when he swung the pistol at him. Doc Holliday, Virgil and Morgan watched the other men closely. Ike continued to grapple with Wyatt while everyone else stood tensely with hands on or close to their guns.

Sensing they weren't going to draw, Doc met the gaze of Frank McClaury and moved his lips in the form of a kiss. Frank made the mistake of going for his gun; Holliday was faster and shot him in the stomach with his revolver. Morgan Earp went for his gun when he saw Frank draw. Billy Clanton drew almost at the same time. Morgan shot Billy in the chest. Tom McLaury still held the reins of his horse and maneuvered the horse in between him and the Earps. Billy Clanton, even though wounded, managed to shoot Morgan Earp, wounding him.

Next, Doc Holliday pulled the double barrel shotgun out from under his long coat and fired one barrel in the air, scaring the horse Tom McLaury was hiding behind. Doc then shot Tom at point blank range with the second barrel, killing him.

Frank McLaury was wounded in the stomach, but was able to shoot Virgil Earp in the leg. Billy Clanton tried to shoot Virgil Earp but missed. Virgil was more accurate, shooting and killing Billy Clanton. Finally, Frank McLaury shot Holliday, wounding him in the hip, but then he was shot by Morgan Earp and killed. The shooting stopped.

Ike Clanton had not been hit. Wyatt Earp had also come out of the gunfight unscathed. Wyatt walked over to tend to his wounded brothers.

Ike was nearly in tears as he knelt beside his brother Billy. His dead brother's gun was lying in the dirt on the other side of his body. Realizing Morgan, Virgil and Doc were wounded, Ike thought about reaching for the weapon. He now wished he had knelt on the other side so he could more likely pick it up unnoticed. Wondering how many bullets were left in the gun, he tried to gauge his chances of killing the three Earps and Holliday. Nobody would blame him, he thought, not after what the Earps had done to his brother and the McClaurys. Or would they? Ike tried to think quickly. He could hang, but thought a jury would let him go free. Looking at the gun, he had almost decided to go for it, but first sneaked a look at the Earps. Wyatt had his back turned to him, and was talking to his brothers. Wyatt was between him and Virgil, so Virgil couldn't see him. Morgan was in pain and had his eyes closed.

Ike took a quick glance at Doc. He saw the gun in Doc's hand, and then saw that Holliday was looking at him. Doc winked. He had been waiting for Ike to go for the gun. Ike was livid and was about to go for the gun anyway, knowing Holliday would kill him. He hoped to at least be able to kill Doc. Suddenly a gust of wind blew dust into Ike's eyes. He hurriedly rubbed them, but by the time he could see again several citizens had arrived to help. Ike looked for Billy's gun, but it was no longer on the ground. One of the local citizens had picked it up and put it in Billy's holster. They were lifting Billy's body right in front of Ike. He had to decide in a split second whether to reach for the gun. The second slipped away, and Ike remained kneeling in the dirt.

Wyatt helped his brothers and Doc Holliday back to the office, and sent someone to get the doctor. Several citizens of Tombstone carried the bodies of the three dead men to the undertaker. Sheriff Behan heard what happened, and talked to a number of citizens who had witnessed the event. Later he talked to the participants. The Earps and Holliday claimed Tom McLaury was armed, but no one else supported that claim. A few townspeople told Behan that some of the lawmen already had their guns drawn, but others said they hadn't. Some said the Earps were just doing their job, but most thought it was akin to murder.

On the following day the sheriff found there was considerable anger in town toward the Earps and Holliday. Even those who were usually supportive of the Earps thought they had overstepped their authority. Many people knew that Ike Clanton had talked earlier of killing Wyatt and Doc. Most believed that was the reason for the gunfight. The bartender at the Alhambra, where the Earps hung out, had quietly told Behan, "There wouldn't have been a gunfight if Johnny Ringo had been in town. Wyatt is scared to death of Ringo."

Two days later Sheriff Behan and Ringo walked together with Ike Clanton while the wagon carried Ike's brother and the McLaurys to the graveyard. Afterwards when Behan had a moment with Ringo, he said quietly, "Well, if there was any doubt how the citizens of Tombstone feel about the McLaurys and Clantons, it's been erased here today. There must be nearly two thousand people come to see them buried. This is the largest funeral I ever heard of in this territory."

Ringo replied, "I wonder if that's why they came. You know, they might be here because they hate the Earps."

Behan nodded, but said nothing for awhile. He didn't want any retaliation. Knowing Wyatt's aggressive tendencies, he was concerned what might happen if any of the "Cowboys" took revenge for the deaths of the three men. Later he finally said, "You know, Johnny, Curly Bill was right though. He told me last night Ike was stupid to be talking about killing Wyatt and Doc. I'd never tell Ike this, but he got his brother and the McLaurys killed. I'm not saying the Earps and Holliday were justified, but it was just plain dumb to be talking like that."

"I know. I reckon all the 'Cowboys' know that except Ike."

During the first week after the funeral many in Tombstone suggested the Earps and Holliday ought to be lynched. Regardless of the talk, the town remained quiet. Finally, the time came for the four men to be brought to trial before Judge Wells Spicer. The judge was a business partner of City Marshal Williams and a friend of the Earps. After the testimony had been presented, the judge called for order and delivered his opinion.

Sheriff Behan's mouth dropped open when Judge Spicer ignored the evidence and dismissed all charges. Most in Tombstone believed the Earps and Holliday were clearly in the wrong, but it wasn't the first time they had seen Judge Spicer turn a blind eye to their misdeeds. After the trial Behan sought out Ringo. He found him outside on the street talking to Ike Clanton and Curly Bill Brocius. The three men grew quiet as the sheriff joined them. Ike glared at

Sheriff Behan; the anger on his face was obvious. Curly Bill looked away.

"That was kind of a surprise," Behan said, not knowing what else to say.

"Surprise isn't what I was thinking," said Ringo.

"Surprise my ass, we should've known that Spicer would let 'em off. We ought to kill that judge and the Earps too," Ike blurted.

"Dammit, Ike, it's that kind of talk that caused all this in the first place," Curly Bill said.

"They killed my brother; I'll say any damn thing I like."

Sheriff Behan had expected Ike to be the angriest. "All the same, Ike, you're going to cause a lot more problems if you don't quit that threatening talk."

"He's right, Ike. You keep it up and we'll find you dead somewhere," Ringo warned.

"So we're just going to let them get away with killing my brother and the McLaurys. I was their friend. Hell, all of you were their friends. Do we just let them get away with it? What the hell kinda men are we?" Ike said in frustration.

Curly Bill spoke next: "Dammit, Ike, why don't you call a town meeting and tell everybody. Don't you know Wyatt and Doc will shoot you down like a dog? If you're going to do something, do it, but don't go around announcing what you'd like to do. Get some sense into your head."

"You've got to quit shooting off your mouth, Ike," Ringo added.

Ike was seething. "Okay, I won't say it no more; I'll just shoot the bastards instead."

Sheriff Behan had heard enough. "Any of you men take revenge and I'll have to arrest you. This is a matter for the law."

After a few seconds of quiet Ringo responded, "The law isn't working so well around here."

"Johnny, keep your cool," Behan said softly. Then he added, "Why don't you fellas go back to your ranches? Stay out of Tombstone for awhile."

Staying out of Tombstone seemed like a good idea to Ringo. As he rode back to his ranch he recalled the night John Franklin told him to stay out of trouble with the law. It was good advice and he planned to take it, although the Earps had probably pushed the "Cowboys" too far in the killings near the OK Corral. Ringo thought sure there would be retaliation and soon. He decided he would not be a part of it and later told Ike he didn't want to know about any plans.

Each day Ringo thought of selling out and quitting, but each day he put it off. He struggled with the commitment he felt toward his friends. He wanted to leave Arizona, but didn't want the other ranchers to feel he had run out on them. Ringo also had a trial to worry about because of drinking too much that night in Galeyville. He wanted to get that resolved before he left, which meant he couldn't leave because his attorney had strongly advised him to wait. Ringo decided to turn his attention to the ranch and sell more cattle and horses.

FIVE

The calm of Tombstone changed drastically on the night of December 28, two months after the gunfight at the OK Corral. Virgil Earp was ambushed late at night on the streets of Tombstone. The bullet shattered the bone, crippling his left arm for life. Who committed the shooting was unknown. Morgan Earp investigated to narrow the list of suspects. He met Wyatt and Doc at the Alhambra. They went to a back room.

"What'd you find out about Ringo?" Wyatt asked.

"Both Carl Baker and Harold Doolin said they saw him in Galeyville buyin supplies around six," Morgan replied. "No way he could've been in Tombstone in time to shoot Virgil. It couldn't a been him."

"How about Ike?" Doc asked.

"Nobody seemed to know where he was that night. The blacksmith said he did see Ike and Curly Bill ride out the day before. They mighta done it."

"Anybody else?" Wyatt asked.

"Some thought Stilwell could've been in on it. They're just guessin. No way to know for sure."

"What are you plannin on doin, Wyatt?" Doc asked.

"Don't know yet. I was planning on running for sheriff. If Ike and Curly Bill suddenly end up dead, everybody will figure we did it."

"That's for sure," said Morgan.

In the weeks that followed Ringo stayed out of Tombstone. Some of the "Cowboys" dropped by his ranch and described the harassment they were receiving from the Earps and Holliday. Ike in particular had complained bitterly about Wyatt. In mid-January Ike and Curly Bill rode up to the cabin just as Ringo was sitting down to eat.

"You in there, Johnny?" Curly Bill called out.

Ringo walked out on the porch.

"Ya ought to shoot that damn Earp," Ike said angrily.

"What'd he do?"

"He told us that if we came into town again he was gonna shoot us and feed us to a couple of shit eatin dawgs," Ike replied.

"Wyatt ain't got no call to be talkin to us like that," Curly Bill added.

Ringo didn't respond right away. He glanced at their faces; both were red with anger. Reluctant to become involved in their controversy with Wyatt, Ringo finally replied, "Reckon he's pissed on account of Virgil getting shot."

"What's that got to do with us?" Ike fired back.

"Reckon he thinks you might have done it."

"Well, if I did I was jest gettin even for Billy. They killed Frank and Tom too. Have ya forgot about all that? Guess it don't matter none to ya. Guess it's okay if they call yur friends food for shit eatin dawgs. Hell, maybe yur just afraid of Wyatt."

Ringo met his gaze, but didn't respond.

"Come on, Ike, let's go," Curly Bill said.

"Thought we could count on ya," Ike said, and then they turned to ride away.

As the sound of their horses grew faint, Ringo walked back inside. His mind started replaying what was said as he sat down to eat. The look Ike and Curly Bill had given him flashed in his mind. He felt like he had let them down. Ringo stood up suddenly, lifting the edge of the table and sending it spinning end over end. He kicked the door as he walked through and sent it slamming against the outside wall of the cabin. Ringo walked to the corral and looked at his black stallion, Thunder. He visualized saddling up the horse and riding away. What would the "Cowboys" think if he just rode off?

Ringo walked back inside and strapped on his guns, and then went out behind the barn and practiced his draw. He tried to forget about the Earps. The gunman did what he did best, draw and fire, draw and fire. That night he didn't sleep well, and when he did the look on Ike and Curly Bill's faces came back again and again.

The next morning, angered by the abuse to his friends, Ringo ignored the advice of his good friend John Franklin. He saddled his bay and rode toward Tombstone to confront Wyatt. That night Ringo slept on the trail and was up before the sun to continue his journey. It was mid-morning on January 17 when he rode into Tombstone. It was less than a month after the wounding of Virgil Earp. As usual the Earps were at the Alhambra. Ringo walked in with both Colt 45s strapped on, clearly in violation of the gun ordinance.

Morgan Earp spoke first, pleasantly saying, "Johnny, you'll need to be checking in your guns if you're going to stay for awhile."

Ringo didn't speak right away; he turned and looked at the men in the saloon. There were three Earp brothers, Doc Holliday and a couple of townsmen he didn't know. Finally, he replied in a serious tone of voice, "I reckon I should, but I might need them here in a minute. You see, I'm real tired of having my friends ride clear over to my place to tell me how you boys have been giving them so much trouble. I know you're the law and all that, but I don't reckon that gives you the right to harass them the way you have. So I'm here to tell you it's got to stop."

"You threatening us, Ringo? Cause if you are we're going to have to lock you up," Wyatt replied.

"Well Wyatt, why don't you come over here and take my guns?" Ringo said, growing angrier, turning toward Wyatt and lowering his hands close to his holsters.

Ringo's reply caught Wyatt by surprise. He had no intention of going against Ringo. Morgan Earp interjected, "Now there's no call for gunplay, Johnny. We all know your reputation with a gun."

"I want you to stop harassing my friends," Ringo said in a voice that clearly indicated his intent.

"One of them bushwhacked Virgil in the dark like a cowardly snake," Wyatt said angrily.

"You don't know that it was a 'Cowboy.' I wonder if it was any more cowardly than using your badge to kill the McLaurys and Billy."

"They didn't have to go for their guns," Doc Holliday jumped in. "We were there to arrest them."

"You're no lawman, you don't arrest anybody. You were there to kill."

"Maybe someone ought to kill you," Holliday said, but made no move to get his hand closer to his gun.

"I'm here to settle things one way or the other, Doc."

"Now hold on. There's no call for any of this," Morgan said, holding up his hands and stepping in front of Ringo. "We know they were your friends, but they did go for their guns. We were just trying to arrest them."

"You were trying to arrest them because of Ike's talk, and I understand that. But I'm here about you harassing the 'Cowboys.' I don't know who shot Virgil, but I want you to lay off my friends."

Morgan looked at the gunman and saw he wasn't bluffing. He tried to calm him once again, "Ringo, we don't want any trouble with you. We know you didn't do it. Let it go at that."

"I want you to leave my friends alone. I'm here to make that happen." Ringo's anger had the best of him.

"Well, Mr. Pistolero, I'm game," Holliday suddenly offered.

Ringo hadn't figured on having to go against Holliday. He hadn't thought any of them would want to draw against him, but then he remembered Doc was dying of a lung sickness anyway. Ringo had played his hand and Holliday had called it. He felt he had no choice but to follow through. At this point it didn't matter; he wasn't afraid of death. Ringo responded as he turned toward Holliday, "You surprise me, Doc. I didn't figure you were brave enough to die."

Doc smiled. "Well, my educated friend…it's such a beautiful day. What do you say we go outside and enjoy it one last time?"

"Sure, why not?" Even as Ringo replied he was amazed. He always figured Doc for a man who would get into a gunfight only if he knew he would win. Doc seemed completely at ease and showed no signs of fear. Ringo showed the same confidence and started to turn to go out on the street. His back was to the door and he hadn't seen the two men standing outside. Just as he started to turn, Behan's deputies stepped quietly through the door and grabbed both of his arms. They took his weapons and escorted him to jail for disturbing the peace.

After the deputies had taken Ringo outside, Wyatt walked up close to Doc and said quietly so no one else would hear, "Wasn't that kinda risky?"

"No, Wyatt, I saw Behan's deputies through the window. They're his friends. They wouldn't let Ringo do something that would get him hanged," Holliday chuckled.

"There for a minute I thought you were gonna try him."

"I'm dying, but I still got some living to do. I don't know if I could take him or not, but I'm not real anxious to find out."

"Let's ease up on the 'Cowboys.' They can't keep him locked up forever."

Doc took a drink of whiskey. "Given any thought to his having an accident?" he asked and watched for Wyatt's reaction.

"Hell no. The 'Cowboys' would go crazy and kill us for sure. We're makin too much money. This silver isn't gonna last forever; we have to cash in on it while we can. Let's just give him a wide berth and ease up on his friends."

"Whatever you say, Wyatt." Doc finished his drink.

Once again Ringo found himself behind bars. It was something he had grown to hate. As he reflected on his actions it was hard not to second-guess himself. He had ignored Franklin's advice and was paying for his mistake. After several days in jail, Ringo decided he would not pull another stunt like challenging Wyatt. The "Cowboys" would have to fight their own battles.

Things remained quiet in Tombstone for the week Ringo was locked in jail. Behan and his deputies kept a close watch to make sure that no one tried to harm him while he was confined. At the end of the week, one of Behan's deputies let him go because the judge had given him a week for the offense. The deputy knew the judge had since extended it to two weeks at the behest of the Earps, but pretended he wasn't aware.

Wyatt was furious with Behan, figuring the sheriff was behind it. He had planned to talk to Ringo before he was let go and make sure there were no remaining animosities. Wyatt asked his brother to form a posse. Seven men volunteered and were led by a deputy. None of the Earps or Holliday went. Inside Tombstone the Earps were the law, but outside the city limits the "Cowboys" were a powerful force with many friends.

The posse headed toward the little town of Charleston, where they heard Ringo had gone. When the eight man posse went up to the only hotel in town to get something to eat, they were confronted by a large number of rifle barrels from behind a nearby adobe wall. A friend of Ringo's had alerted the residents of the posse's approach. After a brief negotiation with the men, the posse agreed to leave town. It was promised Ringo would return on his own. By the time the posse got back to Tombstone, Ringo had already given himself up to Behan and was back in jail.

It was a long week for Ringo. He particularly disliked the monotony of sitting in jail with nothing to do. Behan's deputies were friendly and played cards on occasion. The rest of the time Ringo contemplated what he would do next. Jeff had sent word that he was looking after his livestock. Ike and Curly Bill each stayed a few nights at his cabin to help look after his ranch. Even with the help he received from friends, leaving Arizona as Franklin had suggested seemed very appealing. Wyatt came to his cell at the end of the week, shortly before he was to be released.

"Morning, Ringo," the lawman said pleasantly.

"Wyatt."

"I want you to know we have no ill feeling toward you, and hope you don't have any against us. I understand you were angry and don't blame you a bit for that. Hope you understand why Doc and some of my brothers were upset...on account of Virgil getting crippled like he did."

"I don't know about you, Wyatt, but I'm tired of all this bloodshed. It would help if Doc and your brothers would lay off the 'Cowboys.'"

"I guarantee you I'll see what I can do," the lawman assured him.

Ringo nodded.

Ringo was let go within the hour and returned to his ranch. Jeff had taken Thunder to his place and tried to look after the rest of Ringo's livestock, but a few horses had been stolen in his absence. Ringo did his best to forget the situation in Tombstone. He felt like he had done what he could for his friends. Wyatt apparently was good for his word because the harassment of the "Cowboys" lessened considerably. Ike and Curly Bill both told Ringo later that things weren't as bad as they had been with the lawmen. Nevertheless, several of the "Cowboys" still held a considerable grudge against the Earps. In the weeks that followed Ringo sold nearly all of his livestock.

Two months after the confrontation with the Earps and Holliday, Ringo went to Tombstone to see his lawyer. He wanted to talk to him about selling his ranch. After the meeting, Ringo purchased some supplies and talked with several of his friends. He learned the bad blood many in Tombstone felt toward the Earps and Holiday had worsened. Later that night Ringo heard a rumor that something was planned against the Earps. While he had no love for the lawmen, he wanted nothing more to do with the feud against them. Early the next morning Ringo visited his attorney again.

"Briggs, Could I see you a minute?"

"Sure, John, come on in."

"This is pretty secret stuff."

"Okay, close the door. What gives?"

Ringo closed the door, pulled a chair close to Briggs' desk and then said softly, "Last night I heard...well I heard something might happen to the Earps."

"John, if you know something for certain, you ought to warn Wyatt."

"I don't know anything for certain. I don't know who; I don't know when or what. I didn't hear much, just that the Earps are about to pay."

"That's it?"

"That's it."

"What do you plan to do?"

"I was hoping you could suggest something."

The attorney leaned back in his chair, not sure what Ringo wanted from him. Finally, he asked, "What's your main objective here?"

"Well, it's kinda like you said earlier, I feel like I ought to warn them, but I don't know what to tell them. Hell, Briggs, what I really want to do is sell my ranch and go somewhere else. But like I told you yesterday, I don't want anybody to know that." After a few moments of silence he added, "I guess I don't want any more trouble with the law. I don't want Wyatt thinking I might try to get even. I just want to be left alone."

"Why not tell him that?"

"What?"

"That you don't want any more trouble and you just want to be left alone."

"How would I do that, Briggs?"

"I could tell him for you."

"Would you?"

"Sure, if you want me to."

"Do you think I should warn him about the…whatever is going to happen?"

"You don't know what is going to happen. What would you tell him?"

"Hell, I don't know."

"Let's give him the message that you don't want any more trouble. No, let's say you hold no grudge against him and you just want to be left alone. That way he'll know you want out of this feuding business."

Ringo thought about it for several seconds, then said, "Okay, you give him the message and tell him it's from me."

"I'll do it. Anything else, John?"

"No, sure hope that works."

Later that day, the attorney delivered the secret message to Wyatt. Ringo rode out of town and returned to his ranch. That very night Wyatt was watching his brother Morgan play pool with Bob Hatch. Suddenly two gunshots came through the glass panes in the door facing the alley. Morgan was shot in the back. A shot was fired at Wyatt, but missed by inches. Morgan died an hour later.

With Virgil's left arm crippled, Morgan being killed, and an attempt being made on his own life, Wyatt was enraged and swore revenge on the men he suspected were involved. He and Holliday met alone later that night in Doc's room.

"What now, Wyatt?"

"I mean to kill the yellow-livered assholes that did this."

"Thought you said you didn't see them."

"We know who they are. We know well enough. There was two of 'em that shot at us. I could hear them run out of the alley. Cliff at the livery said he saw three riders heading out of town hellbent right after the shots were fired. Cliff said one of them looked like Indian Charley. My guess is the others were Stilwell, Ike Clanton and Curly Bill."

"That's four. Didn't you say Cliff spotted three?"

"Don't matter none. They all need killin," Wyatt nearly snarled.

The depth of Wyatt's anger surprised Doc. After a short silence he said, "Well...don't matter none to me, but if we're gonna kill that many let's get rid of Barnes too."

"You think he might talk?"

"He might, and I don't like him anyway."

"Suits me, Doc. You know...Ringo sent that message. He could be part of this too."

"He damn sure didn't do the shooting."

"Why's that?"

"You're alive."

"Anybody can miss, Doc."

"Ringo wouldn't miss from that range. Even if he did, a second bullet woulda got you before you could spit. He wasn't one of the shooters, of that I'm certain."

"The message still means he knew."

"Probably, but shootin him won't be so easy."

"First let's get what's left of my brothers and their families on the train in Tucson. Then we'll come back and finish things."

"If anybody sees us we'll be on the run."

"We'll be careful. Besides, you got anything better to do?"

"Hell, I'm dying. Might as well take a few of them bastards with me for company. What about you, Wyatt? If we get caught they'll hang us."

"We won't get caught. We'll be careful. Virgil is crippled, Morgan is dead, and they damn near got me. I mean to get 'em, Doc, one way or the other."

On the evening of March 20, only three days later, most of the Earp clan climbed aboard the train in Tucson. Sherman Macmasters and Turkey Creek Johnston had gone to Tucson with the Earps. It was dark at the station, but Macmasters happened to spot Frank Stilwell in the shadows. Behan had sent him to see if Wyatt Earp and Doc Holliday were leaving with the rest of the Earps. Macmasters told Wyatt about seeing Stilwell. Wyatt was furious that the man he most suspected of shooting Morgan dared to be there. Wyatt and Doc walked toward Stilwell. Macmasters and Johnston followed them. Wyatt carried a shotgun and the other three had rifles. Stilwell was surprised by their approach, thinking he was well hidden.

"Well, Frank, you come all the way over here to see us off?" Wyatt asked, anger evident in his voice.

"No...a friend of mine got on the train. I...I come to see him off," Stilwell replied nervously.

"I think you're lyin," Wyatt nearly hissed at him. "Tell me, Frank, are you the one who shot Morgan or the one who missed me?"

"I don't know what you're talking about. I didn't shoot at nobody."

Wyatt pointed the shotgun at his chest. "Who was with you, Frank?"

"I told ya...I wasn't there."

Doc pointed his rifle at Stilwell, and then Macmasters and Johnston did the same.

"If you tell me who it was, I'll let you live," Wyatt pursued.

"I wasn't there, Wyatt...I swear I wasn't."

"Bad thing to swear just before you die. Last chance, Frank. Who did it?"

"I don't know."

Wyatt pulled the trigger, shooting him in the chest. Doc and the other two fired their rifles while he was still falling. Wyatt fired the second barrel of the shotgun into Stilwell's downed body, and then Doc added a second bullet from his rifle, hitting Stilwell in the heart.

"Is this what you meant by being careful, Wyatt?" Doc asked.

"Careful don't matter now. Let's ride."

Warren Earp, one of Wyatt's brothers, got off the train and joined them. The five men headed toward Tombstone. The next day Florentine Cruz, a Mexican, was found shot in the back with ten bullet holes. Wyatt and the other four riders had just been asking some men where they could find Indian Charley. They apparently killed the Mexican by mistake. The five men knew they would be charged with murder. Already in trouble with the law, they continued their ride of vengeance. Shortly thereafter, Wyatt shot and killed Curly Bill Brocius with a shotgun. John Barnes was killed a short time later.

Behan sent a deputy, Harry Woods, to Ringo's ranch. When he rode up to Ringo's cabin, Ringo, Ike Clanton and Jeff Sloan came out carrying rifles.

"See you're prepared," Woods said.

"Reckon we are," Ringo replied. "With Stilwell getting gunned down like that, we figure Wyatt doesn't care who he shoots."

"They killed Johnny Barnes."

"Why Barnes?" asked Ringo.

"Behan thinks Barnes was with the robbers that tried to hold up the stage a while back. Some say he was the only one still alive that could testify Holliday was with them."

"Makes sense," said Ringo.

"Got more bad news; Wyatt shot Curly Bill."

"Damn sonofabitch!" yelled Ike.

"Is he dead?" asked Ringo.

"Fraid so. Behan wants you and as many 'Cowboys' as we can get together to go after Earp and Holliday. Will you help us, Johnny?"

"Damn straight. Jeff, Ike, Let's round up the 'Cowboys.'"

With a huge posse of over fifty men on their trail, led by Sheriff John Behan and a deputized Johnny Ringo, Wyatt Earp and Doc Holliday fled to Colorado as fugitives.

A week later Ringo received a letter from his sister Fanny Jackson in San Jose. She and his other two sisters still lived in California where the family moved from Liberty, Missouri sixteen years earlier. They had become concerned when they read in the papers about all the killings in and around Tombstone. She invited her oldest brother for a visit hoping to lure him to California where she believed he would be safer. Ringo gave the visit serious consideration, but put it off, believing he needed to stay and decide what to do with the ranch. With Wyatt and Doc gone, he thought it would be safer now.

On Wednesday night, five days later, he dreamt again about the dark figure in the night. He thought about Fanny's invitation, but put it off once more thinking there was no reason to be afraid now.

That Friday Ringo went to Galeyville to get supplies. He was on the road returning to his ranch at night when he heard a gunshot. A bullet whistled close by his head. Ringo kicked his horse and sped away at full gallop, bending low over the horse's neck. He felt a shiver run down his back and anticipated the sound of another gunshot and the impact of a bullet at any moment. Ringo thought back to Franklin's advice to leave Arizona and wished he had taken it. The seconds went by slowly as the horse raced down the dark road. "If I live through this I'm leaving Arizona for sure," he mentally promised himself.

Ringo rode for a mile and then stopped his horse, dismounted and waited in a grove of trees with gun in hand. Even though it was night, there was enough light from the moon to see a rider approach. The sound of his heart was evident as he strained to hear or see any movement on the road. He hoped the attacker would come after him and waited for twenty minutes, but no one came. Ringo doubted that Wyatt or Doc would take the chance of returning, but thought they were the most likely to try to bushwhack him.

The near miss of the rifle bullet made him reflect again on Fanny's invitation and the dream about the dark figure. If he had gone when she invited him, or right after the dream, the near miss wouldn't have occurred. He decided to take her up on the visit. The trip west would allow him to see his sisters, whom he dearly loved, and give him time to plan his next move. He would let his neighbor, Jeff, know he would be gone for awhile.

SIX

The long ride to California gave Ringo time to think. He felt safer on the trail. Whoever wanted him dead had no idea how to find him. Only a few of his closest friends were aware he had sisters, and even they knew only that they lived somewhere in California. Information about his family was something he kept to himself; he wasn't sure why, but he did. As he rode, his mind returned to the question of who wanted to kill him. He also wondered why he had several times dreamt about the dark sinister looking figure. If the dream was a warning, who or what could be sending the message? He was the one having the dream. How could he send himself a message? Ringo knew that some people believed in visions. His mother had often said that she had dreamt of things that later happened. Was it possible then that he also had visions? Was the dream a vision or a warning?

It was a sunny April afternoon in 1882 when Ringo arrived in San Jose. He recalled that it was a year almost to the day since he visited the Franklins in Texas. As he climbed off the bay in front of Fanny Jackson's house, his sister came running out to greet him. She was followed by her husband of two years.

"John!" Fanny exclaimed, as she rushed into his arms. "Gosh, I've missed you."

"Missed you too, little sister. This good looking fellow over here must be Frank."

"It sure is. Honey, I'd like you to meet my brother, John."

"It's good to meet you," Frank said, as he shook hands with his infamous brother-in-law.

"Good to meet you, Frank," Ringo said. "Sorry I couldn't make it to your wedding."

"Oh, that's alright, Mr. Ringo. Sure heard a lot about you...from Fanny I mean."

There was an awkward moment of silence.

"Name is John. You don't want to believe everything Fanny tells you. She never did like me much."

"You know that's not true, big brother. Frank, would you let Mattie and Mary Enna know that John is here?"

"Sure. I guess I'll see you a little later, John."

Mattie and Mary Enna came over a short time later and Ringo spent a delightful afternoon and evening getting reacquainted with his sisters. It had been a long time since they had seen him and they talked well into the night. The three sisters were all curious about the stories they had read in the papers, but had not wanted to bring them up the first day he was back.

The next afternoon when the four of them were in the backyard drinking lemonade, Mattie finally mentioned the newspaper articles. Ringo did his best to explain the earlier problems in Mason County, Texas, and the more recent events in Tombstone. His sisters listened intently and nodded their heads politely as he spoke, but he sensed they were uncertain about his role. Ringo assured them the newspapers often overstated the facts and expanded events to get readers to buy papers. After discussing it for awhile longer, he changed the subject to more pleasant things, asking about their children. That night, after Ringo had gone to bed, the sisters talked about their brother.

"John isn't safe where he is now. I think we need to get him to move here and be with us in California," Fanny said.

"But can we get him to leave Arizona?" questioned Mary Enna.

"We can try. Don't you get the feeling he's sort of lost and not sure what to do?" Fanny asked.

"But what about the stories?" interjected Mattie. "The one article says he even robbed some people."

Fanny bristled, "Oh, I don't believe those stories. John might be a little reckless, but he is not a thief. And John is right you can't believe the newspapers, especially the ones in a place like Tombstone where they've struck silver. We all heard the stories when they found gold here in '49. Remember the claim jumping and killing? There were crooked sheriffs and corrupt politicians all over the place."

"That's true," replied Mary Enna.

"But there isn't just that one story, there's several," Mattie argued. "One paper said that when he was in Texas he threatened a sheriff and was in jail for a long time. Then there was the recent article that said he threatened some lawmen in Tombstone. He spent time in jail there too. We have children, Fanny. What kind of influence would he be for them? We haven't told our kids those stories and they haven't heard them. But, if he's living here, somebody will tell them. You know they will. What'll they think?"

"She's got a point, Fanny," Mary Enna said.

"Maybe we should just suggest he move somewhere else," Mattie offered.

"No, don't do that. He'll think we don't want him here," said Fanny.

"Does he even want to leave Arizona?" Mary Enna asked. "We might be arguing over something that won't happen anyway."

"That's a good question," said Fanny. "You know, I guess we haven't asked him. Maybe with all the killings there he's ready to move. I'll see if I can find out in the morning."

"I tell you the other thing he needs is a woman," Mary Enna said.

"I agree he needs a woman, but first we need to get him out of Arizona," Fanny stated. "He's a good looking man. It's hard to figure why he isn't already married."

"I can remember that John sure attracted the girls," Mary Enna added.

"Well he's good looking," said Mattie, "but I've got to tell you, with all those stories about him...I know several of my friends would be reluctant."

"You might be right," said Mary Enna.

66

"Maybe so," admitted Fanny, "but getting him out of Arizona comes first. Let's worry about a woman later."

"How are you gonna do that and not invite him to move to San Jose?" asked Mattie.

"I'll think of something," Fanny replied.

The three sisters went to bed and planned to get back together at noon. Ringo stayed at Fanny's house and was up before she was. He went out on the porch and sat on a bench attached to the ceiling with chains. He was swinging gently back and forth, and watching the neighbor kids playing across the street. It was quiet and peaceful. The calm reminded him of Franklin's place. After a while Fanny came out with coffee. They talked about things that happened when they were children, and the long trip in the covered wagon to California. Ringo was thoroughly enjoying the time alone with Fanny. He had always been closest to her when they were growing up.

"John, have you ever thought about leaving Arizona? With all the killing going on there we worry about you."

There was silence as Ringo tried to decide what to say. He looked at her and felt the love she had for him. He hadn't planned to say a word, but suddenly opened up to her.

"Actually I have decided to leave. Don't say anything to Mattie or Mary Enna, but just before I left someone took a shot at me. I probably shouldn't be telling you this. Don't want you to worry."

"I was already worried. Oh John, don't go back. You can stay here with me until you know what you want to do."

"I have to go back. I've got to sell the ranch. There's that thing that Mattie mentioned too, the charge against me. I've got to go back and get that cleared up."

"You mean the…"

"Yeah, the robbery," he sighed, regretfully.

"You really robbed somebody?"

"Oh, yes and no." Ringo looked at the floor of the porch and stopped talking. Fanny waited. "One night I drank too much and was losing money playing cards. I got mad at these fellas and sorta…stole it back."

"Sorta stole it?"

"I took it, but I was drunk. It was stupid. I had a friend take the money back the next day. Unfortunately, they had already turned me in. That's been around nine months ago. I haven't been drunk since."

"Good!"

"Anyway, I've got to go back and be tried for that, and I've got to sell the ranch. Then I can leave."

"Any chance you might go to jail?"

Ringo looked off into the distance for several seconds. "Yes…but my attorney thinks they'll drop the charges. That's why he wanted me to wait…to give them time to…to get over it."

"Think it'll work?"

"Well…the attorney does."

"Sure hope he's right."

"Not as much as I do."

Fanny smiled. "I'm glad you told me about all this. I won't say anything about your getting shot at, but can I tell them you're planning on leaving Arizona?"

"Yeah…why not?"

"Have you thought about where you would go?"

"Yeah…some…but I'm just not sure yet; not here though. I don't want to cause problems for you, Mattie and Mary Enna. Seems like wherever I go there's trouble."

"I'm willing to take that chance."

"I can't do that, Fanny. It wouldn't be fair to the three of you."

"Well, if you're not going to move here, then you have to promise to come and visit more often."

"I plan to." He was silent for awhile and then told her about his visit to the Franklins, and how much he admired what his friend had accomplished. He talked about riding up on the hill at Franklin's ranch and wanting a place like that. "His wife Lucy is quite a lovely lady. Sure would like to meet a woman like her someday. She reminded me of you."

Tears came to Fanny Jackson's eyes. He had talked about Franklin's wife as being quite pretty and wonderful to be around. His statement comparing her to Lucy touched Fanny. She was also delighted that her brother was thinking about a wife. Fanny took it as a sign he was finally settling down. She wanted to tell her sisters, but would wait until after he left. It was something personal he shared with her, and she didn't want one of them to ask him about it.

"I sure have missed you, John."

"I've missed you too, Fanny. Seems like I was always able to talk to you."

Mary Enna and Mattie came over at lunchtime. They were midway through the meal when suddenly Fanny said, "John is planning on leaving Arizona."

"Oh really…that's great," said Mary Enna. "When?"

"Well, maybe sooner than you think," he responded almost immediately.

"Where will you go?" Mattie asked, trying not to disclose her concern.

"Not sure…maybe Kansas. I'm still working on where."

After that the mood of his other two sisters changed dramatically for the better. The next day, the four of them left early in the morning for a buggy ride to the coast. Fanny had a friend, Clara Mason, who lived near the ocean. They would stay with her for the night. The three sisters took John to the beach for a picnic. Before eating, he and Fanny took a short stroll and watched the waves as they walked barefoot in the sand. They returned to where Mattie and Mary Enna waited to eat. Later, the four of them watched as a large ship with sails aloft moved slowly by. Right at sunset, the three large sails passed in front of the orange globe just as it touched the water. The colors of the sunset reflected off the waves. It was a beautiful sight and Ringo relished this moment of his life being there with the three women he most loved.

Ringo felt truly saddened five days later as he prepared to leave. He loved his sisters, but realized they were troubled because of what they had read in the papers. Ringo wished he could relive the past and remove the mistakes he had made. He didn't know it at the time, but this experience with his sisters would be the second step in a dramatic change in the direction of his life. The Franklins had provided the first step, although Ringo didn't realize any change within him had occurred. He felt saddened as he left his sisters, but took great joy in their long hugs and smiling faces as they said their good-byes.

As Ringo headed back east his thoughts went to the trial that awaited him in Tombstone. There was the option of not returning to Arizona and not risking the possibility of jail time. He decided it wasn't enough to be free—he wanted to clear his name and be rid of any trouble with the law. After crossing the rugged mountains of California, his horse trudged through Nevada.

Finally, in early May 1882, Ringo rode into Tombstone. The next morning there was an article in the <u>Tombstone Epitaph</u> announcing he was back in town. It went on to talk about the recent shootings by the Earps, and the part he played in running them out of the territory. He had hoped to come back without attracting much attention.

Ringo wasted no time asking his attorney to get a date set for his trial. He didn't want to wait any longer to clear up the matter. It was his penalty for having been drunk and acting on impulse. He hoped for the best. His friend Dave Estes had already been cleared of his part in the escapade. It seemed likely they would let him off, but nothing was certain.

The day finally arrived when Ringo would find out whether he would go to jail. It was May 18, 1882 and the courtroom was crowded, primarily with men whom Ringo considered friends. There were also some that detested him and hoped to see him convicted. Two of the men he had played cards with, Bob and Fred, were there. He avoided making eye contact with them, and looked down at the table in front of him.

His attorney presented the argument that Ringo had consumed too much whiskey that night, and was remorseful about what he had done. Briggs reminded everyone that Ringo had returned the money before he knew that anyone had filed charges. This was proof Ringo had no intention of keeping the money. Briggs also mentioned Ringo had not been drunk since that night. Finally, he reminded everyone that Ringo had bravely served as a deputy sheriff in pursuit of the Earps and Holliday after their killing spree. The attorney used all of his skills to convince the court that this was a good man who had learned his lesson.

Bob and Fred listened. After Briggs sat down, they talked quietly for a few seconds. Fred stood up and told the judge they had a change of heart. The trial concluded with all charges being dismissed. It was a tremendous relief for Ringo, and he thanked Bob and Fred. He told his attorney he appreciated the advice to wait and the persuasive presentation at the trial. Before leaving he walked over and thanked the judge, and then walked out into the sun a free man.

After he left the courtroom many of his friends congratulated him and took him over to the saloon for a drink to celebrate. He kept the number of drinks to a minimum. Late in the evening he headed back toward the hotel. It was dark on the street, and as he walked Ringo felt an uneasiness he couldn't explain. Perhaps it was the article in the paper. By publishing the news of his return, the Epitaph had unwittingly alerted the person who wanted to kill him.

Ringo had just passed the entrance of a saloon when he heard a voice call out his name from behind. He turned his head to see a man in the shadows headed toward him. Out of habit his hand drifted closer to his gun as he turned around. He recognized the voice, but couldn't place it. As the man approached, Ringo couldn't help but recall the dream. Finally the figure walked into the light spilling out from the window of a store.

Ringo couldn't believe his eyes at first; it was Charlie, whom he had known during the time he had spent at William Jewel. Charlie was someone he remembered because they resembled each other. Charlie wasn't as muscular, but he was lean and tall much like Ringo. Now as Charlie walked up, Ringo noticed he was dressed in a nice suit and wore a small derby on his head. Charlie removed his hat and offered his hand. Ringo noticed he looked a little older and his hair was thinning in front. They had not been close friends; in fact Ringo didn't know his last name.

"Well, I'll be! What are you doing in Tombstone?" Ringo asked as they shook hands.

Charlie returned Ringo's gaze, still amazed and in awe of the famous gunman. He had noticed him at school because he had been mistaken for him more than once. One night a beautiful girl with long black hair had come up to him and almost kissed him, mistaking him for this man. She had stepped back embarrassed and apologized.

Earlier in the day Charlie had wanted to attend Ringo's trial, but there was no room left in court. When he had seen this man exit with everybody congratulating him, Charlie realized his old classmate was a big part of the story he had traveled so far west to write about.

"Well, to tell you the truth I came out here a couple of weeks ago to write about the Earps, Clantons, Holliday and Ringo. When I heard that Ringo had returned for his trial, I started hoping I'd get a chance to talk to him. I had no idea you were Johnny Ringo."

Ringo had almost forgotten he hadn't used his real last name while at William Jewell. Many people in Liberty, Missouri knew the Ringos were related to the Youngers. Ringo's Aunt Augusta was married to the uncle of Cole Younger. Cole had become notorious riding with Quantrell and then later with the Jesse James gang. In 1863 Quantrell's Raiders looted and burned the nearby town of Lawrence, Kansas. Since Liberty was only a few miles from the Kansas border, a lot of nearby residents had hard feelings toward Quantrell and the Youngers. It was not uncommon for someone to be beaten or killed in revenge. It had seemed wiser to Ringo at the time to avoid that animosity.

"That's right, I used a different last name back then; I almost forgot. What was it, ten years ago?"

"Nine or ten. I graduated six years ago, then headed to St. Louis," Charlie replied.

"It seems like forever."

"You can't imagine how surprised I was when you walked out of the court room as Johnny Ringo."

"So, you're a writer?" Ringo asked, trying to change the subject.

"For the St. Louis Gazette. They sent me down here to see what I could find out about the gunfights. I've spent the last two weeks talking to people here in Tombstone, trying to piece it all together. Sure would appreciate it, John, if you could tell me what you know. I could probably get the paper to pay you for your story."

"I was planning on leaving town in a day or so. Guess we could talk some until then. I tell you what though, Charlie, I'm pretty tuckered out tonight. Could you wait until morning?"

"You bet I can," Charlie said grinning. He couldn't believe his luck.

"Good! I apologize, Charlie, but I'm kind of done in for the night. Do you want to meet somewhere for breakfast?"

"Sure. Where?"

"Why don't you come to my hotel, the Grand?"

"What time?"

"How about nine? I want to sleep for awhile."

"That would be great! Good night, John."

"Night, Charlie."

The next morning as they sat together at a table waiting for breakfast, Charlie couldn't get used to the idea that he was talking to Johnny Ringo. While a reporter in St. Louis, Charlie had no idea that the man he read and wrote about in the papers was the young man he knew at college.

Later that afternoon, Charlie wrote his notes trying to capture everything his friend had provided. As he reread his narrative he realized he was putting together the most complete documentation of the events that led up to the historic gunfight at the OK Corral. Late in the evening, Ringo let Charlie know he had to be getting back to his ranch and asked Charlie if he wanted to go with him. Charlie was ecstatic. It would take more time than the reporter had planned so he telegraphed the Gazette. By early morning the paper had given him permission to stay and pursue the story. Charlie met Ringo at the hotel for breakfast at the agreed time.

"Do you have your horse and pack ready?" Ringo asked as they ate.

"Horse and pack? I guess I hadn't thought about needing a horse. Uh, I guess I just wasn't thinking," Charlie said, looking embarrassed.

Ringo was surprised but didn't let it show. "I know a good place to get a horse if you want to buy one. A friend of mine has a ranch near Tombstone. He can probably get you a saddle too."

"Great."

"If you don't have a bedroll, we probably ought to get that here in town before we leave."

After breakfast Ringo helped his tenderfoot friend pick out what he would need. They left town riding double, and headed for Sam O'Malley's place. Ringo knew Charlie could get a fair deal from the rancher.

When they rode up to the house O'Malley came out on the porch. What was left of his hair was red and he spoke with an Irish accent.

"How ya be doin today, John Ringo, and who is this ya got with ya here?"

Ringo introduced Charlie and then asked Sam, "Have you got a horse my friend can buy?"

"Got sevrul. Depends on how much he wants to spend. Come on out back." There were at least a dozen horses in the corral, and Ringo noticed that three were too old to consider. After they had time to look at the horses Sam asked Charlie, "Do ya see any that interest ya?"

Charlie looked a bit perplexed and finally turned to Ringo. "What do you think, John?"

"Well, like Sam said it depends on how much you want to spend. If I were looking to buy a good horse I'd want to know about that appaloosa or maybe the palomino over there. How much for the gray appaloosa, Sam?"

"Ya sure know yur horses, John Ringo," Sam chuckled.

Charlie waited in anticipation for the price, but mainly waited to see if Ringo thought the amount sounded okay. He would sell the horse back to Sam when he returned and would be reimbursed by the Gazette for any difference in price. Within an hour he had a horse and saddle, and was ready to ride. Both Ringo and the Irishman agreed the appaloosa was a real beauty.

As they rode away from Sam's place Ringo continued to tell him about his ranch. Later he expanded on the problems they had recently with the Apaches. It was clear Ringo put much of the blame on the Indian Agent at San Carlos. They rode at a leisurely pace and talked much of the way. By the time they stopped to set up camp for the night, Ringo had filled the reporter in on all the recent events. Later, after they had eaten, Charlie noticed Ringo was gazing at the fire, not saying a thing. Finally he asked, "Is everything okay, John? You're being kind of quiet."

"Well Charlie, there is a little more danger out here. You can always get backshot in town, but people are careful because no one wants to get hanged for murder. Out here, a man could get killed and no one would know for days. Can't be sure either that we won't run into some renegade Apache on the way."

Charlie looked around and was struck by the complete darkness. He couldn't see further than the circle of light provided by the fire. Beyond the trees it was pitch black. For the first time he realized they could be sitting ducks to anyone hidden in the surrounding darkness. Suddenly a coyote howled in the distance and Charlie's right leg involuntarily jumped and kicked one of the sticks in the fire.

Ringo couldn't help but laugh, and then apologized to his friend. "I didn't mean to make you worry, Charlie, but a man has to remember the problems with the Mexicans and Apaches are real threats. We should be okay here; we're still pretty close to Tombstone. We'll stay with one of my friends on the way to the ranch. It'll be safer."

"I have to admit I'm not in the habit of sleeping without a roof over my head."

"This is probably a little different than St. Louis, I suspect."

"Sure is."

Ringo once again became serious and was quiet for awhile. Finally he added, "What worries me, Charlie, is that so many of the men in this feud with the Earps are dead. Many of them were my friends, the McLaurys, Billy Clanton, Frank Stilwell and Curly Bill. It's hard to believe that so many have died. The Earps have lost only Morgan, and Virgil got a crippled arm. I guess I worry whether Wyatt is through with his revenge. He and Doc are supposed to be hiding up in Colorado. They don't dare show their faces around here because they would be locked up and probably hanged. But, they might try to sneak down where I live and ambush me. I didn't do any of the ambushing on them, but they don't know that."

"Gosh, I guess I hadn't thought about it still being dangerous. In town one of the reporters said there had been more killings, but he didn't say anything about the Earps coming back."

"I really don't know whether Wyatt would take the chance or not. I haven't told anybody else around here this, but a couple of months ago someone took a shot at me. It was night, and I was riding back to the ranch."

"Holy Cow! Any idea who it was?"

"Not for sure. First person I thought of was Wyatt, and then Doc. You know, Charlie, it's hard not to think about death when so many have been killed. One of the reasons I went to California to see my sisters was to get away from this for awhile."

Ringo looked very serious as he continued staring at the fire. Finally he added, "There's one other thing. I haven't told anybody this. A little over a year ago I had a dream that there was a man in the trees behind my cabin. He was just walking around. I dreamt that I was watching him through the window when he turned and saw me. He started walking toward the cabin. I was just about to see his face when I woke up. I've had that dream several times now. The last time was just before someone took a shot at me."

"Damn. That would scare me shitless. Too bad you didn't see his face."

Ringo was quiet for awhile. "I'm not sure, but I might have seen it in one of the dreams. If I did I don't remember who it was."

"You don't remember?"

"No! I know that sounds odd, but I don't know what he looked like. Maybe I didn't see his face, but at the time it seemed like I did. I just don't know."

"Any idea who it might have been? You know…not based on the dream…but just who might…hold a grudge."

"No, not besides Wyatt and Doc. It seems to me like the dream is…a warning…that someone is trying to kill me."

Charlie was surprised, both to find out this man knew what fear was, after all the stories he had heard about him, and that he had opened up and told him.

"Why don't you leave, go someplace else?"

"Actually, Charlie, I've thought about that a lot lately. Fanny, my sister in California, she also suggested I leave Arizona."

"So why don't you?"

"I plan to. I've made that decision, but I'm not sure where to go or what to do. You saw the papers, Charlie; I ride into town and they write about it. Every now and then a youngster tries to make a name for himself by challenging me to a gunfight. Now somebody is trying to shoot me in the back. If I leave, wouldn't it just be the same thing in a different place? That's my predicament, Charlie. Where would I go that they wouldn't know Johnny Ringo?" Ringo turned his head and looked into the flames of the fire.

Charlie thought about what Ringo had said. "Why don't you change your name again, like you did at school?" he asked softly as the idea formed.

"Change my name?"

"Yeah...go someplace where people won't recognize you." Charlie's eyes sparkled with excitement, as his idea became more tangible. "Have you ever been to Utah? There are canyons there you wouldn't believe. I've seen them. I'm not lying, John. It's beautiful. Go to Utah; change your name. There aren't that many people up there. Lots of Mormons, but they tend to keep to themselves. That would help you keep your identity a secret. Still a lot of land available too."

Ringo's eyes returned to the dancing flames. He was silent for the longest time, contemplating what Charlie had said. First the Franklins and then his sisters had advised him to get out of Arizona. Leaving his identity behind was new. Finally, he turned to Charlie. "You really think it would work?"

Charlie was surprised Ringo might consider it, and suddenly felt like he could be instrumental in the life of his friend. After giving it a little more thought he responded, "It would if we could convince people you had died here. Hell, I'm a reporter. I could write about your death and get famous just because I was the one who reported it."

Charlie laughed a little but stopped when his friend didn't smile. Ringo turned again to look at the fire. There was a long period of silence. Charlie wasn't sure what Ringo was thinking. The silence between them started to become uncomfortable for the reporter. Finally he said, "I'm sorry, John, I didn't mean to laugh about your death like that."

When Charlie apologized, Ringo looked at him confused. Finally, he realized what Charlie meant and replied, "Oh no, Charlie, I was just deep in thought. I want to think about it some more. You might be on to something. Your being a reporter could be a big help. We'll talk tomorrow and think about how we might pull it off."

Charlie had a hard time trying to go to sleep that night. He thought about Indians sneaking up and scalping him, and coyotes lurking in the dark. Mostly he thought about Ringo, and tried to think

77

how they might fake his death. He entertained several possible scenarios, then dismissed them one by one. Finally, after hours of planning first one story, then the next, and hearing every little noise nearby, he drifted off to sleep.

The next morning Ringo didn't say a word about the discussion of the night before. He was quiet, very quiet. Charlie figured he was thinking the idea over and doing the same thing he was doing, trying to concoct a story that would convince everyone. As they were on the road and traveling again, Charlie tried to go over the possibilities.

By midday Ringo was more cheerful, much like he had been when Charlie had talked to him that first morning in Tombstone. They stopped to rest and eat in the shade of a tall oak tree. While munching on a biscuit, Ringo said, "You know, Charlie, it would be great to start over as someone else. I have enough money saved up and could do it. The big problem for me is that it would mean leaving all my friends behind, and maybe never seeing my sisters again. That's a lot to ride away from." After a brief pause he continued. "I guess it depends on how you look at it. If my gut feeling is right and the alternative is being shot, probably killed, then I wouldn't be giving up a thing. I'd just be getting a new start somewhere."

Charlie looked at his friend who was smiling some, but still in a serious mood. "I guess I hadn't thought about not being able to see your family again. You're right though, it would be best not to tell anyone. I've been trying to come up with a good story, a way to fool people into thinking you had died."

"Yeah, me too. Let's keep thinking it over and if you come up with something good, tell me, and I'll do the same. Surely between two bright fellows like us we can come up with something."

"Okay! You know I was thinking that you'd need to change the way you look. You could even wear spectacles like Doc Holliday does."

"But I see fine."

"So get some that are just glass. You could change the way you dress too, you know, more like I do."

"Then I'd get shot for looking like a dude," Ringo said, breaking into a laugh, trying to move the conversation to less serious matters.

Charlie smiled; he thought maybe he did need to consider changing his attire. There were enough men in Tombstone who dressed like he did that he didn't draw much notice. But he had to admit, out here he hadn't seen anybody else dressed in a suit or small hat. "I reckon I ought to buy some new clothes at the next town we come to."

"Well, let me pick them out," Ringo said jokingly.

On the way to his ranch, Ringo stopped at the home of John Yost in the southwestern part of Arizona. Yost had been a friend of Ringo's for a long time, even when they were in Texas. He and Charlie ate dinner with Yost and his family. Afterwards Ringo and Yost went outside alone and talked.

The next morning after a good breakfast of eggs, ham and coffee, Ringo and Charlie were back on the trail. While Charlie was getting outfitted with new clothes in a nearby town, Ringo spent some time with Jim Hughes and his young sister Mary. He had been teaching her to read and write. The little eleven-year old girl had a huge crush on him. She was enthralled with the beautiful ornate writing of her friend John Ringo. He departed their place realizing he would probably never see them again. As he rode he started thinking he would need to quietly put his affairs in order, but be sure not to do anything that would be noticed now or later. Ringo was glad he had already sold the land in Missouri and most of his livestock.

Finally, they reached Ringo's place. Since he had been gone for a few months, Ringo saw the cabin, barn and corral needed repair. Charlie helped him fix a leak in the roof of the cabin and then they started replacing several loose boards on the barn. As they worked they talked about various ways to pull off the deception.

"I shared the idea of faking my death with Yost," Ringo said.

"Do you think that was wise, John? The more that know, the more that can tell."

"Yeah, we can trust Yost. I saved his life when we were in Texas together. I trust him completely."

"I guess with two people claiming you had died it would be easier to get people to believe the story."

Ringo finished nailing a board onto the barn wall, then he replied, "We might want more than two. You see, Charlie, there are so many deaths in Arizona that a small group of people can serve as a coroner's jury. A few men can bury the body, and then go to town and testify to the coroner. They sign a piece of paper describing what they saw and who they buried. That's pretty much it. I have a lot of friends, and we could get several to vouch I was dead."

"But would they all keep quiet? One man tells somebody and then the secret is out."

Ringo thought about that for awhile. "Yeah, you're right, we better keep it limited."

A few minutes later the reporter came up with another idea. "You know, John, remember how you told me someone tried to shoot you? Maybe you ought to start telling other people that; get them thinking that somebody is out to kill you. It wouldn't be too hard to sell because it's true. If people are thinking someone is trying to kill you, it would make your death more believable."

"Good idea, Charlie." Ringo wiped the sweat off his brow with his shirtsleeve, and put the hammer back in the wooden toolbox. "This just might work."

When they ate supper that night, Charlie noticed Ringo was smiling more. He was cracking jokes and laughing. They talked about stunts some of the students had pulled while they were at college. This was the man Charlie remembered from school, carefree and happy.

In the weeks that followed, Charlie came up with a plan, and then they both worked on the details. Now they had to wait for the right time. While they waited, Ringo showed Charlie how to shoot a revolver. Charlie had already been proficient with a rifle, but firing a six-shooter was completely new to him. They practiced a little each day to pass the time. During one afternoon while they were shooting, Charlie came up with yet another piece of the plan.

"It might be a good idea if you went back to Tombstone just ahead of time. It would be a good place to have people see you while you pretend to get drunk. I heard you used to do that now and then. When a man drinks too much he's more likely to talk about things, like being afraid he might be killed. It makes it easier to swallow. If you weren't drunk, why would you be telling a bunch of people something personal like that?"

"Makes sense. In fact, that fits right into the plan. You're pretty good at this, Charlie."

During the next week Ringo quietly made arrangements for his belongings. The remaining horses and cattle were sold to Jeff Sloan. When Ringo went to Tombstone, he would check with his attorney to make certain that the money from the sale of the ranch would go to his three sisters in San Jose. Two weeks later the final piece of the plan fell into place. Ringo was ready to go to Tombstone. Charlie would stay and take care of the place while he was gone.

On his way to Tombstone, Ringo drove a wagon to John Yost's place well after dark. The bay was tied to the back of the wagon. After they ate dinner, Ringo had a long private discussion with Yost. The next morning before daybreak, Ringo got on his bay and continued his journey.

Once in Tombstone he started his charade of drinking. He talked about the possibility of being shot to several of his friends. For the next few days he drank every night and appeared drunk most of the time he was in town. A reporter overheard a man say that Ringo talked of dying. The reporter sought out the gunman that evening. Ringo knew he was a reporter and chose his words carefully; he said he was certain he would be killed, but that he didn't know when.

On the evening of July 12th Charlie arrived at Yost's home leading the black stallion. Yost and Charlie went over the details to make sure that they understood what they were supposed to do. Yost told Charlie he and Ringo decided there were two other men they could trust with the secret. When it was late, just before they turned in for the night, Charlie produced the bag of money Ringo had instructed him to give Yost. Ringo knew Yost would never take the money from him, but hoped he would take it from Charlie.

"I don't need no money to help John R. He saved my life."

"I know; he told me. He knew you would be reluctant to take it. But the other two men might need it even if you don't. It could help buy things for their families. Yours too. Ringo wants to help the men who are going to give him a new life. If you won't take it for yourself, take it for your families."

Yost shook his head and looked at the floor, but didn't reply. Charlie walked over to the corner of the cabin and set the money next to Yost's saddlebags, then went into the back room to sleep.

Early the next morning Charlie rode out toward the small canyon where Ringo said he would meet him. Charlie led the black stallion. According to the plan, Ringo would leave the bay he had been riding. The black stallion was not well known to others, and Ringo planned to ride him away at night after his death was staged. Charlie followed the directions Yost had given him, and before long saw Ringo sitting on his horse waiting under a tree. A smile broke out on Charlie's face as he approached Ringo. He felt proud to have a role in the shaping of this man's future.

"Run into any problems?" Ringo asked.

"Nope, things are all set. How about you?"

"Ran into a fellow I know named Billy Breakenridge—I just acted real drunk and offered him a drink of whiskey."

"Good! It'll help people believe the story later."

Ringo nodded, relieved their plan was about to happen, and at the same time, saddened he would never see his sisters or friends again. Charlie would catch up with him later and show him the places in Utah he had talked about so often. Ringo would repay him by giving him his story. Charlie planned to write about the life and death of Johnny Ringo.

The plan called for them to burn Ringo's cabin with a dead body inside. They would use the one Ringo had found just before going to Tombstone. Bandits had apparently killed the unidentified man near the Mexican border. His body had been left to rot. Ringo had brought the body to Yost's place under a tarp in the wagon. Yost had bought lots of ice and stored the body in a vacant cabin near his home. Now Yost and the others would use the wagon to haul the body back to Ringo's ranch, and set fire to Ringo's cabin that night. The bay would be tied to a tree outside. The three men, plus Charlie, would report that Ringo had been drunk and tipped over a lantern and burned with the cabin.

The story would be all the more believable because Ringo had been seen drinking by so many. Charlie thought it was a great plan. He had come up with it while they were putting a horseshoe on

Thunder. Then they had to wait to find a body that was near Ringo's size. They had gotten lucky in finding one so quickly.

Now everything was set. Ringo and Charlie would ride back to the vacant cabin where the body was stored. Yost and the other two men would meet them there. Ringo could say thanks and goodbye to the men who would free him from his reputation. He would stay at the vacant cabin until late that night, and then would be on his way. Charlie would catch up with him in St. George, Utah.

SEVEN

It was always hot during the summer in Arizona, but this mid-July day was a scorcher. Ringo and Charlie were on their way to the vacant cabin where Yost and the other two men waited. They traveled through a small canyon; Ringo was riding his bay and leading the black stallion. Charlie rode beside him, eager to have his plan carried out to fruition. As they rode, Charlie couldn't help but notice the unbearable heat. He had not yet acclimated to the hot climate. Occasionally there was a slight breeze, which felt cool when it blew across his sweat-laden skin. They talked while they rode.

"Well, you just wait," said Charlie. "There's some mighty pretty women in Utah."

"I don't think I'm quite ready to worry about women just yet."

"I'll bet within two weeks after we get up there, you'll be worrying about them alright."

Ringo chuckled. "Maybe so."

The black stallion tugged on the reins and Ringo turned to look back at him. As he turned he saw movement up in the rocks behind them. There was a man with a rifle aimed right at him. Ringo reacted without thinking. Two shots rang out. Pain tore through Ringo's left shoulder as he fell from the saddle. His head hit the ground and the blow knocked him unconscious.

Charlie had been shocked when Ringo suddenly drew and fired. He turned and saw that Ringo had wounded a man still holding a rifle. Charlie pulled his revolver and shot at the man in the rocks. The attacker now had two wounds, but still stood with gun in hand. A second shot from Charlie's gun downed the man, and then Charlie got off his horse to help Ringo.

Suddenly, more bullets whistled past. Charlie moved quickly to pull his wounded friend to safety. The horses stepped about nervously and for the moment blocked the line of fire between them and the men in the rocks. Charlie had to pull Ringo uphill, making it all the more difficult. Bullets from the guns of several men were hitting the dirt nearby. In a few more nerve-wracking seconds he had Ringo behind a big boulder. Beads of sweat fell from Charlie's forehead as he began returning fire at the men.

The attacker had waited in the rocks in ambush and had the advantage of surprise. Still, he had gotten off only one shot before he succumbed to the deadly speed of Ringo. The bullet had ripped through the man's stomach. Charlie's first shot had hit him in the arm, but the second went through his heart more by luck than aim.

Ringo awakened somewhat dazed with the sound of guns booming in his ears. The wound in his shoulder had a burning sensation like fire on bare skin. He saw the dust in the air as Charlie shifted about firing his weapon. Ringo figured his only chance to remain alive was to be as still as possible and wait it out. The bleeding needed to be stopped, but there was still the problem of men trying to kill them. He looked up at Charlie who had unknowingly placed himself in danger to help him.

"Sorry I got you into this mess," Ringo said. "You should have stayed in St. Louis."

Charlie turned but said nothing; they were in a bad fix and his glance suggested he was afraid this might be the end for them. To get into a gunfight with ordinary men was one thing, but the men in the rocks were experts with a gun. Charlie had seen two of them and knew who they were. He had hoped to write about them. If he could live through this, what a story he could tell. Charlie had become pretty good with a revolver; it was fortunate he had spent so much time practicing lately.

Charlie fired a shot and quickly ducked back down. A bullet ricocheted off the top of the boulder making a wicked sound as it sped off to hit and glance off yet another rock. He turned and looked back at his wounded friend and blew out a big breath of air. Charlie reached over to look at Ringo's wound.

"Don't like our chances. John, it's…"

That was the last thing Charlie ever said. He was about to tell who had ambushed them, but didn't get the words out. Ringo would never know whose bullet it was, but it struck Charlie in the side of the head as he looked back at him. One of the men had slipped over to the side and had been waiting with gun aimed and ready.

The man who took credit wore a white shirt and a black tie, which was unusual garb for that part of the country. Charlie's features were so much like his wounded friend that he thought it was the famous gunman. "I got him," said the man in the black tie, thinking he had just shot Ringo.

Charlie's head fell on Ringo's chest. Ringo started to slide sideways out from under his dead friend, but then he thought better of it. Whoever these men were they were obviously good with guns and he had no way to fend them off. His left shoulder bled heavily, and now the blood from Charlie's head spilled upon his right shoulder. There was nothing he could do for Charlie and he had to think of a way to make it out of this alive. It was important to keep his wits, think ahead, and come up with a way to survive, for this fight had reached its conclusion. They couldn't see him flat on the ground, but with no return fire coming it wouldn't be long before they concluded he and Charlie were either dead or defenseless.

Ringo's head throbbed from the heat of the sun and the uncertainty of what to do next, but then it hit him. He knew what to do. There was only one chance of coming out of this alive. They had to believe he was dead. He pulled Charlie's body further up on him so his friend's open wound bled directly on his face and head, sickening as it was. Most men will do things they never dreamed of when it comes to life and death situations. The will to survive should never be underestimated.

He continued to hold Charlie's head just above his own until he couldn't stand to bear another drop of his friend's blood. The precious fluid was still warm and his stomach nearly revolted when he thought about what he was doing. There was no choice, he told himself, so he let it flow on him as long he could. Finally, he carefully rolled Charlie's body over on its side so no one could tell that it wasn't his own blood covering most of his face and head.

Ringo knew he had only a few seconds at best. He took Charlie's gun and laid it close to his side, and then placed his gun in the space between his and Charlie's bodies. It took only a few seconds to put these things in place, and then he lay on his side with his face against Charlie's shoulder so they wouldn't be able to detect his slight breathing. He could feel the wetness of the blood, both his and Charlie's. He lay still waiting; seconds seemed like minutes.

This day belonged to the man in the black tie. He was death with a gun, but death awaited him also, for he was dying of a sickness in his lungs. He wondered if Ringo had been as fast with a gun as everyone claimed. Some thought he might be as fast, but he had never wanted to find out.

"Good shootin, Doc," the man in the green shirt said to Holliday.

"Why, thank you. Will you check for me and make sure they're dead?" Doc Holliday wanted confirmation from another source that he had killed the gunman.

"Sure, Doc."

Ringo heard footsteps slowly approaching. He lay motionless; blood still oozed from his shoulder. That side of his body was on the bottom so they couldn't tell his heart was still beating, still pumping blood out of the wound. Now his thoughts went completely to being dead. He lay still, trying not to listen or react. He tried to become like the rock he lay behind, inert. Ringo felt the sun on his back heating the moisture that had been life and was now death.

As he lay there the wind blew dust in his face and he breathed some into his lungs. His body cried out to expel the dust with a cough and he struggled to stifle that involuntary reaction. To cough now meant death. He tightened all his neck and chest muscles trying to prevent any sound. The cough was almost there; his lungs felt like they would explode if he didn't allow them to blow the foreign material out, but he would not give in. Finally in a silent expulsion of saliva and a small amount of air he forced the dust from his lungs and into his mouth. Then he opened his mouth and let the filthy fluid drain and mix with the blood on the ground. Now, he concentrated on being a rock—motionless, unfeeling. He knew they would check him, and he had to be prepared for a kick in the ribs or being rolled over. If they rolled him over he would grab his gun and take as many with him as he could. The footsteps were within a few feet. Ringo could feel eyes studying him.

"They're dead alright. Both of them are deader'n hell. Shot in the head just like you said." The pronouncement came from the man standing over the bodies.

Doc had killed many men, but none so feared as Ringo. He wondered now what the man had been like, really like. They had talked, even argued, with the possibility of life and death being decided in a fraction of a second. The man in the green shirt came back just as the lawman walked up next to Doc.

"Never seen so much blood," the man in the green shirt told them.

"Are you sure they're both dead?" the lawman asked.

"Yeah, I'm sure. Head wounds, both of 'em. There's blood everywhere, Wyatt."

Wyatt Earp motioned to another man wearing a brown vest. "Go check. I want to be sure."

After the two men left to look at the bodies, Holliday spoke quietly to Wyatt.

"Being kinda cautious, aren't we?"

"I suppose, but if he isn't dead and knows we ambushed him our lives wouldn't be worth a plug nickel."

The two men returned and the one in the brown vest said, "They're dead alright, dead fur certain."

"Good!" Wyatt said. "You fellas better load up your friend over there. We need to take him with us so nobody will know who did it."

"Let's make it quick," added Holliday. "Somebody might have heard the shooting." After the two men walked away, Doc said to Wyatt, "This is the last of them. I hope you feel your brothers are avenged now."

Wyatt nodded, long since hellbent on avenging the attacks on his brothers. He knew Ringo wouldn't have ambushed Virgil or Morgan, but Ringo had sent the message. That suggested he knew about the plans to kill Morgan and could have warned them.

"I reckon this is the end of it, Doc. Time for us to get on with our lives."

"Or in my case, with death."

"You aren't dead yet, Doc. Look's like they're about done; let's get the hell outta here."

As they began to ride away, the man in the green shirt rode over and grabbed the reins of the black stallion. It would bring a handsome sum. The man with the brown vest rode hurriedly to the bay, went quickly through the saddlebag and swatted the horse on the rump with his hand. The two men caught up with Wyatt and Doc, and they rode off with the sound of hooves echoing off the rocky floor of the canyon.

Ringo heard them leave. The trick had worked, for now. The wound was bad and he was a long way from being out of trouble. He tried to think clearly as to what he should do next. He got up slowly. His head reeled with pain, and spots of light circled in front of his eyes. His black horse Thunder was gone. The bay was a quarter mile away, but Charlie's appaloosa stood nearby.

Holstering his revolver he moved slowly toward the horse. Every small step was painful. Blood covered much of his head and face. At first the appaloosa was skittish and moved away. Ringo talked softly to the horse, and shuffled slowly over to him. The appaloosa smelled his hand and then nuzzled his arm. Slowly and painfully Ringo climbed into the saddle.

He rode to the bay and checked the saddlebags; his heart nearly stopped when he saw the bag of money was gone. It contained the proceeds from the sale of his livestock and the land in Missouri. It was a significant sum and all that he had to his name. Ringo had planned to buy a new ranch with it. Now he wished he had risked death and fought it out with them.

Ringo rode back to where Charlie was, leading the bay. Even though he knew he shouldn't, he picked up Charlie's body and put him over the saddle of the appaloosa. His wounded shoulder throbbed and he became light-headed. He stood there for several seconds and nearly passed out. When his head finally cleared he got on the bay and took Charlie's body toward the cabin where the three men waited. He struggled to remain conscious.

As he rode up, Yost came out with the others. They looked in horror at Ringo's bloody face and head.

"Oh Lordy! What happened, John R?" Yost asked.

"Ambush! Charlie's dead," Ringo replied almost in a whisper. "They think they killed me too."

"Let's get him off of there," Yost told the other two men. "Who did it, John R?" Yost asked as they prepared to help him down.

"Don't know. Heard one of them talk, but didn't recognize his voice."

Ringo started to say something else but passed out and fell from the saddle. Yost caught him, and then he and the other two men took Ringo inside and put him on the table. As they cleaned the blood that covered Ringo's head, they were amazed to discover there was no wound there. After cleaning the shoulder wound they saw that he was still losing blood.

Yost put the blade of his hunting knife in the fire. He had treated bullet wounds before and knew how to stop the bleeding. Yost knew it would probably wake Ringo when they did it and would certainly be painful later, but it was essential he not lose any more blood. When the blade was ready, he took the hunting knife from the red-hot coals and walked over to Ringo.

Yost told the other two men, "Open his mouth. Here, put this stick between his teeth. Now hold him tight cause he's gonna jerk for sure when I lay this on him."

The two men held his arms as Yost put the blade against his wound and counted to three. Ringo's eyes opened wide and he tried to rise up. The pain went crashing through his head; his teeth sank deep into the wood. The sickly smell of seared flesh filled his nostrils. He looked at Yost's face and saw the knife as he moved it away from his shoulder. Yost was saying something to him but he couldn't make it out. He spoke again, saying something about his back. The other two men lifted his upper body off the table. Yost reached behind Ringo where the bullet exited, and again he suffered the horrible pain and smelled the stench of his own burning flesh. The pain was excruciating and after a few more seconds he passed out.

90

They finished bandaging his wound, lifted him off the table and put him on the bunk. The three men stood there looking at one another. The old man had gray hair and whiskers and was missing several front teeth. He had known Ringo for only two years, but considered him a close friend. The old man hated the Earps because of what they had done when they had locked him in jail one night in Tombstone. When they arrested him they bashed him in the teeth with a pistol. The old man didn't know which one of them did it. He had been drunk. A friend told him he thought it was Wyatt.

The second man's name was Smith. He was taller and had reddish brown hair. He had ridden with Ringo a few months earlier when they had helped Sheriff Behan chase the Earps and Holliday after the murders of Frank Stilwell, Curly Bill Brocius and John Barnes. The year before Ringo had helped him recover eight horses that had been rustled by Mexicans. He, Ringo, Yost and three others caught up with them just before they got to Mexico. Ringo had shown no fear, riding straight at them with guns blazing, and they lit out without firing a shot.

"What do we do now?" the old man asked Yost.

Smith spoke first, "Good grief, it's just like he's been saying. Somebody was after him."

After several seconds Yost replied, "Well, John R said whoever shot him thinks he's dead. If that bullet was a couple of inches lower, he would be. Luck was with him today. Let's go take a look at his reporter friend."

They walked outside to see a gunshot wound in Charlie's head. The bullet had entered his right temple and exited through the top of his head. As the three stood there, Yost said, "You know, Charlie sure does look a lot like Ringo. He told me last night that a girlfriend of John R's nearly kissed him once by mistake."

The old man said, "Yeah he does, cept his hair is thin in front."

Yost stood in silence looking at Charlie's body, then said, "If we put a hat on him, people would think it was John R."

The old man wrinkled his nose and looked questioningly at Yost. "What are ya sayin? What do ya mean about people thinkin he's Ringo?"

"Well, I'm sayin we're the only ones within several miles that know John R well, so if we say it's him they'll think so too."

"What does it matter?" countered Smith. "We're gonna burn up that body over there in John R's cabin. Nobody could identify it anyway."

"Yeah, but Charlie there was a reporter," Yost said. "He was gonna vouch it was John R along with us. Now Charlie's dead. They won't believe us about the burnt body. They know we're John R's friends."

"Ya thinkin we gotta do somethin different?" the old man asked.

"Yeah, something different. Somehow we've got to make them believe John R is dead," Yost replied.

"But shouldn't we tell the sheriff?" Smith asked. "Charlie here has been murdered."

Yost was growing impatient with Smith, "Hell, the sheriff couldn't catch them. John R said he didn't know who it was. How can anybody go after them? I say we forget about reportin any murder and go through with saying John R is dead. He would want it that way, and so would Charlie there. He and John R were good friends. What we got to do is figure out exactly what we're gonna do now."

Smith remarked, "Or we could go ahead like we planned. They might believe us."

Yost went on like he hadn't heard Smith. "This reporter fellow looks an awful lot like John R; I say we show his body to a couple of people who don't know him, go to town as a coroner's jury like we planned and say it was John R's body."

Smith looked at Charlie again and shook his head. "I don't think he looks enough like him; it'd be risky."

The three men went on with their discussion. It was half an hour later before they all finally agreed. To help hide the body's identity, they would wait until the next day to officially discover it. As hot as it was the body would be swelling and turning colors. By then it would be much more difficult to recognize. As the other two men continued to talk, the old man inspected Charlie's wound closely.

"It kinda looks like Charlie might have shot hisself, don't it?" the old man asked.

92

Yost and Smith stopped talking and looked again at the wound, then Yost replied, "Well, it does kinda look that way except there's no powder burns."

"Do ya spose we ought to tell 'em we think it was suicide?" asked the old man.

"Oh I don't know about sayin something like that," Smith said doubtfully. "I know John R real well and I don't think he would ever do that. I don't think anybody else would believe it either."

"Well, you're right about those that know him well, but some people might buy it," Yost said rubbing his chin. Then he added, "He's been acting like he was drunk, and talking about dying and all that shit in Tombstone. That was part of the plan, for him to be telling people he thought he was gonna die. With all that kinda talk about death, some people might believe it."

"Well, if nothin else, maybe they'll be wonderin whether he shot hisself or was murdered instead of wonderin if it was John R," the old man added.

"Yeah...yeah they might at that," said Yost, surprised at the old man's insight.

"I still think we oughta just burn the body like we planned," Smith argued.

"Smith, you gotta be with us now if this is gonna work," Yost challenged.

"Oh...I'm with you. It's just that it sounds real complicated...but I'm with you."

They decided to wait until it was nearly dark to move Charlie's body. In the meantime they took the body of the man Ringo found near the border and buried it out behind the trees. Next they put Ringo's spare set of clothes on Charlie. When they started putting Ringo's boots on him, they ran into a problem. Charlie's feet were too big. Yost considered putting Charlie's boots back on, but the top part of his boots were turquoise in color and had fancy stitching.

"Well, they'll never believe John R would wear a pair of boots like those," Yost said.

Smith started getting nervous. He had been concerned about the deception and feared they would get caught. "Well, what now, mister smarty Yost?"

Yost looked at Smith in anger. He didn't reply right away, and focused instead on what to do next. Yost asked thoughtfully, "If a man was on the trail and lost his boots, what would he do to protect his feet?"

The other two looked perplexed. Finally Smith said impatiently, "I don't know."

"I'd wrap some cloth around my feet, a shirt or somethin," the old man said.

"Yeah, that makes sense," Yost replied. "Let's see what we got over here." He went to Ringo's saddlebags and got an undershirt, tore it in two pieces and wrapped a piece around each of Charlie's feet.

The other two watched. The old man nodded and said, "Ought to work."

They were nearly done. It was starting to get dark as they finished dressing Charlie. They decided to take the body somewhere near Smith's house so they could keep an eye on it. The old man had come up with the idea of using a tree. He had sat there once waiting for Smith to return home, and had seen some boys playing there a couple of times. It was an old oak tree that had been cut down to a stump. When it grew out again, the limbs spread out from the trunk, leaving a spot in the middle where a person could sit. Someone had put a heavy rock in the middle of the limbs to serve as a sitting place.

By the time they arrived at the tree, there was barely enough light to see. That helped ensure no one would spot them, but made the task more difficult. They carried Charlie's body to the tree and propped it up like it had been sitting there when it was shot. Smith put Ringo's extra cartridge belts on the body. The old man took the things they had found in Ringo's pockets and put them in Charlie's. Yost put Ringo's hat on Charlie's head so it covered the thin spot. They were about to leave when the old man noticed the gun was in the holster. He took the gun and put it in Charlie's right hand, but it wouldn't stay.

"What are you doing?" Yost asked.

"Tryin to get the gun to stay in his hand. Ya know, like he shot hisself." The old man went back to his horse and took out a piece of cloth. He then tied the hand closed around the gun handle. "By mornin it'll be set hard holdin that gun," the old man explained.

94

"You take the rag off first thing in the morning," Yost said to Smith.

"Alright, but I still don't like the idea. I bet John R won't like it neither."

"Yur probably right about that," the old man admitted.

"We already talked about all that, now let's finish up here," Yost concluded.

"Are you fellas sure this is gonna work?" Smith asked.

The old man replied first: "It'll work. Like I told ya earlier, in this heat the body will be turnin colors. By tomorrow afternoon it'd be real hard for anybody to tell that wasn't John R."

"It'll swell some by then too," Yost added.

"Oh Yeah. We won't have any trouble gettin them to wanna bury it," the old man assured Smith.

"So when do we want to act like we found him?" Smith asked.

"How about around three? That'd be a full day after he was shot," the old man suggested.

"Alright, three it is," Yost said. "Okay, Smith, you're gonna keep an eye on the body, right?"

"Yeah, me or the missus will keep a close lookout the whole time."

"If anybody happens by and finds him before three, we gotta get down here quick. If nobody finds him, and I don't think they will, I'll act like I found him at three sharp. Sound okay?" Yost asked.

"Yep," said the old man.

Smith just nodded, still unsure if they could fool people into thinking it was Ringo. The three men decided that Yost would send his wife to take care of Ringo. The men headed home to get some sleep before morning. Mrs. Yost was shocked when her husband told her what they were doing, but she didn't hesitate to go look after Ringo. He had always been a good friend to their family.

In the middle of the night the old man woke up with a start. He remembered the thinning hair in front and was sure someone would take off the hat to look at the wound, and then discover it was not Ringo. He got out of bed, and for half an hour tried to come up with a solution. Finally, he slipped out of the house and went back to the tree. Asking the Lord's forgiveness, he cut the front part of the scalp off of Charlie's head. He figured everybody would think an Indian had done it. As he left the tree he decided he would never tell Yost or Smith what he had done.

Just before daybreak, Yost awoke and realized they had overlooked something. There was no blood. He got a lantern and went out to the hen house. Yost grabbed a hen, cut off its head and held it upside down over a bucket. He worked quickly killing two more chickens and decided that would be enough.

When Yost got to the tree it was just starting to get light. He was horrified to see someone had scalped the dead body. The sight of the missing skin sent a chill all the way up his spine. Since it was not uncommon for Apaches to raid in the area he immediately assumed it was one of them. He looked all around thinking the Indian that did it might still be close by. Finally, feeling sure he was in no danger, he poured a small amount of the chicken blood over the top of the body's head, and then poured the rest on the entry wound at the temple. Yost was about to leave when Smith showed up to remove the rag tied around the gun hand.

"Oh shit!" Smith yelled. "Oh it's you, Yost. Damn, you scared the shit outta me. Why are you here?"

"A man bleeds when he gets shot. Somebody would have started wonderin why there was no blood. I killed a few chickens and came out here to make it look real."

"You're right. Damn, they would've figured it out for sure. Holy shit, he's been scalped. Damn, did you do that?"

"No, of course not."

"Well, who did then?"

"I don't know. I figured some Indian did it."

"Injun! Have you seen any?" Smith asked loudly.

"Shhh! Would you keep it quiet?"

"Well, did you see any Injuns?"

"No, but who else would've done it?"

"It sure is ugly, ain't it?"

"Yeah! It's getting light. We'd better finish up and get outta here."

Smith untied the rag and both men went quickly back to their homes before anyone saw them. All three were nervous that day.

Smith waited all morning on the front porch. A few people went by but it was far enough from the road that they didn't notice the body. Finally it was close to three. Yost hitched up the wagon and started toward the tree. His dog followed him down the road and went over to the body. Yost ran over to the tree and the other two men came shortly thereafter.

Yost said to the other two, "Now remember to say it's Ringo and act all excited like we just found him."

The other two men each went to a neighbor's house they had chosen in advance. They picked men who had never seen Ringo, or at least they didn't think they had. One of the neighbors that arrived had been on a coroner's jury before and knew that a report had to be completed. To their dismay, the three men had forgotten to bring anything to write on. Smith went quickly to his house to retrieve a pencil and paper. While they waited for Smith, just as the old man had predicted earlier, the two neighbors started debating whether Ringo had shot himself. They also talked about the missing scalp. When Smith returned, one of the men offered to write the report.

The note taker started documenting every little piece of information. By concentrating on detail, the men paid less attention to potential broader questions like whether it was Ringo. They read off the serial numbers on the guns and counted the cartridges in each weapon. One of the neighbors noticed that a cartridge belt was on upside down. Smith had put it on in the dark and failed to notice the cartridges were pointing up rather than down. They all knew that if a man wore it that way for long the cartridges would start falling out. It seemed suspicious, but the old man saved them when he said, "Well, ya know John R has been drinkin an awful lot lately."

The process was taking longer than the three men had hoped and other men were arriving. A man who lived several miles away rode up and stopped to see what was going on. His name was Ward and he had met Ringo. Before long Ward was studying the body closely. Yost noticed and moved closer to him, trying to decide whether it was better to tell him or risk having Ward say something. Finally, Yost tapped Ward on the arm and motioned for him to walk a short distance away where they wouldn't be heard.

"I don't think that's Ringo," Ward said quietly.

"It's not, but don't tell nobody. This fellow was a friend of John R's. They were ambushed yesterday and Charlie here got killed. John R was wounded bad too. We noticed that this fellow looks a lot like John R, so we're sayin it's Ringo. John R wants everybody to think he's dead."

"He does? Are you sure?"

"Yeah I'm sure. He told me himself. I helped him plan it all out, but then they got ambushed."

"Well, I'll be. I never would have guessed."

"I know, I was surprised too, but that's what he wants."

"Do you know who ambushed him?"

"Nope, no way of finding out neither. Are you willing to help us keep John R's secret?"

"Well, hell yes…if that's what he said he wants."

"It is. Now you can't tell nobody, not ever."

"I won't."

"Do you swear it, cause it's awful important to John R?"

"Yes sir. I swear it."

"Good! We'd better get that body buried before somebody else figures it out."

Yost walked over to the old man and said quietly, "This is taking too long; we already have more people here than we wanted. We gotta get the body in the ground. After I get back over there, why don't you say something about burying the body?"

The old man waited about thirty seconds and then said, "Gentlemen, we need to get this body buried. If we don't, it's gonna get mighty unpleasant to be around."

Yost jumped in. "You're right. Smith, why don't you get some shovels from your place and we can have some men start digging a grave?"

"Alright, be right back."

Smith went to his place and brought back three shovels. Several of the men took turns digging. It was hot dirty work and it took a long time. Before long more men had shown up. The conspirators were getting nervous; they hadn't planned on so many seeing the body. So far they had been fortunate; only Ward knew Ringo well enough to pick up the deception. Charlie had his features, and the blood, scalping, swelling and discoloration of the body did the rest. Yost and the others were relieved when the grave was dug.

Yost hollered out, "Grave is ready. Come on, men, help me get the body over there. Be careful now; we need to show proper respect to John R."

Yost, Smith and the old man started lifting the body. The man taking notes laid down his list and helped. After they carried the body over, Yost and the others lost no time lowering it into the grave and covering it with soil. Yost and Smith were sweating profusely, partly because it was hot and shoveling dirt was hard work, but mostly because they had been concerned their secret would be discovered.

Smith often read scripture at church and took it upon himself to quote some phrases from the Bible over the grave. Yost and the old man said a few words of praise for the man they called their friend. Each of the conspirators was beginning to feel relief from having the body out of sight. They gathered rocks to cover the grave, and then the men rode into town to give their testimony to the coroner and sign the report. With so many men coming in to testify it was Johnny Ringo's body they had found and buried, the coroner didn't question that it was Ringo. He did question whether it was suicide as two of the men claimed.

When they got back home, Smith invited his three cohorts into his house and the four of them had a drink of whiskey. Yost explained their original plan in detail to Ward.

"Yost, I'm sure glad you told me when you did. I was just about to say something."

"Whew, I know. I could tell you didn't think it was him." Finally able to relax, Yost chuckled and said, "Smith, you were right. We should have just burnt that other body in John R's cabin. Lordy, I never want to go through something like that again."

The old man said, "That damn fella takin notes was writin everythin down. I'm surprised he didn't count the hairs on Charlie's butt and write that down too."

The other men laughed. They sat in the cabin, drinking and relaxing for a good hour. Later, Yost said, "Tomorrow we better haul in more rocks and cover up that grave good. I don't want nobody digging up the body tryin to make sure it's John R."

Being of a cautious nature, Smith added, "Yeah, I think we ought to get some of those really big rocks from the creek bed."

After a short pause Yost raised his glass into the air and said, "Congratulations, fellars. By damn, we pulled it off."

"We done somethin good for John R; we ought to be proud," Smith said.

"I'll drink to that," the old man added.

"Me too," said Ward.

Yost finally added somberly, "I sure hope Charlie will forgive us for what we done to his body."

They were all silent for a while. Finally, the old man remarked, "Any one of us would've done it for John R. Charlie would want us to do just what we did. I'm sure of it."

EIGHT

Ringo woke a little before noon of the next day, before Charlie's body had been discovered. He immediately felt the pain and remembered that his three friends had seared his wound. When he opened his eyes he saw that Mrs. Yost was at his bedside. Right away she went to get him some soup. While Ringo watched her fill a bowl, he recalled that Charlie had been killed. Charlie had tried to help him and paid with his life. Ringo had seen men die before, but he felt directly responsible for Charlie's death. When Mrs. Yost came back she cautioned him not to talk, and then she told what she knew as she fed him. Ringo was amazed they had decided to show other people Charlie's body, thinking people would never fall for it.

After eating he lay back on the bunk. He figured they would be found out, and he would have to go on being Johnny Ringo. He reasoned that if they tried to fake his death and the plot was uncovered, it would be very difficult to successfully deceive anyone on his death again. He reminded himself that at least he was still alive. Dejected and weary, he went back to sleep.

Ringo didn't wake again until the next morning. It was still early and the light from the morning sun was coming through the rear window of the cabin. There wasn't anyone else inside, but he could hear voices. A minute later he heard footsteps coming through the door. Yost entered and walked over to the wood stove. He stirred something in a small pot and finally looked over at the bunk. Yost smiled at his friend and walked closer.

"Back among the living. How you doing, John R?"

"Well, now I know how it feels to be branded."

"Sorry bout that. We thought it was the best way to heal it up. Reckon it hurts."

"If you ever get a bullet wound, I'll be happy to let you find out."

"Think I'll pass."

Ringo watched his friend get a bowl of soup and bring it over. "Your wife told me you decided to pretend Charlie's body was me." He looked anxiously at his friend.

"It worked, John R. It worked," Yost said with pride.

"It did? When she told me I thought you were crazy. Are you sure they believed it?"

"Yeah, I'm sure. There was eleven of us went into town and testified. Everybody thinks you're dead."

"Eleven? Why on earth so many?"

"Aw, it just kinda happened that way. Everything was taking longer than it was sposed to. But all that's important, John R, is that it worked. In town, the only thing the coroner questioned was whether you was murdered or shot yourself."

Ringo's expression turned to a frown and his voice took a negative tone. "What do you mean, shot myself?"

"Now take it easy, John R. You gotta remember how Charlie's wound looked. It looked to a couple of the fellas like it could've been suicide. You saw his wound, didn't you?"

"Yeah, I saw it."

"Well, one of the men said it looked like he shot himself when they seen it."

"No, it didn't."

"I didn't think so neither; most of the men didn't. But two of 'em told the coroner that's what they thought. Now relax, John R.

The main thing is they think you're dead. That's what you wanted, ain't it?"

"Sorry, I didn't mean to blame you for it."

"That's alright, John R. No offense taken."

Yost changed the subject by telling him about the fourth man, Ward, and how he had taken him aside. Then he told about the neighbor who was being so detailed taking notes. Finally, he relayed how he and the old man had done their best to get the body buried as quickly as they could.

"Guess I owe you some thanks. Sounds like you boys had a rough day."

"Well, not nearly as rough as yours." After a brief pause, Yost added with sincerity in his voice, "Sure glad you made it, John R."

Ringo looked at his friend and saw moisture in Yost's eyes. He said, "Reckon we're even now."

Yost stood up smiling and walked over to the stove. He couldn't help but think back to when Ringo had saved his life in Texas. Yost had been in a burning barn and his leg was trapped under a huge wooden beam that had fallen as he tried to get his horses out. He suspected some Mason County residents had purposely set the fire, but was never able to prove it. As the flames had come dangerously close he tried in vain to free himself from the beam. Yost had finally pulled out his revolver and aimed it at his head. Dying by a bullet was far less painful than burning to death. Yost remembered how he had felt when he started to put his finger on the trigger, the flames of the fire nearly upon him. Ringo had burst through the burning door and thrown a horse blanket over the flames about to scorch him. Then Ringo had grabbed a board and pried the beam up to free him. Shortly after they were out, the barn collapsed. Yost wiped away a few tears as he recalled his terrifying brush with death. He would do anything for Ringo.

The next several days were quiet in the little cabin. The two wives took turns caring for the patient. With each passing day his wound improved and he grew stronger. After the third day he was out of danger and no one stayed with him at night. The women brought food twice each day, but otherwise stayed away from the cabin for fear people would get curious. Before long Ringo was able to sit at the table to eat and had become bored waiting for his body to heal. The next several days passed slowly.

It had been ten days since the ambush when Yost came to visit and told him, "Well, John R, you best be thinking what your new name is gonna be because everybody bought it lock, stock and barrel." The pride Yost felt was evident.

"It's hard to get used to the idea that people think I'm dead."

"Reckon it would be a bit eerie at that. Made me feel kinda funny when I read your obituary. You should see the one in the Epitaph. Longest one I ever saw. Told all about you. Course, don't know that I'd ever want to read mine."

Ringo sat quietly thinking about what Yost said, and finally responded, "Guess I'm not sure whether I will or not."

"One thing though, people have been asking what happened to your horse."

"The black stallion?"

"No, don't think they know about the stallion. Your bay, the one you been riding, they're wondering why it ain't been found," he explained.

"Do you know where he is?" Ringo asked, puzzled.

"He's in Smith's barn; we figured you'd need him since you lost the black."

"What about Charlie's horse?"

"They're both in Smith's barn," Yost explained.

"Has anybody seen them?"

"I spose just his wife and kids."

Ringo's first thought was they should have let the bay loose a long time ago. "Take my horse out tonight and let him go so he can be found. Charlie's horse is better than my bay, and hardly anybody knows about that appaloosa. I'll take him when I leave."

"Okay, John R, we'll do it. Uh…guess there was one other thing. They're wondering about your boots too," Yost added.

"My boots?" Ringo asked, even more puzzled.

Yost explained how his boots were too small to fit Charlie, and they had tied the undershirt around his feet. "We told them your boots were probably hurting your feet so you took them off and wrapped a piece of cloth on each foot to have something to walk on."

"Are you sure people believe I'm dead?" Ringo asked in disbelief.

"Yeah, John R. I wouldn't lie to you. The whole town believes it. Hell, I heard it was even in a newspaper in Los Angeles. Can you believe that, clear out in California? I'm telling you, we fooled 'em good. Everybody thinks you're dead," Yost insisted.

Ringo was surprised to hear it was in a Los Angeles paper. His sisters would have heard by now, and he felt guilty about the grief they must feel. He hadn't really thought about the pain that they would suffer when the news of his death reached them. Ringo began to wonder if he should secretly let them know he was still alive. Finally, he decided that was something he could worry about later. He thought for a few seconds more about the boots.

"Tie the boots on my horse. If I had taken them off, I would have tied them to the saddle horn. Anything else they're wondering about?"

"Nope. We pulled it off, John R. It's hard to believe, I know, but we pulled it off." Yost was grinning ear to ear.

Ringo smiled. He was still surprised the ruse had worked. Yost went outside to get something from his horse. When he came back in Ringo said in a serious tone, "Old friend, I owe you. You not only saved my life, you've given me a chance at a new one."

Yost beamed. He was glad to have been able to help his friend. Even more he was proud to have fooled so many people. Nobody gave him credit for being smart, but this man had put his life in his hands. "John R, if you ever need anything, I'll always be there to help you. You got my word on that."

Ringo smiled again and nodded, sensing his friend's sincerity. After Yost left, Ringo thought about his obituary for a long time. It was impossible not to be curious, but he decided he would never read it. He closed his eyes and went to sleep.

When he woke the next morning Mrs. Yost had just brought breakfast. She was cheerful and made small talk with Ringo. After he finished eating, he decided to mention that someone might get curious and happen by the cabin.

"Ma'am, I reckon I'll need to be leaving here pretty soon. I'd hate for anybody to drop by and find me here."

"John R, you can't leave yet. You aren't healed."

"I'm feeling pretty good, and it's dangerous to stay. You never know; some kid might be out hunting or something and walk right in here. I think I need to get out of here before long."

"Well, not right away you're not. You aren't ready and you don't have a horse until we bring it to you."

Realizing he wouldn't get anywhere with her, Ringo smiled and let the conversation drift to other things. The next time Yost came by, Ringo brought up the need to leave. Yost's wife had already warned him that Ringo wanted to take off soon. After considerable discussion, they finally agreed to a compromise. Ringo would wait four more days. It was less than the week and a half Mrs. Yost recommended, but two days more than he had wanted.

Finally the time had come and Ringo prepared to depart. He said goodbye to the men who had helped stage his death, and to the women who cared for him while he was injured. Late that night he climbed on Charlie's horse and headed north. Ringo stayed away from roads and areas where he might run into people. He rode at night, stopping when it started getting light and then riding on when it grew dark.

On the second day, while waiting in a grove of trees, he noticed the money in his saddlebags. It was at the bottom under the food. Yost and the others had given back all the money he had Charlie leave for them. Ringo shook his head, thankful for the generosity of his friends. Ironic, he thought, what he had given away was now the only money he possessed.

Ringo was not familiar with this area, and continued his journey slowly. He did know that very few people lived in this part of Arizona. After three days he decided to switch and ride during the day and sleep at night. He was far enough away that he thought it unlikely anyone would recognize him, and he could travel faster in the daylight. Ringo had let his beard grow the entire time he was in bed to help hide his identity, and Mrs. Smith had cut his hair shorter. Yost had given him an old pair of boots and a hat.

His wound wasn't completely healed and with each day he became weaker as he rode. After five days in the saddle, Ringo realized he should have waited. Toward the end of that day he was growing weary but continued on until dark, knowing he had to maintain his balance and stay in the saddle.

Ringo looked up and noticed the sun getting low on the horizon. Its rays were breaking through the clouds, almost like it was guiding him in that direction. The red and purple colors of the sunset illuminated the clouds like there was a huge fire in the sky behind them. He looked at the magnificent spectacle; it seemed to him that it represented a beacon beckoning him to ride to safety. Without really thinking why, he headed that way. Ringo wasn't the type who usually noticed the beauty of a setting sun, and he wondered why he did now. Perhaps it was the possibility of getting a fresh start that caused the change, or because he had been at death's door and survived.

That thought brought him back to reality, for indeed he would be dead if he didn't stop and give his wound time to heal. It had started seeping blood the day before, and now it bled more heavily. No sooner had he realized that he must stop than he happened on to a good place to camp for the night.

Ringo knew he had lost a lot of blood, and had little choice but to rest for a few days. There was a stream about six feet wide off to his right. The water looked clear and tasted sweet and clean. Having been on the trail for days he was dirty and smelled. First he took off all his clothes, then stepped into the stream and found a place where it was knee deep. He sat down in the middle and the cool liquid sent a chill through his body. The hairs on his arms stood on end and he shivered.

When he was clean, he got out and put on a spare set of clothes, leaving the shirt off. There was one bottle of whiskey in the saddlebags. He took a couple of swallows and then used it to pour over the wound. Alcohol on an open wound is painful, and he yelled out. After putting on a clean bandage, he built a small campfire and ate. As he lay down on his bedroll, he was thankful he would spend the next few days taking it easy.

Ringo didn't wake until morning. The muscles in his neck were sore and his head throbbed. As he lay there with his eyes closed the first sound he noticed was the birds singing. He could also hear the water gurgling in the nearby stream. Suddenly, he remembered Mrs. Smith had put a good selection of food in his saddlebags; some biscuits, bacon and coffee would make a good breakfast. It was then that he noticed the smell of bacon and coffee.

Alarm raced through Ringo's head as he realized someone was there. He quickly opened his eyes and saw a man sitting about ten yards away. There was a newly built campfire and a skillet over the flame. The man had brown hair with streaks of gray and lines on his face that attested to middle age. He wore a plain blue shirt and tan colored pants. The boots were well worn and his brown hat showed sweat stains around the band. It was pushed back on his head revealing a tanned and handsome face. The sound and smell of eggs frying in bacon grease wafted through the air. After a few seconds the gent looked up from his task and smiled at the wounded man.

"Good morning," he said with a deep pleasant voice and friendly smile. He put eggs and bacon on two plates and brought them over. "Good thing I happened along when I did. Looks like you could use some help."

The night before he had seen the campfire, ridden up and found the man with the wound in his shoulder. After taking the saddle off the appaloosa, he had hobbled the horse along with his own mount. Then he had covered the wounded man with a blanket. The stranger had made supper, but decided the man needed rest more than food and let him sleep.

Now the stranger gave him a plate and set a cup of coffee nearby. His gentle manner reduced Ringo's fears. They began eating the food, which tasted good to Ringo. When he finished breakfast, he took a sip of the hot coffee and once again looked at his visitor. "Much obliged for helping me out. You just happen along?"

"Yep, I was returning from western Montana where I was visiting my sons. Sort of a vacation, I guess. Always come on this side of the Rockies and visit a friend near here, and then head east back to Texas. Seems like I always come to this place near suppertime and camp here for the night. Best drinking water and fishing anywhere on the trip."

"Yeah, it is nice here."

"How'd you come to get shot?" The visitor motioned with his cup toward the wound.

"Got bushwhacked a while back. Guess I'm lucky he wasn't a better marksman. It started bleeding on me again yesterday."

"You do that with your knife?"

"No, a friend of mine did that for me."

"That was nice of him. Maybe you ought to consider getting some new friends. Damn, that musta hurt."

"Sure did," came the brief reply and the first sign of a slight smile. They sat in silence for awhile. The wounded man was appreciative of the lack of questions; it showed proper western respect for privacy. Ringo thought the stranger seemed decent enough, but figured it was best to ride on as quickly as possible to protect his identity.

"I'll need to be moving on here in a bit. Would you mind getting my horse for me?"

"You can't ride yet; you'll open that up again. We ought to stay here today. If your wound doesn't start bleeding by morning I'll help you to a cabin I know where you can get rested up."

Ringo figured insisting on leaving would raise too much suspicion. He decided he didn't really have much choice but to agree with the stranger. "I guess you're right; rest does sound pretty good."

The gent took the plates down to the stream and washed them, and then brought the coffeepot over. As he poured the younger man another cup he asked, "By the way, what's your name?"

Ringo had to think quickly. He should have already picked out a new name, but hadn't. His best friend when he was younger was named Tom, and he decided that would be his first name. He paused only a second more, looking around for help with the last name. "Tom Stone. How about yourself?"

The stranger strongly suspected he had lied. The response came a little too slowly, and in his business it was important to know when someone wasn't telling the truth. "I'm Josh."

Ringo didn't ask for the last name. If he had he would have recognized the name and this man's reputation with a gun. Josh Steel was a Texas Ranger and known as one of the fastest guns in the Lone Star State. The ranger decided not to reveal his identity if he could help it. It always changed the nature of the conversation when he did.

"Well, thanks for helping me out, Josh; reckon I don't feel much like riding today."

Josh poured himself a cup. "You rest now and take it easy. If your shoulder doesn't start bleeding we'll move you in the morning."

"I'll be owing you considerable."

The stranger's calm voice made Ringo…Tom feel more at ease. He took a drink of coffee and closed his eyes while the warm liquid went down his throat, and then he laid his head back on the saddle. Again he listened to the birds and the bubbling sound of the stream. Soon he was asleep.

Josh planned to do some more fishing. He walked down the stream to the little pond. "Guess I'm still on vacation," he said out loud to himself as he sat by the pool and flung his line into the cool, clear water. A big smile drifted across his face as he looked at the canyon walls nearby glistening in the morning sun. A slight breeze brushed softly through his hair and the sun warmed his bare forearms where he had rolled up his shirtsleeves. He leaned against a tree trunk lying on the ground ten feet from the water. As he sat patiently, he noticed the tiny waves sparkling in the pond and he listened to the birds in the nearby tree. Josh closed his eyes to enjoy the sensations around him. He wanted to get the full benefit of peace and tranquility while he could. It was a long ride from Montana to Texas, and some time out of the saddle was welcome. He spent much of the day fishing but checked on his patient every couple of hours. The younger man slept heavily. He talked in his sleep several times, but not while Josh was within earshot. Tom didn't wake until that evening while Josh was preparing supper.

"You seem to always know when there's food being prepared."

Tom smiled. For some reason he couldn't help but feel at ease around Josh. "I'm hungry, alright." Finally, he noticed it was late in the day. "The sun's about to set. You mean I slept all day?"

"Reckon you did, and a good thing too, help you heal." Josh walked over and looked beneath the bandages. "Looks better, still not bleeding. Reckon we can get you under a roof tomorrow."

Josh Steel wasn't just a ranger; he was the most respected and trusted ranger in Texas. He was known as a tough hombre who would go to any length to get his man. Tom hadn't thought much about not getting a last name from Josh. He was just hoping to get away without his secret becoming known. The less anyone said about a name or the type of work he did, the better Tom liked it. Josh had no more questions for him that night and Tom was relieved. They talked about the canyon and the stream, and then the horses. After awhile Tom grew tired and went back to sleep.

The next morning Josh made breakfast and they sat and talked while they ate. The ranger mentioned the birds singing and the wild flowers by the stream. There were an abundant number of yellow and blue flowers and a few white ones mixed in. In the stream where the water was smooth, the colors of the flowers reflected off the surface. It was a sunny day with only a few white clouds in the sky. These were things Tom had never really paid much attention to until the past few days, but took pleasure in now. As they finished up the coffee, Josh told him there was a small town where they could get supplies on the way to the cabin.

When they got near the town, Josh had Tom stay out in a grove of trees. "No sense letting anyone know we have a wounded man."

Josh rode in to what was more a village than a town, and had more Indians than white men. There were just a few homes and one store. The buildings were not well kept and the street was little more than a trail. He went in during the hottest part of the day, when most people were more concerned about staying cool than finding out who the rider passing through might be. Josh spent as little time as possible, and bought the supplies they needed. There were no questions asked and no information offered. As he rode out of town Josh gained a little attention from two Indians, but they did not speak. Tom was waiting under the shade of a tree, and they headed on to the cabin Josh claimed would be as good as a hospital for recovery.

NINE

As they rode toward the back of the canyon, the cabin came into view. It didn't appear anyone was there. No horses were in sight and no tracks in evidence. Tom had felt good when they started, but twenty miles in the saddle had taken its toll. He tried not to show his fatigue, but Josh could tell Tom was nearing the end of his endurance. They rode up to the cabin and Josh helped him inside. Josh checked Tom's bandages, and then took some blankets he bought at the store and laid them on the cot. Tom went to sleep quickly.

Josh took the horses to the little stream behind the corral and gave them their fill. Then he walked them to the corral, unsaddled them, fed them some grain and closed the gate. Josh looked at the two saddles he had just taken off the horses and lugged them one at a time to the cabin. Poor planning, he thought, should have taken the horses to the cabin first and unsaddled them there.

His mind was on the man in the cabin. Josh always found it hard to think straight when something else had captivated his attention. He wasn't sure what it was about the man, but he liked him. Maybe he saw himself in Tom fifteen years earlier. When Josh had first moved to Texas, the war between the North and South had just ended. Many confederate soldiers ended up in that still untamed state. Josh had been young and very quick with a gun, his temper just as quick. There were a lot of things happening in Texas that left good people dead or swindled. A need for the law was not something that the young ex-soldier felt compelled to solve, but his willingness to tackle tough hombres and his speed with a gun caught the attention of a captain in the Texas Rangers. Josh remembered the man who had convinced him to put on a badge. He idolized him. He still wasn't sure what the captain had seen in him, but the ranger had a way about him that changed Josh's life. The captain took him under his wing and put a lot of trust in him. Josh had never disappointed the lawman.

The man in the cabin was a gunfighter; Josh could tell by the gun and holster. He had checked the wanted posters in his saddlebag. This man's picture was not among them. He hadn't expected to find him there. Somehow the ranger sensed he had good in him. Josh retrieved the saddlebags and canteens, took them to the cabin and fixed something to eat. After tidying up the cabin he went outside. The ranger knew it would be easier for Tom to sleep if he busied himself elsewhere. He went down to the stream to catch fish for dinner.

Tom slept through the night and woke while Josh was cooking breakfast. The fact that Josh purposely set the frying pan down on the stove a little harder than usual probably helped.

"Good morning, Josh."

"How you feeling this morning?"

"A little dizzy. Otherwise, I think I'm okay."

"I'm sure the long ride in the saddle didn't do you any good. Would you like some coffee?"

"Coffee sounds good."

"You might want to sit out on the porch. Sure nice out this morning."

Tom was grateful to have a roof over his head and someone to look after him. The little cabin was ideal, just as Josh had said. It had a wood floor, stone fireplace and a bunk in each back corner. There was a window in the front and one on the side looking out toward the corral. On the little table next to the door was a water pitcher and basin. Tom used the small cloth near the basin to wash his face, and then walked out on the porch.

Tom hadn't noticed the beauty of the canyon when they rode in the night before; it had been everything he could do just to stay on the horse. Along with the corral, there was a small shed for the horses.

Apparently, the corral hadn't been used in a long time because the grass was tall. When the grass in the corral ran out there was plenty of pasture within the canyon, and it waved gently back and forth with the breeze much like waves on a lake. It reminded Tom of the wheat fields back in Missouri when he was young.

Josh put the food on two plates, but then decided they should eat on the porch. He set the plates down and carried the small table out. Josh had been watching the sunrise earlier and thought Tom would enjoy eating outside.

"Here's breakfast, Tom. Well, I'd have to say based on my long years of doctoring that you look like you might live at least another day or two."

"Thanks!" Tom replied with a smile. "Appreciate you bringing me here. It's a pretty place."

"It sure is. Cooler than you'd expect for the middle of the summer, and the fishing is great. A man would never go hungry here, provided he could live on fish and rabbits. Stayed here one time when my horse came up lame and needed to rest him a few days. I fell in love with this canyon."

"I can see why."

"Let's eat this food before it gets cold."

Tom ate like a starving bear. He wasn't sure why the food tasted so good; maybe it was Josh's cooking or perhaps just because he was so hungry. It wasn't long before his plate was empty.

"You get enough to eat, Tom?"

"Yeah, sure did. Where'd you learn to cook like that?"

"I was the oldest of four kids and my mother passed away when we were still young. Learned out of necessity I guess. Sure was glad when my sister Katie, she was the youngest, was old enough to take up the cooking duties."

"Is she as good a cook as you are?"

"No!" Josh chuckled. "To be real honest she never did learn to cook very well. My younger brothers tried to get me to start cooking again, but I never did. Well, least ways, not until I was out on my own."

As they sat on the porch Josh told him this place was well away from any trails. A rancher who lived to the north had told him about it. Josh said he used it on occasion as he traveled to and from Montana. The cabin had been built a long time ago, but it was solid. It had a rough look with large spaces between the logs that had been tightly packed with mortar. Whoever built it had done it well, Tom thought. After eating and talking for a while, Tom became tired and again went to sleep.

Later, that evening, Josh was frying fish when Tom woke up.

"Good timing, Tom, supper will be ready shortly."

"Supper? I've sure been sleeping a lot lately."

"You need to. You lost a lot of blood. It'll take you awhile to get your strength back. If you feel up to it you might want to sit on the porch again. The sun's about to go down."

"You really like sunsets and things like that, don't you?"

"Sure do. The beauty of nature is a gift from God. It's something we need to learn to appreciate. If a man can understand nature, he can better figure out what he's supposed to be doing in life."

Tom went outside and watched the horses eating near the trees. Josh came out and sat with him for awhile, but went back in several times to turn the fish. The sunset was somewhat colorful that evening, but not spectacular. After they ate, Tom quickly tired, his body using all its energy for healing. He went inside and went quickly back to sleep.

During the next few days Tom spent almost the whole day in bed, getting up long enough to eat, walk out on the porch and sit for awhile. Josh took care of the horses and made the meals, and then he would head off to fish or hunt. They had rabbit stew one day and catfish the next. Josh was quite the cook. Tom did his best to be an agreeable patient. The bandage would occasionally show some red, and Josh would remove it and put on a clean one. When Josh cleansed the wound he dabbed it with some whiskey before putting on a bandage. It caused some pain, but Josh said it would help it heal. Tom nodded his agreement, not mentioning he had done the same thing earlier.

Josh had little to do all day. Hauling water up from the stream was the most strenuous task he faced. When Tom was awake the two men spent a good deal of time talking. They learned little in the way of each other's background, but much about character. Neither had any idea of the fame of the other. Josh talked about his experiences as a youth growing up, and Tom countered with similar stories of his own. Josh avoided talking about the war or being a ranger, and Tom his days as a gunman.

The more they talked and spent time together, the greater grew the bond between them. Josh was developing a fondness for Tom that he couldn't really explain. Tom enjoyed the time with Josh and absorbed the knowledge and wisdom his stories conveyed. Neither spoke of any closeness, but it formed nevertheless. Each day Tom spent with Josh the less lost he seemed to be. He had desired to start a new life, but hadn't been real sure how to go about doing that. Tom wasn't aware of what the term "mentor" meant, but he had found one and was learning more than he realized.

As the days passed Tom began to spend an increasing amount of time on the front porch. It was hot during the middle of the day, but the mornings and evenings were agreeable. He particularly liked to sit with Josh and watch the sunsets. That time of day seemed to bring out Josh's inner thoughts. After a few more days Tom was feeling better and they were running out of provisions.

After breakfast Josh told Tom, "We're running low on a few things. I think I'll head back to that little town and get coffee, some grain for the horses, flour and some bacon. Anything you want me to get?"

"Some eggs if they have them. I've got some money here in my saddlebag."

"I've got money, Tom. Thanks all the same."

"You paid last time. It's my turn." Tom walked over to his saddlebag and brought back some money. Handing it to Josh he said, "Here, this should cover it."

"And then some. You stay put while I'm gone. No climbing up canyon walls or riding your horse when there's no need to. Just take it easy until I get back."

"Yes, mother Josh."

Josh chuckled, but didn't respond. He saddled his horse and rode into town. As was the case earlier the town was almost empty and no one took much note of his presence. The store clerk was glad for the business and asked few questions. It was one of those little stores that had a little bit of everything, including a drink for those who wanted it. He passed on the drink, but bought a bottle. Josh put the goods in his saddlebags, tied the bag of grain to the pommel of the saddle, and headed back to the cabin.

That afternoon, he and Tom spent a long time on the front porch talking about simple and common things. As he watched the horses in the pasture, Tom was consciously aware he was starting to really like Josh. He wondered what this man did for a living, but never imagined this helpful and generous fellow tracked down desperados. After a while Tom grew tired, and went back inside. They ate supper and Josh rounded up the horses and put them in the corral for the night.

The next few days moved along slowly. While Josh was away, Tom spent much of the time reading one of the books he carried in his saddlebags. He also contemplated what he should do next. Being fast with a gun hadn't proven to be as rewarding as he had first thought. He had come to realize that everything had a price. His reputation with a gun had nearly got him killed.

One morning just as Tom got out of bed, Josh poked his head in the door saying happily, "Good morning! While I get some breakfast ready you ought to come out and see these clouds gathering off to the west. I've been sitting out here watching for a good half hour."

"Thanks! Think I'll bring some coffee with me." Tom got up to pour himself a cup. "Damn, but you make good coffee, Josh."

"Pour me some while you're at it."

Tom poured an extra cup and then stepped out on the porch. He saw the dark clouds Josh had mentioned. "I'd say we definitely have some rain headed our way alright."

Josh went inside and before long the sound of bacon just starting to fry could be heard. He stepped to the door, took a sip of coffee and said, "Always loved storms, at least when I'm not out in them. Do you see how tall that cloud over to the right is? There's going to be a lot of rain, pretty good wind too I imagine."

"It sure looks that way. Glad we've got the cabin." Tom drank coffee and watched as the clouds approached. The scent of bacon drifted out to Tom as Josh brought out the coffeepot and refilled Tom's cup. "Thanks, Josh. I'm beginning to feel spoiled. Why don't you let me help?"

"No help needed; be done in a jiffy." A few minutes later Josh brought out a couple of hot biscuits with butter melting on top. On the table he placed a small jar of peach jam. "The store clerk told me he'd just bought this butter and jam from a farmer's wife. I've been saving it for a time like this."

Tom took a bite and closed his eyes to concentrate on the flavor. It was sweet and tasted just like the butter his mother used to make. On the second biscuit he spread some of the peach jam. He closed his eyes and could see his brother and three sisters sitting around a table eating his mother's biscuits covered with jam. Josh brought out the bacon and eggs, along with more biscuits. They ate their food and before long the breeze picked up. It was cool and bore the scent of rain that always comes before a storm. With a sudden gust of wind the first drops of water spattered onto the dust. It looked like it could rain heavily as the lightning struck off to the west and the wind blew the trees, first one way then the other. A few dust devils swirled by picking up dead grass and leaves.

Josh went inside to make another pot of coffee, and then returned to the porch to watch the lightning approach. His excitement at the coming storm was evident. It was the energy such storms possessed that amazed him. He sat outside like a man about to see the curtains open and a play performed. Putting a little whiskey in their coffee for flavor, Josh and Tom propped their feet up on the porch rail and tilted back in their chairs. Tom remembered how his mother had always scolded him when he tilted back in a chair. As he sat there he remembered the faces of his family, especially the three sisters he would never see again. Later, his thoughts drifted on to other things. He felt the effects of the whiskey and his mind relaxed and enjoyed the feel of the cool gusts of air. It had been peaceful here and it was nice to sit back and watch the gathering storm.

Before long the rain came down in sheets. Josh moved over to the other side of Tom as it came in at an angle getting half of the porch wet. A few drops of rain blew on Tom's face. He found them refreshing. Within minutes puddles began forming out in front of the cabin. The wind continued to blow and Tom closed his eyes and let the air move his hair about.

As Tom sat on the porch he felt like he was capturing some of the energy of the storm, leaving him feeling stronger but at the same time peaceful inside. When he opened his eyes again, the little stream behind the corral was swollen with swirling water. The horses were in the shed and seemed to be doing fine, even though the roof on the shelter had several small leaks. Tom watched the rain for awhile and then began to read his book. When he tired of one, he did the other. They talked occasionally, but mostly each just enjoyed the wonder of the storm.

Finally the rain slackened and came down more gently. The air smelled of wet grass and soil; it was refreshing and clean. Tom couldn't remember ever enjoying a rain this way, at least not since he was a kid. Without realizing it he was absorbing some of the traits of the man beside him, and the result was an increasing appreciation of nature and greater enjoyment of life.

Three days later found both men in good spirits. "It looks like your wound is nearly healed," Josh said.

"Yeah, it's closed up completely. Still feel a little weak now and then, but I think I'm about ready to ride."

"Better give it a couple more days. I'm going to head back into town to get some supplies and go see that rancher I know. Should be back in about four hours. Anything you need?"

"More of that butter and jam if it's there."

"Doubt if we'll be that lucky, but I'll give it a try. Sure was good."

Josh saddled up his horse and headed to town. Tom sat on the porch after Josh left and time passed slowly. It gave him time to consider what to do next. The way things had unfolded everyone thought he was dead. If he could hide who he was, he might be able to walk away from the life of a gunman altogether. In the past he had killed three different men who were trying to outdraw the legend and become one themselves. Two of them had been young men who thought they were fast and wanted to get the big reputation quickly. Both had their bravery supported by liquor. The third man was a true gunslinger who had killed several men and wanted to add him to the list. Tom had been younger and not known at the time, but well known enough to attract a gunslinger trying to add a notch to his gun. The man had been fast, but not in his league. He was buried in Waco.

With these thoughts surfacing, Tom decided he needed to get some practice with his gun while Josh was gone. He went to the very back of the canyon. According to Josh, this canyon was far away from any nearby trails. The sound of gunshots shouldn't be heard by anyone. Tom practiced his draw without firing the greatest majority of the time, but would occasionally draw and fire. He preferred to shoot with every draw, but was limited in ammunition. He practiced for a half-hour then headed back to the cabin, still an hour before Josh was expected back.

Josh had expected it to take four hours because he had planned to go visit a rancher in the next county. What Tom didn't know was that by chance the rancher had been in the little town getting supplies. Josh had returned early and heard the gunshots. He was concerned when he first heard the sound, but as he rode closer he noticed the consistency in shots being fired every twenty or thirty seconds. Having practiced himself, he recognized the meaning. He took the time to circle around and rode up on the canyon wall. Josh dismounted and walked slowly to the edge where he could look down over the rim. There he saw Tom practicing. He hadn't anticipated danger, but was nevertheless relieved everything was fine.

He watched Tom and soon became amazed at what unfolded in the little remote canyon below in the middle of nowhere. Josh went back to his horse and retrieved a small telescope out of the saddlebag. He watched Tom's hand closely, but couldn't detect the movement. His hand was near his gun, and the next instant it was drawn and fired. Josh had been around long enough to realize this man's name wasn't Tom Stone. He had suspected it before when the wounded man gave his name a little too slowly. Now Josh was certain.

The rancher he met in town at the store had told him the big news about the gunman killed in Arizona. Ringo was known as the fastest gun alive. At the time Josh had no reason to believe Ringo wasn't dead. As he watched this man draw with speed such as he had never seen before, Josh knew this had to be the legend himself.

Josh watched in awe. Certainly no other living man could match the draw he witnessed in the canyon down below. Near the end of the practice, Tom fired shots in quick succession. With ammunition running low he placed three rocks on the larger stone, and then drew and fired quickly. Josh watched this exercise in complete amazement. The three shots came so fast that it sounded like one shot. Ringo had been in Texas for several years and was a big part of the Mason County War. Josh had been in a different part of Texas and had never met him. Those rangers that had met him said he was a likeable man.

Josh thought out loud, "The papers have reported him dead. Now he's using a different name and wanting to move on. He let them think he's dead, maybe even set it up. He wants to start over."

After Tom walked back to the cabin, Josh mounted up and rode quietly away. He decided not to say anything about what he had seen. An hour later he rode up as if just returning. His easy manner veiled the knowledge he now possessed. For the next several days Josh continued to talk to Tom about life. One day he brought up the need for good men and women to settle the West, and the need for sheriffs, marshals and rangers.

"Have you ever thought about being a lawman?" Josh asked.

Tom laughed. He had actually been a lawman in Texas for a short while. "If he only knew who I was," Tom thought. Finally he replied, smiling, "Reckon not, but that part about good women sure did interest me."

Josh chuckled. "Well, I guess if I was young and had your looks I'd find me one of those myself."

Tom smiled and shook his head but had no response for his wise friend. Josh was still a handsome man even at his age. Tom had learned earlier that Josh's wife had succumbed to smallpox after she had gone to a nearby town to help others with the illness.

During those final few days, Tom and Josh became as close to each other as either ever had to any other man. The morning finally came when Tom was healed and Josh was ready to head back home. Tom couldn't go to Texas because too many people there knew him. He would dearly miss Josh.

"You know, Tom, there's a lot of opportunities in Texas," Josh said as he saddled his horse. "Sure would be happy to have you come and join me there."

"Thanks, Josh, but I'm afraid I'll have to say no. I can't tell you how much I appreciate what you've done for me. I'm hoping someday I'll have the chance to make it up to you."

Josh nodded, then took off his hat and wiped his brow. "Well, I'll tell you what, Tom. You can repay me by helping somebody else someday. You'll know when the time comes. Someone helped me years ago. I was just repaying my debt to him."

Tom smiled and couldn't help but think what a good man this was. "I'll remember that." He offered his hand and Josh gave him a firm handshake. "So long, Josh."

Josh got on his horse and touched the tip of his hat as a salute goodbye. Tom returned the gesture, and then Josh turned and headed south. Tom checked the cinch on his horse, climbed in the saddle and headed north. Exactly where he would go and what he would do he would decide on the trail.

Rather than returning to Texas right away, Josh headed toward Tombstone so he could research the reported death of Johnny Ringo. At one of the newspaper offices he found a picture of the gunman, confirming that Tom Stone was indeed the legend. He studied the newspaper articles and talked to several of the townspeople, being careful not to rouse any suspicion. After finding out all he could in Tombstone, he went to nearby Tucson and read past articles there. Josh finished his study, finding more inconsistencies than he had anticipated.

Some of the irregularities were minor. The obituary in the Tombstone Epitaph indicated one of the cartridge belts on the body was upside down. In addition, there were no boots; instead there were torn pieces of undershirt wrapped around the feet. Josh had talked to one of the men on the coroner's jury who had seen the body. The man told him he had been surprised when he noticed the pieces of cloth on the body's feet were clean and had not been walked on. The most interesting thing to Josh was that the man said he didn't know Ringo, and that most of the men on the coroner's jury didn't, but several did know him and vouched for the fact that it was indeed the famous gunman.

In the same obituary was another puzzling statement. It read:

"There is, apparently, a part of the scalp gone, including a small portion of the forehead and part of the hair. This looks as if cut out by a knife."

The obituary offered no explanation, nor did Josh find much discussion of this fact in the articles he read. Several of the townspeople indicated they figured an Apache Indian did it. Josh didn't argue with them, but was surprised they accepted that an Indian had scalped him. Just six sentences later the obituary listed the guns, including a rifle and Colt 45 revolver, along with ammunition and cartridge belts. Josh thought to himself, "If an Indian had done it, he would have taken the guns, especially the Colt." Josh couldn't come up with a plausible reason why the body that was found was scalped, but believed it should have raised some questions.

Another thing that didn't make sense to Josh was where the body was found. If a man or group of men were going to kill someone like Ringo, they wouldn't pick a spot in close proximity to where several of his friends lived. Josh also saw no reason for the gunman to take his own life, regardless of the talk about Ringo thinking he was going to be killed. Ringo had lived through the bloody Mason County War in Texas, and then had survived the Earp and "Cowboy" feud in Arizona. It didn't make sense that he would suddenly take his life four months after Wyatt Earp and Doc Holliday fled to Colorado, and two months after he had cleared his name of all charges in court. The same man who had told Josh the pieces of cloth on the feet were clean also told him there were no powder burns on the wound. He couldn't have shot himself.

It was in the Tucson Weekly Citizen that Josh found the issue of the horse. Ringo's horse wasn't found until July 25th, eleven days after the body was discovered. The article read:

"A son of B. F. Smith, says the Tombstone Independent, found John Ringo's horse, on Tuesday last, about two miles from where deceased was found. His saddle was still upon him with Ringo's coat upon the back of it. In one of the pockets were three photographs and a card bearing the name of 'Mrs. Jackson.' It seems strange that the horse should have wandered about all this time without having been discovered before. Mr. Smith brought the horse into town with him. It is a bay, weighing about 1,000 pounds."

The reporter in Tucson who wrote the article realized it was odd that it took so long for the horse to be found. Josh agreed and thought it highly unlikely the horse just wandered around for eleven days without being discovered. Josh went back and read the obituary again. He thought he had seen the name Smith before. In the <u>Tombstone Epitaph,</u> B.F. Smith was one of the men in the coroner's jury who testified that the body was Ringo's, and it was his house that was closest to where the body was found. In the Tucson paper, it was Smith's son who supposedly found the horse, and B.F. Smith himself who brought the horse in. "No doubt about it," thought Josh, "This B.F. Smith is a close friend of Ringo's and helped him stage the death."

Ringo's obituary contained another statement that Josh thought should have raised suspicion.

"He was found by John Yost who was acquainted with him for years both in this territory and Texas."

It would be easy to read right on past the sentence, thought Josh. He found it very interesting that the body was discovered by someone who had been a friend both in Arizona and back in Texas. That made him a long-term friend. Mr. Yost was on the coroner's jury, and no doubt was one of the men who vouched it was Ringo.

Josh understood why people believed the death; after all, a coroner's jury testified. There was no real reason for the average person to doubt what a coroner's jury said. The jury, which was just a group of men who had seen the body, had no apparent motive to tell anything but the truth. Even Ringo had no obvious incentive to fake his death.

Josh discovered that some of the people recognized the inconsistencies, but they told him they thought someone murdered Ringo and tried to cover it up by making it look like a suicide. For some reason they never considered that the death might have been staged. Josh thought there were too many unexplainable facts not to be suspicious. But he reminded himself that if he hadn't known Ringo was alive, he probably wouldn't have doubted the story either.

Since Ringo's grave was on the way to Texas, Josh obtained directions from the man that was on the coroner's jury. When he arrived, Josh was amazed. Before him were the largest rocks he had ever seen on a grave. The huge pile of oversized stones stood four feet high, four feet wide and twelve feet long. Josh couldn't help but laugh, realizing Ringo's friends did it to help secure their secret. With his curiosity satisfied, the ranger turned his horse east and headed toward Texas.

TEN

After saying goodbye to Josh, Tom headed north and east skirting around the edge of Indian country. His route took him through seemingly never ending sand dunes and scraggly trees. As he rode his thoughts often went back to Josh. The man had seemed like an older brother to him. Without being judgmental, Josh had shared his way of looking at the world and the people in it. It almost seemed like he was teaching him—particularly during the last couple of days. Josh had talked about how everyone had a purpose in life. Tom began to wonder about his reason for being. He wished that he could be more like Josh.

Late in the day Tom approached the border between Arizona and Utah. He saw several beautiful stone structures with spires reaching high into the sky. He had seen similar formations here and there in the West, but never so many in such close proximity. Tom was fascinated with them. Some were within a mile of another formation and others were more distant. One of them looked like three people standing next to each other, one taller than the other two. Tom could visualize a father talking to his two sons. The structure that most captured his attention looked from a distance like a tall fence with a few boards missing close to one end. It was nearing sunset and the sky in the west was aglow with bright purple clouds. The tall red walls became brighter as the sun lowered and before long they were ablaze with color. Having seen the natural magnificence of the area, Tom felt certain the Creator had spent extra time when he shaped its splendor.

Tom rode his horse up to the base of the stone structure that looked like a fence. He decided to watch the sunset from a perch in between the pillars of rock. By first standing on the saddle of the appaloosa, he was able to find a foothold and climb to the spot that looked like the gap in the fence. He stood next to the spire at the end of the structure. The stone reached high into the sky, and looking straight up Tom could see clouds floating by above. The movement of the clouds made it seem as though the spire was falling.

Tom watched as the sun started to disappear. The western horizon was bathed in purple and red. Touched by the beauty, he watched until the sun was out of sight. Leaning on the pillar with one hand resting against the stone spire, he could feel the warmth from the rays of the sun. Closing his eyes, he felt as though the pillar was transferring tranquility to him. Tom sensed the past presence of other men, and believed that they had experienced similar feelings.

While he continued standing there with his eyes closed it became a spiritual moment. It seemed to him that the pillar called out to his soul, and he asked God to forgive him for the many wrongs he had done. Continuing to stand there with his hands on the stone spire, he began to feel warmth inside he could not explain. Later, still touching the stone, he opened his eyes to see the Evening Star sparkling above in a most inviting way. The beauty and peacefulness of this place had captured his heart. As it was growing dark he climbed down. When he lay down that night to go to sleep, he felt at peace inside. It was an incredibly calming feeling he had never before experienced.

The next morning Tom woke up and ate breakfast slowly, reluctant to leave. He started out mid-morning and continued north and east. Tom passed one structure where a huge flat rock sat atop a pillar, balanced somehow by nature. There was a small mound in the center of the flat rock, which from a distance gave it the appearance of a large sombrero sitting on a man's head. Later he came to a river with fast moving water. It had a muddy red hue from all the sand and soil it carried. The banks on each side were very steep and he had to travel along the river for miles to find a place to cross. Late in the day he came to some huge red bluffs. A few miles further there were two cylindrical stone towers that were the same size, which looked like two men standing next to each other.

Late in the day as the sun was getting low on the horizon, Tom realized he needed to find a place to camp. Just a short distance away he saw a canyon and rode toward it. He found a little cabin in the back of the canyon not unlike the one where Josh helped him recover. The cabin had come as a surprise; he was just looking for a good place to spend the night and the canyon had drawn him with its beauty. The cabin was near a large grove of trees. It wasn't quite as well built as the one Josh had taken him to, but it beat sleeping on the ground. He gathered wood for the fireplace, made coffee and supper.

After eating, Tom walked outside to enjoy the fresh air. Charlie's horse was nearby eating grass and looked up when he whistled. Grain in his hand brought the horse closer to the cabin. Later, while sitting on the porch, Tom watched the setting sun brighten the red walls of the canyon. That night he sat outside watching the stars, drinking coffee and absorbing the peacefulness. It was late when he went in to retire for the night.

Except for a short break in the afternoon to eat and rest, he rode all the next day. Toward early evening he came to another beautiful Utah canyon. There was no cabin in this one. As he sat before the campfire he listened to the birds in the nearby trees. The wood cracked and popped as the fire heated his pot of coffee. Tom decided that even though he really liked Utah, it was too close to his old stomping grounds. He promised himself that in a few years he would come back. Having never spent much time in the mountains, he decided to cross over them and head toward Kansas. Surely that was far enough to get away from his old identity.

It was a week later and Tom had found the mountains of Colorado breathtaking. He enjoyed their beauty even though it was very cold at night and could get windy up high. In Durango he had purchased a heavy coat and extra blankets. It was incredible scenery and he could travel for days and not see a single person. The mountains were everywhere, with clear streams and lush green valleys. In the distance were snow-covered peaks. On partly cloudy days, the mixture of sun and shadows seemed to dance over the mountaintops. The shadows in the morning, and again in the evening, added texture and contrast to an already majestic picture.

After several nights continually, though very slowly, heading east, he felt closer to nature, maybe to himself. Unsure just what the feeling was, he felt a...newness within him. He stopped at a huge mountain lake with water so smooth it looked like glass. Melting snow from the nearby peaks fed a constant bubbling stream of clean water into the lake. The rocks in the stream were of many colors and sizes and were rounded from the constant rapid flow of water. The lake was clear and Tom was surprised at how easily the fish could be seen.

That night next to the lake, high up in the mountains, it seemed close to heaven as he watched the flames in the campfire and wondered at length about the meaning of his life. At a turning point he pondered the possibilities of his future. He was deathly quick with a gun, and it had seemed his destiny. "Live by the gun and die by the gun," he remembered Josh saying on one of the last few nights. Josh wasn't preaching, he just said it as they sat before the fire and gazed into the flames like Tom was doing now. It hadn't seemed important at the time, but he reflected on it now.

As Tom continued to look at the flames he thought about the gunfights he had been in, and wondered if he should have walked away from them. At the time what seemed important was to be the victor, but now he wished he had tried to defuse the situation and avoided bloodshed. The past trouble in Texas and Arizona seemed unimportant as he sat amidst this vast beautiful wilderness. It was feuding and revenge-filled hatred that led to the deaths of many men in both states. All that hate and bitterness seemed to make little sense to him now.

Looking up at a clear sky Tom noticed the stars were much brighter up in the mountains. As he continued to watch the heavens his eyelids grew heavy and sleep claimed him. That night he dreamt a great deal. He was in the midst of a dream when all of the sudden he sat up awake, or at least it seemed as though he was awake. Tom couldn't believe his eyes and was filled with fear. He looked out before him and saw someone seemingly suspended in air. A large white robe covered the body and a glow of light surrounded the figure. Rubbing his eyes, he shook his head slightly and looked once more. It was still there. Even though apprehensive he did not think about trying to get away. He was too fascinated with the image and curious about its meaning. His body shivered either from cold or the anxiety and fear that enveloped him.

There before Tom, perhaps fifteen feet away, was the figure of a person floating several feet off the ground. Now as he watched, the figure came into focus. It was a young woman. Her facial characteristics seemed to fade in and out, and then all of a sudden he could see her features clearly. She had the most beautiful face he had ever seen, much like a porcelain doll. Her eyes were green and her hair blonde. Surely, he thought, this had to be an angel. Her long white robe covered everything but her face, hands and feet. She was barefoot. The vision seemed to move slowly to the right then back to the left, still off the ground. Enthralled with her absolute beauty, he was still fearful of her intent. It was then that she smiled at him. Slowly the image faded away.

He was taken aback. Who was she? What was she? Was she real? Was this a dream? Was this a vision? He sat there befuddled, trying to think clearly.

The next morning Tom awoke with a start. Getting up quickly he looked all around, hoping to see the girl in the robe again. He searched for any evidence that she might have actually been there, but found nothing to prove she existed or that he had seen anything. He knew it could have just been a dream.

That day he explored near the lake and thought about the image. He stayed another night in the same spot but didn't dream at all, or at least not that he could remember. As he rode out of the mountains, he thought about what it had all meant. Was the girl an angel? Was it a dream or a vision? If she was an angel why would she appear before him? He knew he would never forget that mountain lake, and was determined to pass this way when he returned to Utah.

When Tom reached the foothills on the eastern side, he looked down out over the rim at a flat, seemingly never-ending plain. He hesitated, but knew he would have to move on to make a living. Late that day he turned and looked back at the mountains. He saw low flying clouds lift to go over a snow covered peak, and then bend and fall downward as they came to the near side. The sky was bright blue and the clouds as white as new fallen snow. Tom would miss the beauty of the wilderness contained in the peaks and valleys of Colorado, and the pureness of the clear mountain streams. He decided to camp that night where he could still see the mountains and enjoy their company one last evening.

When Tom awoke the next morning, he fixed breakfast leisurely. He ate flapjacks and drank coffee, looking often back to the west. Finally he saddled up, packed his gear and headed on east. There was ample grass for his horse, but he found the ride boring and unpleasant. The land was barren except for a few sparse trees. The dirt and sand blew with the wind and ended up in his saddlebags, clothes and teeth. While the mountains were beautiful, eastern Colorado was a different story. It took him two more days to reach Kansas. Having no particular notion of where in Kansas he wanted to be, he just kept heading east.

Tom stayed at a few farms doing chores in exchange for food and a barn to sleep in. He found he was becoming more patient with others and tried to be of help. The farmers he encountered saw a man who had a way about him that led them to ask him to stay. Tom sensed that he had become more comfortable around people, but wasn't sure to what it should be attributed. Sometimes at night he reflected on this and wondered if it was because of Josh, or perhaps it was the experience in the mountains that unforgettable night. Whatever the reason, he was friendlier to others and more tolerant of their shortcomings.

It was getting late in the year when Tom decided he needed a home for the winter. He considered Wichita, but it was a large town and he wanted to find someplace where he was less likely to be recognized. He traveled on east and came to a town on the Verdigris River. It was near the Oklahoma border, a little town called Coffeyville. The people were friendly enough and he found a job helping a gunsmith in a hardware store. Working on guns was something he knew a lot about. The store was located across the street from the two banks in town.

Tom had shed his old clothing. He had tended to dress a bit flashy before, wore a mustache and hair longer than most. Now he wore the same type of clothes, pants and shirts as most everyone in town. Growing tired of his beard he shaved it off along with the mustache. He was a good looking fellow and women young and old always said hello. A few of the younger women tried to get to know him, and one asked him to a dance, but Tom didn't meet any he wanted to get to know seriously. He pretty much kept to himself and a small collection of friends.

That winter proved uneventful, and by spring Tom was growing bored. He liked the town and the people, but his life had become...predictable. As the weather warmed he began to think about moving on to another location. After considering several possible towns he decided to go to Abilene, Kansas. Wild Bill Hickock had been a lawman there. Tom wanted to see the town where the legend had been sheriff.

A week later Tom traveled north, riding over endless rolling hills flush with green grass and cattle, but few trees. The verdant hills were like giant swells of an ocean. He topped one hill only to see another and yet another just like it. When he camped at night and looked up at the sky he felt like he was the only person within a hundred miles. One night there was no moon; the sky was clear and he saw three different shooting stars. It was a peaceful and fulfilling night and Tom felt comfortable in the grassy hills. In the morning he fixed breakfast and drank coffee as he listened to the sound of cattle in the distance. He saddled up and continued north, finally riding out of the rolling hills. In another day he reached the town of Abilene. It was a small town situated next to the railroad. In earlier years it had been a huge railhead for cattle-drives.

Tom carried a letter of recommendation from the gunsmith in Coffeyville and soon had a similar job in Abilene. He liked the work and the town, but as before found his life a little boring. After a while he began to frequent the saloons and partake in poker games. Some of the local ranchers would occasionally talk about Wild Bill. Some had seen Hickock when he served as a lawman there and had various opinions about the man.

In mid to late summer the herds of cattle from Texas started arriving routinely. Tom was more careful when drovers from the Lone Star State came into town. He didn't expect to see anyone who knew him, but couldn't be certain. Letting his beard grow again helped hide his identity. He even wore the glass spectacles Charlie had suggested. Only once did a cowboy walk in that he vaguely remembered. Tom left shortly and stayed out of the saloon for a week.

One evening Tom detected a card sharp cheating at poker and winning more than his share. Tom left the game. Calling a man a card cheat was serious business and usually ended in gunplay. He wanted to avoid getting into a gunfight. Tom never drank to excess, which was different than in years past. He had nothing to prove and could relax and enjoy himself and the people around him. Cowboys learned that he was always fair and often invited him to join their game. A couple of times when a cowboy lost all his money, Tom had given them enough to eat and sleep for the evening. He took an interest in those around him and his view of the world was less centered on himself. Without realizing why, his life had become more rewarding.

Tom boarded with Widow Hawkins on the outskirts of town. She was older, heavyset, and very pleasant. Her hair was short, curly and brown with a bit of gray sprinkled throughout. She treated him like a son. Tom would occasionally go to church with her on Sunday, something in which she seemed to take great pleasure. She introduced him to some of the younger women in town, including Mary Simms. Her father owned the general store. Mary was pretty with long brown hair. She was a nice person and Tom took her to dinner a couple of times. Knowing he would have to move on some day, he was reluctant to try to get to know a woman well. Tom was able to put some of his earnings and all of his winnings from poker in the bank. The rest he used to pay Widow Hawkins and buy what he needed.

Summer, fall and winter came and went. After being in Abilene a year, Tom found his life had become pretty mundane except for the cowboys and poker games. He spent some of his time making sure he didn't get rusty on those things that really mattered when the time came. Tom found a good place to practice his draw on Will Parker's ranch, and went twice a week. Loading his own cartridges kept the cost to a minimum.

During the season when herds came in from Texas there would inevitably be arguments. He had witnessed several fistfights at the saloon, but they had not resulted in serious injury. While there had been gunplay, most of the time a few of the cowboys just threatened to draw on each other. Tom had seen only one gunfight. A man had been wounded in the arm. There had been two gunfights where men were killed, but Tom had not been there at the time.

One summer afternoon while Tom was at the saloon, a young cowboy was drinking more than he should and trying to pick a fight. He was part of an outfit that had just brought a herd into town. As was often the case, the ramrod had turned the men loose and they were seeking excitement after being on the trail for months.

A middle-aged farmer named Seth came in for a drink and began playing poker at the same table as Tom. Seth was a homely looking man with stoop shoulders and hair that was never combed. What he lacked in appearance he more than made up for in friendliness and honesty. Also at the table were Will Parker and Bob Gill. It was Will's ranch where Tom practiced his draw. Bob worked at the livery stable and had long been a close friend of Will's. Late in the afternoon, after an hour of card playing, Seth told them he had better get home before his wife came in after him. Seth then went to the bar for one last drink and was getting ready to leave.

The young cowboy—Kid Coulter he called himself—stepped in Seth's path and started making fun of the farmer. The Kid wore two guns; both had notches in the handle. He wore them low and had the bottom of the holsters tied to his legs. There was a glove on his left hand, but not his right. The right hand glove was tucked into his gun belt. His hair was long, dark brown and straight, and his voice unusually nasal. His eyes were set close together. Kid Coulter continued to goad the farmer and did just about everything he could to get him mad. Not wearing a gun, Seth was trying to ignore the overbearing young cowboy. He was getting nervous and doing his best to find a way to leave. The Kid took a gun from one of his friends and stuffed it in the farmer's belt.

"Now you're fully dressed."

"I don't want no trouble," Seth repeated, keeping his hands away from the gun.

"Is that so? Tell me something, are all Kansas sodbusters as ugly as you?"

"I just don't want no trouble," Seth said again. It was a struggle, but he kept his temper and was determined not to fight.

Kid Coulter seemed unable to accept an outcome that didn't result in showing his friends what a fast gun he was. He had bragged all the way up from Texas and it was time to prove his skills. Seth wasn't cooperating no matter how much he was pushed. The Kid could tell the farmer was about to leave so he presented the ultimate insult.

"Well, you know, old farmer, I wasn't gonna tell anybody, but you aren't being very friendly. While you were out in the field, I dropped by your house and saw your wife. In no time at all she was kissing me, pulling my pants off and doing things with my tally whacker you wouldn't want me to talk about. She begged me to come back for more whenever I wanted, and she said to be sure and bring all my friends. Your wife was really something."

The farmer lost his composure at that point. He had been humiliated enough. It was one thing to be insulted, but he wasn't going to let any man talk about his wife that way. Seth turned toward the Kid. He was so mad his whole body was shaking.

"Mister, yur a…a lyin sack of shit."

"Hey, farmer, there's no reason to get all mad at me just cause your wife likes to get into men's pants." The Kid laughed and lowered his hand to his gun, daring the farmer to draw.

Tom knew Seth well. The farmer was honest, hard working and would never cheat anyone. Tom had seen gunslingers push men into fights before, but this would be little more than murder. Seth never carried a gun and Tom doubted he had used anything but a rifle. Tom was sitting at the table, behind and to the right of Seth, not more than ten feet away. He had seen enough. Tom took off his spectacles, got up and walked toward the bar. His path crossed right in front of Seth. As he stepped in front of the farmer, Tom stopped and touched the brim of his hat.

"That's a mighty fine looking gun, Seth. Could I see it?"

Before the farmer could react, Tom had the gun out and was looking at it, taking his time. Tom's back was to the Kid, and Tom seemed to be ignoring him completely. Seth was mad, flustered and not thinking clearly. Tom had always been a friend and seemed like an easygoing fellow. Seth and his wife had Tom out for supper twice, and even introduced him to one of the neighbor girls.

The voice Seth heard from Tom now was different. It wasn't friendly; it was matter of fact. Seth looked into Tom's eyes. They were ice blue, cold, hard and seemed to look right through him. This wasn't the Tom he knew. Seth was angry, but the voice and eyes of this man unnerved him. The man who made the decision to intervene was Tom Stone, but the man who got up from the table was from the past.

Finally Kid Coulter said to Tom in a loud boisterous voice, "Mister, I don't know who you think you are but you better be giving that gun back. This old fellar and I have some unfinished business."

Tom continued to ignore the Kid, looked at Seth and asked, "Weren't you on your way home?" Seth started to reply but Tom's eyes grew even harder and he cut Seth off. "You go on home. I'll take care of this gun and little mister fancy pants over here."

Seth's eyes went wide and he looked bewildered. Tom's face became stern and he motioned with a nod of his head toward the door. The farmer's anger subsided from his shock and amazement at Tom's behavior. It had been quiet in the saloon before, but now there was no sound at all except Seth's boots on the wood floor as he headed toward the door. Seth looked back at Tom, then at Kid Coulter and went on out. He was glad to be alive but still mad as hell at the cowboy who had insulted his wife. After the farmer was gone, Tom tucked the gun into his belt, turned slowly and faced the Kid, lowering his right hand to his holstered gun.

"Well, what about it, fancy pants, do you only fight old farmers? I bet you kick sick dogs and slap little girls too. My guess is you wouldn't draw on a man who knows how to use a gun. Just another punk who strapped on a gun and thinks it makes him a man."

Kid Coulter was caught off guard. He hadn't anticipated any interruption, let alone someone calling him yellow. He tried to regroup and looked back at his friends. One was a round-faced Mexican and the other a tall, skinny cowboy wearing chaps. Their faces glared with surprise and anger; they looked at each other then back to their companion. Finally the Kid regained his composure; after all, he was Kid Coulter.

"I think it's only fair to tell you, mister, I've already killed four men in gunfights."

"Did any of the four have guns? I bet they died with holes in their backs." Tom could have let it go, but how many more men like Seth would die at the hands of this braggart?

The Kid looked again at his two friends and growing anger was evident in their faces as well as his. He could tell what they thought: "Are you going to let him talk to you like that?"

The men in the saloon who knew Tom couldn't believe their eyes and ears. They had never seen Tom anything but friendly. This was a man seemingly without feeling or fear, a gunman who exuded confidence. His very presence seemed to command respect.

The Kid had finally been pushed far enough. He would normally be reluctant to draw on someone so willing to fight, but he had reached a point beyond rational thought. Everyone was looking. Kid Coulter wanted to leave, but he didn't know how. His pride was severely damaged; his friends and everyone in the saloon were waiting to see if he would turn yellow. He couldn't; his pride was too hard to swallow. The Kid didn't stop to realize the tables had just been turned. The hunter had become the prey.

Tom knew he was ready, something he had learned from experience. The Kid went for his gun. Before the gun was halfway out of the holster an explosion sounded, the Kid's head jerked back and the expression on his face went blank. There was a hole in his forehead. His body dropped like dead weight to the floor. His legs buckled under him in an unseemly position, and his hand was still on the half-holstered gun.

Silence turned into the absolute nonexistence of sound. No one made a move except for the astonished looks that came to their faces. An old man's jaw dropped wide open, and then the upper plate of his false teeth fell out of his mouth and plunked into his mug of beer. Some of the liquid splashed onto the table. The splash of the beer was the only sound Tom could hear, and it drew his attention for a split second. Then he immediately looked around the room searching for any movement. There was none. He knew there was danger in this type of confrontation. The Kid might have friends in the saloon in addition to the two behind him, and Tom couldn't be sure who they were.

"Is there anyone who thinks that wasn't a fair fight?" Tom asked as he stepped back against the bar.

"He drew first," one man remarked.

"He deserved to be plugged," another said.

Tom noticed the two behind the Kid changed expression at the last comment, but he noticed no such resentment in the faces of the other men in the saloon. Tom looked directly at the Kid's two friends.

"Do you think it was a fair fight?"

A long period of silence followed.

"Yeah it was a fair fight," the tall one finally said.

"You be sure and tell that to the Sheriff," Tom said and then moved cautiously toward the door.

This was Abilene and these men had seen gunfights before, but Tom's draw was incomprehensibly fast. The men looked at him dumbfounded as he walked out. Will Parker sat silently at the table. He had known Tom for a year and had never seen this side of him. During the whole time he talked to Seth and faced the belligerent young cowboy, it was as though he were someone else entirely. Will thought his actions were those of a man who had been in many gunfights. He could tell Tom knew exactly what he was doing when he challenged the Kid. Even though he had no idea how fast his opponent might be, Tom never showed any sign of fear or hesitation in getting Seth out and confronting Kid Coulter. "He has to be a gunfighter, and a damned good one," Will said to himself. Some of the men in the saloon started talking but Will could hear only a murmur. Finally he realized Bob was saying something to him.

"Did you see that draw?" Bob repeated. Bob was a heavyset man and sat looking straight across the table at his friend.

Will's thoughts came back to the present, "Well, hell yes I saw it. I was sitting right here, wasn't I?"

A couple of cowboys from a different cattle drive joined them, asking who the man was. Since Will and Bob had been playing cards with him, most everyone from the saloon started moseying over to their table. Bob told them, "His name is Tom Stone, and he works at the gunsmith shop. I guess he's been in town about a year. He's a real nice fella. Don't you agree, Will?"

Will had a ranch west of Abilene and had lived there for years. He was shorter than most men and had a nose that looked like the beak of a hawk. His face was wrinkled from too much sun, and his skin was a dark bronze. Those acquainted with Will knew him to be a respected and trustworthy rancher. Will pushed back his black hat and shifted in his seat so he could face where most of the men were standing.

"I've known him for about a year and Bob here is right, he's a helluva nice fellow. He even goes to church sometimes with Widow Hawkins. Tom sure knows a lot about guns, I can tell you that. I just never knew he could handle them so well too."

Will went on to tell them he had been in Abilene back when Bill Hickock was the town sheriff. He had seen Hickock draw on two different occasions. At the time, he didn't think anybody could be faster than Wild Bill. Will told them he had seen the time that Hickock and John Wesley Hardin had met on the streets of Abilene. Several of the cowboys had heard about it, but had never talked to anyone who had actually seen it. They encouraged Will to tell the story. Everyone gathered around as close as they could and listened to Will. He was feeling mighty important about then and he looked up at the men and picked his words carefully and slowly for effect.

"Well you see, it was back in '71. Hickock was the sheriff and he had a town law forbiddin the wearin of guns. Now Hardin, he come into town after a cattle drive up from Texas. It was rumored he killed ten men on that there cattle drive. Hell, the cowboys with Hardin was a tellin everybody about it. Hickock had heard about John Wesley killin all those men, and he saw Hardin wearin his two guns. Wild Bill just walked right up to him. Now who but Wild Bill would've been willin to do that?

"Hickock was an impressive lookin man. He was over six feet tall, wore a black suit and was wearin his two ivory handled guns in a red sash, butt forward like he always did. Everybody includin Hardin and all the Texas cowboys had heard about Hickock and knew how fast he was supposed to be. Well, Wild Bill just walked right up to Hardin and before John Wesley could react, Wild Bill drew a gun and told Hardin to surrender his six-shooters.

"Now while Hickock was all impressive lookin, Hardin looked like any other cowboy. If you didn't know who he was you wouldn't think nuthin about him. John Wesley looked all sheepish like, and then he real slow like pulled both guns out, butt first, and was holdin them out for the sheriff. Now that's where Wild Bill made his mistake. Hickock put his gun back in the sash and started to reach for the two guns Hardin was holdin. Hardin had hold of the barrels with the butt of the guns facing away from him and down, but he also had his fingers in the trigger guards. As Wild Bill started to reach for them, Hardin snapped his wrists and twirled the guns, cocked and ready.

"What exactly was said between them, I couldn't hear, but after a bit Hardin holstered his guns and he and Wild Bill went into the saloon and had a drink. I suspect Hardin realized if he shot the sheriff down while Hickock's guns were holstered, he'd been lynched pretty quick like. Anyways, they headed off to the saloon together like they was old pals. It was probably a big thing for both of them to be standin at the bar talkin to the other, both of them well known gunmen like they were. I don't suspect there were many times a couple of legends like that faced each other with a gun. I was sure privileged to see that encounter, and I've told many a man this story. But I'll tell you this, ain't no man alive or dead I ever seen could match the draw of Tom Stone," Will concluded.

All the men stood there spellbound while Will talked. Several of the men were very familiar with Will and knew he wasn't the type to exaggerate. Afterwards, some nodded their heads in agreement, but others weren't so sure anybody could be faster than Wild Bill. As fast as Tom's draw had been, several argued he couldn't be quicker than the legendary Hickock.

Will repeated what he had said: "Well I seen 'em both, an I'm a tellin ya, that there fella you seen today is the fastest gun there ever was." Not everyone necessarily agreed, but they were all in awe at the speed of his draw.

"Maybe it was Ringo. Those that seen him said he was faster than anybody, includin ole Wild Bill," one of the men said.

"Nah, he got killt out in Arizonie; everybody knows that," a tall lean cowboy from Texas said.

Tom didn't waste any time. He had no desire to stay around and hear men talk about his draw. It would spread like wildfire, especially in a town like Abilene. After this gunfight the name Tom Stone would become known, at least in Abilene and probably most of Kansas. Tom went back to the house where he was staying. After collecting his things, he quickly said goodbye and asked Widow Hawkins to let the gunsmith know he had to move on. He told her what had happened at the saloon. "I just couldn't let him gun down Seth," he explained.

Crying, Widow Hawkins gave him a hug and then helped him pack some food. She would see the banker the next day and make arrangements to send Tom's money to a bank in another town. Tom asked her not to tell anyone but the banker which town. The sun was getting low on the horizon as he rode out of Abilene. It was late that night when he finally found a small creek well off the road to bed down for the night. Sleeping under the stars was something he was used to, even liked, but he would miss the good food and soft bed at the home of Widow Hawkins.

ELEVEN

Tom headed west out of Abilene toward Hays. It was easy to find the way; all he had to do was follow the railroad track. The land was flat, which Tom figured must have made construction of this portion of the track easy. The famous railroad, the one that first connected the East and West Coast, ran through Abilene and Hays. Both were cow towns because of it.

Hays was the name of the town Tom had given to Widow Hawkins for the transfer of his money. He traveled quickly just in case friends of Kid Coulter decided to follow him and settle the score. Around mid-morning Tom rode into Hays, going first to the bank—he wanted to make sure that his money was there. Tom had been concerned ever since leaving Abilene that something could go wrong in getting it transferred.

"May I help you, sir?" the teller asked.

"I had some money sent here from Abilene."

"And the name, sir?"

"Tom Stone."

"Oh yes, that arrived earlier this morning. Is there anything I can do for you today?"

Very relieved, Tom replied, "I need to withdraw some money to get supplies."

When the teller recognized his name, Tom felt like a weight had been removed from his shoulders. He was not wanting to hang around town another day. Planning to get the rest of his money before the end of the day, he noted the closing time as he left.

Tom walked into the saloon down the street and ordered a cup of coffee. There weren't many patrons during that time of morning. Two gents were at a table in the far corner talking about cattle and horses. Both were well dressed and Tom took them to be well-to-do ranchers or businessmen. Neither seemed to be paying much attention to him. Sipping his coffee, Tom chatted with the bartender about everything that came to mind. The bartender, Jack Caper, was a short, fat little man with a long, drooping black mustache and the shiniest bald head Tom had ever seen. Bags under his red-veined eyes attested to the long nights spent tending bar. This time of day he had little to do but wash and dry the glasses used the night before.

"I'll be heading out for Colorado before long. What is there between Hays and Denver?" Tom asked.

"A whole lot of nuthin is what you'll be ridin through."

"Much obliged for the encouraging news." Tom raised his cup in salute, finished his coffee and then headed out the door.

Next he went to the general store to buy needed items, including two new shirts and a hat. They were different colors than he had been wearing. He also decided to get a vest, which he hadn't worn since arriving in Kansas. There was an abundance of army paraphernalia on the shelves, apparently because of the nearby fort. A couple of ladies had the salesclerk occupied showing them the latest rolls of material from the East. Each roll resulted in an opinion from the ladies on the cloth's merits or lack thereof. The store was busy and Tom took his time selecting supplies he would need on the trail. As the storeowner packaged his purchases, Tom mentioned that he planned to head west to Denver. Having left word in two different places that he was going to Colorado, Tom was ready to leave Hays. He went back to the bank, withdrew his money and rode out of town. After he was several miles out of Hays he started to relax.

For most of the afternoon Tom headed west, just as he had said, and then he turned south for Dodge City. He had mentioned he was going to Denver just in case someone had followed him to Hays. Tom wasn't quite ready to go back over the mountains. Dodge had been an interesting place back when Earp and Holliday had been there.

As Tom rode south his thoughts were miles away, but suddenly he realized it was nearing sunset and he needed to look for a place to camp. The clouds just to the left of the sun looked like cobblestones with spaces in between each small cloud. A mixture of yellow and burnt orange burst through the spaces in the cobblestone clouds, and a pinkish red and purple covered the rest of the nearby horizon. Every now and then a beautiful sunset rewards the weary traveler and this was one of those evenings.

Tom had no real worries right now and let his mind drift. He had turned in a direction no one following him would expect. It gave him a renewed sense of security. Now he could relax and enjoy the sunset and the peace and quiet of the wide-open spaces. As the sun lowered the reds became purple and the yellows a dark orange. Tom became even more mellow, and was at peace with himself that night.

The next morning, after eating breakfast, he shaved off his beard. That, along with the new clothes, should help hide his identity. He thought about taking a new last name while he continued south, but didn't settle on anything. It was late in the day when he came upon a wagon that was stopped. A wheel had come off and a man and woman were trying to put it back on the axle. The man wasn't quite strong enough to lift the axle by himself. The woman could help him lift it, but then they couldn't also put the wheel back on the wagon. Tom stopped and helped the man lift while the woman pushed on the wheel. Then Tom helped them load their supplies back into the wagon.

"Much obliged, stranger. We been strugglin for near an hour to get thet wheel back on," the young farmer said.

"No problem at all, glad to be of help."

"It's almost night and we live just up the road if you need a place to stay," the man offered. "You might as well join us for somethin to eat."

"That's awful kind of you, but it's not necessary. Thanks all the same." Tom touched the brim of his hat, nodded to the woman and started to get on his horse.

The woman stepped forward. "We would be pleased if you would stay for supper. It's the least we could do, and we haven't had company for such a long time."

"We'd both feel better about it if you'd at least join us for supper," added the man.

Tom paused for a moment and looked at both of them. Finally he smiled and relented. "Reckon I can't refuse that offer. A good meal sounds pretty tempting."

"Good!" said the man. "My name is Pete Starnes, and this is my wife, Meggy." Pete was of average height and a little thin. His muscles were well defined from hard work. He had light brown hair that came down a couple of inches below his ears. "We can be at our place in no time at all."

The wife had long, curly dark brown hair. Meggy was several inches shorter than her husband. She bore the signs of hard work with strong arms and callused hands. As she climbed into the wagon next to her husband, Tom noticed the lower edge of her skirt had several small tears. He quickly glanced back up before she turned around. They either didn't have much money or material things didn't matter to this couple.

True to their word they reached their home well before nightfall. Pete did the chores quickly while Tom cleaned up behind the house. They had a well there and Meggy provided a basin and towel. He had just enough time to clean up before dinner. As Tom sat through supper he noted the closeness these two shared. They were obviously in love and delighted in doing things for each other. It was something he had yet to share with a woman.

Toward the end of dinner, Pete said, "We're gettin ready to put up our wheat. If you could stay around for a few days I'd be happy to pay you."

Tom sat silent for awhile as he thought it over. He decided he was in no particular hurry. "Well, I reckon I could stay a few days. Never put up wheat before, so I'm not sure I'd know what to do."

"Oh, I can show you. You'll learn in no time, but I'll warn you it's hard work."

"Hard work is good for a man."

"At least some hard work is good for a man. I can't tell you how much I appreciate your stayin."

"We're both delighted you'll help us," Meggy added.

It took a week to finish up the harvest. They had to cut the wheat with a scythe, then pick it up and put it into a standing pile. After they had a wagonload, they would take it to the neighbor's farm. The neighbor had a device that separated the grain from the rest of the stalk. They put the grain in sacks and left them there to get more wheat shocks from the field. When they had enough sacks of grain for a wagonload they hauled it off to town. It was a laborious process and every night Tom felt muscles in his back he didn't know he had, but he felt good about the progress they had made by the end of the day. Meggy was an excellent cook and he ate ravenously. She made the best bread he had ever eaten.

At the end of the week, after they had taken in the last load of grain, it rained for two days solid with high winds. The wheat in the neighbor's fields was flattened down to the ground and would be difficult to harvest. Much of the neighbor's crop was ruined, Pete told him.

They discovered the next day that two miles down the road a farmer's barn had been blown away by a fierce funnel cloud. Fragments of lumber were scattered throughout the nearby field. Luckily the couple had seen the tornado coming and had time to run to a ditch behind the house. The wife was heavy with an unborn child, but had still managed to reach safety in time. The funnel had left the house untouched but hit the barn head on. Several trees on the other side of the barn were blown down and left their roots exposed. The trees on the south side were lying with their roots facing the barn, but the trees to the north were blown down in the opposite direction with the roots facing the other way. Since the funnel cloud was blowing in a circle it knocked the trees down in opposite directions.

During the following week, all the neighbors got together and rebuilt the barn. Tom stayed and helped, thoroughly enjoying the friendliness and helpfulness of the neighbors and the good feeling he had inside at helping the family rebuild. After the barn was complete, Tom stayed on for another week helping mend fences and repair things around the farm that Pete had trouble getting time to do.

Finally, as they ate supper one evening, Tom decided he needed to move on.

"I'll be heading out tomorrow. Wanted to let you both know how much I appreciate your taking me in and treating me like family."

"Are you sure you can't stay a little longer?" Meggy asked. "We've really liked having you here."

"Maybe I can come back this way later."

"I hope so, Tom," Pete said. "You have no idea how much you've helped us."

"We're really going to miss you," Meggy added.

"I'll miss the both of you too."

These were new experiences for Tom. Widow Hawkins had acted the same way when he left Abilene. He realized he was more able to recognize the good in others now; perhaps that somehow let them see the good in him. Tom left the next morning and was truly saddened as he rode away. Meggy's eyes watered, and a few tears found their way down her cheek. Pete shook Tom's hand and wished him well.

Tom told them as he began to ride away, "I hope someday to find a woman that'll make me as happy as the two of you are."

Pete and Meggy each put one arm around the other and stood side-by-side smiling. Tom would never forget them, or the way their closeness to each other caused a void to reopen in him. It happened the first time when he visited the Franklins. He had been attracted to women before, danced with them, kissed them, but never longed for one the way he did after meeting Lucy.

Tom traveled leisurely for two more days before coming to the outskirts of Dodge City. It was getting late, and he decided to head back out of town and spend another night under a lonely tree. He passed by an old farmhouse a little ways off the road. An ugly brown dog barked at him as he rode by. A freckle faced little boy sat on the board fence in front of the house and waved. He was barefoot and wore ragged overalls and a faded shirt with holes in the sleeves. Looking up the lane Tom saw the house needed some repair on the roof and the screen door had a torn screen. About then a woman came out on the porch and watched him ride by. She was probably concerned about the little boy, Tom thought. Tom touched the brim of his hat and nodded. She smiled but did not wave.

The little boy yelled out, "See you, mister."

Tom came to a stream about a half-mile up the road. There were a cluster of tall trees and one of the biggest oaks he had ever seen. A squirrel dashed across the road in front of him and caused his horse to jump to the side. Tom calmed his horse and dismounted. He unsaddled the appaloosa and made camp. After eating he sat before the fire and watched the sun go down. He was tired from the day's ride and his eyelids grew heavy. It had gotten dark and Tom was about ready to turn in; suddenly, he heard a twig break and his horse stamped a hoof and snorted. Tom moved quickly but silently back out of the light close to the trunk of the tree and drew his gun. In a few more seconds he could hear footsteps.

"Are you here, mister?"

Tom recognized the voice of the little boy from the farmhouse and came out in the light of the campfire. "Don't you know you can get shot sneaking up on a man like that in the dark?"

"I wasn't sneaking. I called out, didn't I?" he replied nervously.

Tom softened his voice. "Well, I heard you before you called out. Better be more careful in the future. What are you doing out here anyway? It's late."

"I came down to see if you need a place to stay."

"A place to stay. What do you mean? You don't even know who I am. I could be a bank robber or desperado for all you know."

"My mama asked me to come down and see if you need a place to stay. The fellar that was staying with us got drunk all the time so mama kicked him out. Got a real nice room, and my mama sure can cook. It's a lot cheaper than a hotel in town, and a lot better food too."

"Yeah, well, how do you know I'm not an outlaw or something?"

"Aw shucks, you don't look like no outlaw. Mama seen you, and after supper I told her I thought we should ask you to stay. She said maybe in the morning I could come down and ask you to stop by, but I was afeard you'd be gone. What do you say, mister? Why don't you come and meet my mama? She's a good cook and good lookin too."

"You mean your mother doesn't even know you're here?"

"Ah...nope, but she won't mind. Will you come on up and meet my mama? You might as well sleep in a soft bed."

149

"Tell you what. I'll ride up in the morning and meet your mother then. Okay?"

"Okay, mister," he yelled gleefully and ran toward the house.

Tom figured the boy's father must have run off or got shot or something. His mother must be trying to help make a go of it by renting out a room. The boy's clothes were sure ragged, he thought. They must be pretty desperate to be asking a man they hadn't met to stay with them. He would ride up in the morning to meet with her. Staying with Widow Hawkins had certainly been better than staying in a hotel. He wasn't sure about having a young boy around all the time, but he seemed nice enough. If the house was better inside than out and the woman was pleasant, he thought he might give it a try. If it didn't work out, he would have time to find another place to stay.

As Tom lay down to go to sleep he heard a coyote in the distance, followed by a long howl from the little boy's dog. The air was cool, but his blanket kept him warm. There was a slight breeze and it occasionally blew smoke from the fire in his direction. The smell of the burning wood pleased him. His thoughts drifted and finally he faded off to sleep.

The next morning as Tom woke up he noticed the dark clouds low on the western horizon. It looked like rain was a distinct possibility sometime during the day. He got a campfire going and prepared breakfast. Tom was getting his first cup of coffee when he heard rapid footsteps approaching.

"Howdy, mister! See yur up for breakfast."

"Yep, sure am. Been sitting here watching the sunrise and getting something to eat. Looks like it's going to rain."

"It sure do; just lookit them clouds. Yur gonna come by this morning, ain't ya, and see my mama?"

"I'll be up just as soon as I finish breakfast and get everything put away."

"Do you want me to help?"

"No, that's okay, son. I've got to finish eating first. You run along and I'll be up there before you know it."

"Great!" was all he said as he turned for the house and ran as fast as he could.

Tom didn't hurry. After he finished eating he cleaned up the utensils in the stream, packed everything away and headed to the house. The little boy's mother came to the door as he stepped up onto the porch. She was a pretty woman, just as the boy had said, and had the same little pointy nose as her son. Her dress was green with white lace trim and looked like her Sunday best clothes. There were a few small freckles on her cheeks and long chestnut hair spilled over her shoulders.

"Good morning! I'm Sarah Jones, and this is my son, Ted."

"I'm Tom."

"Tom...?"

As he reflected on it quickly, almost any woman would want to know a stranger's full name before letting him board in her home. Tom had forgotten to think anymore about a last name and had to come up with one on the spot. It was an awkward pause, but finally he thought of the legendary weapon that seemed almost a part of his body.

"Tom Colt."

"Won't you come in, Mr. Colt? Would you like a cup of coffee? I made it fresh just a little while ago."

"Thank you, ma'am." He walked in and took a seat at the table.

"Do you plan to be in Dodge City long?" She poured him a cup and set it in front of him.

"Well, I don't know for sure, ma'am. It could be a month or two, and it could be a year. It just kind of depends on the work I can get here."

"What type of work do you do? If you don't mind me asking."

"Oh no, that's fine, ma'am. I've done a lot of different jobs, salesclerk, businessman, even been a rancher."

"Where are you from?" Sarah was doing her best to size up the stranger quickly. Ted had raved about him all morning.

"Well, I've been in several states but most recently Arizona and here in Kansas. Mostly I've done ranching, but I'm looking to get into something else."

"You seem like the type of man who wouldn't have much trouble getting employment."

"Well, thank you, ma'am. I hope you're right about that."

151

"I guess Ted has already told you we rent out a room, and right now we have a vacancy. Is it possible you might be interested?"

"Yes, ma'am, that is a possibility."

"Would you like to see the room?"

"Sure."

Sarah showed him through the house. It was fairly large and solidly built, although it revealed the need for a man's handy-work. The furniture was old and worn, but it was obvious Sarah was a good housekeeper; everything was clean. His room would be in the back and had ample space for the small table and sofa in addition to the bed. It was larger than the room he had at Widow Hawkins'. There was a small covered porch in the back with a bench wide enough for two people. The back door was in the hall just off of his bedroom. There were several large trees in the back yard, which made for a nice view. The back porch would be a private place to go in the quiet of the evening. There was a small barn, corral and pasture for his horse over to the left.

Tom was pleased with everything and had already decided he would stay. They made their way back to the kitchen and Sarah poured him another cup of coffee. She told Tom they really needed a boarder and offered him a rate that seemed low. He wasn't aware of it, but it was lower than the amount she had charged the man staying there previously.

"That amount does include three meals a day," she concluded.

"And my mom is a real good cook," Ted added.

"I'm sure she is, Ted. Well the room seems nice. Like I said, ma'am, I'm not sure how long I will be in Dodge."

"Oh, I understand. That would be fine." She was unsure whether he intended to accept. "Does the amount seem too high?"

"No, ma'am, not at all. The amount is very reasonable. I just wanted you to know I'm not sure how long I'll be staying in Dodge."

"Oh, that's understood, Mr. Colt. So you'll be staying with us?"

"Yes, ma'am, I believe I will."

"Good!" She smiled at hearing he was staying, but then timidly looked down at the floor. "I usually ask for a week's rent in advance, but if you prefer to pay at the end of the week that would be fine."

"Actually, ma'am, I would prefer to give you a month in advance. That way I don't have to pay as often."

He then gave her half again more than a month's stay would cost based on the price she quoted him. When she looked puzzled he said, "That's the rate I've been paying where I just came from and I figure it cost as much to board and feed someone here as it does there."

She was taken aback and smiled but remained silent. Her hand went up to her lips for a second as she fought her emotions. Tom noticed the tremor in her lips and saw the water swelling in her eyes. Sensing her situation he excused himself, telling her he needed to go to town and would be back for lunch. Ted was ecstatic that Tom would be staying and couldn't hide his delight. Tom sensed Sarah was pleased as well, but also relieved to have a boarder.

As Tom headed toward town, Sarah watched him ride away. Tears came to her eyes and streamed down her face. Ted had gone outside to watch him ride up the road. Sarah went back to the table and sat down, sipped once at her cup of coffee and noticed her hand still had the slight tremor she seemed unable to control. The money he had given her was more than she had left to her name just a few minutes before. She hadn't been sure how she would make it for another month and it had weighed heavily on her. Laying her head on top of her arms, she cried for several minutes with deep choking sobs making it hard for her to breathe. Finally there were no more tears. Thankful that Ted had stayed outside to play, she cleaned up her face and regained her composure before he came back in the house.

Her last boarder had made several passes at her when he was drunk. One night, after he had been drinking heavily, he had come into her room while she was asleep. He got into bed with her and tried to grope her. She shuddered when she thought about what he might have done. After managing to get out from under the sheet, she delivered a kick with great force in a well-placed spot. She had tolerated him as long as she did because she felt she had no choice, but she would not put up with him attempting to assault her. When she told little Ted she was planning to ask the man to leave, the boy told her the man had slapped him two months ago. Had she known that she would have thrown him out then.

The next morning she informed the boarder of her decision; he had refused to go. Sarah went to town and asked the sheriff for help in throwing him out. She told the sheriff about his attempt to molest her and about Ted being slapped. The sheriff wasted no time going to her home and physically throwing him out of the house. He advised him to be on his way to another town.

After that Sarah had prayed, because without a boarder to help pay the costs there wasn't enough money to survive. She didn't know how long Tom would stay, but for now things looked much better. With the amount of money he was paying per month, she would be able to put some aside for the next time they were temporarily without a boarder. Perhaps she could even get Ted some new clothes. She walked outside and looked up toward the sky.

"Thank you, Lord," she whispered.

Tom rode into town to find work. After checking around he quickly discovered there were three options. Help was needed at the livery if he wanted to clean stalls and brush down horses all day, the general store needed a sales clerk, and two different ranches were looking for cowhands. None of these appealed to him and he was beginning to wonder how long he would stay in Dodge. There was the possibility he might have to tell Sarah and Ted he would be leaving. He recalled how she had reacted to the money he had given her for the first month's rent. For no particular reason he decided to stop at a saloon and order coffee. Tom told the bartender he had been looking for a job and hadn't come up with much.

"Do you know of any other jobs hereabouts?" Tom asked.

"I sure don't. Sorry," the barkeep replied.

An old gent with long gray whiskers and no teeth was down the bar about ten feet away. He overheard the conversation. The elderly patron was hard to understand with no teeth.

"Yu mite chek wit de gunsmit un de udder side uh de feed store. De sheruf run a fellar outta town dat wurkd dere."

"Gunsmith, huh? Well I'll be. Thanks, old timer. Let me buy you a drink." Tom gave the bartender the money and headed out of the saloon.

When Tom went to see the gunsmith it turned out the prior employee was the previous boarder of Sarah Jones. Tom let him know

154

that was where he was staying and that while he had never worked in a gun shop before, he knew a lot about guns. The owner asked him several questions about rifles and revolvers. Surprised at the answers he hired Tom on the spot. His wage would be a little less than he had earned at Abilene, but not substantially. Tom was a little concerned about the possibility someone would make the connection between Tom Stone in Abilene who worked at the gunsmith shop, and Tom Colt in Dodge City who also worked as a gunsmith. He knew there was a chance, but decided it was minimal.

The gunsmith asked if he could start tomorrow, and Tom said that would be fine. He was pleased so far with the results here in Dodge. As he walked down the sidewalk with a smile, he tipped his hat to the ladies he met. After wandering around town for awhile he headed back out to the house. As they were eating lunch he shared his news with Sarah and Ted; they were delighted. He proposed they celebrate by going on a picnic for dinner unless the rain came first.

Tom spent the afternoon first surveying the work needed around the house, then going to town for the supplies to do some mending. He made a second trip to get screen for the front door and a windowpane for the side window. There were several hinges needed for the cabinets in the kitchen and one for the back door. On his third trip to town he bought some food for the picnic and candy for Ted. As he finished fixing the hinge on the back door, Sarah brought him a glass of tea.

"I'll pay you for the repairs just as soon as I can. It might take a little while, but I'll reimburse you for the things you've bought and pay you for the work too."

"No you won't," he replied, smiling. "This is just part of the rent."

"But I can't let you do that."

"You don't have any choice. You take the money you would've given me and get something for you and Ted. I really don't need it."

Sarah's eyes filled with tears and this time she couldn't keep them from flowing down her face.

"Thank you, Tom; I...I don't know what to say."

"No need to say anything." Wanting to change the subject, he added, "Ted seems like a really nice boy. You've raised a good one there."

"Thank you!" She smiled with the pride of a mother.

The fortunes of this family seemed to be changing. Even the rain held off while they went several miles to the lake Sarah and Ted sometimes visited on hot summer days. The lake was peaceful, away from the road and quite scenic. The wind was mild and the water had tiny waves that sparkled and reflected the light of the sun. There were ducks on the other side that made wakes wherever they went. While Sarah readied the food, Tom and Ted threw rocks, trying to skip them on the water. The food was delicious, especially the cherry pie. The boy had told the truth when he said his mom could cook. Ted finished first and then spent much of his time walking around the edge of the lake, inspecting anything unusual he came across. Sarah called out to Ted to watch for snakes.

After the picnic they headed home and made it to the house just as it started to sprinkle. Before long it came down steadily. Tom and Ted went out on the front porch to watch the rain. Sarah made hot chocolate and brought it out to them. She sat next to Tom on the bench. They all sat and watched as the rain came down harder. Soon it was pouring.

During the first few weeks Tom got to know several of the people in town, and became more familiar with the various businesses. One afternoon he was looking in the store across the street, trying to find something for Ted. The lady who owned the store, Norma Jackson, already knew he was boarding with Sarah Jones. News travels fast in small towns and the women of Dodge had taken note of this tall, blue eyed, handsome stranger.

While Tom looked at some shirts, Norma struck up a conversation with him. After a few minutes she asked if Sarah was still doing sewing for people. Tom told her she was. Norma said she asked because she could use someone to help her mend clothes that people brought in for repair. Tom said he would check with Sarah to be sure, but thought she would probably welcome additional work. He had learned earlier that Sarah did a lot of sewing for some of the local women to help earn enough money to get by.

Sarah was all smiles when Tom told her about his conversation with Norma, and she told him she was grateful. Later Sarah would learn that she would earn as much from the store as she did from her private customers. This doubled her income from sewing. It was more work, but she had ample time to do it. Finding the work had been the problem. With the additional money she could almost get by without a boarder. By getting so much from Tom and now doubling her sewing money, Sarah found the future looked far brighter for her and Ted.

Dodge was proving to be a quieter town than Tom had anticipated. Even so, he had more to do here than in Abilene. He helped Sarah out by getting the house and barn back in shape. Tom took one little chore at a time, leaving himself plenty of time to enjoy life and go fishing and hunting with Ted now and then. He was good at his work and the days passed quickly.

Tom fell into a routine of playing poker two nights a week. Most evenings were quiet, but on some nights cowboys were in town whooping it up. Tom always played on Friday nights because that was when the cowboys got paid. Several of them had heard how he was helping out the Jones family and they respected him for that. One of the cowboys mentioned that Sarah was an attractive young gal and maybe Tom would be staying around longer than he originally thought. Tom shook his head and chuckled; he guessed there wasn't any way to keep some people from thinking such things. He didn't earn as much in Dodge playing poker as he had in Abilene, but he averaged about an additional day's wages per week. Sometimes he was far less lucky, but he almost always broke even. Just like in Abilene, most of the cowboys weren't very good at cards and the liquor dulled their ability to figure odds.

Sarah was glad to have Tom as a boarder and a friend. He was a pal to Ted, and they got along better than could be expected. She began to hope Tom would be a permanent part of their life. At first she waited for him to show interest in her. When that didn't happen, she purposely brushed against him a few times when he was in the kitchen or elsewhere and the space for her to get by was limited. On some evenings Tom sat out on the back porch and watched the birds and squirrels in the back yard. Several times she brought out hot chocolate or milk and cookies and sat with him on the bench. Sarah sat close enough so that their shoulders or legs occasionally touched. One evening she even rested her head on his shoulder. Tom was always polite but never responded to her subtle hints. He treated her more like a relative and mentioned one evening that she reminded him a great deal of his sister. Over time Sarah came to realize she couldn't get Tom interested romantically. Finally she accepted he was just going to be a good friend.

Before Sarah knew it, winter had come and gone. She and Ted were doing much better now, and she had put money in the bank for leaner times. Since she was working for Norma, she received a discount on material and had made clothes for both her and Ted. Sarah even sewed a new shirt for Tom. Things had changed so much in just eight months.

Tom became aware of some interest in Sarah by a local rancher. His name was Fred Clark, and he owned a small ranch west of Dodge near the Cimarron Crossing. He was several years older than Sarah, and had lost his wife during the birth of their first child three years ago. He was quiet and unassuming. Tom didn't realize his interest at first; he thought Fred was just being nosey about him and Sarah like so many others. But Fred was always careful and respectful in how he asked about her, and it finally dawned on Tom that Fred was sweet on her. Tom started mentioning Sarah and Ted more often to him and how he enjoyed spending time with the boy. He bragged on Sarah's good cooking and quiet disposition. As the weeks passed it became abundantly clear Fred was taking a greater interest.

One Sunday, in early spring, Tom invited Fred to come over and go fishing with him and Ted. Fred readily accepted. While they were at the lake, Sarah arrived with a picnic basket and some snacks. Tom just let things take their course and tried to spend time with Ted, leaving the two alone for awhile. A few Sundays later, Fred and Sarah went on a picnic together alone. Sarah seemed to be floating around the house that night and was happy on into the next week.

On Wednesday, Fred came into the gun shop, purportedly looking for a new rifle. Tom showed him several, but didn't think Fred was really interested in a purchase. Fred finally asked him if he had any objections to his asking Sarah to the dance on Saturday. Tom assured him he didn't, and told him he was hoping the two of them would hit it off. Fred had that lovesick puppy dog look. Tom was happy for both of them, actually all three of them, for Ted really liked Fred.

By late spring Fred was a regular visitor on the weekend, and usually came over for supper once or twice during the week. He also invited Sarah and Ted out to his place. Ted loved the ranch and especially the horses. Tom was invited as well, but didn't go. There was a family developing and he wanted to give it room to grow.

Finally in early July, Sarah was prancing around the house like a little schoolgirl. Neither Tom nor Ted could figure out what had come over her. She moved around the room like she was dancing, hardly touching the floor, and she kept waving her hand around a lot more than normal. Ted would look at Tom and wrinkle his nose, wondering what on earth was wrong with his mama. Finally Tom saw the sparkling ornament on her left hand, but decided to let this play out for awhile. Ted didn't have a clue. It was ornery of Tom to wait and not notice, but he couldn't resist.

Finally, after another fifteen minutes of having her hand waved all around and nearly stuck in his face, Tom yelled, "Well, look at that diamond on your mother's hand, Ted!"

Ted's eyes went wide, and he looked at his mother and asked, "Does this mean you and Fred are getting married?"

"It sure does," she replied with her eyes locked on the ring.

"Whoopee!" yelled Ted.

Later the next day Ted ran down to the stream to play. Sarah took the opportunity to talk to Tom. "Fred and I discussed it and we want you to know you can stay here at the house as long as you like. You've done so much work on it I feel like I should just give it to you."

"Thanks, Sarah, but there is no need for that. I can't tell you how happy I am for you and Ted, and Fred too. There's never been three better people that deserved to find happiness. Ted is gonna love it on that ranch."

Sarah became very serious. "You know for a long time I was hoping you'd take an interest in me, but you never did." She paused for a few seconds looking at the floor, and then continued, "I think Fred will be good for both Ted and me."

She looked into Tom's eyes, and his glance went to the floor as he replied. "Fred is as good a man as I've come across in a long time. And you and Ted, well, a man couldn't ask for more." As Tom looked back up he saw that Sarah was still looking at him; her eyes swelled with tears.

She sobbed just a bit and said, "I still wish it were you, and I think I'll always care for you. I can't tell you how much you've changed our lives. I'll love Fred and be a good wife, but…I guess I just wanted you to know how much you mean to me."

She gave Tom a long hug with tears streaming down her face. Then she pulled back so she was looking right at him. Sarah wiped her tears away, but more came. Putting her arms up around his neck, she looked deep into his eyes and whispered, "Just this one time."

Sarah moved forward slowly and kissed Tom on the lips, her body seeming to melt against his. The kiss lasted a long time and he didn't resist. When she finally pulled away she glanced up to his eyes ever so briefly. Then looking down and pulling away, she said softly, "Thank you! I just needed to do that once."

Tom felt a little guilty, but at the same time knew she had no wrongful intentions, nor did he. It was a way for Sarah to say goodbye to something she had hoped for but wasn't to be.

The wedding was in mid-August, and Tom was the best man. The couple headed off to Wichita for their honeymoon, and Tom stayed with Ted. He had decided he would be on his way after they returned, but would wait until they got back to tell them. Tom told Ted on the day before they arrived. Ted took it better than he expected. The boy had a new life to go to and Fred had already shown him the pony that was to be his.

The next day Tom welcomed the happy couple back home and helped them move some of Sarah's furniture to the ranch. After they had finished with the move and were eating supper, he shared the news with Fred and Sarah that he would be moving on. She looked at Ted, but could tell he already knew. Sarah couldn't stop the tears, but tried not to cry very much. When Tom left that night she walked him out to his horse.

"I'll never forget all you've done for me and Ted, and I'll never, ever stop caring for you. If you ever need help we'll always be here."

She gave him a hug, shorter now, as she was married. Tom rode back to the house. It was lonely there. He was missing Sarah and Ted. The tender feelings she had expressed toward him once again opened that void, only deeper now. That night he wondered about his future, and if he would ever find a woman. He decided it was time to search for his own happiness, his place in life.

TWELVE

Tom headed west across the flat plains between Dodge City and the mountains of Colorado. It was hot during the day and he stopped each afternoon to give his horse a rest. There wasn't much in the way of scenery to break the monotony of the trip. Finally he could see what looked like the outline of mountains in the distance. He couldn't tell for sure if they were clouds way off on the horizon or mountain peaks just beginning to be visible. As he rode toward them they seemed to retreat. After not paying attention for awhile, he glanced up to see dark clouds. It looked like a big storm and he began seeking shelter.

Tom found an old homestead where the cabin had burned down, but a weather-beaten old barn stood vacant. It had two large doors on the front that swung open to the south. He hobbled the horse, letting it graze while he gathered firewood from nearby trees. There was a small loft in the barn and he climbed up to prepare a place to sleep for the evening. The wind came minutes later; it was cool and the strong scent of rain permeated the air. A few drops of rain fell and Tom went to get the horse. There were two stables in the barn and he put him in the cleanest one, feeding him some grain.

Leaving the barn doors wide open, he stood in the doorway while the storm clouds rolled overhead. Within minutes the wind picked up and caused a lot of dust to rise inside the barn. Tom closed the big doors and went up in the hayloft, which was on the side of the barn. There he sat in the open door of the loft with his legs hanging outside as he watched the rain starting to fall. Since the loft opening was to the east, and the wind and rain came from the west, it gave him a nice view of the storm as it blew by.

He could see and hear the power of the wind outside, but where he sat only puffs of air reached him, first from one side then the other. Before long the rain increased to a torrent, soon saturating the top layer of dust and clearing the air outside. While there were several leaks in the roof there were none directly above him.

Tom noticed a clatter on the roof and saw small pellets of ice hitting the ground below. At first they were the size of a pea, but the noise increased and before long the ice pellets were as big as a chicken egg. The roof of the old barn was withstanding the onslaught but the sound of the ice hitting the wooden structure was deafening. After a few minutes the ground outside was covered with stones of ice. The noise reached a crescendo, and then the hail stopped as quickly as it had started.

The rain returned even harder than before. The wind drove it at a sharp angle toward the east, and mist seemed to rise from the ground and be blown along the surface. Tom sat and watched the energy of nature unveil before him. It was soothing to experience its wonder while the rain replenished the earth. It reminded him of the time he and Josh had sat on the porch and watched a similar storm. On that day, so long ago, it had seemed to Tom that he was absorbing some of the energy nature produced. He felt that way again now.

Later the wind subsided and the downpour slackened to a slow steady rain. The night grew quiet and Tom climbed down from the loft and opened the big doors. He used the firewood he had gathered earlier to make a campfire on the ground just inside the doorway, keeping the fire small so there would be no danger of it getting out of control. Sitting and staring at the flames, he ate, drank coffee and thanked his good fortune of finding the barn. Occasionally he looked out at the gentle rain and the stillness of the night. As the night wore on he grew sleepy. Making sure the fire was out he climbed the ladder. The hayloft was a good place to be on this rainy night. He rolled out his bedroll and was asleep in minutes.

When Tom opened his eyes the sun was shining and birds were flying in and out of the rafters above. He climbed down from the loft. The appaloosa, seeing him, was ready to be let out. After breakfast Tom started back over the mountains. As before he did not hurry. Several times he spent a couple of days in a valley, exploring, hunting, and being a part of nature. The air was cold at night and the sun hot in the day. Even when the sun was high and the day at its warmest, the breeze was still cool.

As nice as it was in the summer, Tom had no desire to be there in the winter. He had heard stories about men getting caught in snowstorms and freezing to death in the bitter cold. They were usually not found until spring, their bodies slowly emerging from the snow as it melted around them. Tom thought it would be a slow, torturous way to die, and he never understood why mountain men took such chances. The scenery was beautiful, but nature could be heartless.

Tom looked for familiar landmarks and was able to follow the same route back over the mountains. He was pleased when he found the big mountain lake again. It was just as beautiful and serene as he remembered. He arrived at sunset and nearly a fourth of the sky was aglow. There were many dark purple clouds and a few near the horizon that were bright red. Only a small portion of the sun was visible, mostly hidden by a mountain peak. Since the lake was to the west and the surface was smooth as glass, the water mirrored the beauty of the heavens. Sitting on his horse, gazing out across the water at the mountains and the beautiful sky, he said out loud, "Surely this is as close to heaven as a man can come and still be alive."

Perhaps that was the answer to the question of why mountain men would risk being there. Tom felt a sense of freedom, but it was more than that. He felt as though the eyes of heaven smiled upon him. Finding the spot where he had camped earlier, he began preparing his meal and heard a wolf's lonely call from across the lake. Sitting and watching the fire he could hear the breeze sweeping through the tall pines above. Tom sipped at his coffee and marveled at this masterpiece of nature. The night became still and at length he drifted off to sleep.

Tom awoke the next morning, having slept heavily, and realized he did not dream. He prepared breakfast and poured himself a cup of coffee. The air was cold, but the hot liquid tasted all the better for it. Soon the sun rose higher and warmed things quickly. Tom went down to the lake in the early afternoon, knowing the fishing would be good. After catching two in barely fifteen minutes, he put the fishing pole aside, lay back in the deep grass and gazed at the sky. In the distance a bank of fleecy white clouds touched the tallest peak, rising and splitting apart as it passed the tall trajectory. Tom didn't know the name of the peak and didn't care. "Such beauty as this is to be enjoyed; knowing names or why it occurs doesn't matter. It is the ability to appreciate it that's important," he soliloquized.

Then he laughed at himself. "What do I know about such things?" he thought. He recalled the wisdom of Josh and the weeks they had spent together. "Josh knows of these things," he said out loud, remembering their discussions.

As he lay there content, the cool breeze blew across his face. The sun's rays warmed him, but seemed to provide more than warmth. He felt some healing power within them. When the sun would go behind a cloud for several minutes he would grow cold and pull his coat snug around him, but then it felt all the better when the sun came out and warmed him again. Finally he got up and cooked the fish. After eating he saddled his horse and rode around the lake, which took the rest of the afternoon. When he lay down that evening, he felt completely at peace.

In the middle of the night he awoke, or so it seemed, and there again was the image of the same angel with the beautiful face. She smiled at him and he back at her. He felt no fear this time. Slowly her hand began to reach forward. Tom tried to move his hand but it would not respond. Her arm was soon fully extended, reaching out to him. He tried ever so desperately to make his hand and arm move, but couldn't get them to budge. Then the image began fading away. When it was gone he awoke.

Sitting up he looked all around. The night was dark and cold. It was quiet except for the breeze overhead in the trees. An owl hooted in the distance. Tom pulled his blankets snug around his neck as he was cold. Was it a vision or just a dream? That question was no more answered than after the first time, but he was pleased to have once again experienced such an event and seen the beauty of her face.

The next morning he broke camp and headed west. He no longer felt alone. As Tom rode the appaloosa through the mountain valleys he enjoyed the wildlife, birds, and the varying colors of the trees. When he arrived in Durango he stayed several nights before moving on again. While it was a long and sometimes arduous journey through the mountains of Colorado, he was once again saddened when he reached the other side. He emerged feeling closer to nature.

Tom rode on for another day and then headed into Arizona, deciding to stay for a couple of nights in the cabin where Josh had taken care of him while he healed so long ago. He wasn't sure why he wanted to go that far out of his way, but he felt drawn there. Tom stopped in a small town and got supplies at a little store. The building was dark inside. There was a young couple with a small boy, but they paid little attention to Tom. A man was sitting in the corner, but it was dark there and his hat shadowed his face. He appeared to be dozing.

Getting what he needed, Tom was soon back on the trail. It was early in the afternoon and he wanted to make it to the cabin before nightfall. After traveling for a couple of hours, he left the trail and rode to a large tree with plentiful shade. There he ate the fresh bread and peach jam he had purchased at the store, letting his horse graze while he ate. After about twenty minutes a rider came up from behind. Since Tom was off the trail, he couldn't make out who it was. After resting in the shade for another thirty minutes, Tom saddled up and moved on. There was time to make it to the cabin with an hour of daylight to spare.

Tom moseyed along without a care in the world. It was late in the afternoon and the bright sun was starting to come below the brim of his hat. As he rode along, he heard the piercing sound of an eagle high overhead. Ten minutes later, he turned a bend and was next to a large tree. There was a small clear bubbling stream to his left. Suddenly, a large bird flew from the tree beside him. The sound of the huge fluttering wings startled Tom, and he jerked to the side. At almost the same moment, he heard a blast and pain exploded in his shoulder. Had the bird not startled him, the bullet would have gone through his heart. The force knocked him backward and he fell from his horse, landing hard on the ground. His vision went gray and he nearly passed out. Death was suddenly at hand.

Tom felt his body beginning to give in, but his mind struggled to stay alert. If he lost consciousness now he would surely die, either from loss of blood or another gunshot from his attacker. His vision started to return; he could hear his horse trotting away. Tom was lying on his right shoulder and his hand was under his side. Knowing whoever shot him would be there soon to see if he was dead, he moved his hip upward and pulled his gun from the holster. Ignoring the pain as best he could, he slid his arm backward so his gunhand was under his side. Next he let his wounded left shoulder droop forward with his head touching the ground. He waited, not moving. Memories of his earlier experience flooded into his mind.

"Become like a rock, no movement," he told himself.

Soon he heard a horse approach and then leather creaking as someone dismounted. Tom tried to breathe only slightly. The steps came closer; Tom stopped breathing, no movement at all. Several seconds passed and he wondered if the attacker would shoot again just to make sure. Finally, Tom heard a chuckle.

"I got him, I can't believe it. Ha, ha, ya sonofabitch; I got ya."

The voice was not familiar and definitely had a deep Texas drawl. Suddenly, Tom felt a boot placed on his wounded shoulder and it gave him a push to turn him on his back. He allowed himself to roll like a sack of potatoes and as his right hand came free he pulled the gun up, opening his eyes and firing a quick shot at the center of the figure over him. The man had a gun in his hand and it exploded as he began to fall back. The bullet hit the dirt just to the right of Tom's head. While the attacker fell backward, Tom fired twice more as quickly as he could. The bushwhacker's gun landed by his side.

Tom pulled himself up, and kicked the man's gun further away. It was the man in the shadows from the store. Tom recognized his clothes. The attacker was alive, but red liquid started flowing from the corner of his mouth. Tom knew the man didn't have long to live.

"Why'd you shoot me?" Tom asked.

"Ya kilt my bruther down in Waco, ya no good sonofabitch."

Red foam sprayed from his mouth as he talked. His face was rough and pitted, and his hair long and scraggly. The odor of an unwashed body surrounded the prostrate figure. He was about as ugly a man as Tom had ever seen. Tom remembered being in only one gunfight in Waco, many years ago. It had been with a gunslinger trying to add a notch to his gun.

"Your brother called me out, pushed me into a fight. He drew first."

"He was my bruther," he countered bitterly, more blood coming from his mouth.

"Tell me! Do you know who I am?"

"Yeah, I know ya. My bruther didn't have a chance. I was gonna take your body back down to Tombstone and drag ya thru the streets. Surprise the hell outta them bastards."

The man breathed hard and flinched as the red liquid flowing into his lungs started to overcome him. He coughed and blood fell down his chin. In spite of what the bushwhacker had said, Tom was filled with compassion as he looked at the dying man.

"I don't know how much time you have left here. Is there anybody you want me to write, any next of kin?"

The man looked at Tom with surprise evident on his face. His breathing was labored. Finally, he said, "My mother still lives in Waco. It would be good if she knew."

"What's her name...and yours?"

"Ethel...Ethel Potter. Mine is Zack." There were several seconds of silence and then he added, "Appreciate it." His breathing became even more labored.

Tom had a thought, and after hesitating asked with a soft voice, "Uh...back at the store, did you tell anyone else about me?"

The man looked at Tom, and shook his head. He took a deep breath, or tried to, his lungs filling quickly, and then he coughed a mouthful of blood and died.

Tom had never liked to see death; talking to it was even more gruesome. "Could this be the man from the dream?" he wondered. Zack had been in the shadows at the store. It was similar to the scene of the sinister figure behind his cabin. Tom quickly put that aside. Bleeding badly, he had to get it stopped. He knew what had to be done, and set about it almost mechanically. After stuffing a clean shirt against his wound, he built a campfire. Checking the man's saddlebags Tom found a bottle of whiskey, some food and money. He took these things and whistled for the appaloosa. After putting the food and money in his saddlebag, he started drinking the whiskey. Finally, he put the blade of his hunting knife in the fire.

"Just do it and don't think about it," he told himself.

Tom drank more whiskey, then took off his shirt and sat down close to the fire. As he poured whiskey over the wound, the pain screamed at him. When the knife blade was red hot, he put on a glove and picked up the knife by the handle. Tom began wondering if he would be able to hold it against the wound long enough. Yost had told him earlier it had to be there for three long seconds. Tom decided to lay the knife on a nearby fallen tree. He readied himself then lowered his shoulder onto the knife, grasping the tree trunk with both hands. The smell was sickening, conjuring up memories from the time before. Tom counted to three, biting the stick between his teeth, and then pushed away from the knife. Turning around so the back of his shoulder was over the knife, he slowly lay against it and shook in pain counting to three once more. He rolled off, barely managing to keep from passing out. The pain was even worse than he remembered.

Tom got Zack's horse and then lifted the body, draping it over the saddle. Getting on the appaloosa, he led Zack's horse away from the road. When he was a mile off the trail, he dismounted and took the body off the horse. Next, he unsaddled and unbridled the attacker's horse and let it go. He wanted to bury the body, but decided that if he tried he'd be dead before the grave was finished. Mounting up he headed toward the cabin. It was less than an hour away, and he could still make it before nightfall if he could stay on the horse.

Twice as Tom rode he felt near passing out, but by sheer will stayed conscious. He reached the canyon as the sun went down. It was getting cold and the wind was brisk. His face was wet with sweat, and the cool air was chilling—but felt good to him. There was no sign of anyone in the canyon. He gathered firewood and before long there was a fire in the fireplace. Forcing himself to stay awake, he prepared some food and ate. His wound was incredibly painful, but there was no bleeding. Even with the pain of the wound, sleep was easy in coming once he relinquished control.

Tom slept heavily that night and through half the next day. It seemed his body didn't want to wake. His hunger finally forced him to get up long enough to eat. He then fed the horse and went back to sleep. The next morning he felt stiff and was running a light fever. After eating he went outside and opened the corral gate, letting his horse out to graze in the canyon. Tom thought about hobbling him but decided against it. When he returned to the cabin he was tired and went back to sleep.

That day his health took a turn for the worse. When he woke in the middle of the night, he was hot with fever. He didn't feel like eating, but took a drink of water. Realizing his peril, wounded, alone and with a high fever, he recalled the vision of the angel and said a prayer. Going back to sleep, he knew he was in trouble and that this could be the end for him.

THIRTEEN

Emmett Bailey looked back at the goods in his wagon. He had been to Flagstaff and was returning with a load of merchandise for the ranch. Emmett had made the trip once each year for the last two years, ever since the railroad first came to Flagstaff. The prices were much lower there and he could get supplies that were not available locally. His ranch was in southern Utah and situated in some of the most beautiful canyons in the country. If it weren't for need of supplies Emmett would be happy to stay within the confines of those red walls permanently. He had settled there long ago when the area had seen no white men, or perhaps only a few. Emmett had fallen in love with its natural beauty, and scratched out a ranch from the scenic and promising land. He had faced many natural challenges and still faced the perils of bears, mountain lions, wolves and coyotes. The most dreaded of all was not from nature, but from man. Rustlers were a thorn in every rancher's side.

While in Flagstaff, Emmett searched for new breeding stock and he was returning with three new bulls for his cattle and a red stallion for the mares. The horse had cost him a small fortune, but would be the finest in Utah. All four animals would enhance the bloodlines of his livestock. He knew it was important to get new outside male stock to prevent inbreeding. Having searched earnestly for these animals he couldn't wait to get home and show them off to everyone, especially the horse. They were the best he could find and would be the pride of his ranch.

Emmett had always been frugal in buying supplies, and before going he priced items locally that he was most interested in acquiring. When in Flagstaff he spent considerable time comparing the prices and the differences, along with the weight and bulk of each item. He wanted to save as much money as possible and could carry only so much in the wagon. A new stove was needed for one of the bunkhouses, and he got it for half the cost. Some lanterns, shovels, a barrel of molasses, seed for crops and garden, and rolls of cloth for the ladies rounded out the bulk of the purchases.

Three of his cowboys from the ranch, his adopted daughter, and an old Indian had accompanied him. The men were there primarily for protection. They were good with guns, an unfortunate necessity in this part of the country. The wagonload and breeding stock represented a lot of hard-earned money and the law was scarce in these parts.

Sitting beside Emmett on the wagon was his adopted daughter, Melinda. She was an orphan that Emmett and his wife had taken in as a child and raised as their own. In Flagstaff, Melinda picked out the rolls of cloth and also selected a few cooking utensils and miscellaneous items for the kitchen.

The sun was high overhead and the horses kicked up dust, which occasionally got into Melinda's eyes. They were heading directly into the wind for the moment and she would be glad when they turned more northward again. She had made the trip last year and had enjoyed the change of pace. While she loved the ranch and the way of life they had, an existence required a break in routine now and then. The ride was long and her buttocks complained each time they hit a rock, but she would gladly go again. Much of the trip was scenic, though there were parts that were more like desert.

Melinda liked the cowboys, but at times grew tired of their attention. They would always look away when she glanced in their direction, but she could often feel their eyes upon her. She knew she had little to fear from them; they always acted like gentlemen toward her. One would occasionally try to flirt, but always in a respectful way. She never encouraged them because she had more attention from men than she wanted.

Melinda glanced back at Mescal, the old Indian, and he winked at her. She trusted Mescal more than any other man, except her father. A year ago while returning from her first trip to Flagstaff, they came across him in the desert. The place where they had found him was just ahead, causing both Melinda and Mescal to recall that event.

Mescal remembered he had been shot in the leg and arm by a group of men he believed to be an outlaw gang. They left him to die with no horse and no water. The leader of the gang was called Jack Brock. Mescal had heard one of the men call him by his first name and another by his last. There had been four men in the gang, and Mescal remembered the faces of all of them. The old one, named Gibbs, was about to shoot Mescal when the leader stopped him. "Let him die suffering," Brock had proclaimed.

The old Indian was strong of spirit and had an intense will to survive. Fooling them, and the laws of nature, he had crawled for nearly three miles on the desert floor, and then up on a rock ledge where he could see the road down below. He waited for two days before anyone came into view that he thought might help. The day before he had watched two men on horseback ride by, and decided not to risk alerting them even though he craved water and was starving.

It was the fact there had been a woman this time, and that he had been near death, that made him decide to take a chance and send a signal for help. Building a small fire using what was left of his shirt, he was able to send up enough smoke to be seen. When the wagon stopped, he had waved his loincloth. It was the only form of clothes he had remaining other than his moccasins.

Even though it had been a year, Melinda remembered finding Mescal like it was yesterday. Willie, one of Emmett's most trusted cowboys, had seen the smoke first.

"Look up there on that rock," said Willie.

Emmett had pulled the wagon to a stop and looked in the direction Willie was pointing. Seeing the smoke Emmett asked, "What do you make of it?"

"Don't know…wait a minute. Someone is waving something, like they need help," Willie replied.

"Willie, you and Bud go check it out," Emmett said. "Be careful! Never can tell, it could be a trick."

It was ten minutes before Willie and Bud came back. As they rode up Willie shook his head. "It's an old Indian; he's got a couple of wounds. Looks like he ain't had nothing to eat or drink for awhile. I'd say he's pretty near dead."

"Any hope for him?" Emmett asked.

"Not much if any," Willie replied.

Emmett hesitated for a few seconds and then told them, "Well, take him some food and water so he can at least eat and be comfortable before he dies."

"You can't just leave him there to die," Melinda said to Emmett. She got down off the wagon and told Stuffy, "Let me borrow your horse."

Stuffy looked at Emmett, who reluctantly nodded, and Stuffy climbed off the horse. Melinda took off in the direction of the old Indian; Willie and Bud followed her. She found the old Indian and saw that he looked starved. She gave him a canteen and began to inspect his wounds. As she handed him the canteen she told him, "Don't drink much at first."

The Indian nodded and took a little drink. "Thank you, good lady."

She was pleased he spoke English. It would make it easier to care for him. She stood up and told Willie and Bud, "Let's carry him down to the wagon."

They got off their horses and Bud walked up to Melinda. "That's a long way to carry a man." His tone reflected his hesitancy to comply.

"Well, we're not leaving him here."

Bud took hold of Melinda's arm and led her a short distance away. "Melinda, he's just an old Indian and he's gonna die anyway. He'd be better off if we just made him comfortable and let him die in peace."

"Better for him or easier for us? Let's go ask him what he would prefer to do."

Bud had looked at Willie and thrown his hands up in the air as she walked back to the Indian.

She asked the wounded man in a kind voice, "Do you think you could stay on my horse until we make it down to the wagon?"

The old Indian smiled, nodded and replied, "Crawl many miles. Can ride to wagon."

She helped him as he struggled to stand up. Willie just stood there and Bud shook his head. Melinda gave them a dirty look, and then asked in a pleasant tone, "Could you help me get him on the horse?"

Bud mumbled something to Willie, but Melinda couldn't hear what he said. The two men helped the Indian on Stuffy's horse. Melinda asked him, "Can you stay up there or do I need to ride with you?"

"Me ride to wagon," he replied and smiled at her again.

Melinda started leading the horse back to the wagon, but Willie insisted on doing it and letting Melinda ride his horse. When they got the Indian to the wagon she made a makeshift bed for him using blankets on top of the sacks of seed. She cleansed and bandaged his wounds, and then fed and tended to him on the long trip back to the ranch.

Mescal remembered Melinda demanding they help bring him down when he had been up on the ledge. The two cowboys had tried to talk her out of it, but she hadn't budged. It had been the second time in the last several days he listened to people discussing whether he would live or die. In the case of three days earlier, they let him live only so he could die a more torturous death. Knowing he owed Melinda his life, he had pledged to protect her life with his. He had learned to love her as a relative would a young, innocent child. Melinda loved Mescal as she would an uncle or grandfather. She knew he would not hesitate to give his life to protect her. The bond they held was one few people ever experience.

This trip had provided no such excitement. Melinda had a bit of adventure in Flagstaff when two cowboys engaged her in conversation at the store. She had done her best to discourage them but each tried to outdo the other. Willie noticed the two bothering Melinda and stayed in the store. Mescal had gone with Emmett to help pick out the new bulls and stallion. The old Indian had earned Emmett's respect over the last year, and he sought Mescal's judgement on many issues. Mescal was a superior judge of horseflesh.

Melinda thought back to the two cowboys. They had been hanging around her so long that Willie had finally come over and asked her in a serious tone of voice so both cowboys could hear, "Are these two fellas botherin you, Miss Melinda?"

Melinda wanted no fights over her, and besides Willie was outnumbered and could be hurt. "I'm just fine, Willie, but thank you for inquiring."

One of the two cowboys had red hair and his name was Chester. The other one had long brown hair and was called Lem. Chester had told Willie, "Yes sir, she is just fine. She is in good hands here. Don't you worry none."

"Who was that old coot anyway?" Lem asked Melinda after Willie walked to another part of the store.

"He works for my father."

"Well, he sure is an unfriendly cuss," Chester said. A few seconds later he asked, "Could I carry your packages for you, Melinda?"

"No let me, I was here first," Lem interjected.

"Oh, nobody cares if you were first," Chester countered.

"I can carry them, thanks all the same. Isn't there anything else you gentlemen need to do while you're in town?"

"Like what?" Lem asked with a puzzled look on his face.

"Well, I don't know. Whatever cowboys do when they're in town. Surely there is something you have to do."

Both cowboys had looked at each other baffled, and then continued to follow her. Melinda walked to another part of the store, realizing it had been a mistake to tell Willie she was okay. After that the two cowboys had been even more aggressive, asking to carry her packages again and offering to protect her from other men. She finished shopping and was preparing to walk across the street to the wagon where Bud sat waiting. The two cowboys got into an argument over who would carry her packages and walk her across the street.

Willie had been in the back of the store eyeing a new pair of boots, and hadn't noticed she was done until he saw her walk out the door. He headed out to help her and intervene with the two arguing cowboys, but before he got there the two started swinging away at each other. A few seconds later they were rolling around on the wooden sidewalk, punching and cursing. They continued to fight, so absorbed with their struggle that over three minutes passed. One of them lost a shirtsleeve in the battle and the other had a bloody nose. They were both covered with dirt from the street. When the two cowboys finally stopped and got back on their feet, they saw that Willie and Melinda had already crossed the street and joined Bud in the wagon.

Bud had looked back at the two while they drove away, shaking his head with contempt, and saying loud enough for them to hear, "Couple of the dumbest cowboys I ever saw."

Willie added his opinion in an equally loud voice: "Just a couple of no account, worthless hooligans that don't know how to talk to a lady." Willie had known Melinda would attract more than her share of attention; that was why he had stayed close by in the store. After they traveled a short distance in the wagon, Willie told Melinda, "You should've let me teach those boys some manners back there."

"I guess it did kind of get out of hand, didn't it?" she admitted reluctantly.

"Reckon that's a safe statement of the facts," Bud said, trying to stifle a laugh. Willie then started laughing, and Bud joined him. Melinda's face turned red.

Melinda had always been pretty, but in the last two years she had blossomed into a fully developed young woman. Her sparkling green eyes and short blonde hair made any man take notice, and her face was flawless. Melinda was only a little over five feet tall, making her large breasts even more noticeable.

Later, Willie and Bud had taken great joy in telling Emmett, Mescal and Stuffy about the fight the two-lovestruck cowboys had over her. She had been embarrassed and tried to change the subject, but to no avail. Even Mescal had joined in the merriment at her expense. She had given him a dirty look, but he had just shaken his head and laughed silently. Melinda had never heard Mescal laugh, and even then he made no sound; his body just shook like a small child trying not to giggle.

Melinda smiled as she remembered those events. It was flattering to her, but she perceived the attention as a burden and had grown tired of it because it happened so often. Melinda knew she should probably be grateful for whatever good looks she had, but so far it had brought her only unwanted advances from men and suspicion from wives. She had yet to meet any man she felt really attracted to, but thought surely that day would come. Having always been religious, she prayed each night before she went to sleep. For nearly a year now she had taken to praying that she might meet the right man for her. So far the prayers had not been answered. There were nights when she wondered if she was meant to live her life alone.

Melinda was remembering all this as they neared the canyon where the little cabin stood hidden in the depths of the tall stone walls. When they could see the cabin, they noticed a horse in the tall grass.

"Well, shoot, it looks like somebody is already here," Emmett said. "I didn't think anybody else even knew about this place."

"Do you want us to ride up and say hello?" Willie asked. "You never know, could be someone who's about to leave."

Emmett rubbed the stubble of whiskers on his chin. He had hoped to sleep inside the cabin tonight. "Well, I guess it won't hurt none to find out. If he's stayin, ask him if it would be alright if we camp out in the canyon here somewhere."

Willie and Bud rode on ahead to investigate. When they returned, Willie told Emmett, "There's a wounded man in the cabin. He's been shot in the shoulder. We woke him up and tried talking to him, but he's too sick to know what we were a sayin."

"He looks as close to death as anything I ever seen," added Bud.

Since there was nothing to fear, Emmett drove the wagon up to the cabin to survey the situation for himself. Melinda didn't wait for Emmett's approval. She immediately went into the cabin and inspected the stranger's wound. He had a fever and appeared half starved. She ran out to the wagon for bandages.

"Mescal, would you get some water?" asked Melinda. "No, wait; first get a fire going in the stove. We'll need to boil the water."

"I'll go fetch the water, Miss Melinda," Willie said.

"Thank you, Willie," she said as she rushed back inside.

Melinda woke the stranger. He was delirious but she got him to drink from a canteen. Giving him only a small amount she waited ten minutes or so, woke him again and gave him more. After the water on the stove had boiled for several minutes, she soaked a cloth in it and cleaned his wound. Later she poured whiskey on the seared flesh. He jerked but did not wake. She cooled his head, cleaned his face and arms, and then made the men go outside so she could bathe him. He stunk to high heaven. Later she woke him again long enough for him to drink more water and eat some food. The stranger didn't wake again until the next morning. He was still delirious.

Emmett stayed for a day while Melinda nursed and cared for the wounded man. Mescal had shown him the man's gun and holster. They both thought it looked like it belonged to a gunfighter. Emmett was reluctant to leave Melinda behind, but she refused to leave the stranger. She argued that Mescal could stay to look after her. Emmett was perplexed about what to do; he needed to get back to the ranch.

Emmett waited until the next morning to approach Melinda again. "We've gotta be getting back pretty soon. We could let him ride in the back of the wagon like we did Mescal."

"It would be too hard on him. He's in a lot worse shape than Mescal was. That shoulder wound and fever are serious. I'm afraid it would kill him, Emmett. I'll have to stay here with him."

"Well, we can't just stay forever waiting for him to heal. We've got to get back to the ranch."

"I am not leaving. Mescal can stay here with me. We cannot let this man die."

"I've got to go, and you can't stay here with him. Have you seen his gun? We think he might be a gunfighter for Heaven's sake."

"He is one of God's children is what he is. We can't take him with us and we can't leave him here to die. I'm staying right here. If you need Mescal to help with the ranch then I'll take care of him by myself."

"You're impossible!" Emmett yelled.

As he stormed out of the cabin, Emmett noticed the expression on Mescal's face. He could tell that the Indian wanted to stay and help the man regain his health. The rancher didn't blame him; Mescal no doubt saw his own earlier situation in this man's tragedy. Emmett realized then that he had no choice but to leave them. He knew Melinda would not leave the wounded man, nor agree to take him in the wagon, and he knew Mescal would never leave Melinda.

After Emmett's anger subsided, he realized that Melinda and Mescal would probably be safe hidden in the canyon. It was unlikely anyone would find them there. He finally decided to tell Melinda and Mescal that the rest of them would leave after lunch, and that he would return for them in about ten days. That should give the man enough time to heal and be taken back to the ranch in the wagon.

Emmett had another thought and talked quietly with Mescal. "While we're gone, see what you think of him. If he's a good man and is handy with a gun, we could really use him on the ranch. Talk with him enough that you get a sense of what he's like."

"Me find out. Plenty time."

"Be sure you look after Melinda. Wouldn't want anything to happen to her."

"No worry; safe here."

After Emmett and the three cowboys had left, Mescal did his best to erase their tracks in and out of the canyon. Mescal stayed outside most of the time looking after the horses and making sure no one entered their remote little hideaway unnoticed.

While Mescal was outside Melinda cared for the stranger, cleaned and cooked. She removed his clothes and put on clean ones she found in the wounded man's saddlebag. There was also a razor and she used it to give him a shave. Mescal noticed the fellow was pretty good-looking for a White Man once she got him cleaned up. He knew she had given him at least one bath, but based on the man's appearance and cleanliness he thought surely that she had bathed him more than once.

Melinda enjoyed caring for the stranger and never ventured far away. Emmett and Willie had made quite a fuss over his gun and holster. Melinda didn't believe him to be an outlaw, nor had the others. He didn't have the rough appearance so many of them possessed. While she fed him he opened his eyes and seemed to look at her, but said nothing. She asked him questions but he did not respond. Melinda didn't think he would remember anything that had happened so far. Sometimes while asleep he became agitated and talked about someone named Charlie. At other times he tossed and turned and would bring his hand into the air as though he was firing a gun. He did that several times and beads of sweat rolled down his face.

Melinda wanted to know more about this stranger. His shoulder had been shot before and there were burn scars from that time as well. It was obvious to her that they were put there by a knife. The outline of the point of the blade was clearly distinguishable. When she last fed the stranger he almost came around; it seemed for a moment that he might say something, but he did not. At first she had wondered if he would make it, but now she felt certain his condition was improving. Each night before she went to sleep she prayed for his recovery.

FOURTEEN

When Tom woke next, he saw what he believed to be the angel from the mountain lake. She was smiling and seemed to be saying something to him, but he couldn't make out any words. In a few seconds he fell back asleep.

In the middle of the night he woke again. It was dark and he wasn't able to think clearly. The moon was illuminating the outside. It seemed to him that there was a doorway and it was glowing. As he lay there he recalled seeing the face of the angel. His mind was cloudy and it was difficult for him to put everything together. Unsure what the angel and glowing doorway meant, he thought it might mean he had died. Shortly he fell asleep.

When he opened his eyes the next morning, the girl with the lovely face was putting a spoon in his mouth. He looked at her and she smiled, but he couldn't say anything as he faded out again. Dreams came; he relived being shot, shooting his assailant and the hot knife on his wound. He awoke partially again in the middle of the night, and his mind tried to figure out his situation. Remembering the girl with the spoon he wondered if his mind was playing tricks on him. Still thinking he might have died, he drifted back to sleep.

Thinking more clearly, he woke again the next day. The young woman had short blond hair and green eyes. He just gazed at her for awhile. His mouth felt dry like it was full of dust. He had trouble swallowing, and when he did speak it was with great difficulty.

"Water."

She helped lift his head and held a cup to his mouth. "Here, drink slowly." When he stopped drinking she laid his head back on the pillow.

"Am I dead?"

"No, you are not dead." She laughed softly, but then realized he was serious. "You're doing much better now. I must admit I wondered there for awhile if you were going to make it, but I think the worst is over. Hold on for a second, I'm going to get you some stew." She went to the stove and then returned to his bedside. "Here, let's get some food in you while you're awake."

Her voice sounded as sweet as music to his ears and he still wondered if he might be dreaming, hallucinating perhaps. After several spoonfuls, still staring at her, he asked slowly, having trouble forming the words.

"Who are you?"

"Don't talk now, you are very weak and need to eat. Here, another bite." She smiled and put the spoon to his mouth again. He ate for a few minutes, looking at her the whole time, but then grew weary and went to sleep.

When he woke again she was still there. She fed him without speaking, then washed his face with a wet cloth. It felt cool against his skin. He could tell he still had a fever and watched her as she cleaned his face. She seemed much more human to him now, but he thought the resemblance to the angel in his dreams had to be more than coincidence. Watching her every move he tried to stay awake, but before long sleep conquered him once more.

The next time he woke he felt stronger. As she fed him, she began to tell how they had found him. "We were traveling home and stopped here for the night after going to Flagstaff on business. When we arrived you were hot with fever and nearly dead. It's a miracle anyone found you at all. We only come this way once a year."

"What's your name?"

"Melinda...Melinda Bailey."

"Melinda, that's a pretty name."

"Well, thank you, kind sir."

Tom couldn't help but stare. She continued talking and he tried to listen, but knew he was missing part of it because he was having trouble concentrating. He looked at her face thinking he hadn't seen a woman with such perfect features ever before, except of course in those two dreams. He tried to stay awake but after awhile grew drowsy. She gave him more water, but then he couldn't keep his eyes from closing. Soon he was fast asleep.

Finally he woke again. She was still there. "Good, you are awake. Here, you must eat."

While eating he looked out the cabin door and saw clothes hanging from a rope strung across the porch. He heard the gentle blowing of the wind and the sounds of birds fluttering their wings. Suddenly, a horse whinnied.

"Is my horse okay?"

"Your horse is probably receiving better care than you are. Mescal is here along with me. In the evening he brings your horse to the corral and brushes him, and then in the morning he hobbles him and lets him out to pasture. Your horse is fine, so just concentrate on getting well."

"How long have I been here?"

"We found you four days ago. I'm not sure how long you were here before that. After a day the others had to return to the ranch. Mescal and I remained to take care of you. Well, actually, I stayed to take care of you and Mescal stayed to protect me."

"I guess I haven't thanked you. Appreciate what you've done."

"I'm just glad you made it."

"Yeah, me too."

"Good, some humor; you must be doing better."

"I have some money in the saddlebag. I want to pay you for taking care of me." He paused, realizing how close to death he had come this time. "You've saved my life."

"You are strong; a weaker man would have died. As far as the money, Emmett, I mean Mr. Bailey, will be back in about a week, and you can take that up with him. Let's just worry about getting you well before he gets back."

"Who's Mr. Bailey?"

"He's my father. Let's not worry about that right now. How are you feeling?"

"Like a turtle squashed by a stagecoach."

"When we first got here, that's just how you looked too," she said laughing.

"Glad you came when you did. Thought I was done for."

"I'm glad we did too." Her eyes moistened and she brushed a tear away. "You talked in your sleep about someone named Charlie."

"He was a friend. Charlie was killed a few years ago."

"Oh! I'm sorry." Several seconds later she added, "You know, I've told you my name but I still don't know yours."

Tom's immediate reaction was that was good because apparently he hadn't mentioned who he was in his sleep. He paused ever so slightly trying to decide whether to pick a different name.

"Tom...Tom Colt, and your name is Melinda. That's a pretty name...I guess I've already told you that."

"Yes, you did. Maybe that's something you say a lot...to the ladies."

"No, not really...I'm not that nice."

"A good looking fellow like you, I'll bet you're always nice to the women."

"Only the really pretty ones, like you."

"Oh, we have a charmer."

After they talked awhile longer, Tom suddenly realized she might not be safe with just one person named Mescal. "You never know what kind of trouble might ride in. You could be in danger here."

"Don't worry about that. Hardly anyone knows about this cabin. Besides, the man they left with me provides excellent protection. Mescal might not have a menacing appearance, but he is cunning and good with a gun. I really don't have much reason to fear with him around." She smiled then added, "Now that you're getting well, I have no reason to fear at all."

"Thanks, but I'm afraid I couldn't fight off a rabbit right now."

Tom still couldn't believe his good fortune. This angel of a woman had saved his life, and had the same face as in his dreams. What did it all mean? How did he come to deserve this? He tried not to solve that conundrum; better, he thought, to just live it out. Growing weary and needing rest he went back to sleep.

Melinda began sending Mescal out to the edge of the canyon twice a day to see if anyone was on the nearest trail. By riding out to a peak he could look far off into the distance to see if someone was coming. The next morning, after Mescal rode out and Tom was still asleep, Melinda used the time to clean her patient once more. He was still in no condition to care for his own needs and she preferred a person not have odor. While he could have cleaned some parts of his own body, she had been doing it for several days and saw no reason to stop just yet as long as he stayed asleep. She bathed him completely and was glad he did not wake.

Tom had actually awakened somewhat while she was washing him, but not enough to know what was transpiring, at least not for sure. He could remember sensing that she was cleaning him where no woman had since he was little. His eyes opened only slightly and were not focusing well. She appeared to be washing him, and even though he had looked at her, she was too busy with her task to notice. As often happened while he was asleep, his body was in the seemingly aroused state. He remembered starting to feel embarrassed, but was so drowsy sleep had claimed him almost immediately. Later when he recalled the bathing he thought about asking her, but was too embarrassed to say anything. He wasn't sure it had happened, and couldn't think of how to ask such a thing. Having dreamt many things recently, and hallucinated some as well, he knew this could have been nothing more than a dream.

By the next morning his condition had improved and he was feeling much better. The fever had broken and he was starving. In addition to the young woman, the old Indian was there.

"Good morning! How is our patient this fine day?" Melinda asked cheerfully.

"Better, thank you."

"Tom, I would like you to meet Mescal. He has been taking care of the horses and keeping guard, making sure we're safe."

"Happy to meet you, Mescal," Tom said, holding out his hand. "I sure thank you for staying here while I recover."

186

"Good meet you, Tom Colt," Mescal replied shaking his hand. "Glad you better."

"Me too. Reckon I'd be dead if it weren't for you and Melinda."

"Gentlemen, what do you say we eat breakfast?" Melinda asked. "Why don't the two of you have coffee while I finish up the eggs?"

Tom sensed a good man in Mescal. His smile and handshake seemed sincere and genuine. The Indian had long gray hair and a weather-beaten face. Unusual for an Indian, he wore his gun in front and at an angle. Some men wore guns this way because they were readily available sitting in a chair or on a horse. Tom got the impression that the Indian could handle the gun well—just as Melinda had said. Knowing someone was good with a gun was a knack he had gained from years of experience.

That day for lunch Melinda prepared an excellent meal of roasted rabbit, potatoes, green beans, biscuits and coffee. Tom ate like a wolf, which pleased Melinda. Feeling better he wanted to get outside for awhile. She took a chair out on the porch and put a folded blanket on it. As they sat outside drinking coffee, Tom asked the Indian if he would exercise his horse. Mescal seemed pleased. He took the bridle and rode the horse bareback up the canyon. While the Indian was gone, the girl informed Tom she was an orphan. Her parents had died of sickness while on a wagon train. She had never learned what illness killed them. A Mormon family had taken her in and raised her as their daughter.

During the next few days, Tom spent considerable time sitting on the porch. There were rocks in the nearby stream and it made a constant bubbling sound. Birds flew in and out of the trees and often landed on the top rail of the corral. A crow made its distinctive cawing sound in the distance. There were two of Tom's shirts and a pair of pants hung out to dry. They would occasionally make a flapping noise as wet clothes do in a breeze.

Late one day Mescal was brushing down the appaloosa. Melinda and Tom walked out so he could say hello to his horse. Tom could tell she was enjoying her mothering role now that he was better. Perhaps it was just the sense of accomplishment bringing him back from the dead. He wondered how things could turn out so well when it appeared there was little hope such a short time ago. After Mescal finished brushing the horse, they walked back to the porch. Later, Melinda went down to the stream to get a bucket of water. The old Indian talked little, but while she was away he spoke to Tom.

"Me see your gun. Holster cut down on top. Sight on barrel gone. That for faster draw?"

"Yes, that's right. It helps a little."

"Can I look at it?"

"Sure, go ahead."

The Indian went into the cabin and brought out the gun. He looked it over thoroughly. "Gun look good; done by expert."

Having done the work himself, Tom was pleased with the comment. "Thanks, I just try to do what's needed to get by."

The old Indian smiled, motioned his head toward Tom's shoulder and stated, "Didn't work so good."

Tom laughed a little too hard and it hurt a bit; then he said to Mescal, "My, but aren't you funny?"

Melinda looked questioningly at them when she returned. Finally she asked, "Were you laughing about me?"

Tom smiled and shook his head. Surprised that a woman of her beauty would think anyone would laugh at her, he repeated their conversation and the comments made by the Indian, trying to use his exact words and accent. Mescal smiled as Tom attempted to sound like him.

Melinda laughed. "Yes, I noticed the gun earlier." After a few seconds of silence she offered inquiringly, "In fact, Mr. Bailey said it looked like a gunfighter's gun."

The Indian nodded. "Good gun."

Tom didn't reply to Melinda's statement that sounded more like a question. Instead, he asked, "Mescal, what do you think of the appaloosa?"

"Good horse. Very strong."

They all sat on the porch then and talked about Tom's horse for awhile. No more mention was made of the gun. Later, they talked about the birds, the beautiful view and the pleasantness of the day. The more time he spent with them, the closer and more grateful he became to both. This scene on the porch was repeated for the next several days because Mr. Bailey was overdue in returning. All three were glad for the extra time. It gave Tom more time to heal before the long ride to the ranch on the wagon, and they were enjoying each other's company.

Their companionship gave Tom a feeling of closeness that reminded him of Josh here in this same cabin. They sat and listened to the birds sing, the horses whinny and the wind blow through the trees. Later that day the sun was shining fully on the canyon, and as it lowered the walls took on a splendid reddish glow. As the sun neared sunset it went behind some clouds and shot rays out like the spokes of a wagon wheel extending in all directions.

In the middle of the night it became cold. Melinda put more wood on the fire, and then came over to Tom's bunk. After straightening his blanket, she kissed him delicately on the forehead. He was thoroughly surprised, but pleased. Lying still, he wondered if she knew he was awake. Feeling her breath ever so slightly as she continued standing there made him tingle all over. He wondered if she might be waiting for him to open his eyes. Not certain what to do he did nothing, and in a few moments he could hear her move away.

The day finally arrived when Mr. Bailey returned. The Indian had seen him coming well in advance and had ridden back to the cabin to announce the pending arrival. Tom noticed that both Mescal and Melinda seemed pleased that he was returning, which indicated they thought well of him. Twenty minutes later Tom could see the wagon approaching. Mr. Bailey didn't seem in any particular hurry. A slight wind was coming out of the south and blowing a small amount of dust to the side. There were two horses pulling the wagon. Both roans had a wide white stripe running down their foreheads; they looked like twins. As Mr. Bailey pulled up, Melinda waved from the cabin door and the Indian held the team as the rancher got out of the wagon.

Bailey was a relatively tall, thin man with strong arms and hands. His eyes were somewhat close together and his chin protruded. He was not a handsome man, but not of unpleasant features either. His clothes reflected simple practicality. They were plain and made of coarse, strong material.

"Hello there. My name is Emmett Bailey."

"Glad to meet you. I'm Tom Colt."

"How is the wound progressing?"

"Very well, thanks. I've had the best of care here while you were away."

"I knew Melinda would nurse you back to good health."

"She sure did." Tom became more serious. "I want to thank you for leaving Melinda and Mescal here to look after me. I'd like to repay you for your kindness."

"I'm sure we can work something out. Let's worry about that later."

Emmett explained to Melinda that he was late because of some problems at the ranch. Returning to the wagon he pulled out a wild turkey he had shot. Melinda clapped her hands and took it to prepare for the evening meal. It was only a little after midday and ample time remained to cook the turkey for dinner.

Emmett made some additional small talk with Tom and then asked how he came to get shot. Tom told Emmett about being ambushed by a man he did not know, but that he managed to shoot the fellow when the attacker came to make sure he was dead. He told Emmett he wasn't sure why the man had shot him.

Remembering that Melinda mentioned he had talked about Charlie while he was delirious, he told Emmett about being shot a couple of years ago when he and his good friend had been ambushed. Tom thought it a good idea to reveal how Charlie had talked endlessly about Utah.

Emmett expressed his condolences for the loss. "Charlie liked Utah, huh?" Emmett seemed particularly pleased by that. "Sounds like you kinda have a habit of getting bushwhacked. Hope your luck changes."

The Indian went out to unhitch the horses from the wagon and Tom started to walk out to help him.

"Oh no you don't, you sit down and work hard at getting well," Emmett said.

Emmett helped Mescal while Tom went to see if he could help Melinda. She was in the cabin getting the turkey ready. As she went about her work Tom noticed her blonde hair, newly brushed, shone from the light of the window. Her cheekbones, nose and chin couldn't be any more perfect, he thought. The loose fitting dress she was wearing didn't hide the fact that she was a shapely woman.

"How is it you aren't married to some cowboy yet?"

Tom could hardly believe he had asked the question and wanted to take it back as soon as he realized what he had said. Melinda smiled awkwardly. She was quite surprised and wasn't sure how to take the inquiry. She would normally be evasive, but found she was inwardly pleased.

"I guess the right cowboy just hasn't come along yet. I'll know when he rides in." After a pause she suddenly added, "It could happen anytime now."

Melinda was surprised by her own statement and felt confused. Nevertheless, she looked his way and smiled at him shyly. Her face was radiant and her eyes were gleaming. She seemed unable to control her reaction, which was new to her.

Tom could sense his heart beating faster. He was without words and his face wore a silly smile. Over a minute passed without anything being said.

"You seemed to hit it off pretty well with Mr. Bailey," said Melinda. "That's good. We could use some help at the ranch when you get well."

"What is the ranch like?" Tom asked, relieved at the change in subject.

She had just started telling him when Emmett came in and took up the description. It was clear that there was probably nothing in the world this man would rather do than talk about his ranch. As the rancher continued, Tom noticed the lines of muscles on his arms could be seen easily. It was similar to the way a good horse looks when the muscles flex as it walks. This man's arms, particularly the forearms, looked the same way when he moved them. Only grueling work could harden a man like that.

After a while the Indian finished with the horses and sat out on the front porch. Emmett and Tom joined him and Melinda brought out coffee. They talked leisurely about the weather and what had happened in the last two weeks. Emmett had all kinds of questions he would like to ask Tom, but it wasn't considered good western manners to pry into another man's business, or his past. As the turkey was cooking slowly over the fire, Melinda came out and joined them. She glanced at Tom and he at her, but neither held a prolonged look. Emmett and the Indian were older and more experienced. Both of them could tell by the way Tom and Melinda acted around each other that there must be a considerable attraction between them.

When they had found Tom earlier he was such a mess that Emmett hadn't been able to tell much about him. Now that he was cleaned up, Emmett could see Tom was a handsome fellow. His blue eyes drew attention and his quick smile was captivating. Emmett thought Tom might be a good match for Melinda. She was the apple of every cowboy's eye that had seen her. So far Emmett thought Tom to be very likeable.

When Emmett had asked the Indian earlier, he said "Good man, looking for right path."

"Seems like a good enough fella alright. Any idea how fast he is with a gun?" Emmett asked.

"Not sure. Me think fast."

Mescal had proven to be a good judge of character, and Emmett thought he was also. This man seemed like the type to have around. If he were as good a man as he seemed to be, as well as being good with a gun, he would be a great asset for the ranch.

"Tom, you need to help me figure out what's wrong with Melinda here," Emmett remarked mischievously. "She should be married and have children pulling at her skirt by now."

"Father!" Melinda turned scarlet and couldn't believe he had said it. Emmett was not one to joke around much and she had no idea why he would say something to embarrass her. Tom was surprised, but thought it all in good fun and decided to add to her plight.

"I noticed she was right pretty. I figured she could afford to wait until some good looking fellow comes along and sweeps her off her feet."

Melinda gave him a menacing smile and headed back in the cabin; as she passed Tom she hit his arm gently with the small towel she was carrying. Then Emmett turned to Mescal, who was sitting close to him. Emmett said something softly, but a little louder than he meant to because he was already starting to laugh.

"Reckon she won't have to wait long now."

At that both Emmett and the Indian laughed heartily and Tom turned red. It was the first time Emmett or Melinda had ever heard the Indian laugh out loud. Melinda had overheard what Emmett said and couldn't believe what she was hearing. Were the feelings she was struggling with so obvious? Did this mean Tom might feel the same? She couldn't hope for that much. Then she chastised herself; she didn't know anything about him. Who was he? Was he running from the law? Was Tom Colt really his name? She had never seen or been around anyone like him before. No man had ever made her feel...like what? What was she feeling? What was he feeling? She felt flustered and couldn't remember ever being so confused. "Oh the nerve of that Emmett," she thought. She wasn't sure whether to be mad, whether to say something to Emmett about his manners, or...just what. Deep inside there was a tinge of gladness that the subject had been surfaced, but at once she put that feeling away because she didn't know what to do.

Tom decided he needed to get away from these laughing yahoos. If Melinda did care for him it was probably only because she nursed him to health. She had kissed him on the forehead that night, but that was after he had been sick a long time. To think someone that attractive and nice could be seriously interested in him, not knowing anything about him, was just crazy, he told himself, "just completely and absolutely dadburned crazy."

He walked out to see the appaloosa. "Got to stop thinking of you as Charlie's horse," Tom said out loud. Charlie hadn't given him a name and Tom had just referred to him as "the appaloosa." Deciding he would give him a name kept him from having to ponder the situation with Melinda, at least for now. Different possible names flashed through his mind. One by one he rejected them. Finally he noticed one of the marks on the horse's forehead was in the perfect shape of a diamond, like on a deck of cards.

"That's it, you're Diamond, and a fitting name at that." Tom picked up the brush and smoothed out his mane and sides. With the sun getting lower the horse's coat soon had a lustrous gray sheen. Diamond stood perfectly still as Tom groomed him. Finally, Melinda hollered out that supper was ready.

As they sat down to dinner everyone was quiet. Both Melinda and Tom were ill at ease. Emmett broke the silence by asking Mescal about the canyon, whether he had seen any signs of anyone, and then about the horses. The Indian's replies were short and to the point. Then Emmett filled Melinda in on what the women were doing back at the ranch. Melinda feigned interest, glad to be on a safe subject. She asked about his wife, Margaret, and Margaret's younger sister, Beth. Then she talked about how pleasant it was in the canyon and how they had all enjoyed their time there. The Indian nodded and talked about the ground being rich and growing lots of grass, having plenty of water and being protected from the wind by the canyon walls. He said there was a lot of wildlife and it would be a good place for horses. That was a lot of conversation from someone who usually remained silent. Emmett had never heard him say so much at one time.

"Wouldn't be a bad place to settle if it were closer to other ranches and towns," Tom said.

"You're right, too bad it isn't closer to home," Emmett replied.

"This canyon reminds me of home," Melinda added.

"Yes it does. Wait'll you see the ranch, Tom. You'll love it," Emmett said.

Everyone became more relaxed and enjoyed the meal. Melinda went to get more coffee and filled each of their cups. When she poured some in Tom's he couldn't help glancing at her for just a second. Again their eyes met, but only for a moment. Emmett noticed as did the Indian, but they gave no indication this time. Tom wasn't sure what he was feeling, but it was having a powerful impact. Melinda was a little lightheaded and feeling nervous, so much so that her palms were sweaty and she wiped them on her apron.

The Indian smiled softly to himself. The woman he had sworn to protect had finally met a man with whom she was smitten. It couldn't be more obvious and neither of them appeared to have experienced it before, because they both seemed without a clue.

Melinda couldn't help daydreaming even now, about this canyon, or some canyon…and Tom. She interspersed those thoughts with the realization that he might be a gunman, but thoughts of him kept coming back. Her heart was beating so strongly she was afraid someone would hear it, or perhaps see it. As she looked at her plate of food she felt, and then she saw that her left breast pulsed with each beat, and moved her dress ever so slightly. She shifted in her seat so her breasts didn't fit so tightly against the material.

After dinner Melinda made coffee and they all sat out on the porch in the cool evening air. They were stuffed with turkey, biscuits, green beans and the apple pie Emmett's wife had been so thoughtful to send. As they sat in the slight breeze each enjoyed the sounds of nature around them. Occasionally one of the horses would stomp its hoof and another would whinny. There was a cougar off in the distance and it let out a shrill cry.

Tom became introspective. He couldn't remember when he had ever felt like this; these people seemed almost like family. Mescal appeared to be the type of friend to be trusted without worry. Emmett had a devilish streak in him a mile wide teasing him and Melinda that way. Tom had to smile when he thought about it. If he were ever to settle down, he wanted it to be with someone like Melinda. Her beauty, goodness and tenderness had opened up a part of him he had never known. He had feelings inside he didn't recognize and it left him baffled. This was all mysterious but wonderful to him.

Emmett stood up and stretched. Melinda turned to Tom and suggested he probably needed to get his sleep for the long trip back to the ranch. Tom got up and glanced at the old Indian, who was looking at him. Tom nodded, Mescal smiled and returned the nod. A bond was developing between the two men. Tom then said good night to Emmett and the others and went in to his bunk; he was soon fast asleep.

FIFTEEN

The next morning they set out for Emmett's ranch. Tom rode in the wagon next to Melinda. She had folded two blankets and put them on the front seat to help cushion the ride. Mescal had fashioned a sling for Tom's left arm. Emmett rode Tom's horse. They traveled slowly where the ground was rough, but made good time across the smooth and level areas. Tom admired this team of Morgan horses pulling the wagon. They were strong and seemed to know where to go with Melinda's slightest touch on the reins. She told Tom they were Emmett's favorites, except possibly for the red stallion he had just acquired.

The morning portion of the trip was comfortable. The air had a hint of coolness and there were many clouds in the sky. A little after midday Emmett had Melinda pull the wagon over to a creek where there were tall shade trees. The campsite was off the trail, back in a horseshoe type bend in the stream. The cleared ground and evidence of past campfires revealed it had been used several times before. A couple of old tree trunks were lying on the ground. The bark had long since fallen off the logs and they made good seats for weary travelers. Melinda started to prepare a meal while Emmett and the Indian tended to the horses. Tom got up to help Melinda.

"Tom, you need to sit down and rest. I can prepare the food just fine."

"I can help. I don't have anything else to do."

"No, you sit and rest."

"Really, I'm fine."

"Emmett told me not to let you help," she told him quietly. "He is concerned the long ride might be hard on you."

Tom sat down on one of the big logs and watched. There was plenty of grass for the horses on a low spot close to the water. After Melinda had lunch ready, they ate and then relaxed in the ample shade for another hour. Emmett meant to take it slow so Tom would not have a relapse. It also gave him time to talk to the wounded man. He had a calm and easy manner that Emmett regarded as a sign the man had little to hide.

Tom told Emmett about some of his experiences in Kansas, including working as a gunsmith much of the time. He thought there was little chance anyone here would make the connection between a gunsmith in Kansas and that one gunfight in Abilene. Tom also told them about staying with a farmer long enough to help with the wheat harvest and how they had finished just before a storm flattened much of the crops in the neighbors' fields. After describing the scene left by the funnel cloud at one farmer's place, he told how the others living nearby got together and helped rebuild the barn. Finally, he talked about Sarah and her son Ted and how she got married just before he left. Emmett studied the man as he talked and asked few questions. He knew Tom might not be telling everything, but Emmett believed the man was honorable and honest.

They were back on the trail in the early afternoon. Tom noticed some of the terrain they covered was quite scenic. As he looked around he also occasionally glanced at Melinda. A little later in the afternoon, as it grew warmer, she unfastened the top two buttons of her blouse to stay cool. Before long Tom noticed a third button had also come undone. He thought about telling her, knowing she would be embarrassed, but decided to just sit and enjoy the ride. After being on the move for two hours they stopped the wagon for a quick drink—including the horses. Melinda walked over to Mescal and talked to him briefly.

"How's that shoulder feeling?" Emmett asked Tom.

"It's doing fine, no problem at all."

"Is your wound doing okay, Tom?" Melinda asked as she returned.

"It's fine."

"I'll see for myself." Melinda undid the top part of his shirt and removed the bandage just enough to look at the wound. There was no bleeding. She felt Tom's forehead.

"She'll make a good mother someday, Tom," Emmett said.

Tom and Melinda both looked embarrassed and didn't say a word. Melinda went to get a drink of water and Emmett headed back to the horses, grinning. Mescal had heard what Emmett said and winked at him as he approached.

An hour later they came to a spot known as Lee's Ferry. Melinda explained to Tom that it was the only place nearby to get across the Colorado River. She told him quietly that Emmett had known John Lee, for whom the ferry was named. He was a Mormon that had been exiled from Utah for his part in a raid where a large number of immigrants to Utah were killed. Many years later, John Lee was tried in court and hanged.

After crossing the river they got underway again. Later that day, they could see riders in the distance approaching from the opposite direction. The riders were still far away and it was difficult to make out how many there were. The wagon went down into a low place to cross a small stream with a rough and rocky bottom. By the time they emerged to where they could see the riders again, the distance to them had been reduced to a quarter of a mile. Tom saw there were three. While they were still far away he decided to remove his sling as a precaution. He had nearly died, and suffered going through a lengthy recovery and considerable pain, because he had grown too comfortable and hadn't been cautious enough. He wasn't going to make that same mistake again.

As the riders drew closer, the oldest of the three took note of the wagon approaching. He was a leader of dishonest men, and he and two of his cohorts were on their way to get some rest and relaxation. They had just finished rustling and selling some cattle and were ready to enjoy the rewards their money could bring them. They were headed back to their hideout where other members of their gang had already gone. The leader had stayed with two of his men to complete one last job, and now had a bag full of money. They were tired of working and ready to take on the festive mood of drinking, gambling and the companionship of loose women.

The leader was quick with a gun and sure of himself. As the distance lessened he recognized Emmett Bailey, a rancher they had stolen cattle from just a couple of months ago. One of his men had pointed Emmett out to him nearly a year earlier in town. He felt certain Emmett didn't know who he or his men were.

"That's Emmett Bailey," the leader said to his men. "He's the rancher with the pretty girl. If she's the woman in the wagon, well…wouldn't that be nice."

"You mean the blonde Lester was telling us about?" asked his skinny companion.

"Could be, Slim. She's blonde alright," the leader replied.

As they got closer the leader noticed one of the men was an old Indian whom he saw as no threat. Even at a distance he could tell Emmett had a long barreled revolver in a holster not suitable for quick draw and knew his men could handle him. The man on the wagon wasn't driving the team; that kept his hands free. The leader knew he could be a problem and decided he would take care of him personally.

He quickly formulated his plan and told the skinny man beside him, "Slim, wait for me; you take the Indian."

"That old gray haired Indian?" Slim didn't like being given what seemed to him the easiest target.

"That's what I said."

"If you say so, Bert."

"Well, I say so." Then looking at his other partner Bert said, "And you take Bailey, the other one on the horse. I'll take the man in the wagon." As they rode closer Bert could tell it was the girl all the men raved about. "Let's be careful and not hit the girl. We'll take her with us."

As they approached the wagon he couldn't believe his good fortune running into Emmett Bailey so far from his ranch. He had been planning on relieving the rancher of some more of his cattle. Taking Emmett out now would allow him to take much of his herd and get rich in the process. And the girl, well that would make everything complete, the leader mused. Having this girl to take care of his manly needs, and then cook and clean while he rested, was even more than he could have hoped. As they drew near he saw just how pretty she was; her companionship would be pleasurable. He started imagining taking her clothes off. His blood was pulsing as he said, "This is going to be easy, like taking candy from a baby, and my oh my how I'm going to enjoy the candy."

As the riders drew near, Tom became more alert. Trouble was not normally expected, but it was prudent to be cautious when meeting strangers so far away from towns. All three of these men had a hard appearance, and while each wore a smile, they lacked sincerity. The three riders pulled to a stop well before the wagon came to them.

Tom became very vigilant; he sensed danger, and a feeling of alarm pervaded his body. He couldn't pinpoint any one thing that caused him to be apprehensive. It was just a feeling in his gut that these men were evil. They had seen no other travelers since the ferry crossing. It was unlikely anyone else would hear gunshots. As they approached the riders Tom shifted his right leg so his gun was in an easy position to fast draw. He was glad he had disposed of the sling earlier and felt prepared. If there were going to be gunplay he would rather not have a woman sitting so close to him, especially Melinda. Mescal was also wary and could tell Tom was ill at ease.

As they pulled up to where the men waited, Emmett asked, "How are you gents today?"

Bert, who was the oldest of the three, replied, "Well sir, we've traveled a good distance and still got a long way to go."

"At least you have good weather," Emmett said.

The three men looked like they had been traveling for several days. They were dusty, hadn't shaved and smelled. The youngest of the three was on the right and was overweight. His gut bulged over his belt and his second chin attested to his liking for food. The man in the middle was short, scrawny and had a long narrow nose. Stains from chewing tobacco were on his chin. Tom thought his face was almost as ugly as the one who had ambushed him a couple of weeks ago. The oldest rider had spoken and appeared to be the leader. He wore a brown hat and removed it to wipe his brow. Tom noted he held it with his left hand. His right hand was still visible, but just barely. The hat hid his gun. After removing his hat the leader continued.

"That's right, we sure can't complain about the weather. I'm Bill Smith and these here are my partners Dave and Luke."

"Pleased to meet you," Emmett replied. "I'm Emmett Bailey. In the wagon there is my daughter Melinda and Tom Colt, and this fellow over here is Mescal."

"Good to know you all," said Smith. "Say, we are a little short on grub. Wondered if you might have any extra for some hungry strangers? We'd be happy to pay a fair price for any food you could spare."

"Sure we have plenty, but we don't expect any money for it," Emmett responded, revealing no outward signs of concern. He turned to Melinda. "Would you get them some food out of the back?"

She dismounted from the seat and went to the rear of the wagon. Emmett tried to keep his eye on them and on Melinda. He gave her a glance and she returned it to let him know she understood. She would not get too close to them nor venture into the line of fire.

Tom and the Indian kept their eyes on the three strangers. Tom felt they couldn't be trusted. Sensing something was about to happen he kept his eye on the leader, but didn't focus directly on him. He tried to concentrate on the motions of all the riders.

Melinda collected the food in a white cloth bag and tied the top. She walked up close to the front of the wagon to hand the food to Bill Smith. Staying to his right and keeping her distance, she lifted the bag up holding it by the bottom. It would be nearly impossible for him to grab her without falling off his horse.

"Here you are, sir," Melinda said as she lifted the bag.

"Thank you, miss."

The leader had watched her dismount from the wagon and she felt his eyes study her as she took the food from the wagon. Now that she was close she had expected him to look into her eyes and maybe glance at her breasts, but he barely seemed to notice her as she lifted the bag. The leader first put his hat back on and then reached for the bag with his left hand, but on the right side of the horse. As he pulled the bag up it crossed in front of him. When it was directly in front of his right hand he went for his gun.

Tom couldn't see his hand or gun, but saw his shoulder and upper arm move and didn't hesitate. Even as Tom started his motion, he sensed the man in the middle was starting to go for his gun. An explosion sounded and the leader's head jerked backward as his gun fell from his hand. Before the sound from the first shot ceased, a second blast sounded and the top of the scrawny man's head exploded, throwing his hat into the air. His gun was barely out of its holster and still pointing toward the ground. The blasting sound continued as a third shot found its mark and the final rider's face suddenly had a blotched red spot on his forehead; his gun settled back into the holster. He hadn't cleared leather. All three men fell to the ground almost at the same moment. Once initiated Tom's action was automatic, three targets, three shots, over so quickly it was unbelievable.

One instant three men were alive and felt comfortable they were about to acquire several horses, a wagon and a beautiful woman. The next instant their mental activity came to a sudden halt. The response they received was over so quickly the three men didn't have time to realize their violent fate. Tom had practiced this type of quick draw and rapid fire at multiple targets so many times he didn't have to think about it. He just did it, faster than the eye could see. The Indian had pulled his gun and had it aimed, but had not pulled the trigger. Emmett had gone for his gun, but it was still deep in the holster when he realized it was all over. He sat stunned, watched them fall, and let go of his gun handle.

Everyone was silent. Circumstances had changed completely in the blink of an eye. Emmett stared at the three fallen men in disbelief. The Indian's eyes were wide and his mouth dropped open as he looked at Tom. He had known Tom might be a gunfighter, but the speed of what happened was beyond comprehension.

Melinda was in shock. The gun blasts had scared her. She had seen the leader start to draw as she was moving back, and had the best viewpoint to see him go for his gun. When the first explosion occurred, she grabbed at the nearest Morgan because the horse had reacted to the blast and moved to the side. After the three men fell, she turned to see if any of her men had been hit. In a glance she saw all three were without wounds. Her immediate reaction was relief that they had not been shot. She noticed Tom and Mescal's guns were leveled and assumed those two had shot the men. It didn't register to Melinda that only Tom's gun was smoking.

Tom holstered his revolver and got off the wagon. He checked to make sure none of the three men was alive, and then took their guns and put them in the back of the wagon. Having avoided looking directly at any of the others, he finally glanced quickly at Mescal and Melinda. They were just staring at him. She looked confused.

Back in Kansas when Tom had fought in Abilene, he made a conscious decision. Having made that decision he never second-guessed it. The farmer, Seth, had no chance against Kid Coulter, and when Tom stood up to intervene he became the gunman of the past. The iron will, ice blue eyes and steel-like voice were a part of him; they had dominated his former self. When Kid Coulter was about to murder his friend it wasn't Tom Stone that drew the gun that killed him, it was the man of the legend. These three desperados had meant to kill these innocent men and run off with this angelic girl. As Tom sat waiting for them to go for their guns, it was that former part of him that took control. Afterwards he went through a slow transformation back to his new identity. Tom Colt reemerged.

"Guess we ought to bury these gentlemen," Tom suggested to break the silence.

At first the others didn't respond. Finally Emmett nodded and got off his horse. Mescal dismounted and removed a shovel from the wagon. The Indian surveyed the surrounding area and went over near a big rock. The ground was soft and he started digging. Melinda stood still, the sudden intense violence holding her captive. Emmett knew Mescal had not fired his weapon, and had seen enough men draw to know Tom was no ordinary gunfighter. His initial reaction was that no one could be that fast, but he had seen it. There could be no doubt about it being real. Having accepted that fact, Emmett walked over to the three dead men to see if he could find out who they were. What he found allowed him to return to normal. Emmett got a smile on his face and looked up at Tom.

"This one is Bert Cooper. Says so right here on this letter that was in his vest. Tom, it seems you just got rid of a well-known rustler. He's stolen a lot of cattle and horses from me and the neighbors.

Never seen him before, but sure heard the scoundrel's name often enough. Guess you more than repaid any care you'll get while you recover."

The rancher was all smiles now as he went through the saddlebags. Bert Cooper had terrorized Emmett and his neighbor, Jake Evans, for several years. They had done their best to catch up with Cooper but without success. "Whew boy, Jake will sure be pleased," Emmett added when he finished his search. He took the saddlebags and belongings and threw them in the back. Then he tied the horses to the back of the wagon saying, "Reckon they stole enough from us to cover this and more."

Mescal hadn't said anything. Tom watched the Indian dig to pass the time. Emmett went over to help and give Mescal a rest. They dug three shallow graves, dragged the bodies over and covered them, and then started putting rocks on the graves to keep animals from digging them up. It was hot and tiring work. Melinda started walking over to help carry rocks and Tom followed.

"Tom, you really shouldn't; this trip is hard on your shoulder and we don't want it bleeding again."

He went back to the wagon and used the time to look over their guns. Bert Cooper had a Colt similar to his own. He was moving it around in his hand when Emmett returned for a drink of water.

"I noticed it's like yours, Tom. Why don't you keep it? You never know when you might need an extra gun."

"Thanks, think I will." He put the revolver back in the holster and stored it under the seat. "Who is Jake?"

"He owns a ranch near mine. We been neighbors for a long time. Good man and a good rancher."

Emmett went to help them finish with the graves. When they returned to the wagon he said, "We better get moving; the next camp is a ways off and we lost a little time here."

When Melinda climbed up on the seat next to Tom, she did her best to give him a natural smile. It was a little awkward, but he returned it with a quick smile of his own. It was three more hours before they reached the camp Emmett always used on this part of the trip. They could tell someone had stayed there the night before. The Indian studied the tracks.

"Same horse, same mark," Mescal said, motioning toward the leader's horse.

Emmett looked at the hoof print, then went back to Bert Cooper's horse, moving the horse so he could look at the tracks it had just made. "Sure enough, those fellas stayed here last night."

"Should we stay somewhere else?" Tom asked. He wondered if Melinda would be comfortable camping there.

Emmett gave him a puzzled look, but then understood. "You feel okay about stayin here, Melinda?"

"Yes, that's fine. We always stay here."

"Would you rather go somewhere else?" Emmett asked Tom.

"No! I'm okay."

Emmett looked at Mescal who shrugged his shoulders. They made camp and prepared dinner. Melinda had time afterwards to think of the danger and what could have happened. Later, as they sat around the fire eating, Melinda broke the silence.

"I guess I was a bit rattled by this experience. I should have thanked you, Tom, and you, Mescal, for shooting those evil men. Surely they would have killed us all. Or they would have killed you and heavens knows what they would have done to me."

The Indian looked at Tom, then at Emmett and finally at Melinda. He shook his head and replied, "Me no shoot, Tom shoot. One sound, three bullets."

Melinda looked at Mescal puzzled, and then her mouth dropped open; she was incredulous. "You shot all three men, but there was only one..." She couldn't finish. Who in heaven's name was this man? She even began to be a little afraid, but quickly realized that was silly. She had saved his life and now he had saved hers, and Emmett and Mescal as well. Still she had trouble with the anxiety that seemed to grip her body. Tom saw her reaction, and then looked at the flame in the campfire, not knowing what to say.

After a long and uneasy silence Emmett said, "Tom, I'm hoping this doesn't change your plan to stay with us for awhile. Fact is I'd like you to stay on after you're healthy."

Tom sat silent for several seconds. "I had planned to stay." His throat tightened and he paused. "Word of this will get around. I'll have to move on."

Melinda's heart nearly stopped beating. Mescal grew concerned, realizing Tom's dilemma. Emmett was cognizant of what he meant, but wasn't ready to give up so easily. Many long agonizing seconds passed. Finally Emmett was struck with an idea.

"The only ones who know what happened are all right here. What I saw was that you and Mescal took those three men down...just like Melinda said."

The Indian understood what Emmett meant and quickly nodded agreement. "Me shoot fat one."

Melinda could feel her body trembling when she realized Tom might leave. She heard what Emmett said and then Mescal. Nearly a minute passed before Melinda regained control, and willed her body to stop trembling. They finished eating in silence, each pondering what the future would bring. After they ate, they sat around the campfire, watched the stars come out and listened to coyotes in the distance. In one of the nearby trees a woodpecker hammered away. Emmett had been thinking for a long time about what to say, and finally he spoke.

"Tom, you're a good man. Mescal there, he told me that right off, and I know Melinda thinks an awful lot of you. So do I. You are welcome to stay with us as long as you like. If things work out, and you want to stay in this part of the country, I'll help you get started in ranching. We need men like you."

Tom sensed Emmett's sincerity, but he still didn't know what to say or do. After an awkward silence Emmett continued, "Sure we can use your gun, but I wanted you to stay long before those rustlers came along." Emmett paused again then finished convincingly, "Hell, man, we owe it to you. You saved our lives back there and we all want you to stay."

Tom wanted to stay with these people, especially Melinda. Finally he spoke, his voice revealing his internal struggle. "Well, on saving lives I guess we're even, for you saved mine. I'm in no hurry to leave. We'll see how things go. I sure...I sure like the three of you." Having trouble getting the words out, Tom's voice reflected the emotion he was feeling.

Melinda listened intently and her heart leaped as Tom spoke from the heart. Her chest swelled with emotion and her bosom heaved up and down as she breathed. She settled herself as best she could.

"Tom, the ranch is a great place for you not to be seen. We don't have many visitors because it's so remote, and there's lots of work for you. It's beautiful there; I'll show you around. It'll work out fine. I just know it will."

She looked at Tom while she spoke, and then imploringly at her father. Emmett was pleased with Melinda's remarks and understood the look she gave him.

"Right you are," said Emmett, now feeling like they could convince him. "You'll love the ranch. We do have some problems, dadburned rustlers. But you just got rid of the worst of the bunch. When word gets out my new man, Tom Colt, and Mescal here, took care of Bert Cooper and these men, they'll think a long time before they take cattle from our ranch again. And oh what a ranch! You'll love the canyons, Tom, and who better to show you around than Melinda?"

Tom smiled. They didn't need to say any more to convince him. He looked at Melinda and saw that her green eyes glistened with a trace of tears. "I'll stay. I don't know how to thank you folks for being so kind and inviting to a stranger."

Melinda got up and went over to him, the concerns about his being a gunman overpowered by her strong attraction to the man. She didn't stop to think what her actions were conveying. Walking up to him she bent down and kissed him on the forehead; her lips were trembling. Caught by surprise and not knowing how to respond, he just looked into her eyes and smiled awkwardly.

That evening Tom had trouble going to sleep. His mind raced through the events of the day. It wasn't shooting the men that burdened him; he was glad to have been there. He wondered if he was hoping for too much, hoping that he could stay and have this chance at a better life. Melinda danced through his thoughts. What man wouldn't want to stay with her? Tom lay still, looking up at the stars. Occasionally he could hear the cry of a wolf in the distance. He had always felt kinship to the wolf, alone, feared. The wind blew softly through the trees above and the leaves made a rustling sound. The sweet aroma of burning wood from the campfire drifted by with the cool breeze. Tom's senses absorbed these sounds and smells. With his eyes closed his mind replayed again and again the way she had come over and kissed him. With images of her dominating his thoughts, he drifted off to sleep.

Just before the sun rose they were on their way to the ranch again. Emmett noticed that Tom seemed much more relaxed. He and Melinda were talking. They sat close together, and when the wagon tilted slightly to one side or the other they touched shoulders. The Indian noticed as well, and motioned to Emmett with a smile on his face, nodding in the direction of the two on the wagon. When they stopped for the midday meal, Tom and Melinda did most of the fixing while Emmett and the Indian unsaddled the horses and fed them grain. Emmett took the Indian over to the wagon and opened Bert Cooper's saddlebag. There were a large number of gold coins inside a leather bag. He didn't bother counting them; that could come later.

Emmett motioned toward Tom and Melinda and said, "This ought to help them get started."

The Indian broke into a broad grin. "Good!" was all he said.

SIXTEEN

They reached the ranch late the next day when the sun was low on the horizon. As they turned into the canyon Tom was amazed at what he saw. A bright red sky dominated the horizon with purple clouds covering most of the sun. The tiny portion of the sphere that was visible burst through with bright beams of light. The canyon was immense in size and its walls blazed with the reddish glow of the sunset as though illuminated from within.

The ranch house stood a quarter of a mile out from the stone walls near the canyon entrance. A small spring emerged behind the house and ran through the yard. It meandered out to the stream that wended its way through the length of the canyon. The water reflected the bright colors of the sunset. A variety of wild flowers splashed their colors of white, yellow, blue and violet. Most majestic of all were the spires in the distance where many tall stone formations stood like soldiers on sentry duty.

Melinda and Tom got off the wagon and walked toward the house and onto the bridge that crossed over the stream. There was a waterfall close to the bridge, where a small dam of stone had been built to create a pool. As the water spilled over the top and hit the rocks below, it made a soft bubbling sound. Melinda stopped on the bridge and while holding onto the wooden rail, looked up at the blazing sky and then toward the bright stone spires in the distance.

She looked at Tom, her face brushed with colors of the sunset as she spoke.

"Have you ever seen anything so beautiful?"

Tom looked again at all the color and beauty around him. He shook his head slowly, marveling at a picture no artist could possibly capture. Then he looked back at Melinda, answering in words that were unknown to her, but that sounded exotic and romantic.

"*Unam pulchritudinem vidi unquam quae hanc superat, in eam incidi abhinc complures dies.*"

"What does that mean?" she asked intrigued, waiting with her bosom heaving softly.

"It's Latin. It means…there is only one thing I have ever seen to exceed this beauty, and I met her several days ago."

Out of Tom's educated past came charm he never realized he possessed. He was surprised he had remembered the language well enough to utter such a statement; it sounded eloquent even to him. She felt faint and couldn't help but fall against him, any concerns about his speed with a gun lost to the burning love in her heart and the passion of the moment. Hugging him, she pressed her whole body against his and raised her lips, longing to kiss him. His heart raced, his pulse throbbing in every part of his body. His lips found hers and they kissed there on the bridge, forgetting everyone else, completely taken with the romance captivating their hearts.

Emmett's wife, Margaret, and her younger sister, Beth, came out on the porch just in time to witness Melinda and some stranger locked in a long embrace and kiss. "Good heavens!" exclaimed Margaret. "The girl wouldn't pay any attention to the men around here. Now she's head over heels for some stranger. What is she thinking?"

Beth shook her head, but then smiled. "He's certainly good looking."

"Well, even so she's only known him for a short time. It's a little early to be kissing the man."

"I agree, but he sure is attractive."

Emmett and the Indian had taken the wagon over in front of the barn and as Emmett dismounted he witnessed the same event. The Indian noticed Emmett's stare and looked.

"He no leave now," Mescal said.

"Reckon no man could walk away from Melinda if she decided she wanted him."

Emmett was thoroughly surprised. He knew she was very attracted to Tom, but she had always been so completely proper. To offer a kiss like that to someone she had only recently met was difficult to believe. Perhaps the splendor of the canyon helped surface these actions early. Emmett looked at the sunset and at the spires in the distance that were always beautiful, but were simply spectacular at the moment. A good omen, he hoped, for the ranch, and for these two people.

Emmett and the Indian went into the barn, which was bigger than most. It had many stalls for horses and a huge hayloft. The aroma of hay drifted down to them as they entered the big doors. The loft was brimming with both alfalfa and native grass hay they had put up last month. Down below, there were several rooms used to store tools, feed and saddles.

Taking an old metal box from one of the rooms, Emmett cleaned it out. He had the Indian bring Bert Cooper's saddlebags and put the leather bag full of gold coins in the box. They dug a small hole in the corner back where the tools were stored. That room had always kept dry and no animals could get into it. He buried the box, packing the dirt down solid and placing a large barrel over it. No one would find it.

After unhitching the horses they turned them out to pasture. The two Morgans kicked up their heels and ran to join the small group of horses congregated there. Emmett and Mescal joined Melinda and Tom, and all four headed toward the house. They could tell by the pleasant aroma permeating the air that dinner was ready. When they walked onto the porch, Margaret came out.

"I'm afraid dinner this evening is rather simple. We weren't sure when everyone was returning so we didn't have time to prepare something special."

"It sure smells good to me, ma'am," Tom quickly replied.

Beth came out and gave Tom a warm smile. Emmett realized introductions were in order.

"Everybody, this is Tom Colt. Tom, I would like you to meet my wife, Margaret..."

"Pleased to meet you, Tom."

"The pleasure is mine, ma'am."

"And this is Beth, Margaret's sister," said Emmett.

"I'm very happy to make your acquaintance, Mr. Colt."

"I'm honored, ma'am."

"Tom, this is Stan Brown; he's the foreman," Emmett continued.

"Good to meet you, Tom," Stan said, though there was no smile.

"Glad to know you, Stan."

"Now that the introductions have been taken care of, let's eat," Melinda interjected. "I think we're all starving."

During dinner, both Margaret and Beth were pleasant to Tom and seemed more than a little interested, no doubt partly because of what they had seen between him and Melinda. Margaret was a good wholesome looking woman. While she wasn't unusually attractive, she seemed good of heart, genuinely friendly and a perfect match for Emmett. It was clear she respected and loved her husband. Beth had similar facial characteristics, but appeared to be a little younger. Tom thought she was probably in her late thirties. The foreman was around thirty years old and seemed a little distant, but Tom didn't think too much of it. Some people warm up to strangers more slowly than others do.

They had finished the main course and were just getting into the peach pie when Emmett told them the story of Bert Cooper. They were all attentive listeners as Emmett described in detail how Tom and Mescal had bested the three desperados in the desert. Stan knew the Indian was pretty fast and wasn't too surprised he had beaten Bert's companion. When he heard Tom outdrew Bert Cooper and the other man, it outwardly left an impression on him. Bert was known to be very fast with a gun. Beating him to the draw was no small feat— especially when he drew first.

"Didn't you feel in danger, Tom?" Beth asked.

"Wasn't really much time to think, except when they were first approaching. Once they were there, things just sorta happened."

"Well, I think it was very brave," Margaret offered. "It sounds like you and Mescal saved the day."

After dinner, Emmett, Tom, Mescal and the foreman went out on the porch. Stan filled Emmett in on the details of events while he had been gone. Then Stan went on out to the bunkhouse. Emmett offered Tom a smoke, which he declined. They talked for awhile, and then Mescal headed off to his small cabin.

"Tom, I didn't want to say anything while Mescal was here. You can either stay in the bunkhouse with the men, or with Mescal. His cabin is that small bunkhouse over there. It's plenty big enough for two and might give you more privacy. Mescal offered to have you stay with him, but it's completely up to you. There's plenty of space in the main bunkhouse with the men, and they're easy to get along with."

"Thanks, Emmett. Appreciate the choice. I'll stay with Mescal."

For the next week Tom did little as his body continued to heal. He walked around and became familiar with the barn, corral and outbuildings. Discovering they had a garden behind the house, which was irrigated with the little stream, Tom now realized that was why they had built the rock dam. The pool of water had wood planks over on the side that could be removed to flood the small irrigation ditch.

As the week progressed Tom grew stronger. During the second week Melinda began to show him around the ranch. They spent all of the first morning and some of the afternoon looking at the main canyon. Melinda could tell Tom was growing weary from the ride, so she took him back to the cabin. The two of them sat out on the front porch.

"Does Beth live here or is she just visiting?" Tom asked.

Melinda looked toward the house and was quiet for a few seconds. "She's lived here for about ten years. I was still pretty young when she came. What I understand is that her husband liked alcohol too much, and tended to hit her when he was drunk. His name was Daniel. One time after he beat her, her eyes were nearly swollen shut. She came here to stay with us for awhile. I remember Emmett was furious with what Daniel had done.

"A few days later Daniel simply disappeared. His horse and saddle were gone, along with some of his clothes. Nobody has seen him since, at least not anybody around here. Most people figured he had just run off and left Beth, but there were a few that wondered if Margaret and Beth's brother, Eldon, had dispensed some western justice. I guess the sheriff even asked Emmett about it.

"Eldon was killed three years ago when his horse threw him and broke his neck, so I guess we'll never know if he did anything to Daniel or not. Emmett never talks about it." After a period of silence, she added, "It would probably be better if you didn't bring it up. It's worked out real well with Beth living here. She's a hard worker and easy to get along with."

"I was just curious. No reason for me to mention it."

Tom spent the rest of the day on his own taking it easy. The next several days Melinda rode out with Tom and showed him some of the surrounding canyons. Their time was short so they rode through several without stopping. The expanse of area involved was substantial, and Tom was quite impressed with the potential for the ranch.

The central canyon was cleared of brush, had smooth walls and was well defined. The same was not true of the connecting canyons. Several of them were still undeveloped and under utilized. This was partly due to their rough and jagged walls, and also to the existence of predators that killed both cattle and horses—primarily cougar.

Melinda told him the main factors keeping these other canyons from being more productive were rustlers and cougars. They never saw the rustlers, but would discover their tracks and the disappearance of a small herd after the fact. The size of the canyons involved and the many walls and rock formations made it difficult to catch or eliminate these culprits—either the two or four-legged variety.

Despite the problems of these rougher canyons, Tom felt they were beautiful in their own way. As a boy he often went exploring in the woods or any place where he could be alone with nature. He had been quiet as a child, and enjoyed those times when he could get away by himself. These canyons provided the ultimate in exploring; one could get lost in them.

The second week, while they were in one of the rougher canyons, Melinda rode her horse up an incline strewn with rocks and boulders. Tom urged on his horse and followed. He assumed she was headed for the small grove of trees. When she reached the edge of the grove, she turned and looked to make sure no one else had seen them go up the slope. After dismounting, she led her horse around the trees and through what looked like a large crack in the canyon wall. The split was just large enough for a horse to walk through.

Tom did the same and was completely surprised with this secret opening. The split couldn't be seen from the canyon because of the trees in front. The area behind the split was about twenty yards long and just over ten yards in width. The grass was tall because of the trickle of water coming down the wall of the canyon. It seemed to nearly disappear into the ground, but there was a small puddle for the horses to drink. The water was enough to keep the grass healthy, but none went through the split in the rock. It was completely dry there. Without doubt it was this water that seeped through the soil and fed the grove of trees at the top of the slope.

"This is my secret place. Do you like it?"

"Sure do. I was really surprised when you walked your horse through that stone wall."

"I have something else to show you. Follow me. It'll take a while to get there."

She grabbed the picnic basket and motioned for him to follow. She started climbing the wall next to where the water was coming down. Tom thought it looked a little dangerous, but she seemed to know what she was doing. They climbed for several minutes and both were beginning to tire. Up above on a large ledge, still well below the top, they reached a level place where the water trickled out of the canyon wall. It flowed into a small pool about six feet wide and eight feet long. Next to the pool, in the same area, was a huge flat rock perhaps ten feet in diameter. On the other side of the pool, where it met the canyon wall, a collection of wild flowers grew. They were mostly white flowers, with a few violet ones interspersed.

"Well, here it is, my secret hideaway. I carried the soil up here and then transplanted the flowers. Lovely, aren't they?"

"They sure are. This whole place is. Bet it took some work to get that dirt up here."

"It did, but it was fun."

Tom saw that next to the flowers there was a small cave in the side of the canyon wall. It was oval in shape and no more than one foot wide, too small for a man to crawl in. It was impossible to tell how far back it went and that mystery added to the exotic nature of the spot.

"The pool looks like a big bathtub, doesn't it?" she asked.

"Yes…it sure does."

"The water is about two feet deep. It seeps into the pool from the canyon wall all spring and summer."

"I never would have dreamed this was here."

"If you get on this big flat rock next to the pool, you are not visible from any direction. You can't even be seen from the top of the canyon wall above. If you'll notice, as the wall goes up from here it goes outward. Up above it slopes back. I have been on the rim and you can't see this place from anywhere. When a person is here on this big rock or in this pool of water, they are invisible to the world."

"Incredible!"

"If you walk out between those two large rocks at the edge you can see or be seen from a distance, but if you stay in the area near the pool you won't be seen at all."

As Tom stood on the flat rock, and moved around close to the pool, he realized he could not see into the canyon, nor see any nearby ground or distant canyon wall. He walked between the two large rocks she had mentioned, and was able to see well out into the canyon. He looked down to see their horses. It was nearly two hundred feet up from the floor. It was almost like a small castle or fort built into the canyon wall, but built by nature.

"What a wonderful place to retreat."

"I don't think anybody other than the two of us and Mescal know about it. Mescal found it last year and showed it to me."

Melinda spread a small blanket on the big flat rock next to the pool. Then she opened the picnic basket and arranged a small meal. She had brought fried chicken left over from the night before, fresh rolls and apple pie. They sat and enjoyed the food and the cool breeze. While they ate, they made small talk about this peaceful sanctuary.

"If I had found this place when I was a boy growing up, I would have spent all my free time here."

"I'm pleased that you like it. I was entranced with it from the very first day I saw it."

"Anybody would love it here; it's a fortress in the sky."

"That's a perfect name for it, Fortress in the Sky."

Suddenly Melinda's eyes glinted mischievously and she made Tom promise to keep a secret, which he agreed to do. Then she told him that sometimes when she wanted to get away and be one with nature, she would come here, remove all her clothes, get in the pool of water and then lie out naked on the big rock beside the pool. No one could see her and she enjoyed the freedom of lying out beneath the grand blue sky. Tom imagined the scene she had just described. Then he thought how wonderful it would be to feel the cool of the water in the pool, then the warmth of the sun on the rock.

"What if someone happened by and saw your horse, or followed you and came up? Wouldn't you be in danger?"

"No, Mescal stays down below and keeps watch. He would die before he would let anyone harm me."

Later, as they descended the wall, Tom realized that while Melinda was proper in her actions and a fine lady, she had an adventurous nature within her. He would never have guessed she would have a place so secretive or make such...creative use of it. His thoughts jumped forward to a time he might join her.

After they had gotten back down to the horses and were preparing to leave, Melinda said, "Mescal really likes you. He knows the canyons better than anyone, including Emmett. I think he would be pleased if you asked him to show you around."

Later that day, Tom decided to take Melinda's advice and asked Mescal to show him the ranch. The Indian made plans to start the next morning. They ventured first to the main canyon and spent most of the day there. Tom thought there must be over five thousand acres in that canyon alone. The ground was fertile and had ample water for irrigation. The alfalfa patches were huge, and toward the back of the canyon there were two fields of oats. Even though Tom had seen it with Melinda, Mescal provided additional information about the crops, cattle and horses. The Indian also knew more about the implications of the canyon in regards to the effects of rain, wind, sun and snow on the livestock. Toward late afternoon, Mescal took him into the roughest adjoining canyon and explained the differences between the two extreme environments.

On the following days they started exploring the connecting canyons. Mescal taught him a great deal. Tom wrote it all down in the evenings, trying to capture what the Indian had told him. Mescal showed him the various plants, including cactus, and the strengths and weaknesses of each canyon—they were all unique. He showed him places where there was water that wasn't evident, and where the bear and cougar liked to hunt. The Indian took him to the high spots of the ranch that served as the best places to keep lookout. One thing Mescal didn't show Tom was Melinda's secret spot. Mescal considered it a private place for her use, and not his to disclose.

Tom learned there were no maps of the canyons. In the evenings he began to draw an outline of the area they explored that day, and then would check it for accuracy the next time they were there. He hoped to get a fairly detailed map of the whole ranch, a labor that lasted for several weeks. Carrying the maps in his saddlebag he added detail to them as they came across something new. He showed the maps to Emmett one day and the rancher was pleased. Emmett asked Beth to draw a copy for him.

The rancher explained to Tom that several of the canyons weren't officially part of his ranch. They hadn't been properly claimed yet. Someone would have to improve them and use them successfully. Emmett used the map to show Tom which canyons were still available. He went on to explain that the maps would help substantiate the claim when the time came.

After Tom had become familiar with the lay of the land, he and Mescal began hunting cougar. Tom used the Henry rifle that had belonged to Charlie. During one week they managed to kill three adult cougars, which they took back to the ranch. Emmett delighted in having rugs made out of the hides. He had complained earlier to Tom that the cougars killed a large number of cattle and especially young calves. Each one Tom and Mescal eliminated would increase the future size of the herd.

After shooting a cougar one afternoon, they discovered she had two young ones. They were quite small and too young to be afraid. Tom wasn't sure what to do with them so he took them back to Melinda. She made a small cage and started feeding them cow's milk. It was a trick to get them started and she received a few punctures from their sharp little teeth. Finally they started lapping up the milk with their tongues. As she grew attached to them, Tom wondered how smart it was to have brought them back to the ranch. The foreman, Stan, had looked at Tom and shook his head while Melinda fed the two young cats. Tom had to admit he was probably right, but they had seemed so harmless when he had found them.

He and Stan had not become close, but they had become friendly. It had become clear to Stan that Tom was not after his job, but wanted to someday have his own ranch. At one time, Stan had hoped to interest Melinda. After Tom arrived, it became obvious Melinda was taken with him.

While Tom and Mescal were out exploring, Tom looked for a place where he could practice his fast draw without attracting attention. Having not practiced for a long time, he knew the need for constant attention to that exercise. Finally one day, Tom asked Mescal and he showed him a good spot. Mescal joined him. Tom practiced drawing and shooting until the natural feeling came back. The Indian had a surprisingly quick draw and good aim. Mescal was amazed at the speed of Tom's draw and the incredible accuracy of his shots, even when he fired several in rapid succession.

They began to spend at least an hour practicing once or twice a week. The Indian's speed and accuracy improved. Mescal returned the favor by showing Tom how to use a bow and arrow. There were times when "No noise good," as Mescal put it. Tom was pathetically poor with the bow at first, missing his first rabbit by ten feet, but he learned quickly. He doubted he would ever gain Mescal's level of expertise.

One afternoon, when they were checking one of the more remote canyons, they saw three men working with a small herd of cattle. Tom and Mescal had come into the canyon through a pass that had required some rough and treacherous riding. There were numerous rocks and scrub trees to work around. Because of the trees and brush they were not readily visible to the three men, so Tom and Mescal dismounted and watched to see what they were up to.

A heavyset man was on a black and white paint; it was sleek and muscled and appeared as fast as the wind. He seemed to be directing the other two. They were getting the cattle together, bringing them out of the washes and crags where the strays had wandered. After an hour they had close to two hundred head and started moving them away from Emmett's ranch.

Tom wanted to be sure of their intentions so he and Mescal trailed them for several miles. Once they were well off of Emmett's ranch they headed east. Mescal told him there was no nearby ranch in that direction. "Where rustlers go," offered Mescal. The Indian motioned Tom to follow and they went around a huge rock formation so they wouldn't be seen. Then the Indian led him through a pass, down the length of another canyon and to a deep, dry streambed. They followed the streambed that meandered like a snake for what seemed like a long distance. Finally, the Indian stopped, got off his horse and peered over the edge. "They come, we wait."

Before long, Tom could hear the cattle and soon the dust they kicked up started floating over the streambed. Within minutes a few head began crossing fifty yards further down. Tom and Mescal rode up the steep bank and rode slowly toward the closest of the three riders. One was behind the herd and the other two on each flank. The one nearest stopped when he saw them. He waited there, not sure what to do. Tom and Mescal approached leisurely like they were just out for a ride.

The other two riders rode over at a brisk trot. They didn't want a couple of drifters interfering with their money making scheme. As they pulled up, the heavyset man on the paint recognized the Indian as being one of Emmett's men and his apprehension grew. He hadn't expected anyone from the Bailey ranch because Tom and Mescal had come from the opposite direction. It was too late to run now. He didn't recognize the Indian's companion, but had heard Emmett had a new man who had outgunned Bert Cooper. They all knew rustling was a hanging offense, and when rustlers were caught in this part of the country, no one waited for judge or jury. If this was Emmett's new man they were in trouble.

Tom rode right up to the three men. Mescal stayed to his right about five yards away. "Where you all headed?" Tom asked matter of factly. There were a couple of nervous looks among the men.

"Some of Mr. Evans' cows strayed over this way and we just come to bring 'em back," the youngest one blurted out.

Mescal had already told Tom that Evans' ranch was toward the north, and they were definitely not headed there. Tom also knew the cattle had Emmett's brand, not Evans'. "Are you the leader here?"

There was a short period of silence when no one spoke. "No, that would be me," said the heavyset man who sat atop the black and white paint.

"Who do you work for?" Tom inquired still very matter of factly.

"We work for Evans of course, if that's any of your business," the heavyset man replied quickly and irritably.

"What's your name?" Tom asked without any reaction to the tone.

The man was getting agitated. He knew they had been caught red handed, but this fellow wanted to carry on a conversation like they had just met outside church. "Well, I guess I was wonderin who's doin the askin?"

"Name is Tom Colt." Tom could tell they reacted to his name.

The heavyset man had feared it was the new man who bested Cooper. He knew Bert was deadly fast with a gun, and that he had no chance with Cooper. That meant the likelihood of outdrawing this stranger was not promising.

"What do you want with us, Tom Colt?" the heavyset man asked.

"I want you to unbuckle your gunbelts and step down off your horses."

If any of the three had a doubt about the mess they were in, it had just been removed. If they did what was asked, they would probably be taken back to Emmett's ranch and hanged as examples of what happens to rustlers.

The heavyset man had seen two men that had been hanged. He had gone to check on them because they were overdue getting back from what was supposed to be a simple job. When he saw those men they had been hanging for three days. As he rode up, vultures were standing on the men's shoulders, picking at their eyes. One of the large ugly birds started picking away at an ear, trying to get to the tender flesh inside. The men's heads were various shades of black and a hideous display of death. When he rode close to the two bodies suspended in air he heard the buzz of flies. Then he saw the maggots in what used to be their mouths. He swore to himself he would not be hanged. No matter what his chances were here, he would not be hanged.

His horse seemed to sense his tension and fidgeted, moving slightly to the left. Without warning he went for his gun and a fraction of a second later so did the man next to him. Tom had expected them to draw, as foreshadowed by the sudden change in the tone of conversation. As long as there was a chance they might talk their way out, Tom figured they wouldn't go for their guns. When he changed the direction to surrender their weapons and dismount, they had little choice but to comply or draw. It was a lot easier to react when he knew it was coming. Two bullets were fired and each found its target. Both men were lying on the ground dead a few seconds later.

The youngest man, who had spoken initially, put his hands in the air. Tom and Mescal had their guns leveled on him. Tom's gun smoked. He had come close to releasing the hammer one more time, but the youngster hadn't made any move for his weapon. The young man wasn't sure what to do, but he knew going for his gun would leave him dead like the others. He knew he might hang, but that wasn't immediate, and he had no past images of hanged men to horrify him. He thought for a second about making a run for it but knew he had no chance.

"Don't shoot, don't shoot." Snail-like the young man lowered his left hand to unbuckle his gunbelt, letting it drop to the ground, and then slowly got off his horse. He was visibly shaking. "I don't want to hang, I don't want to hang. It was Simpson's idea. He was the leader. He said it would be easy, said he had done it lots of times. I can't believe I was so stupid. I just needed the money. I don't wanna hang."

"What's your name?"

"It's Jeff...Jeff Short."

Tom waited, trying to size him up and letting him stew. "Will you answer a few questions?"

"Anything, sure, anything," he replied quickly, hoping some fate other than death awaited.

"Were you rustling for someone other than Simpson here?"

"No, just Simpson. He said with Cooper gone we should make one last grab and get outta this part of the country. I just helped him

222

one other time. Once you help, they pretty much make you do it again. But he said this was it. We'd grab a good size herd and get outta here."

"Are you working for Evans?" Tom pursued.

"Yes, but he don't know nothin about this. We all work for Evans, but Simpson was in with Cooper. He would tell Bert when to hit and where. I don't want to hang, Mr. Colt. I'm real sorry I got into this. I just needed the money. I don't want to hang."

Tom pondered what to do. He figured the boy just fell in with bad company. Chances were good he would go straight after this, and he could carry a message that might slow up rustling of Emmett's cattle for a long time to come.

"We'll keep the guns. Let's load up your friends. You take them to Evans, tell him what Simpson has been doing and what happened here today. Then you ride out of Utah and never come back. Is that a deal?"

"Yes, sir. Yes, Mr. Colt." Jeff looked at him incredulously, nodding his head hurriedly while he spoke. "I'll do it, just like you said. I'll tell Jake, and I'll leave Utah and I'll never rustle again."

After they loaded Simpson on his horse, Jeff opened Simpson's saddlebag. Both the Indian and Tom's hands went to their guns. The youngster jumped back and held up his hands. "Don't shoot, Mister Colt, there's something in here I want to show you." Tom nodded but both he and Mescal kept their guns leveled on the youngster. Slowly he pulled out a thick leather pouch and opened it to show Tom the money inside.

"This was the payoff from last time. There's some in Cully's saddlebag too. Guess it belongs to you now."

"Why didn't you just ride off with it?"

"Because you gave me back my life; I owe it to you. I have some money in my saddlebag too, and you're welcome to it as well."

He decided if the boy was honest enough to turn over the majority of the money, he should have some reward. "No, you keep it, Jeff."

Tom soon discovered there was a sizeable amount of money in the two saddlebags, but Simpson's must have had three times what Cully's did. As he and the youngster loaded Cully's body, Tom noted the Indian was eyeing Simpson's horse.

"Who owns the paint, Evans or Simpson?" Tom asked.

"That's Simpson's horse; you can have him if you want. Simpson didn't have no family."

Tom had noticed long ago that the Indian's horse wasn't much to look at, nor was his saddle. Tom walked over to Mescal. "Why don't you take the horse, and the saddle too? Like he said, it doesn't really have an owner."

Inside Mescal was ecstatic, but he showed no emotion and just grunted and nodded. He led his horse over so they could put Simpson on it, transferred his belongings and climbed on his new horse. Tom had to smile at the proud look that came to the Indian's face once he was on the paint.

Jake Evans was surprised and saddened to hear his own men were involved with the rustling. At the same time he was happy to hear both Simpson and Cully had been caught in the act. Jake felt certain the killing of Bert Cooper and Paul Simpson would have a substantial effect on the rustling of cattle, at least for him and Emmett. Jake wasn't so sure about the idea of letting the youngster go free, but he believed his story about Tom Colt letting him ride off on the provision he tell what happened. Jake would honor Tom's wish to release him.

"Okay, Jeff, you be on your way now."

"Goodbye, Mr. Evans. I'm real sorry I got hooked up with Simpson on this. You can tell Mr. Colt I'm gonna make good on my promise. I'm through with rustling. I'm gonna get a job and work hard. Will you tell him for me?"

"Yeah, I'll tell him."

As Jeff was about to leave he gave Jake the name of the man he believed to be the buyer who had been purchasing the cattle from Cooper. He told Jake he had never met the buyer, but had overheard Simpson talking to Cooper and they mentioned his name.

Jake decided he would have to get over and meet this Tom Colt; maybe a gift of some sort would be in order. He had heard Tom and Mescal were out killing cougar. Jake also wanted to talk to Emmett about the man who might be the buyer of their stolen cattle.

SEVENTEEN

It had rained the night before and Tom could smell the freshness of the grass and the musky smell of the soil. The canyon, and all its contents, had received a thorough cleaning from the wind driven water. The sun glimmered on the tall stone walls surrounding the ranch house. The wind blew softly, turning the weather vane on the barn ever so slightly, causing a small squeak each time it changed direction. The windmill spun slowly, pumping water from the stream into the large holding tank for the livestock in the corral.

It would take at least two days for the grass, alfalfa and ground to dry enough for cutting hay. It would be the second cutting of the year. The hay would be needed for the winter months. The canyons provided shelter and food even in winter, but there would be snowfalls that would cover nearly everything at times. With so many livestock, there had to be abundant hay for those periods. The hay harvest had been planned for tomorrow, but would have to wait for a couple of days.

This meant today was a time to relax, at least for the morning. In the afternoon Tom and Mescal planned to check one of the canyons where a pesky cougar had managed to elude their efforts to track him down. Perhaps the wet, soft ground would give them a better opportunity. Melinda brought Tom a cup of coffee as he sat on the porch waiting for Mescal. The Indian had gone out to check on their horses. Melinda sat next to Tom and they both looked out toward the pasture.

Diamond whinnied in the distance as the Indian approached. Two young calves raced toward the stream, then turned and raced back toward their mothers. Melinda pointed at a flock of birds by the barn feasting on worms that had found their homes too wet. Emmett, Margaret and Beth had gone to town for food and supplies that would be needed for the hay harvest. This left Tom and Melinda alone, which was rare at the ranch house. Emmett had suggested something to Melinda and she decided to broach the idea to Tom on this pleasant morning.

"Have you given any thought to starting your own ranch in some of the remote canyons? Emmett mentioned something about it the other day. I think he was wondering if you were considering the possibility."

Tom wasn't surprised Melinda asked him, but was surprised Emmett had said something to her because he had not said anything to him, at least nothing so direct. Emmett had talked about Tom settling down here, along with telling him he would help him get started in ranching. When Emmett had talked about the remote canyons, Tom thought he might be hinting about letting him use them for some cattle of his own, but Emmett hadn't said anything explicitly. Perhaps this was Emmett's way of conveying the idea, using Melinda as the messenger.

"Mescal and I have talked about it, but we aren't in any position to buy cattle or the other things needed for a ranch just yet, even a small one. Emmett has sure helped all he could. He insisted Mescal and I keep the money that was on Simpson and Cully's horses. It's a substantial sum, but not nearly enough to start a ranch."

"So you're thinking when you do get a ranch that Mescal will be a part of it?"

"Oh yeah, we'll be partners. He and I have talked about it."

"I'm sure you're right about it taking a lot of money to get started. Ranching is a big investment."

"Cattle alone are expensive, and it takes more than cattle."

"Emmett might help you get started." Actually Emmett had told Melinda that he would, but she was hesitant to push the subject.

"He's already done too much. I couldn't ask for more." Tom didn't want Melinda to think the situation was hopeless. "We've been saving all the money we can, and hope to have enough before too long. Mescal has talked about buying some cattle and putting them in one of the remote canyons. I told him we would have to wait until we've got the cougar problem solved. Right now we'd lose too many calves."

"There's still too many cougar, you think?"

"Yes, but we're working on it. We'll get them thinned out."

"With both you and Mescal saving money, you'll get enough that much quicker."

"Yeah, should be able to. I've kind of gotten to where I like that old Indian."

"Me too!" Melinda laughed. She was delighted that Tom wanted him to be a partner. "My, but it's a beautiful day," she said happily, changing the subject.

Melinda felt like she had accomplished what she had set after. She would let Emmett know everything Tom had said. Pleased with the results of their discussion, she dreamt about their own ranch and more importantly, at least for her, their own house.

Emmett always tried to put more hay aside than would normally be needed, in case a hard winter set in. For several years he had ended up with more than required, but was able to sell it to neighbors or use it through the summer. Having ample hay available was a convenience in most years and a necessity in a few. He hadn't come up short for years. During that year, so long ago, he lost many cattle to the cold and ice, but mostly to hunger. That winter nearly broke him financially and the mental strain took its toll. He swore he would never be short again. Cutting and storing hay was strenuous and tiring work. Each year Emmett brought in some of the neighbors and additional help from town, including some of the older boys who jumped at the opportunity to earn extra money.

Two days later the workers arrived early in the morning and the operation commenced. With so many workers, camaraderie soon developed. Spirits were high as they began cutting and storing the hay. Over the years Emmett had learned whom he should employ. It was hard work, but there was a certain satisfaction in seeing how much could be accomplished by the end of the day.

Tom enjoyed meeting the men and getting to know them. Initially he had some concern he might run into someone from Texas or Arizona who knew his earlier identity. Even though he had altered his appearance, someone who had known him might look past those changes and recognize who he was. Tom had avoided going to towns for that reason, going only once so he could send a letter to Ethel Potter in Waco, Texas, about the accidental death of her son Zack. There had been a barn dance at a ranch west of Jake's place two weeks ago, but neither Tom nor Melinda attended so he could avoid the exposure. Here on Emmett's ranch Tom couldn't avoid having people see him, but the number was limited and he hadn't seen anyone he remembered. After the first day of cutting hay, Tom stopped worrying.

With so many extra hands, progress was good. After three days the loft was filled to overflowing. In the following days haystacks were built out in the main canyon up against the stone walls where the hay could easily be fenced off from the cattle. This hay did not have to be transported far, and would be readily available to the herds when the heavy snows came. The men nailed together old lumber to form a makeshift roof over each haystack for protection from the elements.

Every day all the workers would go up to the ranch house for lunch. With so many men the only practical way to feed them was to put the food outside on tables under a big shade tree. They filled their own plates and found a place to sit and eat. Many sat on blankets under a tree, on the porch of the house or out in the yard. It presented the opportunity for Tom to get to know some of the neighbors and folks from town.

All helped in the harvest of the hay. Melinda, Margaret and Beth were kept busy getting food ready and serving lemonade and tea. The young men gave a lot of attention to Melinda while they were eating and often asked for more lemonade, as she was the one serving it. They had heard that Tom Colt and Melinda liked each other, so no one became "too friendly." Melinda was not one who enjoyed attention. She wore loose fitting and plain attire, but it didn't seem to matter.

In the evening they would have another meal and then some of the neighbors would go home to sleep. Many of those from town slept in the few available spots in the bunkhouse or on the porch. Some of the men preferred to sleep under canvas tents. Those that slept in the barn had to get use to the cry of the cougar. Melinda's pets were noisier than usual; they were ill at ease with so many unknown people around. On the second day Melinda laughed when she found a rope tied around the cats' enclosure to give extra protection from possible escape.

"Who put all this rope around their cage?" she asked Stan who was standing nearby.

"A couple of Jake's men did that late last night. I swore to them I wouldn't give any names."

Bud overheard the conversation and walked up. "They just aren't real men over there on the Evans place, Miss Melinda. Those cats don't scare us cowboys here on the Bailey spread."

"While they're in the cage, that is," Stan said. "Don't suppose you'd mind if we told those boys of Jake's what you just said."

"Ah, if you did that, they'd get mad and start a fight. I'd hate to have to whup those boys, and get 'em all broke up. We need 'em to help with the hay."

"Guess we better not tell them then," Melinda said laughing. "We want to get the hay up as soon as possible don't we?"

"That'd be the smart thing to do, Miss Melinda. It would be a lot better for Jake's boys if we didn't say anything."

It was a festive atmosphere in the evenings. Many sat around the campfire out in the yard and shared stories of the day. There were ample bouts of humor and teasing of others in good fun. On the porch of the main bunkhouse one of the cowboys got out his guitar and played some tunes. Later one of Jake's men joined in with his harmonica. But most of the men gathered around the campfire, and listened to the tall tales. With such a large group there were bound to be men who could tell some whoppers.

An older bowlegged cowboy named Gumpy was the king of story telling around these parts. He had been working on the Bailey ranch almost since Emmett got started. Gumpy told only one story each night. He would wait until after everyone else had told their stories then he would top them all, stopping every so often to spit his tobacco juice for effect. On the fifth night, all the cowboys gathered around and were anxious to hear Gumpy tell his tale to see if it would be better than the night before. Gumpy strolled forward.

"Last year I visited a friend of mine up near Provo. He told me this here true story about a newly converted Mormon. It seems he was looking to buy him a ranch. He told all the local ranchers up there he'd pay top dollar for their place, but he had one stipulation. There couldn't be no mosquitoes whatsoever. Now most of the ranchers didn't want to sell, cause ranchin was all they knew. Three ranchers did contact him and soon discovered he was offerin a powerful amount of money.

"Well, this fellar wantin to buy a place went out to the home of the first rancher that approached him. Now this fellar spent nearly a whole day a ridin around that ranch, includin in the trees. An hour before sunset he rode back to the house with two mosquito bites. 'This ranch will never do,' he told the first rancher. The next day he rode over to the second ranch. Again he spent the whole day and then part of the evening, but sure enough bout suppertime he had himself another mosquito bite.

"That fellar was disgusted, and he went back to town and told people he was a leavin cause he felt like those two ranchers lied to him. When the third rancher heard about it, he hurried up and rode into town. He wanted to sell his place real bad cause he had a gimpy back and couldn't work much no more. He found that fellar at the saloon and was tryin to convince him to come out and check his ranch. But the fellar told him if the other two ranches had mosquitoes then surely his did too. 'Oh no!' the rancher said. 'In all the years I've lived there, I've never had one bite from a mosquito.'

"The newly converted Mormon was pretty impressed by that claim. But he told the third rancher that the other two had also claimed they didn't have no mosquitoes, and he wasn't sure it was worth the effort to check another place. The third rancher was stubborn and wouldn't give up. He said, 'I'll tell you what, we'll tie you naked to a tree out in my pasture. If even so much as one mosquito bites you during the whole night, the ranch is yours for free. But if you don't get bit, then you pay me half again more than you quoted me the other day. I'm that sure there ain't no mosquitoes on my ranch.' Well, that fellar thought about it and decided he'd do it. They had a lawyer draw up the paperwork, and that night they tied the fellar naked to a tree.

"The next morning the rancher was surprised to see over a dozen men waitin out in his yard. This was such a high stakes gamble, they wanted to see if a mosquito bit that fellar. Several of them was a makin bets among themselves. That whole group of men went with the rancher as he walked out into the pasture. When they got within hearin distance, they could hear the newly converted Mormon a moanin somethin turrible. He was just a hangin limp against the rope and surely would've fallen if he weren't tied to that there tree. When the rancher heard him, he was horrified. The rancher and all the other men ran the rest of the way just as fast as they could. All the while that fellar moaned and moaned so loud he didn't even hear the men a comin. The rancher ran right up to him and hollered out, 'Oh no! Did the mosquitoes get you?' That fellar looks up at the rancher all glassy eyed and says, 'No, but don't that calf have a mother?'"

The men that had gathered around Gumpy roared in laughter. Margaret, Beth and Melinda had listened from a distance, and after the initial shock turned quickly toward the house. When the men noticed their quick departure they laughed even harder. There wasn't any doubt among those present that Gumpy had outdone them once again. Tom was embarrassed for the women, but felt certain they also thought it was funny.

On the last day the men were washing up, collecting their pay and saying their good-byes. Jake Evans had come to see Emmett and told him what he had learned from the young rustler about the possible buyer for their stolen cattle. Emmett, like Jake, had heard the name but didn't know the man. They agreed they needed to figure out a way to check out the story. Jake also told Emmett he had brought a gift for Tom for helping with the rustlers. He hung around until everyone from town and the various neighbors had departed, then he pulled a long object wrapped in a blanket out of his wagon. Jake walked up on the front porch of Emmett's ranch house where Tom and Mescal had joined Emmett to lounge after the others had left.

"Hello there, you must be Tom. I'm Jake Evans."

"Pleased to meet you, Jake. Emmett has sure talked about you often enough. Met some of your men while we were putting up hay."

"That's what Ben and Sam told me. They said you were a pretty good ranch hand."

"Well, I don't know about that, but thank you, Jake."

"Tom, I've been lookin for the right time to give you this. It's my way of sayin thanks for takin care of those rustlers. I also hear you've done more than your share of gettin rid of cougars."

"Jake, you sure didn't need to bring a gift. I've just been doing my job, that's all." Tom slowly unwrapped the blanket to reveal one of the nice new hunting rifles with a scope. "Lordy, look at this rifle. I've only seen these in catalogs. Jake, these are expensive. You shouldn't have done that."

"I ordered it all the way from Chicago. There's not another one like it in Utah, or at least I don't think there is. That ought to help you get some more of those cougars."

Tom was pleased, but felt ill at ease accepting such a nice gift. It was the type for long distance shooting and used big cartridges. He didn't know quite what to tell the neighboring rancher.

"Thanks, Jake, I really do appreciate it. You're right, by golly; we ought to be able to get a few more critters with this."

"Tom, you have no idea how much you saved me in cattle and horses by gettin rid of those rustlers and by ridin the range. This rifle will help give you an edge over those cougars you've been huntin, and it might come in handy with rustlers. We haven't lost any cattle since the story got out about Cooper and Simpson. This rifle doesn't begin to cover what I owe you, but I thought it would be a start."

Tom thanked him again, and showed it to Emmett and Mescal. Later, Tom went to the cabin and set the rifle on the table. He couldn't help but think back to the last time that someone had given him a rifle. He was only fourteen when his family was moving by wagon train from Missouri to California. His father had given him a small caliber rifle and he used it to hunt for food along the way. Tom could still remember the men on the wagon train sitting around the campfire at night talking about what a crack shot he was. He had been proud when they talked about him like that, especially when his father did.

The next day Tom and Mescal set out to break in the new rifle and try to eliminate the elusive cougar. They had failed in every other attempt. Stopping at their favorite spot for target practice they put the rifle to the test. Mescal used the Henry, while Tom got familiar with using the scope and setting distance and windage. Tom was surprised at the kick to his shoulder. The big cartridge packed a lot of gunpowder. Once he had the weapon targeted, they moved on to get the cougar. It didn't take long to see fresh tracks, for it had downed a young calf the night before. The big cat would most likely be sleeping after stuffing itself with the new kill.

Mescal tracked it for over two hours, intent on getting it this time. When they started up a rocky formation, Mescal went up first, motioning for Tom to wait. The Indian thought there was a good chance the cougar was nearby. Mescal climbed to the top, peered over the edge for the longest time and suddenly froze. He signaled Tom up with the slightest movement of his hand.

Tom climbed carefully so he wouldn't make any sound. The cougar was a good two hundred yards away lying on top of a rock. Tom couldn't see him until Mescal slowly pointed. The Indian's vision was incredible for someone his age, far better than Tom's. The younger man thought Mescal's eyesight was the product of a wild land where only the fittest managed to survive.

With the naked eye Tom could see only a slight difference in color and shape from the stone around it. When he looked through the rifle's scope, he had no problem picking the cat out from the various colors and deformities in the rock. Tom judged the wind and distance and made the adjustments. He took careful aim, for the slightest movement of the barrel at such a distance would take it well off target. Slowly he squeezed the trigger.

Tom couldn't tell whether he hit the cat or not because the gun bucked when he fired, but Mescal could. When they walked up to the cougar they found he was shot cleanly through the head. Tom was amazed that the bullet had struck almost exactly where he had targeted. The Henry was accurate, but couldn't hope to compete with this long distance weapon. The cougar was a big fellow and would make a beautiful fur rug to go in front of a fireplace. Tom planned to give that hide to Jake.

For the next several weeks Tom and Mescal went out nearly every day. They were able to track and shoot several more cougars and one bear. While they were out looking for cougar, they occasionally came across deer. If the ranch needed meat, they would shoot one and pack it back to the ranch. Emmett was able to save several cows by using venison to feed family and ranch-hands rather than beef. It also gave them some variety in meat, for which all were grateful. Tom and Mescal had shot so many cougar and deer over the past month that Emmett started selling the hides in town. He gave the money to the two hunters. Tom realized they were going to have to take up another duty because the varmint problems were pretty close to being eliminated. The new rifle greatly increased their effectiveness in this process.

Tom and Mescal then went over to Jake's ranch, and within a month had removed most of the cougars and two bears. They also gave Jake a deer each week while they were there. The rancher thanked them both and tried to compensate them, but they wouldn't accept payment. Jake argued they had saved him a lot of livestock. Tom and Mescal still refused. They sold the hides and added to their savings.

Emmett bought some additional cattle and had his men move them into the remote canyons. It was a safer place to put cattle now with rustlers and cougars at low ebb. Even after the new cattle were added there was a surplus of grass available. Emmett suggested to Tom that he and Mescal buy some cattle, using the money they had collected, and put them in the remote canyons.

Mescal and Tom were delighted. Tom couldn't help but wonder if Melinda had said something to Emmett. They used what they had earned from the hides, and the money from Simpson and Cully's saddlebag. By becoming partners, they were able to buy 300 head of cattle with their combined sums. They bought some of the cattle from nearby ranchers, but most of them from Jake. The ranchers sold them at a very reasonable price, but Jake charged even less. Tom wondered if the price wasn't too low and mentioned that to him. Jake said, "This

234

is the price for you and that's that." Tom started to say something, but the rancher held up his hand. He patted Tom on the shoulder and said, "You're a good man."

The day came for them to put their mark on the cattle they purchased. Tom and Mescal decided on the image of a six-shooter and an arrow forming an X. They took great pride in applying the brand to their new herd. Several of the men helped. As they spent the second day with the branding iron, Tom was surprised at how long it was taking. It was starting to look like they wouldn't finish until the next day. Melinda came out to watch in the afternoon. She sat on the top rail of the corral and the sun made her blonde hair shine. Her green eyes were sparkling. Tom walked over to her.

"This sure is taking longer than I figured. I thought we'd be done by now."

"Oh, Mescal knows why, he's just not telling."

"What do you mean he knows? Not telling what?"

She smiled and shook her head; she seemed inwardly pleased but also humorously mysterious. "I'm not going to tell."

"Not going to tell what? Is somebody trying to slow us down on purpose? Heck, I think we're branding them as fast as we can go."

"That's not it."

"Come on now. I've got to get back to work. Tell me."

"Well, okay. Emmett and Jake each added a 100 head to help repay you for getting rid of the rustlers and cougars. You and Mescal have 500 head of cattle; that's a pretty good start."

"These folks around here are too good to me."

"Guess they want you to stay."

Tom felt water coming to his eyes, and tightness developed in his throat. He turned away and went over to the water bucket to get a drink. Melinda had seen the moisture in his eyes. She couldn't prevent the few tears that now flowed down her cheeks. She was happy for him, and pleased because he worked hard and was good to those around him. Melinda found it almost impossible to believe he had done bad things in his past. If he had, he was a new man, new except for the blazing speed of his six-gun.

Mescal had told her how they practiced together and that Tom's speed was beyond belief. "The gun just appears in his hand and

235

explodes," he had told her. "Whatever he shoots at, he hits." This part scared Melinda, not because she was afraid of him, but because if he became too well known, gunslingers would want to kill him. Emmett and Mescal had talked about it one day on the front porch, not knowing she overheard them. Melinda decided that if Tom became convinced he had to leave, she would go with him.

Over the next week Tom, Mescal, and two of Emmett's men used wagons to haul some of the hay into the remote canyons. The additional cattle would need their own haystacks in the coming winter. In the remote canyons, this was a simpler task because of their rough nature. They had many places where the hay could be easily enclosed with fence between two walls that protruded out.

On the maps Tom had created, they started naming the canyons, keeping track of the approximate number of head in each canyon and even the location of the stacks of hay. The maps also showed the location of streams, springs and watering spots. As winter was drawing close Tom also looked for places where the cattle would likely go to get out of the harsh winter winds. The canyons provided natural shelters. Mescal explained that a favored location would be a north canyon wall. It would break the cold north wind, but allow the warmth of the sun to hit the cattle from the south.

In the time remaining that fall, they eliminated three more cougar. If anyone found a killed cow or calf, Tom and Mescal immediately set out to track down the culprit. With constant vigilance they soon eliminated the threat, at least for the moment. Cougars were mobile and young calves provided easy meals. They went back over to Jake's ranch and spent a week there. They killed two cougar during that time, but had seen the tracks of one or two others they couldn't catch. They had to be getting back to Emmett's place; it was getting cold and they needed to make sure everything was ready for the winter.

During that summer and fall Tom and Melinda had several opportunities to go back to their secret spot high up on the canyon wall. Melinda wanted to go there one more time before winter. They dressed warmly and particularly enjoyed eating on the big flat rock in the warm sun. Melinda had never been happier. She couldn't help but think ahead to what might be and dream of their own ranch, and the wonderful house they would build.

EIGHTEEN

The winter had been uneventful except for the snow. If there were any cougar or bear left on Emmett's ranch they were not in evidence, and the rustler problem had subsided. A snowstorm in December required the haystacks to be opened throughout the canyons. A second heavy snowfall came in February and the stacks were nearly depleted.

As soon as weather permitted Emmett had his men begin taking wagonloads of hay to replenish the stacks. It took four men using two separate wagons a total of five days to do the work. The men traded off each day so no one got too tired. Since there was not much to do in the winter, the men enjoyed the break in routine. A snowball fight while unloading the hay was not unusual. Tom and Mescal took their turn on the third day and it seemed more like fun than work. Tom thought Emmett used good management to shift this work around. Doing it all five days would have been a burden, but doing it only once was more like an adventure.

A blizzard in March required the exercise to be done again. The snowfall had been much heavier this winter than normal, and the hay reserves were almost gone. Emmett couldn't remember having so much snow except for the year he lost many livestock. His conservative nature paid off and there was very little loss of horse or cattle.

237

All winters come to an end. Soon the days were warming and the pastures were turning green. With the adequate supply of hay, the cattle came through the winter in good shape and were calving in the spring. When Tom and Mescal rode the range in early May, they saw new life everywhere. With no cougars to deplete the ranks, calves seemed as plentiful as wildflowers growing in every nook and cranny. The grass was lush and flowers were blooming. Everywhere they rode the color green was abundant and the wildflowers added red, white, yellow, purple and blue. The snow and ice higher up was beginning to melt, and the stream in the canyon was flowing with sparkling clear icy water.

"It's sure pretty out this time of year," Tom told Melinda after coming in for supper.

"You mean the flowers?"

"That's part of it, but I really like watching the newborn calves and colts. I guess it's seeing so much new life that makes it special."

"Gee, I'd like to see that. I bet Margaret and Beth would too. I think I'll ask. Maybe we could all go for a ride and see them."

Melinda said something to Margaret and Beth, and they wanted to see for themselves. Tom and Mescal took a wagon so Emmett, Margaret, Beth and Melinda could go with them to enjoy the spectacle. The women delighted in seeing the various colors of the wildflowers and mentioned them by name. There were columbines, asters, violets and bellflowers. They observed several newborn calves struggling to stand up, still trying to find their legs. Others were suckling for the first time. Those that were a little older were learning how to run. They raced to an imaginary goal, only to turn back and race again, kicking their back hooves into the air.

There were also newborn horses. They had long spindly legs and the ability to stand must have seemed insurmountable at first. The young colts kept trying and eventually succeeded. Once they managed to stand and walk it wasn't long before they could run. While the calves liked to frolic, they were slow compared to the young horses that could run like the wind. The colts stuck their tails high in the air as they raced each other across the canyon floor. Tom didn't know if he had ever seen a prettier sight—except the sunrises and sunsets in the canyon. Suddenly Melinda pointed to the left.

"Oh how pretty; look over there at the red horse."

"He's not pretty, he's handsome," Emmett interjected. "That's a stallion in case you didn't notice. I could explain how you tell the difference if you need for me to."

Everybody in the wagon laughed except Melinda.

"Oh I know the difference." Her face reddened as she replied.

"He is beautiful, isn't he?" Beth remarked.

"Yes, he is," replied Margaret.

The big red stallion had come out from one of the side canyons leading a large number of mares and colts. The stallion stopped when he saw them and let out a piercing whistle. Then he reared on his hind legs, pawing his front hooves into the air. The horse was majestic. He stood shaking his head and pawing the ground with his right front leg, as if to say, "This canyon is mine." The big stallion ran toward his mares and herded them back into the side canyon. He stopped for a few seconds looking at the wagon, then headed after the mares, gaining ground with every stride and overtaking them quickly. Melinda remembered when Emmett had purchased the horse on the trip down to Flagstaff.

"He's the fastest horse in Utah," Emmett proclaimed. "I'd bet any amount of money on it."

"Have you named him yet?" Melinda asked.

"Well, you know, I guess I haven't. I tried for awhile but just couldn't come up with anything that suited him. He is some horse, isn't he?"

"Yes he is," Melinda replied. "When I saw him rear up and challenge us like that, the name that came to me was Wildfire." She looked at Tom and Mescal, and they nodded.

"You're right, that's just the name for that stallion," Emmett said. "Wildfire it is."

Melinda was pleased and admired the great horse as he raced away with the mares. Emmett was proud of the stallion, his ranch, cattle and all the new calves and colts that seemed everywhere. As they continued on in the wagon, Emmett talked at length about when he had first arrived and tried to make a go of it in the big canyon. They had all heard it before but attentively listened again. There were many obstacles for the rancher, but over the years they were overcome. The other canyons had been his nemesis for they harbored many predators, and the cattle would drift there and be subject to cougar, bear and rustler. With the remote canyons in good order, his ranch had become a perfect place for livestock. Melinda had never seen him so happy.

"The extra cattle I bought, even along with those Tom and Mescal added, still don't come anywhere close to filling the other canyons. If we have a few more years like this last one we'll be in awfully good shape. We'll have to put up plenty of hay this summer to feed all the livestock come winter."

"Mescal and I will keep the cougar population down," Tom offered.

"If only the rustlers will leave us bc, and they will if they know what's good fur 'em," Emmett said.

"I think Wildfire is the finest horse anywhere," Melinda said, still entranced with the stallion.

"He sure is," Emmett replied. "Best I ever seen, that's for sure. Before long this ranch will have some of the finest horses in the territory." Thoughtfully he added, "Do your work, Wildfire."

That spring was one of unprecedented optimism for the ranch. Emmett's discussions were now of expansion and prosperity rather than centering on problems. Tom and Melinda were caught up in the enthusiasm and went out several times for picnics. Sometimes Mescal joined them, and at other times he let them have their time alone. They went to different canyons and enjoyed various places to stop, eat and have some time away from the others.

As Melinda and Tom rode in the canyons, she couldn't help but look for that perfect spot for a house and imagine a yard and garden. Tom looked for things like good water, good shade from the hot summer sun and protection from the cold North wind. They rarely spoke of these things as pertaining to a possible future place for their home. When they did talk about places in the canyons it was of their beauty and how nice a spot it was for a picnic, but both knew by the nature of the discussion they were both thinking about that perfect place for a ranch house. There were some locations beautiful by the nature of their ruggedness, and others more resembling the perfect pastoral scene. The canyons had many faces and many places where one could start a ranch and build a home.

Tom and Melinda also sometimes went to their secret place in the canyon, trying not to go too often to protect it from being discovered by others. Whenever they did picnic at the fortress, Melinda brought her growing pet cougars. She had finally given them names, Ember and Flame, chosen one night when she and Tom sat in front of the fireplace. Tom thought they were amazingly well behaved and appeared to be totally obedient to Melinda. When she first talked about taking them out to the fortress, he thought she was crazy. Tom tried to talk her out of it, arguing they would surely run off.

The first day they had gone, Melinda feared he was right. She and Tom went behind the split in the rock and started climbing; the cats came up right behind them. While Tom and Melinda ate, Ember and Flame began to explore the area. After several minutes both cats drank from the pool, crouching down and lapping up the water with their long tongues. Flame climbed up on one of the big rocks at the edge of the canyon wall; Ember returned and lay next to Melinda. When it was time to leave, nobody had been more surprised than Tom to see the two pet cougars following Melinda back down.

Occasionally Tom let Melinda go up alone with the big cats. She still enjoyed bathing naked in the sun on the large flat rock. As she lay on the rock the big cats chased each other and play fought. If they saw a little animal anywhere in the rocks, they stalked it just as they did the mice and rats in the barn. At the ranch Melinda had begun taking the horses out of the barn and putting them in the corral temporarily. Then she closed all the windows and doors and let the cats have full access to the barn. When Melinda first began doing this, there were many little rodents. Now there were none, or if any came they lived a short life.

There were other visitors brought to the barn. Wildfire and the other stallions had to be kept separate from the mares for several months so there wouldn't be births in the middle of winter. During that time the stallions were kept in the barn and out in the corral. Melinda spent a lot of time with Wildfire, often feeding him a carrot and brushing him down. The red stallion became more attached to her each day, and she began to ride him a little in the corral to give him exercise.

As spring progressed, Tom and Mescal kept up their vigilance on the range and often slept out in the canyons. They had developed several favorite lookout points, which allowed them to patrol the area in a routine systematic way. They tried not to be predictable in which canyons they rode through on any given day. This gave them a chance to keep an eye on possible rustling, and to look for evidence of four-legged culprits. Any cougar or bear that strayed onto the ranch soon became a fur rug. They had become expert adversaries to the cougar, knowing their ways and able to track them quickly. They had also both become experts with their respective rifles. Tom's present from Jake had proved itself a remarkable weapon.

The rough canyons now made for excellent cattle range. As the spring months passed the calves and young horses grew. Tom and Mescal loved to ride through the canyon where their cattle grazed and watch the young calves play. The first harvest of hay came and went with many neighbors and townsmen brought in to help. Even though the work was hard, the evenings were so enjoyable that Tom looked forward to the event.

It seemed all too easy, Tom thought, just check on things and watch the cattle grow. Any varmints that came along added to their money collection from the sale of hides. Occasionally Tom and Mescal saw a rider or two. They always rode up to them and introduced themselves. They were polite but careful. Tom tried to convey the idea that these canyons were closely watched, but to do so in a way that didn't seem accusatory. They came across tracks now and then, and followed them to see where they went. If they went straight, they assumed the riders were just passing through. But if the tracks meandered, then Tom and Mescal became more suspicious. They followed the tracks until they found the riders—or until the tracks left the area.

As spring neared an end, there were fewer unknown riders passing through. Word had gotten around about the canyons protected by Tom Colt and his Indian friend. They had become known as "The Gunman and the Tracker." If there were any rustlers still around, they weren't choosing Emmett Bailey's ranch as a source for easy pickings. Tom and Mescal rode back to the ranch house one afternoon to see several of Jake Evans' hired hands in front of the house talking to Stan Brown. Jake came out with Emmett as they approached.

"Glad to see you fellas back," Jake said as Tom and Mescal dismounted. He had a serious look about him, as did his men. They were packing a lot of hardware and it was evident there had been trouble. "We've been hit by rustlers. Sam said there were five of them and they headed off to the east."

"How long ago?" Tom asked.

"Sam thinks about a day, maybe a day and a half. Actually we were lucky. Sam and Ben just started checkin more often like you and Mescal do, and got suspicious when they came across the tracks of too many cattle. Should be able to catch 'em, wouldn't you say?"

"I'd think so," Tom said and turned to Mescal. "What do you think?"

The old Indian nodded. "Take plenty food, extra horses for supplies."

Mescal went ahead to Jake's ranch to pick up their tracks and get a bead on where they were headed. The rest would ride to Candle Lake and wait for him. Within an hour they had two packhorses loaded with all the food they would need for a week.

Mescal had no trouble finding the rustlers' tracks. One drawback of stealing a herd was that cows don't move very fast. Rustling a few head couldn't be noticed easily, but taking a large herd all headed in the same direction left tracks easy to detect and follow. Mescal made good time, and before long found where the rustlers had camped the first night.

The Indian became more cautious the further he got from the ranch. He could tell by the softness of the droppings left by the horses and cattle how far they were ahead in terms of time. Mescal knew it was possible they might leave a man to see if they were being followed. If the man left behind spotted just one tracker, an ambush was likely. Mescal was pretty sure of the general direction they were headed. He moved at an angle away from the trail taken by the

243

rustlers, and swung clear of rock formations. Later, he went back toward their suspected route, coming at it from the side.

He came upon their tracks crossing Amber Creek where the land was level and an ambush wasn't likely. Based on the signs, Mescal was confident they were headed for Butcher's Pass. He thought chances were good he could meet Tom and the others and be there before the rustlers. The Indian pointed the paint in the direction of Candle Lake, and asked the faithful mount to run hard and fast for a long distance. The horse was fleet and of good stock and responded to being given free rein. Mescal couldn't help but feel a thrill through his bones as the horse ran at full speed. The Indian's face felt the sting of the wind; his hair blew back and the trees and shrubs raced by, slowing only in rough terrain.

It was night when Mescal reached the lake. Everyone there had gotten a couple of hours sleep by the time he rode in. After waking Tom, he woke Emmett and Jake. Mescal told them there was enough moonlight to travel slowly in the dark. The two ranchers wanted to get there before morning, and decided to go ahead and wake everybody. If Mescal were wrong, there would be a lot of sleepy and unhappy cowboys.

After several hours of riding, they were within a few miles of Butcher's Pass. Mescal had them wait while he rode ahead to make sure the herd hadn't already been driven through. He was hoping the rustlers hadn't yet reached the pass because it made an excellent spot for an ambush.

Even though it was dark, a herd of cattle left a lot of tracks and the old Indian found very few in the pass. Tying a piece of heavy cloth on each hoof he walked his horse through, being careful not to leave any tracks. When safely on the other side, he rode on to find the location of the herd. Mescal found the cattle near a stream where there was good grass. He hadn't spotted the rustlers, but didn't need to see them; he knew they were close by and didn't want to take the chance of being discovered. He returned to Butcher's Pass just before sunrise, now certain the rustlers were headed there.

After informing the ranchers that the rustlers were camped about eight miles to the west, he told them they would likely be at the pass shortly after sunup. Jake and Emmett planned the locations for their men as it was just getting light. Jake told the men to keep well hidden; they were to keep out of sight and not try to see approaching men. He explained it took only one lookout and he didn't want the other men trying to see and giving away their presence. Tom took a position up high to keep watch with his long-range weapon should any attempt be made to flee.

It was a little over an hour past sunrise when they started hearing the sound of cattle. Tom could tell the rustlers were a little apprehensive as they neared the pass. They stopped and talked for awhile and then sent a rider ahead. The rustler rode through the pass and looked for tracks, and then rode back in the other direction. It wasn't a thorough inspection, and it was evident he expected no trouble.

The men in the rocks waited patiently just as they had been instructed. It was a good size herd that approached, nearing six hundred head of cattle. There were two riders behind the herd, two on the side and one in front. Tom waited until the nucleus of the herd was in the middle of the pass then signaled Emmett and Jake. Suddenly, Jake stood up and yelled:

"This is Jake Evans and those are my cattle. We have a dozen men up here. Drop your guns."

Everyone in the rocks brought his rifle up and aimed at one of the rustlers. It was an ominous sight for the rustlers to see so many rifles pointed at them, and at the same time to know what usually happens to rustlers when they are caught. One of the men, who had been behind the cattle, fired at Jake with his revolver and then turned his horse to run. The other rider in the back didn't bother with a shot; he just turned his horse and spurred him viciously. All of the men in the rocks opened fire on the two riders. They both dropped within a few seconds, and one of their horses was hit as well. The rider in front of the herd also rode off at full gallop. Tom took careful aim with his long-range weapon and squeezed the trigger. The rider fell from his horse.

The two men who had been on the flank were in the pass, within easy distance of the rifles, and had no chance of survival. One rider hesitated only a few seconds more, dropped his revolver and then his rifle. The other suddenly spurred his horse to make a run for it. Ben was closest and shot him in the shoulder. The man slouched over his saddle and then fell to the ground.

The wounded rustler was put back on his horse. He was the older of the two, and appeared to be about thirty. His broad nose was crooked and appeared to have been broken once. Set deep in the sockets, his eyes were wider than most. The captured rustler looked more mad than scared.

The other rustler was young, not quite twenty. His sandy red hair and freckles gave him a youthful appearance. He wore a blue and white checkered shirt and a brown leather vest. The two that were captured were brought in front of Jake with their hands tied behind their backs. The rancher questioned them about their gang but they offered nothing at first. Jake explained, in a manner not to be misunderstood, how rustlers were treated in this part of Utah. He made it clear ranchers don't have time for judges and juries.

"You boys must not be from around these parts," Jake said. "This here fella is Tom Colt and that's Mescal. They're called the Gunman and Tracker. You ever heard of 'em?"

The older rustler showed no indication but the younger one nodded.

"Then why did you try to rustle our cattle?" Jake pursued.

"We heard it was just the big canyon ranch they patrolled."

"Shut up, you fool, it won't help none," the older rustler derided him.

All the while Jake was talking to them, Tom could tell he was trying to figure which one was most likely to talk. After a little more questioning the older rustler became clearly defiant.

"Go to hell."

"Ain't me that's about to pay the Devil a visit," Jake replied.

Jake signaled to Sam and Ben, and they threw two ropes over a nearby tree limb. It was a huge Oak and the limb was at least twenty feet high. They sat the rustlers on their horses and led them up to the ropes. Jake asked them again if they wanted to talk. The youngster with sandy hair started to say something but the other man glared at him. The young man remained silent. Walking up and taking hold of the bridle of each horse, Jake signaled Sam to put a noose around the neck of the older rustler. When the rope was firmly around his neck

Jake relinquished control of the man's horse to Sam. He continued to hold the bridle of the younger one's mount. Jake gave the older rustler another chance to talk, but the outspoken man glared straight ahead. The youngster looked scared enough to die without being hanged.

"Do you have any last words?" Jake asked the older rustler.

"I already told you: go to hell."

"Is there any next of kin you want notified?"

"Let's get this over with," The rustler answered.

The wound in his shoulder was painful, but was the least of his worries. As he sat waiting he wished he had been killed when he tried to ride away. There was no way out for him now; he knew he was going to die one way or the other. He was wanted for murder in Ogden, so if they took him to jail the wanted posters would be seen and he would be hanged anyway. He figured getting caught was just bad luck, but the last thing he wanted to do was help the men that were about to hang him.

Jake motioned to Sam and he let go of the horse; Ben slapped it on the flank. The horse forged ahead, its hooves throwing up dust. The rustler moved forward with the horse only a few feet, and then came out of the saddle and swung back and forth like a pendulum. The tree limb creaked from the added weight and the rustler spun around slowly. As he swung he started kicking and wriggling to no avail. His face looked contorted and full of hate and fear. He tried to say something but nothing escaped but a low gurgling sound. As he turned slowly in the air his face came around to where he was looking at the younger rustler.

The youngster watched the horror in the hanged man's face. It was another thirty or forty seconds before he stopped kicking. Jake waited an extra minute until all the involuntary movements of the dead man ceased. The rustler's neck was stretched and looked much longer than it should. It was red and purple where the rope had burned into his skin. His eyes bulged and the look on his face was of macabre death. The young rustler looked on in dread. Jake watched the youngster, making sure the full impact of the hanging took effect.

"Sometimes the neck snaps and then it don't take so long to die," Jake said. When he uttered the word "snaps" he turned his fist with a jerk.

Jake had held the bridle of the young man's horse the whole time. Now he stepped closer to him, and then looked at Ben who walked to the flank of the horse. Jake waited to be sure the youngster saw him looking at Ben. Slowly he looked up at the young man. Jake had a stern punishing expression on his face, giving every indication the young rustler's time had come. Jake nodded to Sam and he put the noose around the youngster's neck. When Sam started to take the reins of the horse, the rancher held up his hand and looked up at the young rustler.

"This is your last chance, son. Would you prefer to talk?"

The young man couldn't speak and his whole body started trembling. His forehead was wet with beads of sweat and tears started flowing freely from his eyes. He sobbed for several seconds, and then began nodding his head.

Jake and Emmett took him off his horse and over to some nearby rocks. They had him take a seat where he could see his companion still swinging from the tree. It was far enough away the other men couldn't hear the young rustler's words or sobs. Tom went with them.

"What's your name, son?" Jake asked.

"Billy."

"Where were you takin these cattle?"

"I don't know. They're real careful about stuff like that. Only two of them knew, and you just hung one of 'em. The other one was Guthrow, and he was the first one shot."

"What can you tell us?" Jake pursued.

"There were two other groups hitting other ranches at the same time."

"Which ranches?"

"I don't know. They didn't tell us."

"Well, son, what do you know?" Jake asked, impatience evident in his voice.

"I know we were supposed to meet up with the other two groups and drive one big herd on from there. The fellow you just hung told me yesterday it would be three or four more days before we met up with the others."

"Is that all you know?" Jake asked.

"Yes, sir, it is. Honest, sir. It's the truth."

"The herd could be moved a long way in four days," Tom remarked dejectedly. "It would be hard to figure where they would meet."

"I just joined the gang a few weeks ago. That's why I don't know much. I never met him, but I do know the top man is Ben Caisson."

"Oh shit, Ben Caisson," Jake cursed.

"He's the big rustler outlaw in Arizona, isn't he?" Emmett asked.

"Yep!" Jake replied.

Tom had also heard of him. Ben Caisson was known as a well-organized rustler and it was thought he had a large gang of twenty to thirty men. It was bad news he was coming into this territory.

"Well, Billy, that's good information," Jake said. "But we need to know either where this herd was being taken or how to find Caisson's hideout."

"I'd help you if I could, but I just don't know."

"Do you know how to find any of the rest of the gang?" Emmett asked.

"No, sir, I don't."

"That's just not enough information to save you, son," Jake told him. "I'm afraid we're gonna have to hang you."

"But I've told you everything I know."

"Well, like I said, it's not enough," Jake repeated.

Jake motioned for Sam and Ben to come over and get him. The young man looked at the ground as they walked over. When they took him away, one on each side, his knees weakened and he sobbed. Sam and Ben held him up so he wouldn't fall to the ground. When they were about five yards away, Tom came up with an idea.

"Billy!"

Sam and Ben stopped and turned the young rustler so he could look at Tom.

"Could you recognize someone from the rest of the gang if you saw them?"

"Most of them I could. I saw at least ten of them."

"What are you thinkin, Tom?" Jake asked.

"I figure they'll send some men this way after these fellows don't show up. It wouldn't be hard for them to find this pass and figure it out, especially if we leave old slick there a swinging. If they send

249

some men back, then they'll probably turn around and head back to the others. If we were real lucky they might lead us to their hideout. Billy here could identify them. That way we wouldn't just be tracking some strangers. Mescal and I could follow them, maybe even find that hideout. Then we could come back and figure how to capture them."

"That's a good idea," said Emmett.

"Sounds like a long shot, Tom," Jake interjected. "They might not come at all, and if they do they might not go to the hideout. They might just meet up with some of their friends, or go to a town and spend their rustlin money."

"If they do come, Mescal can track them at a distance. We can just keep following them until they do head toward the hideout. If they don't go to the hideout at all, we could capture one of them and bring him back to see what could be pried out."

"Hell, Jake, it's better than just hanging the boy," Emmett said. It was the first time most of them had heard Emmett curse. He was a religious man and didn't normally use swear words. Tom had only heard him use that word one other time. That was when the rancher was trying to convince him to stay after he outdrew Bert Cooper.

"And what about the boy here?" Jake asked.

"Well, I guess if he helps us find them, we ought to let him go," Tom answered.

The young rustler had a glimmer of hope for the first time. Jake didn't like the idea of possibly letting the young rustler go. At the same time he realized it would probably help get the boy to cooperate. Jake shook his head at first.

"Well maybe, but not until after we find their hideout and show Caisson the door to his Maker," Jake said.

"I doubt if he'll ever meet his Maker, but he'll sure leave this world," Emmett remarked. They all chuckled, except the youngster, who waited to hear if he would live or die.

"Billy, are you willing to identify the men for us when they come here?" Tom asked.

"Yes, sir."

"If they come to check and you identify them, you'll be held at the ranch while we go after them," Tom told him. "If we find their hideout, we'll let you go after we take care of the gang. Is that agreeable?"

"Yes, sir, it is," the youngster said quickly with great relief on his face. To come so near such a gruesome death as hanging, and then have the possibility of being let go was quite a switch in fortune. Still it wasn't a sure thing.

"What if they don't send anyone?" Billy asked.

"Then we hang you," Jake said emphatically.

"Guess you best pray they do send somebody," Emmett said to the youngster as Jake walked away.

All of the cowboys rounded up the cattle, and then Jake's men drove them back toward the ranch. Some of Emmett's men stayed to dig four graves, putting the rustlers that were shot in three of them. Jake told them to throw an old log into the fourth and cover it with rocks just like the others to make it appear they killed and buried Billy. The other rustler would be left hanging. Jake joined Emmett and the rest of his men in going to the Bailey Ranch. They left one of the packhorses loaded with supplies. Tom, Mescal, Billy and one of Jake's men would stay near the pass. The extra man, Carney, would take Billy back to Jake's ranch after the youngster identified a rider as a member of the gang.

NINETEEN

After they arrived at the ranch, Jake told Emmett he wanted to talk to him in private about the Caisson gang. They walked out to Mescal's cabin so as not to be overheard. Jake didn't want to alarm anyone, particularly the women.

"Rumor is they not only rustled a lot of cattle in Arizona but killed a lot of cowboys while they were at it. The men are likely to hear about that. If we start havin some men shot by them cow thieves, the others will start thinking about ranches that are safer places to work. Most cowhands know they might get shot at once or twice in their life. A little risk comes with the job. That's a lot different than goin up against an organized gang of men who are good with guns and aren't afraid to shoot first. After a shootin war starts a cowboy knows his chances of gettin killed go way up."

Emmett saw his point; cowboys were pretty faithful as long as a boss was good to them. Most cowboys weren't afraid of danger and none wanted to be thought of as yellow. On the other hand, cowboys didn't get paid enough to get into a shootout with an outlaw gang. Emmett greatly respected Jake's opinion. It was nearly five years ago when he discovered Jake had been a Texas Ranger. The bottom of an old box gave out while Emmett was helping move some belongings into Jake's then new house. He was carrying it into the bedroom, and out of the underneath came some old wanted posters and a ranger badge. Jake was also there when it dropped to the floor and he decided to tell Emmett about his years as a lawman.

Jake explained that his last name had been Lowery. He had arrested a lot of men in his four years as a ranger. During one gun battle with outlaws he had killed a wealthy rancher's son who had gone bad. The father swore he'd get even and had the men to do it. After that Jake moved to Utah and changed his name. He told Emmett it was safer for him if people didn't know who he really was.

They had been standing just inside the door of Mescal's cabin when Emmett noticed the coffee was ready. Jake sat down at the table while Emmett retrieved the coffeepot from the stove and poured them both a cup. Jake's face showed signs of worry. As he sat at the table he picked at a big scab on his forearm, deep in thought. Emmett watched him. One of Jake's men had told Emmett how it happened. Jake was trying to break a new colt.

"It was a damned fool thing for Jake to be trying to do," Sam had said. "Hell, that young bronco sent him flying into the top railing of the corral fence. He busted the wood clean in two. Jake got up, put his hat back on, blood rolling down his arm, got back on that crazy horse and finally got the better of him. Damned fool thing for him to do at his age, I tell ya." Emmett sipped at his coffee while Jake rolled a smoke, and then the ex-ranger continued.

"One of the reasons gangs like Caisson's are so successful is that after they get started, ranchers have trouble keepin enough men. Only the big ranches can afford to bring in enough hired guns to go after that type of gang. It gets real expensive and some of these outlaws get back at the rancher by goin after him."

Emmett shook his head. If Jake was trying to get him concerned, he had gotten the job done. Any way Emmett looked at it, this gang could be real trouble for both him and Jake. No doubt Tom and Mescal had been the reason his cattle had been left alone, but if Caisson got a foothold in this part of Utah, even Tom wouldn't stand much of a chance against so many.

"I'll tell you what, Emmett, I'm glad Tom came up with the idea of waitin for others in the gang to show up and then trackin 'em. I just hadn't thought of it, but then I'm not used to having someone like Mescal to do the trackin. If we can catch that gang by surprise, we just might be able to put Caisson out of business before he gets a good start."

Jake got up to get more coffee, and then had another thought.

"We need to try and hide Tom and Mescal's identity. It isn't good enough to just find out where the gang is, they need to have time to come back and get the rest of us. If Caisson realized his hideout had been discovered, he'd just find his gang a new place. Why don't you send out a couple of new horses and some different clothes for Tom and Mescal? Since they've been ridin the range and talkin to riders that have been passin through, there's a good chance some of those rustlers will know who they are even at a distance."

"You aren't thinking we should send someone else, are you, Jake?"

"Naw, Mescal has to go; nobody can track like him. Without that Indian we wouldn't have a chance of followin the rustlers all the way to their hideout. As for Tom, he'll know what to do when they catch up with them scoundrels. I guess it's your call, Emmett; after all they're your men."

Emmett didn't like putting the two men at risk. He knew if something happened to Tom, Melinda would have a hard time forgiving him. It had seemed easy when they were at Butcher's Pass. Tom had come up with the idea and just sort of volunteered the two of them. Now that Emmett heard what Jake had to say, he more readily understood the danger involved. Tom and Mescal were probably the best men around for what had to be done. "That's what pretty much dictates they are the ones that have to do it," Emmett concluded silently.

"I think you're right, Jake; they ought to be the ones."

"Reckon I feel I'm imposin on you a bit, bein those are my cattle and it's your men goin to track the rustlers. Ain't nobody better than the Gunman and the Tracker, but like I said, they're your men. It's your call."

"Hell, you're not imposing, Jake; we've been through too much together for you to think that. I know you'd do the same. I suspect Tom and Mescal wouldn't have it any other way. If I'm showing any reluctance it's because I know Melinda will be worried."

Jake stayed in Mescal's cabin that night and was gone before the sun came up. After breakfast, Emmett went to the bunkhouse and asked his men to loan him some clothes that would allow both Tom and Mescal to change their appearance. He explained Jake's idea about protecting their identity.

"I'd give up some of my own, but my clothes wouldn't fit either one of them," Emmett said.

"What do you think about Mescal wearing a hat?" Stan asked.

"That's a good idea," replied Emmett. "Wearing a hat is something Mescal has never done, least ways not in the two years I've known him."

"I just bought a new hat a few months ago. Still got the old one over there by the back door a hangin on that wooden peg. It's pretty worn looking, but that ought to help more than hurt."

"Ought to work just fine if it'll fit him."

The ranch hands laid out some clothes. Emmett picked out a couple of shirts and a pair of pants for each, and then went back to his cabin and got his Winchester for Tom. The long distance rifle Tom carried had become a trademark, Jake had reasoned, and would be too easily recognized. Finally, Emmett got the bag of food and sack of grain Melinda had prepared. He asked Willie and Bud to take the new horses and extra provisions to Tom and Mescal.

Melinda had a strange feeling something would happen to Tom. Last night she dreamt that he was lying on a floor with blood around his body. Awakened by her own scream she was thankful to discover it was only a nightmare, but fearful it could be a premonition. Melinda promised herself she would not tell Tom; he had enough to worry about without her dreams. She decided not to tell Emmett either. She wanted to talk to her father, but waited until he finished with Willie and Bud.

When the two cowboys headed back toward the bunkhouse, she walked outside. Emmett was standing on the porch of the ranch house, looking up at the morning sky. He was silent and gave the appearance of concentrating on the task at hand. Walking up to him she stood close so their shoulders nearly touched. He glanced at her and then stood watching Willie and Bud ride away.

"Any idea how long Tom and Mescal might be gone?" Melinda asked.

"It's hard to tell. They might just be gone five days or so. If no one comes back to check on those rustlers, then we're pretty much outta luck finding them."

Melinda showed no sign of relief from his answer. She stood there thinking, worrying and getting control of her emotions for some time before she got the courage to try again. Having grown close to Tom she was concerned what her life might be like without him. This past year had given her a whole new reason for living. Never before had she dreamed of having a ranch and a family, now she dreamed of little else.

"But if the rustlers come and they track them, he...he could be gone a long time. How long before...I have to think...he might not come back?" She failed to keep her voice from faltering or prevent the tears from swelling in her eyes and a few flowing down her cheeks.

"They'll be careful, Melinda. Mescal is the best tracker I ever saw and he knows how to stay out of trouble. Tom won't take chances; he's too smart for that." Emmett paused trying to think what else he could say to reassure her. "He loves you, Melinda; he'll be careful."

"Couldn't someone else go? Tom is needed here to look after the canyons." she couldn't control her emotions any longer, and tears streamed down her face.

"You know he has to go. Be strong. In this land you have to be strong. That's just the way it is, and if you want to be part of this territory you just have to accept it. This is the sort of thing Tom and Mescal do best. This is what they're good at. You know that. You know Tom wouldn't have it any other way." Emmett lifted her chin and looked straight into her eyes. "Don't you?"

She nodded and then lowered her face so she could wipe her tears away, trying again to control her sobs and failing. Emmett walked to the front edge of the porch, then turned to look back at the house, making sure neither Margaret nor Beth were within earshot.

"Melinda, you are the most beautiful and wonderful woman I have ever known, and Tom is the perfect man for you. I think the world of...that boy." Emmett's voice began to break and he paused.

After a few seconds he continued. "The good Lord will see him home safe; you can count on it."

"I'll pray you're right. I'll pray every night. I love him more than anyone can imagine. I don't know what I'll do if he doesn't come back." Crying, she stepped forward and buried her face in his shoulder, her body shaking as she unloaded her tears, unable to stop.

Emmett's eyes became moist as he patted her on the back and let her cry. He waited until after she regained control to continue. "He'll be back, Melinda, and so will Mescal. If it makes you feel any better, I'll be praying for them too."

Mescal found a spot at Butcher's Pass that would allow them to see riders at a distance. The lookout would be in the shade in the afternoon, keeping him cooler and providing shadows to help hide his presence. They decided only one person would be on lookout at any given time. There was less chance of being seen, and each man would stay more alert if watching only part of the time. The others would wait below out of sight, but close enough to get to the lookout spot quickly.

When Willie and Bud arrived with the supplies it was nearly sunset. Willie explained Jake's thoughts about the horses, clothes and rifle. Mescal suggested they leave when it got dark, and ride to where the rustlers had camped prior to coming to Butcher's Pass. The campsite could be reached quickly by horse, but was far enough away that a campfire couldn't be seen from the pass. When they got there, Tom thought it was an ideal place to camp. It had more grass for the horses and plenty of water. Melinda had sent food for the evening meal.

After they finished eating, Carney took Willie to the nearby trees and spoke to him in private. When they returned, Willie offered to stay with Tom and Mescal and then take Billy to Jake's ranch when the time came. Carney explained that he would like to get back to roping and branding cattle, and cussing at cowboys. He had been quiet and ill at ease with Tom and Mescal. Tom was glad to have Willie because of his congeniality. The jabber from his outgoing personality would help the time go faster.

That night was restful. There was a slight breeze and the coyotes kept to their nightly vigil. At the nearby stream the crickets' sound was loud and unmistakable. As time for sleep approached, they were careful to tie up Billy tight. No matter how friendly the youngster seemed to be, it was impossible to be sure he wouldn't slit their throats or just slip away in the night to warn the gang.

Before dawn the next morning a lookout was back in the perch on the rocks. Mescal went early taking the first shift. After breakfast, Bud headed back toward Emmett's ranch and Carney toward Jake's. Tom, Willie and Billy arrived at the pass a short time later.

Two long days dragged by. Tom noticed Mescal took the waiting without complaint. Neither he nor Willie were as patient, and after two additional days they began to wonder if anyone would return to look for the missing five men. Fortunately Willie had brought a deck of cards, and that provided some relief to what Tom could only think of as anxious boredom.

On the sixth day a gentle rain started just before noon and lasted four hours. Those not on lookout stretched a tarpaulin over them to stay dry. The rain helped kill the heat and the monotony. The afternoon dragged on slowly and Tom began to wonder if the wait was for nothing. Late that night, as they sat in front of the campfire, Billy worried about what Jake said would happen if he couldn't help them with their cause.

"It ain't lookin so good for me, is it?" Billy asked.

"I have to admit I'm beginning to wonder if maybe they aren't comin back to check," Willie replied.

"We don't have to give up just yet, Billy," Tom said. "What do you think, Mescal?"

"Good chance they come," Mescal answered.

"How much longer we plannin on stayin?" Willie asked Tom.

Tom considered Willie's question. He had his doubts on how good the chances were, but Mescal had been right many times in the past about similar things. The old Indian seemed to have an uncanny ability to guess what men would do. No doubt that was part of the reason he was such a good tracker. Tom also wanted to allow ample time for Billy's sake.

"Well, I reckon if we waited this long we ought to give them a few more days."

"I guess sittin around in these rocks is no worse than chasin cows and mendin fence," said Willie.

"Well, I sure hope they show up," Billy said.

The seventh day was hot and windy. By afternoon the sand and soil on top were dry. The moisture from the rain of yesterday had been baked away. Adding to the discomfort was the nuisance of trying to keep the sand out of their eyes. In the late afternoon the wind finally subsided, but not the heat. It was the most disagreeable day of the wait and even Mescal showed some signs of losing his patience. No one felt like playing cards and they all kept to themselves. It was evident from Billy's demeanor that he was growing concerned about his chances for living much longer.

On the eighth day, about mid morning, Willie came down hurriedly off the lookout perch. "There's two riders approachin from the east."

"Billy, let's get you up there where you can see," Tom said excitedly. "Maybe all this waiting is going to pay off after all."

The riders stopped where the rustler still hung from the tree. One rode an iron gray colored horse and the taller rider was on a cinnamon bay. They dismounted and walked over to the four graves Emmett's men had dug. In front stood one crude headstone made of wood. It was only ten inches wide and two feet tall. It read, "Hung Rustlers."

The taller of the two men kicked the tombstone down and stomped away from the graves. He wore chaps that couldn't hide the extreme bow in his legs. Riding horses too many days had left its mark. He walked hastily over to the tree and started to cut down the rustler still hanging, but the other man stopped him. No doubt the stench from the corpse exposed to the elements added to the man's fury. It was easy to tell the two were arguing. The taller one was flailing his arms and shouting at the other. Those watching in the rocks could hear sounds but couldn't make out any words. After the two riders argued for several minutes, they moved away from the lifeless form. The shorter man walked back to where the graves were and replaced the tombstone. It was clear he had decided they shouldn't leave any sign that part of the gang had been there.

"That tall fellar sure is mad," Willie whispered.

"You recognize either one of them, Billy?" Tom asked quietly.

Billy had plenty of time to observe both of them with the field glass. "No, I don't know 'em. Sorry!"

Tom was displeased they didn't have confirmation. They would have to use their best judgement as to whether these two were part of the gang. If they were not, he and Mescal could spend a lot of time on a wild goose chase, and they could miss the real rustlers when they came. After what seemed an endless discussion, the two mounted their horses and headed back to the east. The taller man on the cinnamon bay was obviously not happy.

Tom expelled a sigh of relief. If these men weren't the rustlers, they would likely have kept going in the same direction they were headed. Since they turned and went back where they came from, they almost had to be Caisson's men. The reaction of the more demonstrative bow-legged rider added weight to the argument these two were part of the gang.

"I don't think there's much doubt they're in Caisson's gang," Tom said. "What do you guys think?"

"I'm with you. As pissed off as that tall fellar was, they gotta be with Caisson," Willie said.

Tom looked at Mescal. The Indian nodded. "Caisson's men."

They could afford to let the rustlers get a head start. The four men climbed down out of the rocks, and then Willie and Billy walked to their horses. They had left them a good distance away so a horse's whinny wouldn't give up their presence. Willie tied Billy's hands to the saddle horn. Since he would be the only one watching the young rustler, he would have to be more careful. Billy sat on the horse with a deep frown. He was concerned because he hadn't been able to identify the men. Willie walked back to where Tom and Mescal stood.

"There's a good chance Jake will hang him," Willie said quietly.

"Yeah, I was thinking that too," Tom replied. He studied Willie's face for a few seconds and then continued. "You know Billy could have told us he recognized one of them even though he didn't, just to save his neck. Billy was honest." Tom paused for a bit studying

Willie's reaction. "We pretty much know they're part of the gang. Wouldn't you agree, Willie?"

"Yep."

The three men discussed it a while longer and then all three walked over to Billy. Tom told him what they had decided. He concluded, "So the story is, Billy, that you knew one of them was part of the gang. Is that alright with you?"

"It sure is."

Willie was glad he could take Billy back with some chance of living. Still he felt bad for having to tie him up, and he sure didn't want to tell Billy about the shackles. Jake had told Carney he would send Ben to town and have the blacksmith fashion a set of shackles. Jake said it wasn't for any dislike of the boy, but for the protection of Tom and Mescal. It was also because capturing the rustlers was extremely important to the ranchers. Willie rode off with Billy's horse tethered to his.

Mescal wanted to wait. He said the rustlers would be easy to track and they might return to cut down their friend. If they didn't come back within the first two hours, then he thought it would be safe to start tracking them. After a long wait, Mescal looked at Tom and nodded. They went over to where the riders' horses had been. Mescal made a mental note of the hoof prints, looking for little differences he could use later to be sure he was following the right horses. They set off at an easy pace. Later, as the sun was getting low on the horizon, Mescal pulled on the reins of his horse.

"We stop, they no hurry."

"You'd think they would as mad as that one fellow was."

"Rustlers not careful. No sign they worry about being followed. No backtrack. No ride to high spot and look back to see trail."

Tom hadn't thought about it much, but Mescal was right. There was a chance they would backtrack, swinging around and coming up on their own tracks an hour or so later. In this way they could see if they were being followed by anyone, provided the trackers were that close. Mescal had told him earlier when they were hunting that bears were known to do this and attack a man from behind.

Mescal was careful in selecting the campsite that evening. There was a canyon wall just to their east. Even if the rustlers were fairly close they could not see their campfire. Tom gathered firewood; Mescal had long ago shown him which types of wood gave off little smoke. The Indian had been silent while they ate and seemed deep in thought.

"Mebbe no reason hide tracks, hideout still far away. Mebbe fool us, follow too close, then shoot us."

Tom nodded, glad for his partner's experience. Mescal suggested they take turns standing watch with two-hour shifts. He had studied the rustlers' horse droppings and estimated they were around four hours ahead of them. If the rustlers returned, it would be within the first four hours of dark. After four hours both could sleep. Mescal offered to take the second shift. He had that uncanny ability to lie down and go to sleep within minutes. Tom was grateful for how considerate the man was because he was beat.

Willie rode in to Jake's ranch late that night. Jake had been anxious and was glad to hear the news.

"Thanks for ridin all this way, Willie. It's late; you best stay the night in the bunkhouse. Sam will get you some food and show you a bunk you can use."

"Thanks, Jake, but I reckon it would be best if I rode on through the night. Emmett will want to know as soon as possible."

"Emmett would want you to leave in the mornin. You go on and get somethin to eat and get some sleep."

"Some good food and a soft bed do sound pretty temptin right now."

"I didn't say anything about the food being good or bed being soft, but you're sure welcome to it nevertheless."

"Thanks, Jake."

In the morning Willie left for the Bailey ranch and arrived at lunchtime. Emmett was pleased but lost his smile when he saw Melinda watching. He started to walk up to her but she retreated to the ranch house and then to her room. Later Emmett knocked on her door.

"Yes?" she responded, but didn't open the door.

"They'll be okay, Melinda. They'll come back okay."

"Thank you, Emmett."

His footsteps could be heard as he walked back out of the house. Melinda knew her father was happy because they had a chance to find the rustler gang. She appreciated that he took the time to think about how she felt. In the days that followed she tried to spend more time in the garden helping Margaret and Beth, playing with Ember and Flame in the barn, riding Wildfire in the corral, doing more cleaning in the house, helping to cook the meals, and anything else to speed up the day. At night before she went to bed she prayed for Tom and Mescal's safe return. She was thankful the old Indian was with him; Mescal seemed to have a sixth sense when danger was near.

Tom and Mescal had taken their time at breakfast and then were back on the trail. By midday, they had come upon the rustlers' campsite from the night before. After inspecting, Mescal said they were about six hours ahead. "We catch up time," he said and led off at a faster pace than before. As they tracked the rustlers that afternoon, Mescal found one place where they had turned long enough to look back from a high ridge. They could see for a good fifteen miles from that point.

Tom was glad for the quicker pace; it seemed to make the day go faster. It would be easy to become impatient when tracking. Mescal seemed to think of everything. He almost seemed to be able to think like the person he was following. He studied the campsite area, noticed little nuances in where they chose to ride, be it around a clump of trees or through a stream. It seemed to Tom that Mescal gathered information from everything the riders did.

By the end of the second day the horses were showing signs of tiring. It had been hot through the day and the terrain much rougher. Mescal found another campsite. This area was rocky with many washes, scrub trees and cactus. They found good clear water in a small stream. The grass nearby was not plentiful, but with grain would be adequate to feed the horses for one night.

The water in the stream was warm due to the heat and because it had a shallow rocky bottom. Tom went upstream and found a pool about three feet deep. It was just the type of spot he had been looking for. It was a good fifty yards from the campsite and deep enough to sit in. He took off his clothes and stepped slowly into the water. His

263

body welcomed the relief from the heat. Immersing his head he tried to get the dust out of his hair. When Tom got out of the water he sat naked on the rocks. Even though the sun was low, he could still feel its heat.

Being naked in the sun reminded him of Melinda's secret spot. They had spent a lot of time at the fortress and one day there they had kissed for only the second time. A month later they were back at the fortress again and had kissed passionately while they sat on the rock. Over the summer Tom had grown to care for her deeply. The beauty she possessed made it easy to love her, but it was the beauty in her heart that he admired most of all. Several weeks later, Melinda had finally consented to their getting into the pool together and then lying naked in the sun. Her body was even more exquisite than he had imagined.

He remembered after they had been lying there for awhile that she stood and stretched. The muscles in her legs were toned and her skin was tanned. As she stretched she arched her back, her large firm breasts and small pink nipples pointing straight out in front of her. Tom couldn't help but feel passion swelling as the blood raced through his veins. She turned and saw him staring at her breasts, and then she looked at his unclothed body. Her eyes sparkled and she smiled at him. Tom wasn't embarrassed at his body's aroused response to her action. He was surprised when she leaned over and kissed him on the forehead, the nipples of her breasts clearly visible out in front of him. He started to move forward to kiss one of them but she drew back, smiling and shaking her head.

"Not until we're married." As she lay back down on the rock she had said, "Now that you've seen me naked, I guess we'll have to get married."

She laughed and so did he. Later they had kissed again, but nothing more. Tom had since decided he would ask her to marry him. He wanted to be able to start a ranch before he proposed. Right now he missed her greatly.

As Tom sat there his thoughts came back to the present; he saw that remembering her naked body had a similar effect on him now. His body was dry, and he got up and put on his second set of clothes. When he returned to camp Mescal was surprised at his clean, fresh appearance. Tom told him about the pool and hung his wet clothes on a nearby dead tree. Mescal ate quickly and headed that way with his spare clothes.

As Tom sat drinking coffee he studied the scraggly dead Pinyon-Juniper tree where he had hung his pants and shirt. The tree had gone through a tough fight for survival before succumbing to the elements. It had somehow grown out of a crack in the rock floor and the trunk and limbs had twisted about in contorted fashion from its struggle. Tom thought it beautiful in its own tough rugged way.

In the morning they had bacon, flapjacks and coffee. With the good bath, deep sleep and bountiful breakfast their energy was renewed and they set out on their task. The horses were fresh, but Mescal took the slower pace of before, not wanting to push their luck and risk being discovered.

Near midday they came to the riders' campsite from the night before. Their tracks headed toward the desert. Mescal said it would be easy to track them, but very hot. They rested the horses and ate before setting out again. It would take several hours and they would have to cross the desert in the heat of the day. Mescal knew the area well and thought there was a good chance the rustlers would stop for the night at a place known as Indian Waters.

Tom usually fared well in the heat, but the desert was incredibly hot. Finally, late in the afternoon, Mescal broke to the left of the rustlers' trail and went at an angle for several miles. He told Tom the riders were headed for the place he had mentioned. "We go different spot. Pick up tracks in morning." It was getting late when they came out of the desert. They were exhausted. Tom's head felt heavy and ached inside.

"No chance they find us here; sleep all night," Mescal said after they ate. "Tomorrow, go to Indian Waters, good water, take bath."

When Tom opened his eyes in the morning, the sun was just coming up. As he started to get up his head ached. Mescal noticed that he put his hand on his head. The Indian got a towel and soaked it in the cool stream. He motioned for Tom to lay his head back on the saddle, and then he put the wet towel on his head. In ten minutes Tom felt better; the pain was nearly gone. No doubt, he thought, it was something the Indians had learned from living near the desert. They waited until two hours after sunup before heading to Indian Waters. When they got close Tom stayed with the horses. Mescal went ahead on foot, returning ten minutes later. "Gone," was all he said.

The surrounding terrain was desert with scraggly trees and shrubs, but Indian Waters was an oasis. There were tall trees and lush green grass. The most beautiful part was the pond, which had sparkling blue water. Mescal grabbed his clean set of clothes and told Tom, "Me first, you keep watch." That was fine with Tom as he enjoyed the cool fresh air of the morning. He made a small fire and put on a pot of coffee. Then he laid back, enjoyed the scenery and drank the hot familiar liquid.

After Mescal came back, Tom took his clothes and razor down to the stream. It was cool, but bearable. He shaved while he sat in the stream and let his dirty clothes sit in the middle of the running water with rocks on top to keep them from floating away. When he was completely acclimated to the cold, he put his head under several times to wash his hair. When he returned to the camp, Mescal had already put things away and had seen where the rustlers were headed.

"They go to White Cloud, small town, easy follow."

He explained to Tom there was no need to follow them to town. If it proved not to be their destination, they could always come back and pick up their tracks here. The Indian thought it was safer going to White Cloud by a different route.

TWENTY

They reached the outskirts of White Cloud before nightfall. Mescal had no difficulty finding the tracks of the rustlers heading into town. Tom and Mescal were on top of a small mound about half a mile away, and could see the rooftops of several buildings and homes. Smoke streamed up from the chimneys of the cabins. As it was nearing dusk, they needed to find a place to camp. The horses were tired and needed water. Tom felt fatigued, having not completely recovered from the trip across the desert.

Mescal led them away from town and well off the main road. He found a spot under an abundance of tall trees that provided a natural canopy for the ground below. There was a small creek nearby for water. While Tom made camp, Mescal swung around the town and checked the trail on the other side of White Cloud. He could not find their tracks, which made it very likely they were still in town.

Riding into White Cloud, Mescal proceeded slowly down the middle of the main street. Since he was coming into town from the opposite direction, he thought it doubtful they would suspect he was following them even if they saw him. As he rode, the only sound he could hear was the steady clip clop of his horse's hooves on the packed earth of the street. Mescal kept his head down as though tired and sleepy. With his eyes on the ground he studied hoof prints as he rode through town. He had been able to make out the prints of both horses in front of the saloon, but had not seen them until then. He acted as though he paid no attention to the horses tied out front. From the corner of his eyes he could see three mounts there, but not the gray nor the cinnamon bay. With a quick glance he could see the silhouettes of several men in the saloon, but couldn't tell if the two riders were inside.

The general store was across the street from the saloon, and as Mescal rode by an old man sitting on the bench in front of the store looked up and spit tobacco juice on the sidewalk. After looking at Mescal for a few seconds he wiped his mouth with his coat-sleeve. The old man closed his eyes and sat there like he didn't have a care in the world. Mescal noticed that the old man's shoes had a hole in each of the soles. His hair and beard were white and his mouth misshapen from the absence of teeth.

In front of the livery Mescal once again saw evidence of their tracks. As he rode by the livery, one of the big barn doors creaked and it seemed natural for him to look in that direction. The doors were open and there was a lantern inside, but it gave off very little light. He was unable to see the gray or cinnamon bay.

Returning to camp, Mescal discovered that Tom had caught a couple of fish and was frying them. He had also made biscuits and a pot of coffee. The old Indian was glad; he was tired and ready to eat.

"They stay in town or go on through?"

"Rustlers in town. Me ride other side, tracks go in, not come out."

"Well, they might have softer beds than we do tonight, but I bet their supper isn't any better than this."

"Good, me hungry."

"You pour the coffee and I'll put this on a couple of plates."

They sat in front of the campfire eating and watched the flames consume the wood. As the night wore on the embers glowed an increasingly bright red. When a gust of air made its way through the center of camp the fire would flicker as though dancing to the night breeze.

Tom and Mescal began to make plans for the next day. The only interruptions to their discussion were the soft sounds of an owl hooting across the creek, and the occasional popping of the burning wood. The smoky smell of fried fish lingered in the air. After much discussion it was decided Mescal would go into town early in the morning to get supplies. He would find out for certain whether the riders were still there.

"Why don't you wear one of the blankets over your shoulders when you go through town?" Tom suggested. "If anybody saw you tonight, they would be less likely to know it was you."

"Blanket good idea."

"You might also want to wear my hat and ride my horse. That would make it pretty certain nobody would recognize you."

"You worry about old Indian?"

"Well, somebody has to take care of you."

Mescal smiled but did not respond. Tom thought that with these changes there was little chance of his friend being identified. As they talked over their plans they had not noticed the change in weather. It had become quiet and Mescal noticed a sudden gust of wind. He stood, turned to the breeze and detected the smell of rain. The wind increased and started to gust more noticeably, kicking up dust and leaves. Mescal's action and the increasing wind gained Tom's attention. The Indian watched the nearby trees reacting to the gusts. Huge clouds were rolling in and lightning began to flash in the sky.

"Big storm, much wind, much rain."

Mescal motioned toward the horses and they hobbled their mounts. Tom hobbled the packhorse and tethered them all to a tree. The Indian searched about and found a tree with a large low branch about five feet off the ground. He began cutting the small sprigs off with his tomahawk both above and below the limb. Mescal asked Tom to get the tarpaulins that had been on the packhorse. They draped the larger of the two tarps over the branch for a roof. Mescal then found dead limbs not too far from the camp and they drug them over. They secured both ends of the tarpaulin to the ground with a dead limb on each side.

Next they gathered many spruce branches and spread them on the ground under the makeshift tent. They continued to add to the pile of soft green growth until it was several inches thick. Mescal then covered them with the second smaller tarpaulin, folded to fit the space. They gathered the supplies and put them under the shelter, leaving ample room for the two of them. Mescal explained the spruce branches underneath should keep them dry even if the ground beneath became wet. Both stood by the edge of the tent and looked at the coming storm. There was an unusual amount of lightning and accompanying thunder.

"Rain come soon," Mescal said.

The air became very still, and then suddenly a huge gust of wind blew hard against the shelter causing it to make a loud snapping sound. Mescal's hat blew off and he quickly retrieved it. Tom thought surely the tarp would come loose, but it was securely tied to the limbs on the ground. A few drops of rain fell and more hard gusts of wind followed. They both decided it was time to get into the tent. The thunder grew louder as the lightning began to explode nearby. Soon it was flashing all around them and lit up the night at intervals. It was one of those times when nature took command; man and beast could only huddle and hope all went well.

The lightning flashed across the sky and the thunder roared and echoed through the trees. Tom looked out to see the horses pulling at their reins. The horses pulled away from the tree, then moved close to the tree trunk, stamping their hooves nervously when the sound subsided. The rain was holding off except for a few drops. Tom put on his slicker and went to make sure the horses were well tied, giving the reins an extra knot. He had nearly gotten back under the tarpaulin when there was a burst of rain and a tremendous blast of wind, thunder and lightning. It seemed to boom all around even more ferocious than before.

Tom wasn't normally afraid of storms, but the constant presence of lightning was giving him cause for concern. He was relieved to be back under the shelter. When he looked out the edge of the tarp he saw fingers of lightning tearing through the clouds above. As soon as it grew dark from one blaze of light, another would flash across the sky. Some of the lightning was hitting the ground, but it was high up in the sky where the streaks of light were putting on a show. The lightning seemed to be flashing from one cloud to the next and it was marvelous to watch.

For the next several minutes the wind continued to blow. The lightning flashed and the thunder roared. Suddenly a blast of light exploded. Sparks filled the area under the trees and entered the tarp on each side. Tom saw the brilliant light and sparks, but then his vision went blank. He had heard of men being struck by lightning and killed or severely injured. Thoughts of possible death entered his mind.

The image of a man with a burnt and crippled hand who had been hit by lightning flashed before him. The man had been the friend of a neighbor when they lived in Missouri. Tom never knew how to act around him. His right hand was mostly scar tissue and some of the fingers had melted together. Tom had always felt sorry for him; now he was horrified with the thought that the same thing could happen to him.

Seconds later Tom's vision returned and he realized he was lying flat on the floor of the tent. As he regained his senses, the sound of crashing tree limbs and a loud thump reached his ears. The earth beneath him trembled as the force of the landing vibrated through his body. Tom jumped up and hit his head on the branch under the tarpaulin. His first reaction was that the tree must be falling down on them and he had to get out of the tent. Tom felt Mescal's hand on his shoulder, signaling him to stay put. Tom's head hurt and he was dazed, but he was still conscious. In another second the crash of tree limbs and branches subsided.

First Mescal, then Tom, looked out the side of the tarp and saw that the tree twenty feet in front of them had been hit. The rain came again and then increased rapidly, stopped for several seconds and then quickly accelerated. The pouring rain snuffed out the flames that had been ignited seconds earlier by the lightning. Smoke curled up from the blackened tree trunk. The tree was split at the base of the trunk and a huge section had fallen to their left. The branches closest to them had just grazed their shelter, but did not tear the tarpaulin.

The air cooled as the rain came down in sheets with hard gusts of wind blowing through the trees. Several small twigs fell from the trees and glanced off the side of the tarp. Tom and Mescal held the open ends of the tarp together as far down as they could. There was still an opening at the bottom on each side, but the brunt of the wind came from the back and their shelter was keeping them dry.

As they sat under the shelter the rain kept coming. Every now and then a clump of leaves or twigs fell near the shelter. A few drops of water dripped from the top of the tarpaulin, but it fell on their hats and slickers. Thirty minutes later the rain finally slackened to a light drizzle. In another ten minutes it quit altogether. It was one of those storms in Utah that develops suddenly, packs a tremendous punch and then ends just as quickly.

The tarp on the floor of the tent was dry. Tom was glad they had piled the spruce branches so high underneath, because the ground outside was soaked. He decided to go check on the horses. When he returned he started to say something to Mescal, but then noticed his friend was asleep. Tom wished he could do the same so easily. Soon the horses and the surroundings were quiet and peaceful, and finally he drifted off to sleep.

The next morning when Tom woke up, Mescal had already started breakfast. The sun had risen and streams of light came through the canopy of branches and leaves high overhead. Water vapor floated in the air causing the rays of the sun to take on an aura of wonder. Tom marveled at the sight. The tree hit by lightning looked as though a giant had swung an axe down its middle and laid it open from top to bottom. Tom wondered what would have become of them had the lightning hit their tree instead. He surveyed the damage surrounding the camp and saw several large tree limbs on the ground. Branches, leaves and twigs were everywhere, but neither he nor Mescal had suffered any damage other than Tom's sore head. The horses had settled down and weren't injured.

When Tom and Mescal were finished with breakfast, they packed up and rode to the other side of town, following the route Mescal had used the day before. They had to cross the creek and the level of water had risen substantially, but Mescal found a place to reach the other side without incident. As they had decided last night, Tom stayed to watch the main road going out of town while Mescal went in on Tom's horse to get supplies and determine if the men were still there. Tom's post was on high ground with ample trees and boulders where he could observe the trail and not be seen.

As the old Indian rode into town he saw leaves and twigs strewn about and puddles where wagon wheels had left ruts in the street. He pulled up to the hitching post outside the general store. The buildings of the town had a rough and run down look. Those that had been

272

painted didn't show evidence of a brush being applied for a long spell. Some of the planks on the boardwalk were cracked and others broken off on the end nearest the street. Stains from tobacco juice spotted the wood sidewalk in front of the store. Mud from the shoes of patrons was in clumps on the edge of the planks where they had scraped the bottoms of their shoes before entering. The sign on the store, as well as the one over the saloon, was faded. The sign over the livery, down the street, was swinging by one end. It must have come undone during the storm; Mescal was sure it had not been loose when he rode through last evening.

As Mescal went into the store he noticed there were now five horses in front of the saloon and two more further down the street. The iron gray and cinnamon bay were next to three other horses in front of the saloon. Inside the store he saw only the sales clerk, a homely looking middle-aged woman and her daughter. Mescal took his time, picking up a needed item every few minutes and spending a goodly amount of time looking at items he didn't need. As the opportunity presented itself, he would steal a glance through the front window toward the saloon.

The clerk was short and skinny and combed long strands of hair from one side of his scalp clear across to the other. It was all slicked down, but did a poor job of covering a large bald spot on the top of his head. The clerk moved quickly and seemed impatient even though there were few customers. He had grease smeared on his white pants and smelled profusely of alcohol. Twice the clerk asked Mescal if he needed any help; each time the Indian shook his head no.

The woman ignored Mescal, but the little girl kept looking his way. She had no shoes and wore a ragged blue dress. Her hair and eyes were brown and she had a pretty face. Noticing the little girl was looking at him, Mescal smiled and gave her a quick wink. The mother saw the little girl smiling at the old Indian and gave her a bit of a nudge. The little girl looked down, but stole another peek as they left the store.

"Saloon have many men," Mescal said to the clerk when he went to pay for his goods.

"Yes, it is busy this mornin, more than usual. You weren't thinkin of goin over there, were you?"

Mescal shook his head. As the clerk packaged up his supplies Mescal looked out the window at the horses, which were clearly visible.

"Good horses. Think they sell one?"

The clerk turned and looked at them briefly. "I don't know. They're not from here. I don't know if you ought to ask them or not. I wouldn't if I were you." The clerk finished wrapping his packages and gave them to Mescal. "You just passin through?"

The clerk was looking at the Indian when he asked the question and his breath smelled like fermenting grain. Mescal nodded, handed the clerk the money and moved slowly to the door. He took note of the horses across the street. One of the three horses next to the two riders' mounts had the same brand as the cinnamon bay. It was Mescal's guess that at least one of the other horses belonged to a member of the same gang. He didn't want to arouse any more suspicion, so he headed toward his horse and out of town without looking at the saloon or horses again.

It wasn't long before he met up with Tom. They waited for much of the day and observed several men going in and out of town, but neither of the two riders passed. Finally, late in the afternoon, they decided Mescal should ride to the other side of town and come in from that direction. It took him an hour and when he returned Tom was waiting.

"Saw riders going by half an hour ago," Tom said. "The two we've been following were with them."

"Me see tracks, five men."

"It's about another hour to sunset. Should we follow them now or wait?"

"Wait. Easy track; ground soft from rain. They stop soon for night. We go back camp. Spend night there. Easy pick up tracks in morning."

They returned to their camp of the night before. For supper they had eggs and bacon purchased that morning. It was food usually meant for breakfast, but both of them had the hankering for eggs. Mescal had gotten them fresh at the store and there was plenty of time that evening to cook and relax. Later Mescal got out a loaf of fresh bread and a jar of jam. The store wasn't big but it had a diverse supply of food. The evening was still and quiet. The owl revealed its presence once more and coyotes could be heard intermittently. The sounds of frogs and crickets from the nearby creek helped soothe the two riders to sleep. The evening produced no dramatic weather and they slept uninterrupted for the night.

The next morning they were up early and returned to where they had last seen the riders. Their tracks followed a trail into some of the strangest looking rock Tom had ever seen. Some of the steep, sloping, sand-colored stone looked like molten rock that had suddenly cooled. Other huge mounds of stone were more of a dirty chalk color and had cracks in the stone running perpendicular to each other. After meandering through the unusual rock formations, they finally found the riders' campsite ten miles outside of White Cloud. The tracks continued on for another mile, then headed north into rough hill country. Mescal said they would have to be more careful now. Following on an often-traveled trail was not suspicious, but tracking through country usually avoided was a different matter. The riders were at least four or five hours ahead of them. Mescal had little trouble since the ground was wet. Tom and Mescal had gone perhaps ten miles, meandering through the hills, when the Indian noticed there were suddenly six sets of tracks.

"Horse come from side." After studying for a few seconds he added, "Here tracks same horse. One man double back, see if followed. Being careful. Hideout close."

Two miles further up the road Mescal stopped again. "Here where rider turn off to double back. Others wait there."

"What do you think we should do?"

"Hideout close. May leave man on trail, see if followed. Better we not follow tracks. Go off side, look for tracks further down."

"So if they leave a man on the trail we'll go around him?"

"Mebbe. Still chance man see us. We not following tracks, come from side. Mebbe not shoot us if come from side."

"Yeah, you're right. What do we do if somebody wants to know why we're out here in the middle of nowhere?"

"Tie man up. Better he disappear than tell about Indian and White man. Mebbe he tell where hideout is."

Mescal led off to the left and went for what seemed miles. It was difficult to judge distance in such rough country. Finally, Tom asked, "How far you reckon we've gone since leaving their trail?"

Mescal replied, "One, mebbe two miles." He continued for a short distance, and then worked back to the right. Suddenly Mescal held up his hand; Tom stopped and his hand just naturally lowered to his gun. Mescal sat motionless for a while then dismounted. "Wait," was all he said. He was gone twenty minutes and then came back. "Tracks, all five, head that way," he said, pointing off to the Northeast. "Close now, we go that way, make camp." He pointed in the opposite direction.

Tom nodded. It was an hour before sundown. After riding less than a mile they came upon a noticeable landmark. There was a boulder seven feet in diameter that rested atop a smaller flatter rock. The boulder had probably sat there for centuries, but it had the appearance of being ready to fall with the slightest push. Mescal continued on heading directly away from where he thought the hideout was. They rode for nearly an hour. Mescal wanted to be well away from the rustler's location. He found a good place to camp. There was a stream for water, grass for the horses and tall trees for shade. They ate and rested.

"Better if me go alone to find hideout," Mescal said after they ate. "At sunrise, me ride back to big rock, hide horse near there. Me go from rock on foot. Moccasin no leave track. Not easy see man on foot."

"Won't it take longer to find the hideout?"

"No matter, plenty time. Must not be seen."

"Can't argue with that, but what do I do while you're gone?"

"Do what White Man do best," Mescal said, shrugging his shoulders.

"What's that?"

"Nothing."

Tom smiled but didn't respond. After a few minutes he asked, "What if they see you? I won't be able to help from here. I wouldn't even know they had captured you."

"If see Mescal, me act like lost old Indian."

"Yeah, you're pretty good at that."

The old Indian smiled.

"I don't like the idea of sitting around doing nothing."

"It good plan. You rest."

"Okay, my friend, but you be careful." Tom knew Mescal had a better chance of finding the hideout without being seen by going alone.

Mescal set off prior to sunup the next day while Tom was still asleep. The Indian rode back to the balanced rock where they had been the night before. He found a heavily wooded area one-quarter mile to the west for his mount. He unsaddled and hobbled the horse. It was unlikely anyone would happen across the secluded area. Mescal took his revolver, knife and tomahawk. A tomahawk was a good weapon up close if he happened on a sentry and had no choice.

He set off in a direction parallel to the tracks left by the five riders. He continued to use the technique of swinging around and coming back to the expected trail a mile or so ahead. At times he would not find tracks where he anticipated, and he just continued to swing in a wide semicircle until he did. Mescal stayed under the shadow of trees as much as possible. He avoided walking across open areas. Because he was on foot and being careful progress was slow. By late afternoon he still hadn't spotted anyone. Mescal continued his cautious tracking, continuing to swing away from the trail.

It was nearly evening and he had just walked out from under the cover of trees when he suddenly spotted a man high on a ledge. Seeing the guard startled him. Mescal moved back under the shadows of the trees as quickly as he could. He carefully looked through a gap in the leaves up toward the guard. The man began relieving himself over the edge of the rim, the yellow liquid landing on the rocks below.

The placement of the sentry was good. He was high on a canyon wall and had good visibility, but the guard wasn't making much effort to conceal his presence. A man riding on a horse would probably not have seen him first, but on foot the advantage was with the intruder.

There were enough trees along the edge of the canyon floor that Mescal had little difficulty working around the sentry. After making his way to the other side, he found a place to scale the canyon wall. The climb up was not easy and Mescal was beginning to tire. When he reached the top he looked out and could see for miles. He continued progressing toward the canyon rim where he suspected there would be another guard. If there was another man located on this side, it was assured the hideout was further back.

It was dusk now and more difficult to see. There were an abundance of trees, which made stealth easy. As he got within a hundred feet of the wall, his foot struck something and a rattling noise rang out. Looking down he saw a string tied between two trees with a can attached near one of the trees. When he hit the string the can shook. There had to be a rock in it because of the loud noise it made. The canyon wall was not far away and a guard would likely be there soon. Mescal could get away by running and thought about it for a second, but decided against it. If he ran he would be heard even if not seen. To be discovered now would ruin the element of surprise for Jake and Emmett.

Mescal knew he had to decide what to do quickly. The tree he was under was tall, but was a pine and would not hide him well. There was a tall leafy deciduous tree over to the right. He walked quickly to it and swung up on the lowest big branch. Then he climbed rapidly, but quietly, up the tree reaching a fork in the trunk twenty-five feet off the ground. When he straddled the fork he could hear footsteps approaching. He hugged the limb and remained motionless.

The sentry walked slowly as he drew close, looking all around with rifle at the ready. He moved carefully under the pine tree and studied the ground under each of the trees where the string was tied. He looked up briefly into the pine tree. Next he walked toward the tree where Mescal sat motionless, but was looking at the ground for footprints. Mescal remained perfectly still. He knew it was movement that caught the eye of man—movement and bright colors. The man looked into the tree for a few seconds, but suddenly there was a slight noise like rustling leaves under a nearby tree, and then a scampering sound along the ground about thirty feet away. After a few seconds Mescal heard the guard say, "Damn rabbit, you scared the pee wadden outta me." The sentry lowered his rifle and walked away.

Mescal waited until after dark to start descending the tree. He thought surely by now the guard would have gone back to the hideout. When Mescal landed on the ground he turned his ankle and nearly fell down. There was pain, but he could still walk. Light from the moon allowed him to make his way through the trees. Heading away from the sentry's post he continued until he thought it was safe to stop and sleep for the night. He ate sparingly of the little food he brought and drank from the canteen. As best he could he covered himself with leaves for warmth and went to sleep. He woke several times during the night because his ankle was in pain and he was cold. Sleeping would have been more comfortable down on the canyon floor where there was less wind, but he didn't want to chance going down the canyon wall in the dark.

Mescal was up the next morning when the first signs of light began to appear. It was chilly and his body felt stiff from being cold all night. His ankle was swollen slightly and when he stood it hurt. Cutting a strip off the end of his trousers he wrapped it tightly around the injured joint. He moved back toward the rim of the canyon, but away from the entrance where the guard had been. Mescal walked slowly and made his way at least a hundred yards further back and found the rim, but saw no signs of a hideout below. Moving away from the ridge he again made his way toward the back of the canyon. His ankle was becoming more painful, and he decided he needed to end his search soon and return to camp. First he wanted to locate the cabin. Before he and Tom returned to tell Emmett and Jake, Mescal wanted to be able to tell them he had seen it with his own eyes.

After traveling toward the back of the canyon for some time, he again worked his way toward the edge. Seeing no sentries, he came up to the rim at a low point between two large rocks. At first he saw nothing, but then he noticed a thin line of smoke just starting to come up through the trees. He was too far toward the back of the canyon. Moving toward the telltale signs of smoke, he could finally see the roof of a large cabin. To the side there was a corral with at least ten horses. He couldn't see all of them, but recognized the iron gray and one of the other horses that were in front of the saloon at White Cloud.

Having found the hideout, Mescal wanted to get back to camp before nightfall. It would be a long way to go on a bad ankle. He was careful not to leave any signs someone had been there. Within a couple of hours he was well away from the canyon and hadn't seen any prints of horse or man. He estimated the hideout to be three miles from the spot where he left his horse and another four miles to the campsite where Tom was. A streak of pain shot through his leg with every step. The three miles seemed like thirty. Mescal had endured worse, but his ankle was about to give out.

The painful journey made him recall when he was younger and he and his father had tried to escape from soldiers. While they fled, Mescal had hurt his ankle when he jumped from a large boulder. His father hid him behind the rocks, and then led the soldiers away. In a box canyon his father's tracks had simply disappeared, and the soldiers fanned out on foot trying to find him. While they searched he slipped by unnoticed and surprised the soldier left to take care of the horses. His father rode one of the mounts and led the others tied to a rope.

Mescal could still remember how surprised he was when his father came riding back leading all those cavalry horses. He and his father had stopped high on a ridge and watched the men walking back to the fort. The man left to guard the horses had a bandage around his head. Mescal's brother and sister often asked their father to retell this story of outwitting the blue coats. His father had repeated it many times, and they never tired of hearing it.

The sun was close to setting when Mescal reached the secluded area where he had left his mount. Approaching carefully, he walked in a full circle around the horse's location. He looked for tracks but there were none. The horse was grazing peacefully with the hobble still securely around his front legs. As Mescal came into the open, the horse looked up and saw him. He whinnied, snorted and shook his head, then started moving slowly toward Mescal. After removing the hobble, the Indian quickly saddled him and rode back to camp thankful his horse did the walking the rest of the way.

Tom stood as Mescal rode in. "I was getting worried. Was beginning to think something happened to you."

"Hideout far," Mescal said as he climbed off the horse.

"What happened to your leg?" Tom asked when he noticed the Indian was limping.

"Hurt ankle. Go to stream, soak in water."

Tom helped him walk down to the stream. Mescal found a place where he could sit on a small boulder with his ankle in the cool water. Tom unwrapped the cloth from Mescal's ankle to see it was swollen. He had no idea how far Mescal had walked on it.

"Not hurt bad," Mescal said.

"Looks like it hurts like hell."

Mescal smiled and let his leg soak in the cool water. After awhile, he wrapped it back up, and then set it again in the cool water, wrap and all. "Get big if not tight."

Tom got some food for Mescal and then took care of his horse. He waited until his friend had finished eating.

"Where'd you find the hideout?"

"Canyon, very far."

Mescal was tired and Tom sensed he wasn't ready to talk. As they sat by the stream they saw the movement of fish on the surface of the water. It was dark enough they couldn't see them, just the wake they left. Tom told him he had caught several while he had waited there, releasing most. He had explored the stream earlier to pass the time and found a small pool where he had washed up. Tom took Mescal there and left him so he could clean himself. It was dark except for the moon above. It was a clear sky and it was light enough to sit peacefully in the water.

After Mescal returned to camp, they sat and drank hot coffee in the cool air of the night. Mescal filled him in on the hideout and they spent the rest of the evening discussing what to do next.

"Me rest ankle, then go back. Find out more. You go back to ranch, get Emmett and Jake."

"No, I think you ought to go back to the ranch with me. If you're here you could be discovered."

"Mescal not be found. Me find out plenty while you gone."

"There's no way to know whether you'd be seen or not. It could happen, just like your ankle was injured. It could happen."

"Mescal stay here, me be careful." The Indian's voice revealed he was growing impatient.

"Sorry, old friend. I want you to go back with me. If you were caught, I might be bringing Jake, Emmett and the men into an ambush. We can't risk that. You've got to go back with me. The danger to the rest of the men isn't worth what you'd learn while you were here. When we come back, we can bring the men here and stay for a night to rest. You can lead us close to the hideout and we'll stay camped somewhere near while you go back and do some more scouting. Sound okay?"

Mescal was convinced because of the argument of danger to everyone else. He nodded and then told the remaining details of his journey, including how his ankle was injured. After he finished they settled down for the evening.

Tom was anxious to get back to the ranch with the news. It had been much easier than he expected, although he readily admitted that was because of Mescal. He could track almost anything and leave no tracks himself. Tom went over in his mind some of the things he had learned from him, like circling back to find tracks. The Indian had told him about staying in the shadows and stopping often to look for movement and listen for sounds. If Mescal hadn't been there, Tom had to admit he probably would have blundered in and been seen by the lookouts—if he had made it that far. Chances are he would have followed too close and been taken by surprise by the rider who had backtracked. Mescal had told him about walking into the rustlers' string and can alarm. Neither of them had heard of using cans that way. It was such a simple idea. Mescal was lucky the rabbit had been nearby. Most amazing to Tom was walking all that way on a sore ankle. Tom had a similar injury when he was younger and the pain had been excruciating.

As Tom lay in his bedroll he reflected on their discussion. Mescal had told Tom it was important not to bring too many men. With a smaller posse it would be easier to get them in without being seen or heard. Tom agreed that sounded like good advice. He looked over at his friend to see him already asleep. Thoughts were racing through Tom's head as he went over everything Mescal had done in finding the hideout. He also remembered he would get to see Melinda, and more importantly let her know they were safe. Tom envisioned her smile and relief upon their return. Listening to the wind in the trees overhead he became drowsy and went to sleep.

TWENTY- ONE

Tom and Mescal didn't go back the way they came for fear of running into men from Caisson's gang. They left at sunrise in the general direction of the road that led back to White Cloud. The terrain was rough and on two occasions they had to dismount and walk up steep inclines, sliding on loose stone. Tom helped Mescal up the slope and then went back to lead the packhorse. Sweat was rolling off his forehead; there was little breeze and the humidity hung in the air. Tom wondered if man had ever seen the area that they were passing through. They traveled through canyons where rabbits and wild turkey were thick in the shrub and safe from predators because of the dense undergrowth. They saw deer and cougar tracks, but no sign horses or man had ever been there. They forged ahead, often having to push through thick brush with long thorns when there was no other way to proceed.

It was late morning before they reached the road. Both men's pant legs showed traces of blood where the thorns had cut through. When they came to the outskirts of White Cloud, Tom circled around and waited for Mescal. The Indian went through town, stopping to get supplies needed for the trip home. Mescal limped around the store and saw two separate families purchasing goods. One of the women looked at Mescal then whispered something to her husband. The farmers were poorly dressed and were buying only essential items.

Two of the children wanted their father to buy them some candy. All Mescal could hear were the words, "Can't afford it."

Spending as little time as possible getting supplies, he went to pay for the goods. On the front counter there was a glass jar containing big sticks of red and white candy; he added three pieces to his purchases. After Mescal paid the clerk, he walked up to the first child who was with her mother. Mescal asked the woman, "Okay give child candy?" The woman looked surprised, and then finally smiled and nodded. The little girl had a big grin on her face when she took the stick of candy. The other children had seen this. When Mescal headed toward them, they looked up to their father. Mescal walked up and just looked at the father. He nodded and Mescal gave each of them a stick of candy. It was only then that the woman who had whispered earlier smiled at Mescal.

Leaving the store he saw there were several horses in front of the saloon, and got the impression members of Caisson's gang came here fairly often to pass the time. He rode out of town unnoticed by the men in the saloon, and before long met up with Tom. The two of them made good time on the trail since they didn't have to worry about pacing their speed. Both wanted to be back at Indian Waters by nightfall, and then get an early start in the morning to go across the desert as early in the day as possible. They pushed the horses along at a good clip. In the afternoon they met three different riders that they didn't recognize, coming from the opposite direction. Each of them traveled alone. Two looked like local farmers. One was on a wagon and the other rode a mule. The third man was well armed, had a good mount, and could have been one of the rustlers.

A little before sunset they reached the campsite at Indian Waters and Mescal prepared the meal while Tom went for his bath. The water was cold but soothing. He cleaned off two cuts left by thorns. One had broken off in his skin but he was able to dig it out with his knife. When he got back to camp he poured whiskey over the cuts. Mescal prepared biscuits and surprised Tom with two steaks he picked up at the store. It was the steaks that had caused the woman to whisper because they were expensive. Mescal cooked them over the campfire and they ate well that evening. There were plenty of fresh supplies at the store, and Mescal showed him the eggs they would have for breakfast. Tom washed up the eating utensils and saw to the horses while Mescal went to get cleaned up.

While Mescal was gone Tom had time to gather in the beauty of the spot. The sun was setting, giving the horizon a reddish-orange glow. Birds fluttered in and out of the nearby trees. It was refreshing to get a bath, Tom thought, but to do so in the middle of a place like this made it extra special. He lay back and took in the sounds and the sweetness of the air. When Mescal returned Tom noticed the Indian's ankle was still swollen. Tom tried to do all the camp chores to save his friend from further pain. They both got to sleep early. Tomorrow would be a hot day and neither looked forward to crossing the desert.

They started early in the morning and were two thirds of the way across, when they saw a red cloud in front of them. Both knew a sandstorm was approaching. They rode over to a clump of large cactus and brush where they could get some protection. Tom hobbled the horses while Mescal got the biggest tarpaulin. They both stood on one end, then sitting down folded the other end over them. Within a few minutes the wind picked up with force and they could hear the sand pelting the tarp. It wasn't long before the full blast of sand and wind was upon them. Even though the tarp created a shelter almost like a cocoon, they soon began to feel the sand in their teeth. The strong hot sand-laden wind lasted less than half an hour.

Once the wind subsided they brushed the sand off, checked on the horses, packed up and continued on their way. They reached the other side of the desert and rode until coming to a stream. There they ate, rested and gave the horses a drink. By early evening they arrived at the campsite they had used on the trip down. They could have gone on for another hour, but both wanted to take advantage of the little pool Tom had found on the way down. Tom went upstream first. It had been a hot and dusty day, and the cool water was an immense relief. He stayed longer than before, recuperating in the water. Tom had told the Indian to leave the work for him, but he did not. Mescal unsaddled their mounts, took the supplies off the packhorse and set up camp. After Tom returned Mescal went to get his bath; his limp wasn't quite as noticeable now. Tom started a campfire then started brushing down the horses. They were caked with dust and sand from the desert.

While Mescal was away getting his bath, two riders approached. They had seen the smoke and were riding in. Tom was still brushing Mescal's horse and had his back turned to them. As they drew near he heard them and continued brushing but ambled over to the other side to observe without being easily identified. As they pulled up Tom could see the two riders by peering out from under his hat, which shadowed his face. One wore a blue shirt and sat atop a palomino. The other man wore an old brown shirt.

The man in the blue shirt called out, "Hello there, we got some grub here. If ya don't mind some company we'd appreciate sharing yur fire."

Tom quickly replied without stepping out from behind the horse. "Sure, step on down, friend."

He had recognized the palomino and then the men. They were two of the riders he and Mescal had come across while patrolling one of the remote canyons only four or five weeks before. They hadn't acted too friendly then and Tom had been almost certain they were rustlers. He was pretty sure they would recognize him as soon as they got a good look. Tom thought there was a good chance they were part of Caisson's gang. Waiting until both had dismounted, he put the curry brush down and stepped out where they could see him.

They both stopped dead in their tracks. It was useless for the two riders to try to pretend they didn't recognize him; their reaction had been too abrupt. The man in the blue shirt was quick with a gun, but he had heard about Tom Colt and was reluctant to try and outdraw him. His partner was also good with a six-shooter. Handling a gun was just a part of their trade.

"Yur a long way from home, ain't ya?" The man in the blue shirt asked, trying to appear calm.

"Sure am."

"If ya don't mind me askin, what brings ya down this way?"

"Been tracking some rustlers."

"Did ya find 'em?"

"Nope, we lost them in the desert. A sandstorm covered up their tracks. We're headed back."

The man in blue took off his hat with his gun hand and wiped his brow with his shirtsleeve. "That day we met earlier ya had an Indian with ya. Reckon he's here somewhere since ya got extra horses there?"

"Yep! Not sure when he'll be back. Sometimes he likes to hunt for supper."

The other man, whose name was Jim, looked around, gazing at the rocks around the area. He knew the Indian could be anywhere. He put his thumbs in his belt up front and tried to follow the lead of his companion in looking relaxed. Even if they could shoot this fellow named Colt, they would still have to deal with the Indian. Colt had the reputation of outgunning Bert Cooper and Paul Simpson. Both had been known as fast guns, especially Cooper. "We sure rode into a rotten mess," Jim thought. The smart thing to do would be to ride on out, but he doubted his partner Jeb would do that. Jeb was very fast with a gun, knew no fear and was always taking chances. He had a way about him though and always found a way to come out okay. That was the reason Jim had stuck with him so long. He always seemed to have the luck.

Jeb knew the Indian could be hiding in the rocks, but didn't think that was likely. Jeb figured he went somewhere for awhile, otherwise he would have come out to stand with his partner. Jeb decided their best chance was to act friendly and get the drop on Colt as soon as they could, before the Indian had a chance to return.

"My name is Jeb and this here is Jim. Yur name is Colt, isn't it, Tom Colt?"

Tom nodded and returned the smile. "Yeah, that's right. Surprised you remembered."

"Do ya mind if we sit down? It's been a long day and we could sure use somethin to eat. There's plenty of food in Jim's saddlebag. We'd be happy to share it with ya."

Tom figured it was a ploy, but it seemed like a good way to resolve things. He couldn't be sure these fellows were rustlers, so he didn't feel like he could just tie them up and take them back to the ranch. On the other hand, if they were part of the gang, he didn't want them riding to the hideout and telling Caisson how they had come across Tom Colt and the Indian this far from home. He wished he had said something besides tracking rustlers. Tom didn't want to sit down and eat supper with them, having to worry when they might make their move. He wanted them to try something now while he was ready for it.

"Sure; that'd be fine. I'm hungry and I'm sure Mescal will be too when he gets back."

"Good! Jim, see what we got in there to eat."

Jim made momentary eye contact with Jeb. Since the food was in Jeb's saddlebags, Jim knew what he was supposed to do. "Sounds like the Indian is off somewhere," he thought. Jim turned and walked to his horse. He kept his body between Colt and the saddlebag.

Tom noticed the quick glance between the two. Jeb started talking to Tom just as Jim put his hand in the bag. Tom turned his face more toward Jeb, but concentrated on Jim. Suddenly Jim wheeled with gun in hand and Jeb went for his gun. The sound of gunshots filled the air. Tom had fired at Jim and then toward Jeb. Smoke rolled out the end of Jim's gun barrel. Jeb grabbed his right arm, his unfired gun lying on the ground behind him.

Jim stepped forward; his shoulder was bleeding. He had gotten off one shot, but it hit the ground in front of him. Now he was raising his gun to fire again. Tom's gun exploded a third time and Jim cringed in pain, grabbing his side with his hand. Jim's gun was pointing at the ground and now he tried once more to raise it. Another explosion occurred from a gun with a different sound. Jim fell on his knees and then on his face. The latest shot ripped a lethal wound through his chest. It came from a rifle in the rocks.

Jeb was sitting on the ground, his gun arm hanging uselessly in front of him. He was faster than Tom had expected and had managed to clear his holster when Tom's bullet found its mark. Mescal emerged from the rocks keeping his rifle on Jeb. Mescal's wet body glistened in the sunlight, naked, his hair still wet and dripping. He limped slightly as he strode into the campsite. Tom looked at him surprised; he had never seen him without clothes.

"You never know what some men will do for a little attention," Tom said.

"Good I come back, your aim bad." Mescal shook his head and started back toward the pool of water.

"You go ahead and finish your bath; I'll take care of everything here."

The old Indian shook his head again, surprised his friend had taken the chance of only wounding the men in the gunfight. Finally he replied to his impertinent friend, "Get clothes."

Tom had been trying not to kill the men so he could get information out of them. Tom dressed Jeb's wound and then tied his hands. The bullet had passed through the flesh and did not break any bones. Next, Tom got a shovel and dug a shallow grave for the dead man. He had just finished covering the grave with rocks when Mescal returned. Tom walked over to the rustlers' horses and started going through their saddlebags to see if there was anything that would provide useful information.

"Ya asshole!" Jeb called out sarcastically. "Can't ya wait until I'm dead to steal my stuff?"

Mescal walked over and picked up some pieces of wood like he was carrying them to the fire. When he got close to Jeb, he dropped the load on the rider's feet. Then he picked up one of the pieces of firewood, and brought it up hard against Jeb's forehead. It knocked him backward and left a bloody set of scratch marks where the rough bark brought red to the surface. Mescal picked up the rest of the wood and took it over to the campfire.

It seemed to Tom like a good time to interrogate. He walked over to Jeb and asked, "Is Jeb your real name?"

"Well, maybe it is and maybe it isn't."

"Do you work for Caisson?"

"I don't work for nobody, but wouldn't tell ya if I did."

Tom shook his head. Extracting information from a prisoner was new to him. Mescal was standing over to the side and behind Jeb; he looked at Tom and pointed toward himself. Jeb couldn't see the motion.

"You go back to ranch, me stay, me talk with him."

It didn't take Tom long to figure out what his friend was up to. "Aw, Mescal, I don't want you to do that again. Let's take him back to the ranch. Let Emmett talk to him."

Mescal replied, "Me stay, you go, come back, know everything." The words were said quickly and louder than before.

Tom shook his head and started to say something again, getting only a few words out. "Come on now…"

Mescal walked quickly forward with determination until he was standing right in front of Jeb. He drew his knife with a wild look on his face; his head shook and saliva sprayed out of his mouth as his voice took on a deep guttural sound. "Me Apache. Rustlers kill wife and child, me stay, White man talk."

Tom stepped back; he had not seen this side of Mescal and wasn't quite sure what to think. He knew his friend wouldn't hurt him but the Indian's words were convincing, to the point that Tom wouldn't think of challenging him. He held up both hands before him. "Okay, okay, you stay here. I'll go to the ranch."

As Tom stepped away he stole a glance at Jeb and saw he was looking at the Indian. His eyes were wide and his mouth open. Mescal looked down at the wounded man. Where there had been contempt there was now fear. Tom avoided looking at Jeb the rest of the evening. He had no doubt Mescal would make him talk; whether it would be by fear or pain, he wasn't certain.

As it got late Tom went to sleep, or at least so he pretended. Mescal walked away from camp for a short time and returned wearing only a loincloth. He painted markings on his face and chest with black paint, made of soot and water. Putting more wood on the fire he sat before the flames and began chanting. Suddenly he stood and made wild thrusts in the air with his knife. There was an angry expression on his face, as if he were warding off demons. He began circling the campfire in an Indian dance. His shadow from the fire moved like a giant dark figure in the surrounding landscape. Occasionally he stopped and raised his hands high into the air, chanting in a solemn death-like voice. He put the blade of his knife in the embers of the fire. Later, when the blade was red-hot, Mescal held the knife up to the night air and looked over at his captive. It was late that night before he went to sleep.

Jeb watched the whole time. An uncontrollable tremor developed in his body. He had heard about all sorts of torture Indians had used. Jeb had heard about two fellows they tied upside down over a slow fire and let the heat of the flame slowly cook their brains. Another man had told how they took one fellow and buried him next to an anthill with just his head showing, and then poured honey on him. The victim screamed for hours on end and didn't die for over a day.

Jeb had heard how another man had been tied to a tree and slits cut slowly into his skin. That man had lived for nearly three days. He also heard there was a fellow whose arms and legs were tied to four different horses. The Indians whipped the ponies until they pulled and pulled and tore the man apart. Jeb had heard many such stories, but had never imagined he might be the one tortured. All the while he watched the Indian doing his ceremony, different pictures of a horrible fate flashed before his eyes. He had to go take a leak but wasn't about to ask, finally urinating in his pants.

The next morning Tom didn't say anything to Mescal or Jeb. He and Mescal ate in silence. Neither offered Jeb any food or coffee. As Tom walked toward his horse to leave, Jeb was horrified at the thought of being left alone with the Indian. Jeb pleaded in a whisper. "Yur not gonna leave me here with that savage are ya? What kinda White man are ya anyway?"

Tom didn't speak to him, didn't even glance his way. Climbing into the saddle Tom rode to the edge of camp. He was looking straight ahead, away from Mescal and Jeb. "Where will I find you when we come back?" Tom asked.

Mescal walked over in front of Tom and pointed to a tall dark rock that stood well above the rest about half a mile off the trail. "Death Rock!" the Indian said.

Tom nudged his horse and started off at a trot. After he was a good distance away he breathed out a sigh of relief, glad that he wasn't Jeb.

"Death Rock!" Tom said out loud. "That fellow has got to be scared to death."

Fact was, Tom had to admit, he had no idea what Mescal would do to get the information. As he recalled Mescal's behavior from the night before, a shiver ran up his body and the hair on his arms and neck stood on end. Emmett had told Tom earlier that Mescal was Apache. There was no Indian tribe in the Southwest the White man feared more.

Mescal kept up the evil facade; his actions were decisive and seemed filled with anger. Finally, he walked over and grabbed the man, pulling him up by his hair. The pain to the top of Jeb's head was considerable, but all he could think about was being scalped. Mescal

291

nearly threw him on his horse. The outlaw's head and bound hands were hanging on one side and his legs on the other. Mescal took a rope underneath the horse and tied Jeb's hands to his legs. When he took him over to Death Rock, he rode at a trot so the man was jostled by the gait.

He left Jeb on the horse while he made a campfire, and put war paint on his face again. This time his whole face was red and black so that no normal flesh color was showing, looking as evil as possible. When taken off the horse, Jeb saw the Indian's face and gasped. Mescal led him roughly and tied him to a tree near the fire. Jeb saw the blade of the hunting knife in the red-hot embers. Mescal retrieved the knife, and then walked up to Jeb.

Suddenly the Indian started cutting the rustler's shirt with swift violent slashes, coming close, but never touching his skin. The Indian's face was filled with anger as he took what was left of Jeb's shirt and ripped it off of him. Mescal cut Jeb's belt. Then, growling with an animal-like sound from deep within, he cut the man's pants at the waist until they dropped to his ankles. With one slash of the knife he cut away his underpants. Jeb's naked body was shaking in terror and his face was the epitome of fright.

Glaring at him, Mescal turned and walked over to the fire. He put the blade of the knife back in the embers and started chanting. Five minutes later he picked up the knife. The blade was so hot the point was bright red and smoke trailed behind as he moved. He walked within a few feet of Jeb, glaring with eyes of hate. Mescal lifted both hands to the sky and chanted for several seconds. Next he stared hard at Jeb with his red and black evil-looking face. As he started making an animal-like noise, he let his hand with the knife drop ever so slowly down until it was below his waist. Then he moved forward, slowly lowering his gaze and growling a deep guttural sound, moving the knife toward the prisoner's crotch. Jeb could tell the torture was about to begin and thought he knew the first action was to remove his manhood.

Jeb broke down and sobbed. "I'll tell whatever you want, please anything you want...don't...please don't."

Mescal moved close to his face. He was so close they nearly touched noses. He brought the knife up so close to the side of the rustler's face that Jeb could feel the heat. Mescal spoke more like an animal than a man; the voice seemed to reverberate out of his chest, saliva spraying from his mouth as he spoke.

"One chance, one chance only, all truth, or you die slow terrible screaming death."

Jeb nodded furiously. "I will, I promise, anything…anything."

Mescal growled again, raised his voice and lowered the knife. The blade was now nearly touching the rustler's manhood. The Indian's arm was shaking with tension and hate. "Truth…one chance!" Mescal shouted.

Jeb shook uncontrollably, all semblance of manhood vaporized by fear. "Yes, yes. I will tell truth...truth," he sputtered. His legs gave way, urine streamed down his leg and he slouched against the tree sobbing and crying.

Mescal waited for Jeb to talk. Information poured from him. Mescal brought the man paper and pencil that he had asked Tom for in the morning while Jeb still slept. He cut the bonds from his hands and Jeb listed the names of the men in the gang. There were twenty-two names. Finally Mescal had all the information from the rustler he could possibly think to ask. He untied Jeb's legs and let him clean himself in the nearby stream. The dead man, Jim, had a second set of clothes in his saddlebag. Mescal gave them to Jeb to put on, and then fed him. After Jeb ate, Mescal tied him to the tree again, but in a comfortable sitting position.

Later during the night, Mescal once again painted his face the evil-looking red and black. He woke Jeb up and asked him the same questions, threatening to slit his throat if he lied. Before daybreak he repeated the procedure, waking him once again. This time Jeb remembered something else.

"In the canyon where the hideout is, Caisson hid a lot of money. It's the money from the cattle he stole."

"Where money?"

"I don't know, but it's a bunch. You'd be rich if you found it."

"How you know about money?"

"I overheard Caisson talking to his brother. They didn't know I was there. I couldn't hear everything, but they talked about the money they hid."

293

"Where money?" Mescal growled.

"I don't know," Jeb said, trembling. "It's got to be in the canyon somewhere. I swear...I don't know where."

"How many know about money?"

"Nobody cept me. Well, Ben Caisson...his brother Matt...no one else. I heard 'em...in the back of the canyon. Caisson thinks it's a secret. They were talkin real soft...I couldn't hear very well. It sounded like a lot of money...a whole lot of money," he said with his jaw quivering.

"You tell anyone else about money?"

"Nobody. I was hopin to find it. I didn't tell nobody."

Mescal held the knife to his throat. "You no tell anyone else. No one." Mescal moved the knife down to Jeb's chest. "You tell...I cut your heart out. Understand, White man?"

"I understand...I won't tell. I promise."

On the following days Mescal untied Jeb a few times each day so he could eat and relieve himself. Mescal didn't talk to Jeb, and didn't let the rustler see him in daylight any more than necessary. He didn't want Jeb to think of him as a normal man, but rather as a wild Indian who might torture him. It was important the rustler still be willing to talk when Jake and Emmett returned. They might have additional questions for him.

TWENTY-TWO

Tom arrived at the ranch several days later in the early evening. Both he and the horse were covered with sweat and dirt. After riding wearily up to the ranch house, he dismounted and brushed off some of the dust from his shirt. Several people stood on the porch as he walked toward them. Melinda spoke first. The apprehension in her voice was evident.

"Mescal?"

"He's fine."

Melinda breathed out a sigh of relief.

Tom looked at Emmett and nodded. "We found it."

The rancher was anxious to hear the rest, but waited as Tom washed his face and hands. Melinda went inside and brought him a cool drink of lemonade and a thick slice of fresh bread covered with grape jam. When Tom finished, he told Emmett how Mescal had found the hideout, and briefly told the story of the gun battle with the two rustlers on the return trip. He relayed how Mescal had stayed with the one remaining rustler to obtain more information, and that Mescal thought it best to bring a posse of no more than a dozen men because of the need to get in undetected.

Emmett agreed and the two of them picked four men. After walking to the bunkhouse Emmett told the men selected to join him at the house for the evening meal. He sent Willie to the Evans ranch to tell Jake to bring himself and his best five gunmen. They were to meet them at noon at Butcher's Pass.

After Emmett left to go to the bunkhouse, Melinda took advantage of the time to spend a few moments with Tom. Others were nearby, so they walked slowly to Mescal's cabin and stood on the porch. Melinda gave him a big hug. They talked alone for several minutes, and then Melinda indicated she needed to get back to the house soon to help Margaret and Beth.

"I'm so glad you're okay, Tom. I worried about you."

"I thought about you too."

"When did you think about me?" she asked playfully.

"Often, but especially in the evenings. We found a couple of good places to take a bath in the streams on the way down. After I got out of the water at one place, I sat on the rocks to dry. I couldn't help but think about you. Reminded me of when we were up at your secret spot and we lay there naked together."

"Shhh…Tom, somebody might hear you."

"Wouldn't they be surprised?"

"Tom…don't talk about that. That's our secret. You'd never tell anybody, would you?"

"No, of course not. But it sure was nice thinking about you all naked like that."

Melinda smiled and asked, "Did anything…" She paused, embarrassed, but tried again to finish her question. "Did anything get…?"

"Bigger?"

"Shhh…yes," she said, blushing.

"I'll say, as big as a stallion's."

Melinda blushed even more and looked around to make sure nobody had heard. While he was gone she had also thought of that time at the fortress when they had both lay in the sun nude. Her heart had quickened when she had seen him aroused, and her body had reacted in ways she could only think of as warm and passionate. At the fortress when she felt her body becoming aroused, she had resisted the temptation to give in to him. Her body reacted similarly now, arousal throbbing in her veins. Melinda changed the subject.

"Are you sure you're not hurt?"

"I'm not. Other than Mescal's ankle we're both fine."

"Well, you'd better be getting cleaned up, and I need to help get dinner ready."

There was a lot of activity at the ranch and the intensity level was high. Tom went to the bunkhouse and saw that the cowboys who were going with them were methodically getting their packs ready. While walking back to Mescal's cabin, he reflected on the actions of the men. They seemed like soldiers preparing for war. Guns and ammunition were being checked and rechecked, and much time was spent deciding what to take. Hank had suggested to Emmett that they take an additional packhorse to carry rifles and ammunition. Hank, Bud and Stuffy were the three who were going in addition to Willie.

Later, the three cowboys came to the house for the evening meal. Emmett also had his cousin Brad join them. Hank had remembered that someone would need to stay with Jeb. Hank was an ornery cowboy who didn't take a bath often enough, but he was good with a gun and was always thinking about details. He was valuable for that reason alone. Emmett, Tom and the men planned while they ate. Tom told them how Mescal had readied his prisoner for interrogation.

"The last thing he said when I left was 'Death Rock.' I can't imagine the look on Jeb's face when he heard those words."

"I shore wouldn't wanna be in that Jeb's boots right about now," Bud said, shaking his head.

"Me neither," said Hank.

"But Mescal isn't violent like that," Melinda interjected.

"I'm not sure any of us know what he is capable of doing," Tom countered. "He's lived a different life. An Apache does whatever is necessary to survive. Even if Mescal wouldn't carry it through, all he has to do is make Jeb think he would."

"Well, I don't believe he would torture someone," Melinda said.

After Melinda went into the other room, Hank said softly, "I think he'd do whatever it takes." Others nodded in agreement.

Melinda was worried about Tom's safety, but felt better now that so many were going. Based on the conversation at the dinner table, they now had the advantage. The rustlers didn't know they had been discovered. She had listened silently while Tom told the men about the shootout with Jeb and Jim. After supper, Melinda joined Tom out on the porch.

"Why did you take such a chance only wounding those two men?"

Tom looked into her sparkling green eyes and could see the moisture collected in the corners. He was surprised at her question because it suggested she wanted him to kill them, which wasn't like her. As he recalled the gunfight, he realized the risk he had taken. The rustler Jeb had been fast. If Tom hadn't been able to get the second shot off quickly, he would have been killed.

"I felt like we needed all the information we could get."

"Well, be more careful on this trip."

She stepped forward and put her arms around him, her short blonde hair blowing softly in the evening breeze. Finally she released her hug, kissed him, and then went back in the house to help prepare the food that would be taken on their dangerous journey.

The next morning as the day was just beginning to lighten, the horses stood in front of the ranch house. It was still well before sunup; the sky to the east was a hazy gray. Melinda watched as the cowboys loaded up their supplies. She noticed that the men went about their preparations with a sense of purpose and there was little discussion among them. As Bud loaded the food on the packhorse, he looked up and saw Melinda watching them. When she gazed directly at him, he touched the brim of his hat. She smiled, feeling she had a small part in this adventure. Melinda had no desire to hunt men down, and refused to let herself think what these good friends might do to the rustlers when they found them.

The horses seemed to sense the excitement of the moment. They stepped nervously about. Their hooves could be heard above the sound of creaking leather as the men climbed on their saddles. Tom was on Diamond as there was no reason now to hide his identity as Tom Colt. Margaret and Beth joined Melinda on the porch, as the men were ready to ride out. Bud, Stuffy, Hank and Brad all nodded their heads or touched their hats as a parting salute. These women and the ranch represented the reason they were riding off to put their lives at risk. If outlaws were allowed to roam at will, the very essence of law and order would be destroyed. Rustlers had to be stopped. They represented the greatest danger to successful ranches and decent jobs for good men. Most every cowboy hoped to have his own ranch someday. The men felt pride, not fear, as they nudged their mounts to depart. Tom gave Melinda a quick smile and wink, and she smiled and waved. Everyone remaining at the ranch stood outside and watched them ride away, like soldiers marching off to war.

As they headed east the sun was just emerging above the canyon wall. In the center of the canyon the surface of the stream glittered with the reflection of the rising sun behind it. The men rode down the valley and as their horses plunged into the stream droplets of water sprayed out to the side, sparkling with the light of the sunrise. The men rode the remaining length of the huge canyon, around the bend and out of sight.

Melinda watched until she could no longer see them, and then looked at the sky. The sun had gone behind a cloud low on the horizon. The rays of the golden sphere spread like fingers of light from a giant hand. Melinda took it as a good sign and said a silent prayer that Tom and the others would return safely.

Just before noon, the six riders met Jake and his men at Butcher's Pass. Willie was with them. They had arrived twenty minutes earlier and had a campfire going. There was coffee on the fire and food being cooked. Sam, Ben, Red, Henry and Steve from Jake's ranch had the same look of determination. They offered a nod as a salute hello, but the easygoing nature of cowboys was not present.

Jake and Emmett conferred and told the men as much as they knew. Tom provided added details. Jake's men wanted to know more about the shootout, and Tom told them a shortened version. He also told them about Mescal having the prisoner at "Death Rock" and the scene the old Indian had created at the campfire that night. The men listened eagerly as they would to a ghost story. Some raised their eyebrows and shook their heads. Each imagined how he would feel if he were Mescal's prisoner. The Indian had developed a reputation during the last year. It was clear to Tom they respected Mescal, and now feared him.

Tom noted Jake had brought Steve Larson. Steve was young and quick with a gun. He liked to demonstrate his speed and had been practicing at Jake's ranch earlier that spring. Tom and Mescal rode in after hunting cougar. Tom recalled the event vividly.

There had been five cowboys, including Steve, practicing their quick draw out by the corral, competing with one another. Steve had been the victor and was feeling his oats. He was friendly enough, but pressed Tom to show them his draw. Steve had placed a can on the top rail and then drew and shot it off. Tom noted that he was pretty quick, but not nearly as fast as many of the men he had faced. Steve goaded him, though still in a friendly way. Tom was feeling a lot of pressure to comply, but resisted. Demonstrating his fantastic speed was how his reputation had spread.

Mescal had been about to intervene in Tom's behalf, when a man suddenly interrupted. Mescal didn't know him, but did notice he had been talking to Jake. Tom had recognized him immediately and wondered what he meant to do.

The man walked right up to them, never looking at Tom, and said to Steve, "So you think you might be able to outdraw our friend here. Well, I tell you what, let's see how you do against an aging drifter. I need the practice anyway."

There was a little gray in this man's hair. At first Steve had just smiled, but then he shrugged his shoulders and replied, "Why not!" Steve walked over to the fence and put two cans on the middle rail, which was about waist high. He set the cans about four feet apart and strode proudly back to where the man stood waiting. The young cowboy looked over at his friends, smiling confidently, sure of himself, and shrugged his shoulders again. He thought he would have little trouble outdrawing this middle-aged cowpoke. Steve gave the stranger instructions.

"We'll both face the fence, and old Henry over there will toss a rock up high behind us so we can't see it. When it hits the ground, we draw. The can with the red label is yours. Any questions?"

"Think I got it."

Henry looked at both of them with a rock in his hand about the size of his fist. "You both ready?"

Both men nodded and Henry threw the rock up high, well behind them. When it landed, a gun blast quickly followed and the can with the red label flew off the fence. Steve hadn't cleared his holster when the blast occurred; the sound of his opponent's gun had startled him and he stood there holding his gun pointed toward the ground unfired. The men had fallen silent, and there were no smiles to be seen except from Jake.

The stranger holstered his gun, and without looking at Steve said softly, "Well, I'm older, had lots more practice." Then he turned and walked back to where the ranch owner stood grinning.

Tom had been relieved when this older man stepped into the fray. Afterwards, Tom walked toward Jake and the man whose speed with a gun had caught him by surprise. Tom walked right up to him and held out his hand to his old friend. "It's good to see you, Josh. How'd you happen to be here?"

Jake looked puzzled, surprised Tom knew Josh's name.

Josh chuckled, knowing the surprise his presence must have caused. "I've been up to Montana seeing my boys again," Josh said. Tom's expression revealed that he was still puzzled why Josh was at Jake's ranch. Finally Josh smiled and added, "I always stop by to see Jake. He used to ride with me down in Texas."

Tom nodded, putting two and two together. "Were you a ranger too, Jake?"

Josh had a surprised look on his face, as did Jake. Tom had known this man's first name was Josh, but hadn't known his last name. As soon as he saw his draw Tom figured this had to be Josh Steel, the well known Texas Ranger.

"There can't be two men in Texas named Josh that quick with a gun," Tom explained.

"Being a ranger is something I never told the men," Jake said quietly.

"I see no reason to tell anybody," Tom replied.

When Josh had come to the ranch earlier, Jake told him about a young man named Tom Colt who was awfully quick with a gun, and how he had done much to help him and Emmett. Because of the description, Josh had wondered if it was the man he had known as Tom Stone, and wasn't surprised when Tom had ridden in. He and Jake had been watching the cowboys practice their fast draw, and witnessed the audacity of the young cowboy Steve. He didn't seem like a bad sort, Josh thought, just inflicted with over zealous boyish stupidity.

Josh felt like he had to intervene; Tom was developing a new life for himself. The ranger didn't want something as unimportant as this to undo all the work the legend had accomplished in building a new identity. Everybody knew Josh Steel was quick with a gun, so he had little to lose if they found out who he was. It had also been a pleasure putting the boy in his place.

Tom had spent several days with Josh getting reacquainted. He told the ranger about his experiences in Kansas and then how he had been shot again when he returned to Arizona. On the second day Tom had taken Josh over to Emmett's ranch and introduced him to Melinda.

"Well, I bet it was more fun having that pretty young girl for a nurse than this tired old ranger," he had chided Tom.

"Why didn't you tell me you were a ranger?" Tom had finally asked.

"Didn't seem important at the time."

Josh hadn't wanted to because he wasn't sure how the younger man would react. The ranger thought it was easier to find out about someone when they believed he was just another cowboy on the trail. The two men spent a few days together. Tom had a feeling inside he couldn't quite describe. It was a sense of contentment and being at peace with his inner self. Tom wished he could have spent more time with the lawman, but Josh told him he had to get back to Texas. The ranger never let on that he knew who Tom really was.

Tom hadn't seen Steve again since then. He thought about asking Jake if bringing the youngster was a good idea, but they were already half a day's ride from the ranch. Bringing someone else or sending Steve home at this point wouldn't be practical. Tom had learned to prefer the more experienced cowboys in tough situations. Young men were courageous, but not always wise. Steve was pretty good with a gun, which no doubt was why Jake had brought him. Deciding not to say anything about the youngster, Tom hoped for the best.

After everyone finished eating and things were packed away, they all mounted and rode through the pass. The sun was high and the tall stone walls glistened with tiny specks of light amidst the reddish hue of the rock. They rode past the tree where the rustler had been hung earlier. It seemed only to add to their sense of purpose. The dozen men rode at a brisk pace. Tom could feel the sense of pride and purpose in Jake and Emmett, protecting what was theirs, fighting for a just and worthy cause. It was men such as these that would save Utah and the West from the type of men Caisson and his gang represented.

Looking over his shoulder Tom saw stern, serious looking cowboys ready to do battle. His long-range rifle and the Henry were on the Paint, who for now was serving as one of the packhorses. Tom glanced at Jake and could sense the determination the rancher felt. He would not let crooked men destroy what had taken him so long to build. Jake, like Emmett, had dealt with many obstacles in building a ranch. There had been scrapes with Indians, predators to eliminate, droughts and blizzards to endure, and rustlers to overcome. Such events killed many men, but those that survived were hardened. They had built a way of life. Jake and Emmett would kill Caisson or be killed in the process. Tom had no doubts about the ferocity of Jake or Emmett. Of the two, he would least want to be the enemy of Jake.

When they camped that night the men were much more silent than usual. The harmless chatter so normal for men of this calling was absent. They went about their business of caring for the horses. Some cleaned their guns, though they had been cleaned the night before and not fired since. When the food was ready the men ate mostly in silence, glad to have something to consume the minutes until it was time for sleep. After supper, several of the men smoked and some drank coffee. The flames of the campfire captured the attention of the eyes of the men. They stared into the bright fingers of fire moving randomly in the night air, giving off heat and warming their tired bodies.

Two days later they approached the dark peak Mescal had referred to as "Death Rock." The huge stone cast a long shadow as it was late in the afternoon. It had been hot earlier in the day, but was reasonably mild as the sun lowered on the horizon. Ten minutes later they rode into Mescal's camp. The rustler was not in sight. The old Indian greeted them and had coffee brewing. He had seen them coming some time ago. The men dismounted and tended to their horses.

Mescal met with Jake, Emmett and Tom. After telling them what he had learned from the rustler, he took the three men back to talk to the captive. Jeb had a blindfold on and his clothes were dirty. There were no obvious signs of violence other than the wound he had received in the gunfight with Tom. As they approached, Jeb began to shake. He was a pitiful sight.

Jake took off his blindfold and Jeb was visibly relieved to see them. He began to sob; his spirit was broken. This was not the same man Tom had left several days earlier. His confidence and pride had vanished. Jeb avoided eye contact with Tom but looked imploringly at Jake and Emmett. They asked him every question they could think of and he responded immediately. Mescal stood behind and to the left of Jeb.

When the ranchers finished, Jake told him, "If everything you've told us turns out to be true, and we get Caisson, we'll let you go. But if you've lied to us, we'll give you back to Mescal to finish what he started. Is there anything else you want to tell us, or do you want to change anything you've said?"

He glanced quickly at Mescal, and replied stammering, "No...no, told you the truth." Then he looked at Jake with some hope in his eyes. "If you...you get him, you'll let me go?"

"That's right," Jake said strongly. "If you've told the truth and we get Caisson, I guarantee you'll be let go."

The man looked at Jake, and then looked at the ground to help hide the tears. Jake told Brad to bring Jeb a plate of food and some clean clothes, let him wash himself, and then tie him back up. Brad would be left behind to guard Jeb. The information Jeb gave them was helpful. He had known the date when all of the gang was supposed to be back at the hideout.

After conferring with Tom and Mescal, Jake and Emmett discovered they had ample time to get there. They headed over to the spot where Tom and Mescal had made camp before. There was better water and more space there. Tom told them about the place to take a bath and several went to take advantage of it. The rest made camp for the night, unsaddled their horses and started preparing supper.

The men were told all of the gang would be at the hideout and they had more than enough time to get there. Spirits were high and the cowboys became more talkative. The information given by the rustler provided a plan and removed some of the unknown. Tom knew men feared the unknown. When a man knows what he is up against it reduces much of the anxiety. Having a workable plan with the inside knowledge provided by the captured rustler was icing on the cake. It was evident tension had been reduced and confidence increased. Tom could see camaraderie developing. While they belonged to two different ranches, they were now one group with one purpose. Tom had been on such missions before, and knew that experiences of this nature result in strong bonds that last a lifetime.

Darkness had settled in and the men relaxed after eating supper. The wind died down and blew softly through the pine trees above. A few coyotes could be heard howling, and unseen birds sang in the trees. The men talked of other times and daring deeds. They were more like their old selves now, doing what cowboys like to do. The story telling had gone on for a good hour. Willie was telling them about a saloon girl in Amarillo. The men listened eagerly, having become totally enthralled with Willie's description of the voluptuous lady.

Suddenly, something struck the ground just behind Willie and rolled on the ground a short distance. Willie, Red and Henry, who had been next to him, jerked this way and that, and hands went flying toward guns. Only two of the men had cleared leather when they realized the attack was by a large pinecone from a limb high above. Willie threw the cone into the fire with a sheepish look on his face. All the rest of the men laughed not so quietly about the harmless pinecone that had caused such a fright.

Mescal laughed along with the rest. He was glad to be back among his friends. His time at the camp had allowed his ankle to heal, and he now walked without a limp. The days spent with the rustler had been a distasteful experience for the old Indian, but he knew extracting the information was necessary. It would save lives. There was still danger, but less than before. For the last several days he had little to do to pass the time of day. The man had broken completely during the first day Tom was gone. Mescal had made certain he was telling the truth by awakening the rustler in the middle of the night and making him answer the questions again, quickly, without time for thought. The man had complied, and then he had remembered Caisson's secret.

Standing near Jeb while Jake and Emmett talked to him, Mescal had made it a point to let the rustler know he was there. The Indian knew the man was nervous and might slip and talk about Caisson's secret, but he did not. Later, as the men were preparing to go to the other camp, Mescal had walked silently back to the tree where the rustler was tied. No one else was within hearing distance. Jeb was on the other side of the tree and hadn't seen or heard Mescal approach.

Suddenly, in a quiet but strong voice Mescal had told him, "Remember, White man, no talk about Caisson's money."

A nervous, sobbing whispered reply came back: "I won't, I won't, I promise I won't tell."

As it got later many of the cowboys slept; others stayed up to talk. There was a half moon lighting the sky, but clouds drifted by and made it dark now and then. Tom put his bedroll so his feet were close to the campfire, as did many of the men. Closing his eyes he listened to the sounds of the night. He enjoyed it all, the wind, the coyotes and the cowboys. At first he could make out who was talking, but after awhile it became an intermittent soothing murmur. Tom could feel the warmth of the fire on the bottom of his boots and the cool of the breeze on his cheeks. He was listening to the relaxing sound of the wind in the trees overhead, and then the next thing he knew Bud nudged him and told him it was time to get up.

That morning the men were up before the sun and breakfast was quickly prepared. This would be the toughest day of the trip. They wanted to get an early start to cross the desert before it became too hot. The men ate heartily; there was a new air of confidence. The ride in the desert was okay at first, but as the sun went higher the heat rose from the sand as though they were in an oven. When they neared the other side, Mescal went ahead to see if the campsite at Indian Waters was clear. It was a good place for men to rest before taking on a dangerous endeavor. It would also be a good respite from the long trek through the desert. Mescal returned and gave the all clear signal.

When they arrived, Tom went to get his bath and several others followed. There was ample room for a dozen men, but there were never more than three or four at any given time. Hank took his turn and the men were surprised, for he rarely took a bath. Most of his friends had never seen him without clothes before. The cowboy's skinny legs were white as chalk, and the rest couldn't help but look.

When Hank noticed them staring, he blurted out, "Well, ain't ya never seen a man take a bath afor?"

Tobacco juice spilled down his chin as he spoke, adding to his frustration. He turned and spit the brown wad of chewing tobacco toward the bank. It didn't quite make it, but fortunately Hank was down stream from the others and it floated away. Bud and Stuffy shook their heads and smiled at one another, but said nothing.

The cool water was refreshing after the long hot day. The cowboys felt clean and fresh and were in an even better mood than the night before. As they sat around the campfire the aroma of coffee, beans and bacon were in the air. The men lounged about, the reason for their long ride seemingly forgotten as they enjoyed the beauty and calm of Indian Waters.

After supper, Tom, Mescal, Jake and Emmett talked about plans for getting to the hideout. Mescal had learned much from the captured rustler. He knew the landmarks the rustler had described, but believed they had a better chance getting in undetected using a route other than the one Jeb suggested. Mescal would lead them in by backtracking where he and Tom had come out when they headed back to the ranch. It would be rough going because of the terrain, but the chance of being seen was almost nonexistent. Tom headed back to the campfire and once again listened to the men and their stories. On this night there were no tall trees overhead which might drop pinecones.

Later Hank went away from the campfire to take a leak. As he returned he stopped, picked up a stick and threw it so it fell just behind some of the men. The men close by jumped to their feet. When they heard the loud guffaws of the ornery cowboy, there were several bad words that were said, followed by laughter from the rest. This night proved to be as enjoyable as the one before.

As Tom lay down he thought of Melinda. Looking up into the dark sky overhead, he saw a brilliant shooting star lasting for several seconds. Somehow he just knew she had seen it too. Mescal was already asleep. Jake and Emmett were still at the campfire, drinking coffee and having a last smoke. Most of the men were making their way to their spots for the night. Tom could hear the stream nearby, and an occasional snort or stomp of a hoof on the ground by one of the horses. He drifted into a deep sleep.

In the middle of the night Willie woke Tom for his shift on guard duty. They had posted one guard just to be safe. No trouble was expected, but this campsite was used often and they had to be careful from here on out. There was a certain safety in numbers and they had plenty of guns as long as there was someone to rouse them.

As Tom wandered around the perimeter of camp he went down by the stream for a drink. The moon was low on the horizon and as he looked up the length of the stream the reflection of the moon sparkled in the water. He sat on a nearby log and enjoyed the peace and quiet of the night. Looking at his watch he realized it was the end of his shift. After waking Red, he climbed back into his bedroll and was asleep seconds after he lay down.

When Tom woke in the morning he stayed in his bedroll for awhile enjoying the warmth, for the air outside was cool. Finally it was time to get up and prepare for the day's travel. The men were in good spirits; they ate, joked and enjoyed the charm of the place. As they broke camp and prepared to ride the men grew more silent.

TWENTY-THREE

The posse circled around the small town of White Cloud on the chance some of Caisson's men might be there. Mescal led them using the same route he and Tom had taken earlier, and they rejoined the trail on the other side of town. Now closer to the location of the hideout, Mescal was concerned about being seen by someone in the gang riding into White Cloud. He would have taken the posse off the main road, but the surrounding countryside was impassable. The huge walls seemed everywhere and the men couldn't help but stare. Willie was particularly fascinated with the stone that looked like molten rock that had suddenly cooled.

Hank and Ben were at the rear of the posse, and both kept looking behind them. This looked like an excellent spot for an ambush. Red and Henry glanced often at the stone walls, looking high on the sides, thinking men could be up there with rifles. They rode by chalk colored stone mountains with lines similar to a checkerboard. Finally, they passed the place in the trail where the gang turned into the hills. Everyone relaxed, as there was little likelihood of running into the rustlers now.

Later, they reached the place where Tom and Mescal had exited from the hills when they returned to the ranch. The posse left the trail and trudged through the rough terrain of rock, shrub and thorny brush. It was a long, treacherous and uncomfortable journey, and the men began to wonder what Tom and Mescal had gotten them into. Tom had warned them, but it was proving worse than they had imagined. The riders had to make a trail through some of the most unforgiving land they had seen. Those in front created a path for the riders that followed, making it easier for those in the rear. Small shrubs, branches and thorns tore at their legs as they forced their way through the brush. The sharp, prickly spines of cactus penetrated the boots and chaps of a few men. Stuffy had gotten more than his share of thorns and was cursing a "blue streak."

Having been fortunate and not incurring so much as a scratch, Hank gave the other cowboys a rough time. "Wal, I sure don't know what yur complainin about. I've been in a lot tougher places than this." Hank laughed under his breath making a silly huffing sound as he rode.

Red was in front of him and had two thorns of his own. He retorted, "One more crack like that, Hank, and we'll make sure this is the roughest ride you ever had."

The chatter continued as they made their way through the rocks, brush and cactus. It was hotter and more humid than when Tom and Mescal had been there before. The men were drenched in sweat. Everyone had to dismount in two places to negotiate the terrain. More than one cowboy had a sore butt after sliding down loose stone on one steep slope.

Finally they came to the campsite where Tom had waited while Mescal found the hideout. It had been tough coming in, but Jake and Emmett agreed no gang would ever expect a posse to approach from that direction. Nearly all of the men had at least one thorn in their boot or leg. Those with thick chaps had fared best. Two of the horses had cuts on their legs that required attention. Somehow Hank had made it without the slightest injury, much to the chagrin of the other cowboys. Hank asked several of the less fortunate if their wounds were "serious." Tom overheard him say to Bud, "Oh, gosh darn, that's too bad," and then Hank walked away making that silly laugh of his.

While the men were eating, they listened while Jake and Emmett explained the plans. Afterwards they sat around the fire and talked quietly in small groups of twos and threes. Some rolled a smoke and others drank coffee. The smell of tobacco, coffee and burning wood drifted in the air. In a couple of hours all were bedded down and asleep except for the guard. The six men who did not do guard duty the night before would each take their turn tonight. Tom would get a full night's sleep.

In the morning a light rain started falling, and the men got up long enough to take shelter under the trees. Most went back to sleep. Jake and Emmett had told them the night before they could get up whenever they liked. Because of the tough ride yesterday, many were tired and continued to doze. Mescal told the ranchers there was no hurry. They had plenty of time to get to the hideout and didn't want to arrive until just before dark to reduce the chance of discovery.

Jeb had told them everyone in Caisson's gang was supposed to be at the hideout before sunset on Thursday, which was today. Jake and Emmett had decided to wait until dawn of the next morning. They hoped to catch them still asleep and apprehend the rustlers with no shots fired. If it did turn into a battle, they would have all day. Jake wanted to avoid having to fight them in the dark. It would be too easy for the rustlers to slip away undetected in the night.

The men were glad for the morning of rest. Ben and Sam set up a couple of tarpaulins to keep from getting wet. Under one of the tarps, some of the men were playing poker. As always Willie had his deck of cards. On the other side of the tree there was a campfire with steaming coffee. The coffeepot was filled and emptied three times. As the morning passed and midday approached, they prepared lunch and ate wherever they could find a dry spot to sit. After eating, everyone mounted up. Each man had several biscuits and some beef-jerky in his saddlebags for later. The rain let up, but it was overcast and looked like it could rain again.

Mescal was in the lead. Several times he stopped, dismounted and went ahead. He would return and lead on again. The rain caused the scent of grass, leaves and rotting wood to be heavy and pungent in the air. It competed with the smell of wet horseflesh. As they rode Tom heard the sounds of leather saddles creaking, horses snorting, soft thudding of hooves, and an occasional twig being broken by a horse. After passing Whistler's Peak, they came to a stream with very steep banks on the other side. Mescal crossed the stream, and then dismounted, leading his horse up the slippery dirt incline.

The men behind followed suit, some of them having more difficulty negotiating the steep bank. The water in the stream wasn't deep, but the incline was slippery from the rain. Red and Stuffy both ended up sliding down the slope and getting their boots muddy in the stream bottom, cursing loudly. They climbed up the incline by holding onto roots and kicking the toes of their boots into the side of the slope. Other than getting wet and muddy, they came through it none the worse for wear.

Hank laughed his stupid silent laugh, and both of the muddy cowboys shook an angry fist at him. Next Hank took his turn. Unlike the rest he planned to show them how a real cowboy did it. Leaning way forward in the saddle, he spurred his horse to climb the incline. He was almost up the bank when Red suddenly appeared at the top of the steep dirt bank, directly in front of Hank's horse, yelling and waving his hat. The horse stopped and slid backwards most of the way down to the water. Suddenly, the horse caught its footing and stopped with a jerk that jolted poor Hank out of the saddle and plopped him backwards into the muddy water. He was sitting in the middle of the stream with arms and legs sprawled out.

Stuffy laughed so hard he fell to his knees holding his sides, and finally rolled onto the ground still laughing. The other cowboys laughed and several imitated the huffing sounds Hank made earlier. The angry cowboy got out of the water, made his way up the incline, red face and all, slinging mud off his boots by kicking toward Red and Stuffy.

"Ya no account laughing dumbass goodfurnuthin wannabe cowboys. Couldn't play fair, could ya? I had that horse up the bank. Would've made it too. Ya dumb shitheads."

Stuffy couldn't stop laughing long enough to reply. Red managed to form some words between laughs. "Ya shoudda...seen yurself, butt first...plopping into...that water."

"Any chance the rustlers might hear?" Emmett asked Mescal.

"Rustlers far, not hear."

Emmett rode up to Hank and said, "Get yourself cleaned up, cowboy. We don't have time to play in the mud."

312

Stuffy stopped laughing long enough to say, "Hank, you let us know if you need some help cleanin up that muddy butt."

With that, even Mescal joined in the laughter, and Stuffy rolled on the ground once more. Hank wiped himself off as best he could and climbed back in the saddle. As Hank rode by Red, he said, "Now ya know, Red, I'll be getting even with ya one of these nights, but you'll never know when it's a comin."

"Whatever it is, it'll be worth it," Red replied.

After they crossed the stream the terrain became more level and there were fewer trees and less undergrowth. They were able to put the horses at a trot, and traveled several miles in a short amount of time. When they were a little over a mile from the hideout Mescal went ahead on foot. The men dismounted and waited under the trees.

It was a little over an hour later when Mescal returned. He told Tom, Jake and Emmett that the guards were posted at the same locations. Having not detected anyone other than the guards, Mescal said it was safe for the men to proceed closer. He told them he had found a good spot for the horses to be kept for the night. Jake reminded everyone to keep quiet.

Riding ahead slowly, they reached the place Mescal had mentioned without incident. It was a tiny canyon with only one way in and out. The entrance was no more than ten yards across. They put the horses in and built a retaining fence by placing fallen limbs and brush across the narrow opening, being careful not to make much noise.

Tom, Emmett and Jake went with Mescal while the others stayed behind. It was over half a mile to the hideout. They made their way slowly, and then climbed the wall where Mescal had before. The Indian led them well away from the sentry posts and back toward the spot where he had seen the hideout earlier. They looked over the edge and could see the cabin where Caisson's men were. Mescal pointed out the locations of the two guards on duty. He told them the guards were well positioned for someone entering the mouth of the canyon, but not for men dropping down the walls in back.

Jake and Emmett went over the plans they had drawn up earlier. They spoke softly because there was little sound other than the breeze through the trees. After discussing possible approaches and determining the best locations to climb down the canyon wall, they were ready to leave. Night was fast approaching and Jake wanted to get back before dark.

Camping that night without a fire, the men ate cold beans, biscuits and beef jerky. Those who wanted to smoke finally persuaded Jake to let them before hitting the sack. The glow of the cigarettes couldn't be seen because of the canyon walls. Jake had been more concerned about the smell of cigarette smoke reaching the hideout, but since the rustlers were upwind he thought it was safe. Jake decided two men would be on guard duty at all times during this night.

Everyone found a place to sit and tried to relax. Tom observed that they talked quietly and were much more subdued; the time for battle was near at hand. They did not take lightly the taking of a life, even a rustler's. Though they had courage, they also found it hard not to think about their own possible death. Tom knew from earlier experience that men handle such situations differently. Some of those that seemed fearless wouldn't be in the face of battle, and some that were quiet and meek might be the bravest.

As the night progressed, each cowboy handled his fear in his own way. Some had to rationalize the merits of the mission in light of the danger to their personal safety. Others never considered such matters; they had a job to do and that was that. In the past Tom would have been part of the latter group. He had so much more to live for now, finding he too had to remind himself of the importance of what they were doing. As it grew late, each of the men found a spot to sleep. It was very dark on this night. There was no fire, and the moon was behind the clouds.

Two hours before sunrise the men on guard duty woke Jake and Emmett, and then began waking the rest of the men. Breakfast consisted of more biscuits and beef-jerky. The men ate sparingly; none of them seemed hungry. Jake and Emmett assigned the men to two groups. Four men would go with Tom and Mescal, and five with Jake and Emmett. The group with Tom and Mescal went first because they had to go around the back of the canyon and make their way to the other side. An hour later both groups were atop the canyon wall near the back of the canyon, well behind the entrance where the guards would be.

Hank and Henry would stay up on the canyon walls, one on each side. They were both better shots with a rifle than a revolver. Their job was to make their way up toward the entrance. Henry would go to the sentry post closest to where they climbed the canyon wall. Hank would work his way around to the other side. Jake was hopeful the men dropping down into the canyon would be ready to take the gang before the guards left the cabin. If the guards went before the posse was in position, Hank and Henry were to get the drop on them.

Warning them about the string and cans, Mescal told them they would have to be careful approaching the sentry locations. If they hit the string and the guard was already there, they would have a battle on their hands and that would wake the men in the cabin. After checking to see if the guards were there, Hank and Henry were to go back toward the cabin so they could provide cover for the men below.

Jake gave the signal and the men began their descent to the floor of the canyon. They had brought two ropes, one for each side. Fifteen minutes later it had become obvious it was going to take longer than they anticipated for the men to get down. The cowboys had experience roping calves, but not letting themselves down the side of a canyon. Tom realized now this was something they should have practiced earlier. Some of the men didn't like heights. Others went down quickly.

It looked for awhile to Tom that he was going to have to go up and get Stuffy, who stopped halfway down. He was avoiding looking down and appeared petrified. It was getting light, which was helpful when going down a canyon wall, but they needed to get to the cabin before the rustlers started waking.

The last man to go down, Steve, was halfway to the bottom when he knocked loose a rock from the side of the canyon wall. It fell and struck another bigger rock at the bottom. The sound seemed even louder because of the canyon's stillness. All of the men in the posse listened intently to see if they could hear anything from the cabin. No sound came and they proceeded cautiously.

Henry had made it to the guard post on the near side long ago. Hank had been moving slowly toward the other sentry location when he heard the sound caused by the falling rock. He stopped and listened, trying to determine whether the rustlers had heard. Not hearing any gunfire, Hank proceeded to the sentry location. He walked fast, knowing things could break loose at any moment, and looked as best he could for the string and cans that Mescal had mentioned. As he drew close to the sentry point, his foot hit something and he heard the noise of a rattling can. Crouching behind a tree he strained to hear the movement of another man atop the canyon wall. He knew they couldn't hear the noise down below, but if the guard were in position he would have heard for sure.

The men on the floor of the canyon continued to move closer to the cabin, but stayed well within the cover of the surrounding trees. All knew it was possible the men inside had heard the falling rock and were waiting for them. When they were near the cabin, Tom looked up to see if Hank and Henry were in position above. They were supposed to be at the edge and give a thumb's up. There were so many trees Tom couldn't see the entire ridge. Jake was on the other side doing the same thing, looking for the men above. Both were getting nervous and were concerned that it was taking too long. As the minutes passed it was getting lighter.

Finally, Tom started to head toward the cabin. Steve held up his hand, then pointed toward himself. Tom realized that Steve felt he was the one who made the mistake of knocking the rock loose and added to the risk. Now he wanted to make amends by being the one to sneak up to the cabin. Tom nodded and stepped back behind a boulder. Steve tried to use the trees to keep from being seen.

It took Steve a few minutes to creep quietly under one of the windows. Removing his hat he peered through the glass. At first he couldn't see a thing, but after a few seconds he could make out the figures of men lying on the floor. Pulling his head down he moved to the other side of the window, and raised up slowly to look inside toward the other end of the cabin.

A gun blast broke the silence of the morning, echoing through the canyon, and ending Steve's young life. Several seconds later rifle shots rang out from high up on the canyon walls. Next came the sound of men yelling inside the cabin. Soon glass was breaking and shots were being fired from the windows. Within moments there were many guns shooting from the rocks and trees. Pandemonium had broken out. Red was hit a few seconds later and the men outside retreated back to safer positions. Ben helped Red move behind a cluster of trees. Hank and Henry kept firing from above, and a man yelled inside the cabin when hit.

Tom was in good cover and fired into the windows when he saw something move. He was certain he had hit one of the rustlers. The gunfire continued for another minute and then Jake yelled out for the men to hold their fire. The shooting stopped. Tom was toward the rear of the cabin and not far from where Jake was stationed. Slipping back into the trees he made his way up to the big rock Jake was behind.

"Looks like we're going to have to think of something else," Tom said. "They have the advantage in that cabin."

"Yeah, we'll take a beating. If it wasn't so wet we could smoke 'em out. Got any ideas?"

"Wish I did. That cabin is built like a fort. We'll run out of ammunition if we keep firing away like we have been," Tom said as Emmett joined them.

Emmett smiled. "I brought along something special just in case."

"What might that be?" Jake asked.

Emmett just smiled and motioned for Willie to join them. He had come up with a plan he was quite proud of and wasn't ready to tip his hand just yet. When Willie came up with the saddlebags, Emmett reached in and showed his special weapon.

"This ought to do the trick, don't you think?" Emmett asked.

"Well, that ought to put some excitement in their breakfast," Jake replied, grinning ear to ear. After a brief pause, he added, "How we gonna get close enough, though?"

"I dunno," Emmett replied. He took off his hat and scratched his head. "Maybe somebody could work their way up through those trees over yonder."

"I think I know a way," Tom offered. "Willie, could you go find Mescal and send him over here?" While they were waiting, Tom explained his idea to Jake and Emmett.

The rustlers inside the cabin took the two bodies of their dead and put them in the corner of the back room. There were two other men with wounds. One had a broken arm and was in intense pain. Buck took care of him first, putting the arm in a sling. He would still be able to fire a gun with his left hand. The other man was just nicked in the upper left shoulder. There were no bones broken and he was quickly bandaged and ready to rejoin the battle.

Two of the men inside the cabin had heard the rock when it hit earlier. They had looked at each other and one of them had just about gone back to sleep. But the other man, Pete Mangley, was the leader in Caisson's absence and he jerked his head, motioning for the other man to get up and check it out. Lefty had gotten up, looked out all the windows and had seen nothing. He was about to walk back and lie down when he saw movement in the trees. Lefty saw one man and motioned to Pete. They watched and waited to see if he was alone. Not seeing anyone else they decided he must be by himself. Watching quietly while he crept up to the cabin, they just waited and gave him a loud greeting with a six-gun. They were caught off guard when the shots from up above started coming in the windows. Lefty then saw other men approaching through the trees. Realizing this involved many men he yelled for the others to help.

Willie found Mescal and brought him back. Tom told Mescal what they were up to and the Indian thought he could do it. First he shot an arrow in the other direction for practice, because it included more weight than normal. Then Mescal went to the trees Emmett had suggested. From there he could see the front of the cabin and crept up as close as he could and still remain in cover. When Mescal was ready, Jake yelled out to the rustlers.

"Caisson, are you in there? This is Jake Evans and I wanna talk to you."

He waited almost a minute for a response.

"Caisson, it's best we talk about this," Jake repeated.

After several seconds, a reply finally came from the cabin. "What do you want?"

"I want you to surrender."

That was followed by a long period of gunshots coming from the cabin and then return fire from the trees.

"Hold your fire, men!" Jake yelled.

Silence followed. Suddenly, an arrow flew through the air and landed with a thud just outside the cabin door. A few seconds later a tremendous explosion sounded and the door of the cabin blasted inward. The remaining glass in the windows was blown outward. Outside the cabin the blast had thrown dirt high into the air.

Inside the cabin all the rustlers were knocked to the floor. Buck had seen the Indian sneaking through the trees earlier. Now he asked excitedly, "What the hell do we do, Pete? That Indian and his dynamite will blow us all to hell."

Pete wasn't sure what to do and wished that Caisson were there. Minutes earlier he thought they had the edge. The cabin provided better protection than rocks and trees but Buck was right, the dynamite could destroy the cabin and them with it. They heard the man who called himself Jake Evans yelling again outside.

"The next one goes in a window. Now you men throw out your guns and come out of there with your hands up."

"What do we do now, Pete?" young Kelly Jones nervously repeated Buck's question.

"Wal, we ain't givin up just to get hung," Pete Mangley said with determination. He thought for a few moments and then asked, "Are there some boards we can nail over the windows?"

"There's some, but not enough," young Kelly told him, fear apparent in his voice.

"Hell, Pete, he'd just put an arrow on the window and blow it to smithereens," Buck said. "We'd have pieces of wood sticking out of us like porcupines."

Pete realized he was right and thought for a moment about other options. Finally he said, "We'll make a break for the horses. Everybody, load up your guns."

Kelly's eyes got big. "But Pete, they'll shoot us to bits out there. The horses are too far off and there's men everywhere."

They could hear the man outside yelling again to surrender or else. Pete blurted an angry response to young Kelly: "They'll hang us. Have you ever seen a man hung? Unless somebody's got a better idea, the only chance we got is to shoot our way out. Now get ready to make a run fur it." Pete walked back to the window and yelled out, "Give us a little more time, we have some wounded men in here."

Pete gave his men some further instructions. Twenty seconds later they bolted out the front door shooting at anything that moved.

The would-be captors were caught by surprise and the rustlers nearly made it to the cover of the overhanging trees before the rifles above barked out. Two outlaws fell dead. Bud and Stuffy were behind the trees by the corral and killed three more before the fleeing men managed to shoot both of them. That part of the perimeter was breached and the rustlers charged toward the corral. The horses were already saddled, something an outlaw just gets in the habit of doing. They climbed into the corral and ran toward their mounts, all the while Jake and Emmett's men were making their way through the trees to get a shot at them. Sam and Ben were the closest and were firing at the rustlers.

The horses jumped around the corral, skittish from the scurrying men and rapid gunfire. Dust, the yells of fleeing men and the snorts of frightened horses dominated the scene. Sam hit one of the rustlers just as he climbed in the saddle. The man fell and was stepped on by his nervous horse. As Pete grabbed the reins of his mount a streak of saliva from the scared animal splashed across his face. Without thought he wiped it away with his shirtsleeve, and then he heard a bullet whistle past his ear.

The rustlers were trying to put their feet in moving stirrups and get the horses under control. Ben hit a man just as he got in the saddle. The wounded man turned and fired at Ben but missed. Ben shot him again and the man fell dead. Pete had told them in the cabin to stay put in the corral and leave as a bunch so the men up above with rifles couldn't pick them off one at a time as they rode out. The men already mounted were firing at the men in the trees trying to keep them at bay. Tom, Jake and Mescal had moved quickly in that direction and got behind cover. Just as they arrived the remaining rustlers were mounted and started out of the corral yelling at the top of their lungs, encouraging their horses to run like hellfire. Kelly Jones spurred his horse, but then fell from two gunshot wounds.

Of the fourteen men who had made it to the horses, twelve were mounted and about to ride away when Jake and Tom downed Kelly Jones. The rustlers rode around the south side of the cabin because there was less gunfire coming from that direction. Tom and Jake were on the north, but Tom took a quick shot before they turned the corner and wounded a man, though he did not fall. As they rode away in front of the cabin, Mescal let loose an arrow that fell in their midst but exploded a few seconds too late. Only the final rider felt the impact of the explosion that blew him right out of his saddle and the horse over on its side. The horse got up and ran off, but the rustler was unconscious. Had the dynamite exploded a little earlier, it would have gotten most of the fleeing rustlers. Hank and Henry up on the canyon walls shot down two more men before they rode out of sight. Eight rustlers made it out of the canyon.

There had been twenty-one men in the cabin that morning. Now nine were dead and four lay wounded. Jake and Emmett kept their guns on the wounded rustlers while Ben and Willie tied them up. The ranchers soon discovered Ben Caisson was not among the thirteen rustlers still in the canyon.

Tom and Mescal checked on the men to see who was wounded and tally their losses. Steve and Stuffy were dead. Red and Bud were hit, but would be able to ride. Three other men had minor wounds. Jake was upset that so many rustlers got away, but didn't want to show it. They had just lost a couple of men and needed to bury them. Sam hollered up to Hank and Henry to come on down. Henry yelled something in return but Sam was having trouble hearing him.

The rustlers had gone around the corner of the canyon wall. They were out of sight from the two men with rifles up above. Buck had been wounded by one of them seconds earlier. He stopped his horse and rode back as close as he dared. His left arm was bleeding, but he hadn't finished fighting yet. Staying close to the stone wall and using trees for cover, he made his way on foot back to where he could see one of the men up on the wall. As he looked through the foliage of the trees, it appeared to Buck that the man was yelling to someone on the canyon floor. He rested his rifle barrel against the trunk of a tree to get steady aim. Slowly he squeezed off a shot and saw the man bend over at the stomach and disappear from view. Buck ran and climbed on his horse and rode to catch up with the rest of the gang. Pete had told them earlier that they would head for White Cloud.

Jake, Emmett and all the remaining men in the posse were surprised at the delayed shot. Hank hollered out from above, "Henry's been hit." Raising his rifle, Hank searched in vain for the man who fired the shot. Willie climbed on one of the rustler's horses to go after the culprit, but Jake yelled at him to stay put. He walked up to Willie, who worked for Emmett, and told him, "Willie, there might be a whole bunch of outlaws waiting. It could be a trick to get some of us to ride right into an ambush."

Willie nodded and climbed off the horse. Jake sent Sam and Ben to check on Henry. While Sam and Ben climbed the wall, Emmett, Willie, Tom and Mescal went to dig graves for Steve and Stuffy between two huge oak trees. It was the prettiest part of the canyon.

When Sam and Ben reached the top, they found Henry bleeding heavily from his stomach. He died shortly after they arrived. They used a rope to lower his body. Emmett and Willie went to help Jake with Henry's body as it came down the canyon wall. Tom and Mescal began digging a third grave. After Henry's body was down, they carried him over and laid him next to Steve and Stuffy. Jake had known Henry for many years and was saddened and angered by his death. After they laid him down, Jake slapped his gloves against his leg and walked briskly over to the four rustlers tied to the trees.

Emmett and Tom followed him. Both knew Jake had a temper and were unsure what the rancher intended to do. Jake began interrogating the four men. Emmett and Tom listened from a distance. It didn't take Tom long to realize Jake was using the same method as he had at Butcher's Pass. Saying many of the same things he had there, he was trying to determine which of the men were least likely to talk.

Tom touched Emmett's arm and then motioned for him to walk away. When they were far enough distant to carry on a private conversation, Tom told Emmett about Mescal's plan. The Indian had made the suggestion to Tom while they were digging Henry's grave.

"Mescal wants him and me to stay in the canyon in case Caisson returns. I know it sounds like a long shot, but Mescal has a hunch that Caisson will come back. We could keep the long-distance rifle Jake gave me, and Mescal's Henry rifle. Mescal seems to have a knack for guessing what men will do. I think we should stay, and who knows, we just might get Caisson."

"Well, it sounds doubtful, but I guess it's worth a try."

Taking two of the rustlers' horses, Tom and Mescal rode to the little canyon where the posse had left their mounts. They left the two horses that belonged to the rustlers penned up in the little canyon, and rode Diamond and Paint back, leading the rest by tying them to a rope. Mescal had made the suggestion to keep the two extra mounts in case theirs were somehow found and taken.

Tom was glad to have the chore of leaving to get the horses. It gave him a reason to leave the vicinity of the hangings. He still remembered when they hanged the man at Butcher's Pass. Tom had never seen a hanging before and didn't want to see one again. He recalled watching the rustler struggling desperately to breathe while the noose tightened around his neck, kicking his feet and bending his neck in various ways trying to get air. The rustler had taken a long time to die, and it seemed to Tom a cruel way to put someone to death.

It was one thing to fight for a worthy cause and to shoot men who were trying to kill him, but Tom disliked this drawn out ceremony, letting a man die slowly, and making the others watch until it was their turn. Perhaps those who were hanged first were fortunate. At least they didn't have to watch the others die, anticipating what it was going to be like for them. Tom decided that if he were a rustler, seeing one man hanged would be all it would take to cure him. He had two nightmares since that first hanging, dreaming he was the one being hanged, waking with his body wet with sweat, gasping for air. He understood why Jake and Emmett would hang the men; rustling was a significant problem and they believed it necessary to discourage it.

As he and Mescal walked back, they saw the last of the four men kicking his feet as he struggled in vain. Tom said to Mescal, "What a brutal way to die."

Mescal paused for a few seconds, looked at Tom, then back at the four rustlers hanging under the tree. Finally, he replied with some anger in his voice, "Hanging not brutal. Rustlers deserve die. My niece watch soldiers raid camp. Soldiers take babies from mothers, throw babies on ground, bash babies' heads with rifles. Make women watch. Soldiers rape women, many times. When done, tie women all together, put in hut, set hut on fire. They burn alive. Me lose wife…and child. Hanging easy way die."

Mescal's voice had softened and broke ever so slightly when he mentioned his wife and child, and then sounded angry again as he repeated that hanging was an easy way to die. Tom watched the last rustler stop struggling under the tree while Mescal spoke. He sensed that Mescal's anger was not directed toward him, but he detected a tremendous amount of resentment and little sympathy for the rustlers.

Tom had heard many stories of Indians attacking settlers and wagon trains, and of the murdering, raping and torturing of White men and women. This was the first time he had heard the Indians' side of the story. The acts his friend described both shocked and made him feel ashamed for what Mescal's family and tribe had endured. The White man had encroached upon their land, and the soldiers, at least those soldiers, had committed atrocities against innocent women and children. Tom wondered who committed the first sin in this battle between the White man and the Indian, for he knew one atrocity begets another. He finally decided that didn't matter; barbarous acts simply shouldn't occur.

Tom disagreed with Mescal on one thing. Hanging was brutal, even if these men were guilty. At the same time he had to admit, hanging paled in comparison to the horrific event Mescal had described. Tom recalled that when Mescal had scared Jeb that night, he had said that rustlers had killed his wife and child. At the time Tom thought he was making it up to scare Jeb. He remembered Mescal's anger had been convincing. Now Tom knew why. Even though it was soldiers rather than rustlers, Mescal recalled the event and was livid, as any man would be whose family had been so inhumanly murdered.

When Jake finished his morbid task, he went over to talk to Emmett about what to do next. The two ranchers walked out of hearing distance.

"You know, Emmett, this battle belongs to you and me. These cowboys came here and fought for us, but it's not their war. We've lost the element of surprise, and Caisson knows this area better than we do. If we chase after 'em, chances are we'd lose more men than Caisson. Besides, that damn rustler gang still has as many men as us. We got three men dead and several wounded. I don't think we ought to ask these cowboys to ride into an ambush. If I was Caisson, that's exactly what I'd have waitin for a posse."

Jake paused for a few seconds, giving Emmett an opportunity to offer his opinion. Emmett just waited, listening and learning from this ex-Texas Ranger. Finally, Jake continued, "I really want to get that outlaw, but I don't want to underestimate him. He's got to be smart to get away with rustlin as long as he has. If we chase after him, Caisson can pick the time and place. If we don't, he will likely ride out of Utah and never come back, at least that's what I'm hopin."

"Yur right, Jake, we've hit Caisson hard. He's lost a lot of men here. He might have trouble getting any more men to join him, or even keeping the ones that got away today."

Emmett paused for a second and then told Jake about Tom and Mescal's plan to stay and wait for Caisson. Jake thought it pretty unlikely Caisson would come back, but they were Emmett's men and it was his decision.

"Well, let's hope they get him," Jake replied.

When Jake and Emmett finished their discussion, they walked over and took their turns with the shovels. There were thirteen rustlers to bury. They dug the graves out by the corral where they could be seen easily by anyone coming to the cabin. As before, one of the men carved a wood tombstone, which read: "Hung Rustlers."

The ranchers and their men walked over to the gravesites of Steve, Stuffy and Henry. There were many grim faces as each of the three dead men was lowered into his grave. After all three were buried and their graves covered with rocks, Jake said, "Lord, we leave three brave men here for you to look after. Any one of them would help a stranger in need, and they always worked hard and were good to be around. We hope you'll forgive 'em for the few faults they had, and invite 'em to stay with you there in Heaven."

Jake looked toward Emmett, who added a quote from the Bible. Then Emmett said, "Lord forgive these men for any sins they have committed, for as humans we are not perfect. None of us are, but we have faith in your forgiving nature. May these men enjoy the wonder of being in your presence, and experience the unequalled beauty of Heaven. Amen." All the rest repeated, "Amen."

After the men finished paying last respects to their fallen comrades, they made their way back to the horses. When they were all mounted, the posse rode out of the canyon and headed for White Cloud. Jake wanted to eat there and then travel on to Indian Waters. It would give them a good place to get cleaned up and stay the night. The men had enjoyed staying there on the trip down. The beautiful setting and clean water beckoned to them. After a battle, with so much blood and dying, Jake sensed that men always had the desire to cleanse themselves of the darkness of death.

TWENTY- FOUR

The posse took most of the horses, guns and saddles, but Jake and Emmett had been in such a hurry to return home that they left everything else behind. There was an abundance of food, cooking utensils and other supplies from the cabin. Mescal was relieved to have two of the rustlers' horses stowed away in the little hidden canyon. He had told Tom earlier that it would be a long walk to White Cloud if their mounts were taken. The real reason for keeping them was they might be needed if Jeb was telling the truth about Caisson's secret.

Mescal and Tom decided it would be safer in the evenings to camp in the back of the canyon rather than in the cabin. There was some danger of having a campfire in the evening, but they both thought the risk was minimal. The old Indian thought the rustlers would not be able to travel through the rough terrain during the night. Therefore, if Caisson and his men returned at dark it would be early in the evening. Mescal suggested they delay lighting the campfire until later for that reason. He also suggested they use the string and can alarm technique that was so effective for the guard up on the canyon wall.

By the time they were ready to go to sleep, they had the camp well protected with numerous cans. Anyone approaching in the dark was sure to run into one of them. Mescal took the extra precaution of making it appear that they were sleeping next to the campfire at night. Using some of the rustlers' belongings from the cabin, Mescal stuffed several blankets in each of two bedrolls and then put hats on the end. Tom admired the Indian's handiwork.

"I have to admit, it sure would fool me into believing two men were sleeping there."

"If rustler come, make noise, we hear, give big surprise. We sleep over there. Close enough to hear, far enough not be seen."

The first morning they cleaned up around the cabin, washing away the signs of battle with buckets of water. Cleaning up the blood of gunshot wounds was something neither enjoyed, but it didn't bother Tom nearly as much as walking by the wooden tombstone. By its placement, it appeared that all thirteen men were hanged.

After they had the inside of the cabin cleaned, they filled the hole in the ground caused by the dynamite. By late morning everything looked much as it had before, except for the missing glass and numerous bullet holes in the wood. Tom managed to bend the hinges back in shape and then put the door back where it belonged. They spent the rest of the morning outside under the trees eating an early lunch.

"One man on guard enough. Up on lookout can see far," Mescal said.

"Reckon that's right."

"If on guard all day, get tired, not keep lookout. If take turns, stay awake, keep better lookout."

"Sounds okay to me, but what do we do the rest of the time?"

"Look around, sleep, hunt, but use bow. No gun, rustlers hear."

"Okay, I'll be on guard first. You take your bow and get us something for dinner."

Tom discovered Mescal was right, it was difficult to remain alert. His thoughts often drifted back to the hangings. At other times he would think of the ranch and Melinda, knowing she was probably worried about him and didn't like the idea of his staying an extra week. To try to keep his mind on the task, he set up a routine of walking to three different spots on the ridge where he could look out in different directions. He showed Mescal his idea, which the Indian thought was helpful. Mescal told Tom how he spotted the guard, and suggested they try to keep out of view when they went to the edge by standing behind a tree or bush.

When not on guard duty, Tom spent the time exploring. The canyon walls consisted mostly of reddish stone, and the highest point stood approximately two hundred feet high. They were slightly taller in the back of the canyon, which was the east wall. Since the entrance was to the west, and Whistler's Peak was in that direction, the sunsets from the cabin were picturesque. There was a spring that came from the south wall and a small pool of water. It was remarkably clear and sweet tasting, not filled with minerals the way some springs are. There were Maple trees, as well as some Aspen, Birch and Oak. The grass in the canyon was abundant. Tom discovered there was a lot of wildlife, particularly rabbits.

Mescal had made the suggestion to take turns because he would need the time alone to search for Caisson's secret while Tom was on guard duty. His idea that the outlaw leader might return was more than a hunch. If Jeb had told the truth, Caisson was sure to come. The question was when. Whether it would be sooner or later would likely depend on how well Caisson had hid it. There was a substantial area to search and Mescal felt a sense of urgency to find it soon. He knew they couldn't wait around the canyon forever, or probably even for more than a week. Tom would be ready to head back soon. No doubt, he would be missing Melinda and want to get back to the ranch.

Mescal searched the cabin thoroughly; even while they were cleaning it up that first morning he looked everywhere something could be hidden. While Tom was outside, the Indian checked the fireplace that had been built out of stone. He didn't see any loose rocks on it. A quick check of the walls revealed no loose logs or boards. Later, while Tom was standing guard, Mescal went back to the cabin and inspected all those things more carefully. Prying up some floorboards he looked underneath the cabin; nothing was there. He finally decided it was not in the cabin.

The canyon had many possible hiding places. Mescal thought it was likely in a cave nearby or buried beneath some easily recognizable rock or other distinguishable landmark. During the times Tom was on guard, Mescal searched. When he was on guard duty he tried to think of any place he might have missed. After two days he decided the most likely place was in one of the several caves in the canyon walls.

The next morning he approached the first cave. It was taller than a man, but only went into the canyon wall about fifteen feet. It would be a great place to get out of the rain, but the walls were smooth rock and offered no hiding place. There were no loose rocks and the floor was stone, not dirt. Mescal decided it couldn't be in there.

A second cave on the south wall was east of the spring. It was difficult to get in and only three feet across at the widest part. The floor was dirt and something could be buried there, but the cave was so small it was difficult to move around. After investigating, Mescal saw ample evidence it was full of tarantulas. There were holes about an inch in diameter in the ceiling and the walls. He thought it unlikely Caisson would have wanted to go in there.

It was the third cave he found at the back of the Canyon that seemed most likely to contain the secret. The cave went straight back into the canyon wall about ten paces, and then there was a slight bend in the cave to the right. It was just tall enough for a man to walk. After he took several more steps, Mescal discovered it split into three areas. One of those three areas was about the size of a small closet and had a dirt floor. The second was somewhat larger and had several holes in one of the walls. In one of those holes, the opening went further back than Mescal could see, but wasn't big enough to allow a man to crawl into it.

The third area was as big as a small room, perhaps eight feet by ten feet. He could tell people had been there before. Some of the dirt on the floor looked like it had been brushed smooth. Having just found this cave he was anxious to investigate it at length, but would have to wait until tomorrow morning. It was his turn on guard duty.

That night they had rabbit stew. Tom had shot the rabbit earlier in the afternoon with Mescal's bow.

"Feel good in canyon, much birds, rabbits. Not bad place. You like canyon?" Mescal asked.

"Reckon I do, but I'm beginning to think we might be wasting our time."

"Mebbe not." Mescal added after a brief pause, "If not get Caisson, rustling mebbe come back."

"I guess as much time as we spent coming down here, we ought to stick it out for awhile. You're right, though, not getting Caisson made this whole thing only half successful."

"Mebbe he still come," the old Indian said, and got himself another cup of coffee. "Nice canyon! We stay, mebbe he come back."

"Well, I have to tell you, old friend, it seems like a long shot."

The next day when Tom took over guard duty, Mescal got a shovel from the cabin and headed for the third cave. Going to the small room in the back of the cave, he dug several holes looking for soil that wasn't packed. If anything had been buried there, the dirt would be less packed. Checking every square foot, he found no soft spots. Next, he inspected the walls, but without success. The Indian leveled the dirt and stomped it down as best he could, and then spread dust on top. By the time he was done it looked much like it did before he started, but the work was time consuming. He was getting frustrated and went outside for a few moments of rest.

Before going back in to check the area that had several holes in the wall, he fashioned a long torch. Once inside the light revealed several of the holes had rough walls and floors, but it didn't appear anything of significance could be hidden there. The large hole that went far back wasn't as rough, but it had a blind spot he couldn't see and wasn't big enough to crawl in. Mescal decided if he couldn't get in, then neither could Caisson. He looked again in the last area of the third cave with no better results. He was beginning to wonder if Jeb had lied to him or if the rustler had been mistaken about what he had heard. Dejected and tired, Mescal went to relieve Tom on guard duty. He would get another chance in the afternoon. Tom noticed the dirt on the Indian's clothes.

"Looks like you've been rolling around in the dirt. You been chasing a rabbit or something?"

"Me fall."

"Don't suppose you want to tell me how."

Mescal didn't want to explain. He was quiet for a few seconds, then smiled slightly and folded his arms in front of him.

"Apache princess come from nowhere, beg me ride away with her. Me tell her, 'No can go; White man get lost in wilderness.' She take off all her clothes, want old Indian real bad. Me say to her, 'Sorry, must stay, help friend find way home.' She get angry, knock Mescal down with horse, ride horse on old Indian, get dirt on clothes. She beautiful princess, hate to make her sad."

Tom smiled and shook his head. "Sorry I asked."

In the afternoon Mescal inspected all three areas again. He decided there were only two possible hiding places in the caves. One was the cave that appeared to be filled with tarantulas. The other was the one with all the holes, particularly the hole that had the blind spot. While either was a possibility, it didn't seem likely to Mescal. He decided to look in the canyon for a conspicuous rock that Caisson might have used to hide the money under. Except while on guard duty, he spent that afternoon and all the next day looking for such a hiding place. Moving many rocks, he found nothing but undisturbed dirt. He had only two days left and didn't sleep well that night.

In the morning he continued his search, but again without luck. Late in the day he went back to the cabin feeling a sense of desperation. After tonight he would have one day left. Mescal looked all through the cabin yet again. There were lots of miscellaneous items in wooden boxes. In a room that must have been Caisson's, there was a mirror on the wall. There was also a smaller mirror on the shelf. It was round with a handle on it, much like a female would use. Caisson must be vain, Mescal thought, or perhaps he had a woman there occasionally. It was easy to tell Caisson or someone had used it a lot because the handle was rough.

Mescal went back in the main room and sat at the table. It was growing dark and he knew Tom would be coming off the canyon wall and heading back to camp. The old Indian shook his head; he was disgusted. Standing up he was about to leave the cabin, but then with a sudden impulse he looked quickly about the room. Next he rushed to the other room where the rest of the men must have slept. His mind was moving quickly; he couldn't really put the pieces together yet, at least consciously. It seemed as though the answer was there, but he couldn't quite construe what it was in a way that made sense. It was like something or someone was trying to show him, but his mind wasn't articulating the message.

Suddenly he thought of the small mirror and knew it was a missing piece of the puzzle, but he couldn't surface what the other pieces were. He looked around the room, thinking about the items he came across. One by one he rejected each as not being what he needed. Then finally he spied it. There behind a bunk was a long pole that curved on the end. It was around ten feet long. There was a metal hook fastened prominently on one end. There were also marks on the pole like something had been tied on that same end.

The old Indian had noticed the pole earlier, but couldn't figure out what it was for. It could have been used to hang things on the rafters, but nothing was hanging up there. It was something he hadn't been able to solve and had decided to put aside. Later he saw the small mirror. He had seen it several times before and thought it was also odd; perhaps that was what put the two together out on the fringes of his consciousness. It wasn't until he saw the pole again with its unexplainable hook, and then the mirror again, that he put it all together.

He remembered the cave with all the holes and the one opening with the blind spot where he could not see. If he put a torch in the hole, then tied the mirror on the end of the pole, he would be able to see the area not now visible. If something were there, then that would explain the hook. Could Caisson be that smart? Mescal sensed that he had found the answer, but he would have to wait until morning to be sure. It was growing dark and Tom would be looking for him back at camp.

"You seem a little happier tonight," Tom said.

"Go home soon."

"Thought you liked being here."

"Good canyon, but be good get home. Stay one more day."

"If you say so. I'm ready to go now."

"Why you want go back so bad?"

"Well, you know, get back to the ranch, help out, chores and things."

The old Indian knew Tom was missing Melinda. Mescal smiled and said, "You want walk out under moon with Wildfire. Kiss horse on neck?"

"Getting funny in your old age, aren't you? I suppose you want to stay here and see if that Indian princess comes back?"

Mescal laughed softly. "No, me ready go back soon. Women too much trouble."

"Yeah, it probably wasn't a princess anyway. I bet you just made that up. It was probably that female bear I saw earlier. Looked like she was in season. You probably chased after her, then rolled around in the dirt with her until she got a big smile on her face."

Mescal laughed loudly, and then said, "If Mescal did, bear still be moaning."

Tom nearly fell to the ground laughing. He laughed harder than he had for a long time. "Well, I hope she doesn't come into camp tonight thinking I might be interested too."

"You mebbe not want go back to ranch. Stay here with bear."

Tom shook his head, but had no more to add to this conversation. He would be glad to go home, having already seen everything he wanted to explore. With nothing else to do he had spent the last several days looking for game and practicing with Mescal's bow. He had improved his aim significantly.

That night as Tom was trying to go to sleep, he reflected on what had happened since they arrived. The first few days they had both been in good spirits, hoping to catch Caisson. Mescal in particular had been enthusiastic, but after the first several days the old Indian had become quiet like his mind was a thousand miles away. Tom had decided to give him the time he needed and leave him alone. It was hard to say what was troubling his friend. Both had been through a lot lately. The posse had lost three men and killed a large number of rustlers. Mescal had the right to do some soul searching—or whatever it was he needed to do. Suddenly tonight, Mescal's spirits were up and he was much more talkative.

The next morning Mescal was up before light and had their breakfast ready. "You take first watch? Me want go for walk."

"Fine with me. Take your time."

Tom didn't really care. It was their last day and he didn't know whether to be glad the week was over or sad that they had waited a whole week on Caisson and he didn't show. For Tom it was just another long day. He didn't see Mescal again until it was his shift for the morning. When Tom was off duty, he just napped. When he came back to relieve Mescal, the old Indian was quickly off. Tom noticed he was in an even better mood than last night.

Mescal's time for guard duty came and he didn't show up. It was another hour before he finally arrived. Tom was curious, but didn't say anything. Another hour meant nothing; he was just going to lie down under a tree and sleep anyway.

That evening Mescal was enthusiastic. He had packed several saddlebags to take back on the two extra horses, as well as some bags of goods. There were pots and pans, a couple of lanterns, six canteens, three water flasks, and a couple bags of other stuff in addition to the saddlebags. It was everything the two horses could carry.

"Did you turn into a packrat last night?" Tom asked.

"Good stuff, no reason leave, horses can carry."

"Guess so, but what'll we do with it?"

"When have own place some day, come in handy."

"Reckon that's so."

Tom would like to have a ranch too, but that would take a lot more money than they had now. With the cattle they did have a start, and he and Mescal had saved more money since then. Tom also still had much of the money he had put aside while in Kansas. Even so, they needed several more years to have enough to try starting their own ranch. He thought Melinda was the only one who wanted a place more than he did. Tom had told Mescal earlier that when he and Melinda did get a ranch they wanted him to not only be a partner, but also to live with them. The old Indian had been pleased but had not mentioned the subject since. On this night he talked about a ranch a great deal. Tom was a little curious why the Indian brought it up now, but didn't ask. He just wanted to get home.

One thing that had worried Mescal earlier was what Caisson would do when he got back and discovered his secret treasure was gone. If he came back soon, he would follow their trail with a vengeance. Most people can't track far. Once horses have gone on a well-traveled road and their hoof prints are covered by other tracks, it takes a pretty good tracker to pick them up again. On the other hand, Caisson knew how to find Emmett's ranch so it was important he not know that they took it. After Mescal had removed Caisson's money, he thought better of it and returned part of what he had found. He returned enough to hide the fact the rest was gone unless substantial effort was taken.

If Caisson were just checking, he wouldn't notice the rest wasn't there. If he did discover the loss, since some was left to disguise the absence of the rest, he would likely suspect one of his own men was the culprit. Mescal reasoned that Caisson would think only someone in his gang would leave some of it behind, trying to hide the fact it had been discovered. With the possible danger minimized, the old Indian was pleased. If he could get back to the ranch with everything intact, their future would look a lot brighter.

The next morning they were up early and headed out of the canyon. They took the easy way out, following the same trail the rustlers had used coming and going. While there was some danger in taking that route, they both decided it was minimal and didn't justify taking the longer and tougher trail they had used to reach the hideout. After making it back to the road they headed toward White Cloud. They passed by another rider heading away from town. Neither Tom nor Mescal recognized him. Whoever it was seemed to pay no attention to them.

They circled White Cloud as before and then traveled to Indian Waters and made camp. Mescal took care of the horses, unloading all the junk he had put on that morning. While eating they decided to take shifts on guard duty that night because of the one rider they had seen. Caisson could still be around somewhere and Indian Waters was often used as a campsite.

The next day they hit the trail and made good time. Mescal seemed more wary than usual and had already checked once to see if they were being followed. Later, he checked a second time.

"Do you think somebody might be on our trail?"

"Mebbe Caisson."

"Clear out here?"

Mescal shrugged his shoulders. "Mebbe not."

"I wouldn't think so."

Later when they had nearly finished crossing the desert, Mescal started to feel safer. After they reached the other side, they stopped to rest the horses. Mescal had gone up on a small peak to check for followers again, and then returned to where Tom sat on his horse waiting.

"Bout give up on Caisson," Mescal said.

"I suspect we've seen the last of him."

Tom didn't think Caisson would hurry after them, or could even follow them at this point. For some reason Mescal seemed worried, or maybe it was just his cautious nature. They traveled on and then made camp where they had before. Mescal had ridden over to Death Rock. Apparently Jake and Emmett had taken Jeb, or let him go, because there was no sign of him there. The Indian returned and found Tom was just leaving for the little pool in the stream. After taking his bath he came back and Mescal had supper ready. They ate and then Mescal went for his bath. Each had their own dreams as they sat quietly around the campfire that night. It was hard for Mescal not to smile.

TWENTY- FIVE

Ben Caisson had stayed in White Cloud waiting for his brother to return from a trip to St. George. Matt was a day late; otherwise he and Ben would have been at the hideout when the posse attacked. Ben's brother finally rode in. They were standing in front of the saloon and were about to head to the hideout when eight of their men came into White Cloud. Matt saw them first.

"Look, Ben! It's Pete and some of the men. They're all shot up."

"What the hell happened?" Ben asked, as they pulled up.

"Posse hit us at the hideout," Pete replied. "Musta been at least thirty men."

"Were the guards asleep?" Ben asked in anger. The outlaw leader was surprised that a posse could find the gang in that canyon. He considered it the best hideout he ever had.

"It was too early in the mornin, boss," Pete replied, shaking his head and getting off his horse. "We hadn't even sent the guards up yet. They hit us before daybreak. It was that Indian that led 'em in there, I tell you. You know the one I mean; they call him the Tracker, the Gunman and the Tracker. Ain't nobody else could sneak in on us like that."

"Oh shit! Those are the two you were worried about," Matt said to Ben.

Ben was puzzled when he heard Tom Colt and the Indian were with the posse. He had heard about them and had left Emmett Bailey's ranch alone just because of their reputation. Now they had attacked him anyway.

"Why would the Gunman and the Tracker be coming down here?" Ben yelled to no one in particular.

"I dunno, boss, but the man runnin the show called hisself Jake Evans," Pete replied.

"Damn, he's their neighbor," Ben said. "Some of the men hit his ranch a few weeks ago. Kessler and Johnson found one man hung and the others buried. That damn Indian must have tracked them back here."

"Those idiots! They should've been more careful," Matt interjected.

"Well, they're dead now," Pete said. "Both of 'em took a bullet at the hideout."

"Shit for luck. Hell, let's go inside," Ben said angrily.

They all went into the saloon and Ben sent the owner out so they could talk. Pete proceeded to tell Ben how they held them off at first.

"We thought we was doing okay and then all hell broke loose. That damn Indian tied dynamite to an arrow and blasted the door. Then that there rancher, that Jake Evans, he threatened to have an arrow with dynamite shot in through a window and kill us all."

"Them sonsabitches," Matt said.

"Those lousy bastards used dynamite on us, huh? Did you see that Gunman, that Tom Colt?" Ben asked.

"Don't know that I spotted him in particular, but we was sure losin men, boss," Pete replied. "After they threatened to blow us up if we didn't surrender, we made a run for the horses. I figured we'd all be hung if we didn't. We lost more men than I thought we was a gonna, though. Musta been that damn Gunman."

"I saw him, boss, that Colt fellar, saw that Indian too," Lefty added. "Recognized 'em from when I seen 'em both on the Big Canyon ranch. That Indian just about blew us all to hell as we was ridin out. Clark was right behind me and that damn dynamite blew him clean off his horse."

Ben was angry but quickly got his emotions under control. He realized these were the last of his men and that he needed them.

"You did right, Pete. Doesn't sound like you had much choice. You're right; those miserable asshole ranchers probably would've hanged you all, like they was the damn law or something. At least some of you got out. I would've done the same as you did."

The men nodded agreeably with Ben's statement. Lefty was still bleeding from his leg, but he believed in Pete and offered his opinion.

"Pete done good, boss, and we shot a bunch of them bastards, you can bet."

"We ought to kill all them sonsabitches," Matt stated.

"You'd be proud of me, boss," Buck told Ben. "After we got outta there, I went back to the edge of the canyon and plugged one of the men they had up on the wall. I saw him fall."

"Good job, Buck, and you too, Pete." Ben kept the momentum going. "Hell, you men did as well as I could've. Those of you that are wounded need to hold up a while longer. I'll take you out to another hideout Matt and I found and give you all time to heal. Matt, you know the cabin I'm talkin about. You and Harry get some grub, bullets and bandages and catch up with us."

"Come on, men." With a wave of his hand Ben motioned for the rest to follow. He led them outside and could tell the oldest man, Dub, needed help getting on his horse. "Let me help you, Dub," Ben offered. Nobody knew how he got a name like Dub, and when anybody asked he would stroke his graying whiskers and say, "Dubbed if I know." Then Ben helped the young rider, Sammy. The youngster was overly confident and was the last person Ben would want to sit and talk to, but he overlooked the shortcomings of the cowboy. He would need Sammy because he was quick with a gun.

Matt and Harry followed Ben's lead and helped the other wounded men get on their horses. After Ben mounted up, he turned his horse and looked at each one of the riders. Then he got a proud and stern look on his face and said, "Now, let's ride, men." Ben's voice was loud and strong; he felt it was important to have his men see him in control, knowing what to do and when. He wanted them to see this loss as just a temporary setback.

Because of the large number of men in the posse—Pete said there were about thirty—Ben wanted to get out of town quickly. Several of the men had bullet holes so he rode at an easy gait. He glanced back now and then to check on the wounded. When he looked at Sammy, the young man returned the gaze. Ben nodded at him. After what they had been through, the men needed reassurance. It was a hard ride to the new hideout for wounded men, but they made it with everyone still in the saddle. The cabin wasn't as big or nice as the old hideout, but it would have to do. The five men would need time to recover.

The outlaw leader was down to so few men he needed every rider, and would have to get more in the meantime. Arriving at the cabin he helped the men get settled inside, then he and Pete went to take care of the horses. Ben told Zeke to start a fire and boil water so they could clean the wounds. An hour later Matt and Harry brought food, bandages, ammunition and other supplies. Remembering that the posse had the Indian to track them, Ben was concerned they might follow.

"Matt, you stay long enough to get these men bandaged and whatever else they need. I'll take the rest and go set up an ambush in the pass. When you're done here, come out and join us. We'll need every gun we've got to hold off that posse. Pete, how many men did you say they had?"

"Well, I reckon we shot at least ten or twelve. Guess there'd be about twenty left."

"Okay, let's take plenty of ammunition. Wish I had some dynamite; I'd give 'em a taste of their own medicine."

Ben, Pete, Harry and Zeke went to the pass. It was a good place for an ambush and they would be able to do a lot of damage to the posse, at least for awhile. Matt joined them later. Ben kept his brother close by just in case the posse did come. He wanted to be able to ride out with Matt if things started looking hopeless. By nightfall the posse still hadn't come.

"I wish if they was a comin they'd hurry up and get here," Matt said.

"If they have twenty men left, I'd just as soon they didn't show up. But if they do and we kill enough of 'em, the rest won't be in any hurry to try again. There's so many though, we'd have to get lucky just to stop 'em."

"We going to stay out here all night?"

"Hell, I don't know, Matt. That's a good question though. Go get Pete and we'll talk about it."

After discussing with Matt and Pete, Ben decided they would sleep out in the rocks that night. He told Harry to go back and cook some food and get their bedrolls. Two men would be awake at all times just in case the posse tried to sneak in during the night.

The next morning they waited in the rocks. Harry went to the cabin to get them breakfast. They couldn't make a fire at the pass because the smoke would alert the posse. A little after noon, Ben sent Harry back to the cabin for more food. They waited, poised for a battle the rest of that day, but no one came. That night Ben left Pete and Harry at the pass. They were to send one man back to the cabin to wake the other two men halfway through the night.

The following day Ben called the men together. "I need somebody to ride into White Cloud and see what the posse is up to."

There was a long period of silence. Matt finally spoke up. "I reckon I could go."

"No, Matt, too many people know you. I need one of you other men to go and see if that damn posse headed back north."

Everyone remained quiet. Finally, Ben said, "Pete, you got the most experience at this sort of thing. Go in and find out what happened to them. If they're still there, just come on back, but make certain you can't be followed."

"Okay, boss!" Pete thought going to White Cloud was risky, but didn't want to argue with Ben. Putting on his spare shirt, he asked Matt if he could borrow his horse. Pete didn't want the posse to recognize him. Riding toward White Cloud, he saw a lot of tracks at the cutoff heading for town. While talking to the saloon owner he discovered the posse had been through two days earlier. They had arrived in town a few hours after the gang had departed. The bartender said the posse only stayed long enough to eat and get supplies. He assured Pete that nobody in town said anything to the posse about Ben and his gang. Pete believed him because the posse hadn't come after them.

Pete learned as much as he could in town. According to the store clerk, one of the men said they had destroyed Caisson's gang. The old gent with white hair sitting in front of the store said the posse claimed to have lost only three men. Pete learned there were eight men in the posse that came to White Cloud. There had to be more than that, Pete thought. He figured the others must still be around looking for them. Based on the tracks headed out of town, this part of the posse had headed back home. Pete had no idea where the rest were, but wanted to get back and tell Ben what he had found out. He decided not to repeat what the old man said about only three men in the posse being killed.

After hearing what Pete had found out, Ben decided to keep men at the pass. Two men stayed during the night, working in shifts. Another day came and went with no sign of the posse. While taking his turn waiting in the rocks, Ben tried to decide whether to give up rustling or try to rebuild the gang. He had stored away enough money to live in affluence for the rest of his life. It was the dream he had worked so hard to accomplish for these many years. When things went bad in Arizona, he and Matt had moved his treasure to Utah. First the two of them had ridden up alone and found the canyon, then they brought up the loot and hid it.

After the fourth day Ben made his decision and told the men he was going to Arizona to recruit more men. Matt and the others were to stay and guard the pass during the day, and give the wounded time to heal. Leaving Matt in charge, Ben rode out the next morning.

A few days later Matt sent Zeke to White Cloud to get additional supplies. They were about out of food and Matt wanted some whiskey to help placate the men. Zeke had worn a plaid shirt during the shootout, but today he wore a plain blue denim. As he was returning from White Cloud with the supplies, he rode right by the Gunman and the Tracker going in the opposite direction with two packhorses. After going another mile up the road, he rode his horse behind some trees. He waited almost an hour to see if they had recognized him and turned to follow, but they did not come. Finally, he headed on to the hideout and told Matt about seeing the two men.

"Are you sure it was them?" Matt asked.

"I'm sure." Zeke was changing back into his plaid shirt and gave the blue denim back to Lefty. "One of 'em was an Indian on a Paint, and the other a White man on an Appaloosa. They sure fit the description Lefty gave. I'm tellin you, Matt, it was them."

"Maybe the others left and those two stayed to look for us," Pete said.

"Yeah, could be. I wonder why they had two packhorses?" Matt asked, more as a question to himself.

"I don't know. Sure had a lot of stuff on 'em though," Zeke replied.

Matt wondered for a second if they had somehow found Ben's secret. He thought silently to himself, "Surely not, it's too well hid. But if they did I've got to catch 'em." Matt also remembered how angry Ben was about Tom Colt and the Indian coming down and attacking the hideout. "Big Brother would sure be proud if I could kill those two," he thought to himself. Matt knew if he was to have any chance of following them, he would have to leave right away.

"Do you think we can catch 'em?" Matt asked Pete.

"Sure, if we can pick up their tracks on the other side of White Cloud."

"That settles it." Matt smiled as he thought about how happy Ben would be. He believed the men would respect him more as well. "Okay, men, let's get ready to ride. Pete, you and Harry get the horses. Zeke, get some food packed. Let's hurry, men." Just before going out the door he turned to the wounded men. "The rest of you stay in the cabin and wait. If Ben comes back before we do, tell him we'll be bringing back two bodies crost their saddles. The Gunman and the Tracker won't be causing us any more trouble."

"Hadn't you better wait until Ben gets back?" Sammy asked.

Matt scowled and shook his head. "If we leave now we can overtake them. If we wait, we get nothing."

Minutes later the four men rode off. Matt pushed the horses hard, but had to stop well short of Indian Waters that night. Their horses were exhausted and needed the rest. They camped on the trail and got an early start the next morning, reaching Indian Waters just before noon. Pete said it was clear that two men had stayed there last night. Taking out after them, they were able to follow their tracks easily in the desert. Matt knew they had to hurry. Once the Gunman and the Tracker got across the desert and into the rocky hills on the other side, it would be difficult to follow them.

By the time they crossed the desert it was getting dark and they stopped for the night. They had pushed the horses to their limit and the desert heat nearly did them in. The next morning Matt was tired and his head ached, but as soon as they finished eating they mounted up and pushed on. He knew the men were exhausted and so were the horses, but he wanted to catch up with the two riders today. It wasn't long before they found where the Gunman and the Tracker had camped last night. Pete thought they were still a couple of hours ahead. The four took after them, trying to close the distance. When they got closer, Matt wanted to slow up and approach more carefully. He was now confident they would catch up with them later today.

Mescal was finally feeling safe. Last night they had both slept heavily. The next morning they took their time, let the horses rest and got a late start. They traveled slowly, as there was no particular hurry. After they had climbed a pass between two large peaks, Mescal went up on high ground to look back. It was the first time that day he bothered to check their back-trail. He had almost decided not to make the effort, but it was his nature to be careful.

To his surprise, Mescal saw a small cloud of dust in the distance. It was faint and far away, but visible to the keen eyes of the old Indian. Getting out the telescope they used when hunting cougar, he saw four riders in a big hurry. Mescal felt a sense of relief that he had taken the precaution of checking. He hadn't thought Caisson's men could follow this far, although it might not be them. Continuing to look in the telescope, he recognized one of the men that had escaped from Caisson's hideout. The plaid shirt stood out even at a long distance.

Mescal kicked the Paint and returned to Tom in a hurry. "Caisson's men coming," he said. They hid the mounts behind some rocks and went back to prepare for the rustlers. Mescal had spotted them well in advance, giving him and Tom time to come up with a quick plan. Locating two well-positioned trees, Mescal remembered a trick his Chief, Victorio, had used on pursuing soldiers. They worked hurriedly with the rope; it took several minutes to put it all together. They discussed strategy for a few seconds, and then Mescal held his hand up to his ear. Several seconds later Tom could hear the sound of horses approaching. They quickly took their positions.

When the four men came around the bend, Tom recognized one of them from the shootout. Just as they reached the chosen spot, Mescal pulled on the rope that released a knot and triggered the surprise. A rope sprang up directly in front of the riders between the two trees. Twigs, tin cups and rags were tied to the rope and flew above the rope and then quickly down. The sudden appearance of an obstruction scared the horses. The two in front slid to a stop and then reared on their hind legs. The horses in back nearly ran into the two in front. The men were occupied trying to remain mounted and attempting to regain control.

"Put up your hands," Tom yelled as he stepped from behind a rock with his gun leveled.

"What the hell?" Matt exclaimed in shock.

Tom was behind them on the right side of the trail. As they turned to face him, Pete and Harry went for their guns; Tom shot the two and quickly moved back behind the rock. Harry fell dead; Pete slouched over his saddle. Matt Caisson was still trying to get his horse under control. The final rider, Zeke, was nearest the barricade. He drew and fired, hitting the rock Tom was behind.

Mescal was on the other side of the trail opposite Tom. When he saw Tom go behind the rock, he stepped out and shot the man in the plaid shirt. Mescal just as rapidly started moving back behind the tree. Matt drew his gun and shot Mescal in the arm, the only part of the Indian's body not protected by the tree when he fired.

Tom once again came from behind the rock and shot Matt before he had time to turn. The only brother of Ben Caisson grabbed his side and then raised his gun to fire at Tom. He never got the shot off. A second bullet hit him between the eyes and he fell from his horse. Pete was still slouched in his saddle, but now brought up his gun to shoot at Tom. He was too slow. Tom and Mescal shot at the same time and Pete was dead before he hit the ground.

Mescal walked out and checked each of the men to see if any were alive. They were not. There were only four left in Caisson's gang now, and Ben Caisson could be one of these four dead men. Neither Tom nor Mescal knew what he looked like.

The Indian's left arm hung limp. The bullet had gone through and there was no apparent damage to the bone. Tom searched the rustlers' saddlebags and found some bandages. Mescal sat while Tom patched him up, and pondered how fortunate they were to spot the men. If the four had been more careful, or had come up on them in the desert, it could have been a tough situation.

Mescal reflected on what had led him to go back and check. The rustlers had been foolish to be riding so fast; the dust was what caught his eye. Mescal thought it could just be luck to come to the high place at the right time to spot them, and then again maybe it was more than luck; perhaps it was a destiny of sorts.

Tom had spoken of such things to him and Melinda late one afternoon at her secret spot. The three of them were sitting on the big flat rock. Tom was looking off into the distance and telling them about Josh, and the profound impact the man had on his view of the world. Melinda mentioned that perhaps Josh had been sent as a divine messenger. She reminded Tom that when she had nursed him back to health, she had told him then that it was a miracle they had found him. Tom had looked at her, and then his gaze had returned to the small white clouds low on the horizon. He had finally nodded, and then said what remained unanswered for him was why all that had happened. If Josh were a messenger, and their finding him when he had been shot was a miracle, what was the reason? Why had he been saved? It was a quality of Tom's that Mescal admired deeply. Tom obviously believed in the powers of the Great One, and now lived for the purpose of fulfilling his destiny.

As Mescal recalled the gunfight with the four men, he thought Tom's suggestion to shoot and hide had worked well, except he had moved a little too slow and the one rustler had been too fast. Mescal knew Jake and Emmett would be pleased, especially if one of the four dead men were Caisson. If Ben wasn't among them, there was still the concern that he might come for his treasure. But no, Mescal remembered, there wasn't any way the outlaw leader would know who had taken it. He smiled at the thought of Caisson chasing off after his own men. The old Indian felt his shoulders rise a little in spite of the pain from the wound. He believed Caisson was to be forgotten now.

Two days later they rode toward the ranch house. Emmett came out to see them approaching with a string of six horses in tow. Four of the horses carried bodies draped over the saddles. Tom and Mescal had been close enough to the ranch that they decided to bring along the dead men just in case one of them was Ben Caisson.

Melinda and Beth came out on the porch. Five cowboys working out in the corral hurried up to the house. While Emmett began talking to Tom, several of the men went to inspect the four bodies. Willie called out to Emmett, "Caisson's brother Matt." One of the other cowboys went hurriedly to the horse and confirmed the news. Emmett patted Tom on the shoulder. He looked for Mescal but saw that the old Indian was already over by the barn.

Mescal led his horse and the two packhorses inside. While the men were all excited about identifying one of the rustlers, the old Indian carefully hid several saddlebags where they wouldn't be found until he could move them. The rest of the goods he piled in plain sight next to a stable. When he walked back and joined the men, Emmett and Willie were talking to Tom.

"Did any of them get away?" Emmett asked.

"Only the four of them came up from behind," Tom replied. "They seemed to be tracking us. Not sure what happened to Ben Caisson or the other three. I guess these four followed us and meant to even the score some."

"You fellows done shot Matt Caisson, Ben's brother," Willie announced to Mescal.

"You and Tom did good," Emmett added. "I reckon Ben Caisson will find some other range to ride."

While the rest of the men talked to Tom about their stay in the canyon and the gun battle with the four rustlers, Melinda took Mescal into the house so she could treat his wound. She and Beth cleansed Mescal's arm and put on new bandages. He was glad to have some time away from the men. Going over the details of a gun battle was not something in which he took great joy. He had never been the type to do a brave deed and want to tell about it. Mescal knew Tom didn't particularly care for the task either, but the cowboys were curious and would pester him until he had told the story. The old Indian thought it was far smarter to let these women fuss over him. He closed his eyes and left himself in their kind and gentle hands.

Emmett sent a rider over to Jake with the news, and then told Willie to take Caisson's brother and the other three bodies into town the next day. Knowing there was a bounty on Matt Caisson, he told Willie to have the sheriff send the reward money to Tom and Mescal.

The next morning before daylight, and well before anyone else was up, Mescal, wound and all, had saddled up his horse and ridden out. It was after breakfast when he returned. Mescal smiled as he walked back to the cabin. Tom had gotten a plate of food for him and it was on the table. The old Indian sat silently and ate. He never did say where he went. Tom noticed Mescal seemed happy all day. He was probably just glad it was over and they could get back to doing the things they liked to do.

Mescal wondered how long he should keep the secret from his friend, and finally decided he would tell him sometime during the winter. Tom could decide when to tell Melinda. Next spring, Melinda and Tom could get married and have their ranch and home.

TWENTY- SIX

When the rope barricade sprang up in front of their horses, Matt and the other men hardly knew what hit them. Matt heard some shots, saw the Indian, pulled his gun and fired. Matt was nearly as quick as his brother Ben. Turning he saw a man with a gun. Matt tried to move his gun toward him, but doom pervaded his body as he realized it was the Gunman. He saw fire explode from the man's gun barrel.

In the following days the five men at the hideout, recovering from their wounds, wondered what had happened to Matt and the others. Buck rode into town to get supplies, hoping to find out something. He talked to the bartender and the store clerk, but discovered nothing. Afraid something had gone wrong, he hoped Matt wasn't dead. Ben loved his brother dearly and would take his death hard.

A week later Ben Caisson returned with six additional men for the gang; he was proud of being able to find new riders so quickly. Lefty, Buck and the others walked out on the porch as Ben rode up.

"This here's Jack Stanton and his men," Ben said, smiling as he dismounted. "They'll be joining us."

"Howdy! Glad to meet you fellas," Jack said.

All of the men began shaking hands and telling each other their names.

"Where's Matt?" Ben asked.

He noticed the men fell silent, and became concerned at the look on their faces.

"Where's Matt?" he repeated, louder than before.

"Matt and the others went after Tom Colt and the Indian," Buck said reluctantly.

"What? They shouldn't have done that," Ben blurted out. "Tell me what happened, Buck."

"Matt sent Zeke into town to get supplies, and Zeke spotted Colt and the Indian. When Matt heard, he really wanted to go after 'em. We tried to talk him out of it, but he...well, he sorta...was determined."

"How long ago did they go after them?"

"I guess it's been a little over a week," Buck said quietly.

"A week? Shit!"

Ben had always looked after his younger brother; Matt was more like a son to him. The outlaw leader was angry, but mostly at himself. Matt had often complained to him about living under the shadow of his older brother. Remembering there were six new men present, Ben kept his emotions under control. He realized Matt was probably dead, but held out hope that he wasn't.

"Buck, tomorrow morning you ride into White Cloud and see what you can find out. Lefty, you and Sammy go to St. George."

Buck came back the following afternoon with no new information. Lefty and Sammy rode in three days later. Ben went outside as they rode up to the cabin.

"What did you find out?"

"The story is that Matt and the others were brought into a little town up north," Lefty said in a somber tone. "I couldn't find out the name of the town. Nobody seemed to know."

"So they were captured?" Ben asked hopefully.

"Sorry to have to be the one to tell you, boss. All four are dead. The fellow we talked to said that Tom Colt and his Indian friend collected the reward on Matt. Sure am sorry, boss."

Ben was angry; he couldn't look at his men. Walking away to be by himself, he wanted to think it through for awhile. He wished now that he had quit two weeks ago and took Matt with him. They had all the money they would ever need. Ben got on his horse and rode out to the pass, sitting where he and Matt had waited in the rocks to ambush the posse. After much contemplation he decided there was no sense in second-guessing himself. It wouldn't help Matt to question his earlier decision. He had to deal with the fact that Matt was dead. Tom Colt had killed him. Perhaps the Indian had killed him; which of the two didn't really matter. He blamed the man known as the Gunman. Ben wasn't the type to weep; instead he turned his sorrow into anger. He cursed Tom Colt, and then he swore that he would kill him.

The outlaw leader decided he had to avenge Matt. Then he would leave Utah and live the life of luxury in New Orleans, surround himself with beautiful women, good food and fine whiskey. It was Tom Colt and the Indian that led the posse into his hideout and nearly destroyed his gang. Now Colt and his partner had killed Matt and collected the bounty. Ben couldn't let that go; he wouldn't be able to ride away and enjoy the money while Tom Colt still lived. He had to have revenge.

The next day Ben started out for St. George, which was the nearest town with a telegraph. When he got there he tried to find out more about Matt, but was careful lest someone get suspicious. Finally he confirmed the story Lefty had told him, and he sent a telegram. Ben was sending for a man he met in Arizona. While recruiting the six men that had returned with him, he had met the most well known gunman in the Southwest. His name was Bart Sanders. Curtis Wilson, a man who had ridden with Ben years before, introduced him to the famous gunman. Ben had bought the gunslinger a drink and tried to recruit him for his gang, without luck. He couldn't interest the man.

Sanders had told Ben, "Don't do rustling. I'm a gunfighter, a very expensive gunfighter."

Ben sent Curtis Wilson the telegram. He had told Curtis earlier about Tom Colt and the Indian causing him so much trouble. Ben's telegram read: "NEED ASSISTANCE WITH A COLT CAUSING PROBLEM. CONTACT FRIEND. HAVE HIM SEND AMOUNT OF REQUIRED FEE." Ben knew Curtis would understand and get the message to Bart.

The telegram that came back was directly from Bart Sanders. The figure it included was excessive, the most Ben had ever heard for one man. He knew the price was ridiculous. It was way too much to pay for having one man killed, but the more Ben thought about it the more he decided the cost didn't matter. He could pay that much and many times more. Ben sent a telegram back to Bart Sanders with a short message: "COME TO WHITE CLOUD. THE JOB IS YOURS."

Ben knew his men would be impressed. Even if Sanders were there for only one task, he would ride with them and seem like part of the gang until it was over. It would help Ben reestablish his importance in the eyes of the men, and in the eyes of his foe. If people learned Bart Sanders rode with Ben Caisson's gang, it would put fear in their hearts.

Ben left St. George, but before riding back to join his men, he went up to the old hideout. He had hidden a lot of loot in the canyon and would need a portion of it for Sanders and the six men he brought up from Arizona. Ben dug up three bags he had buried near a tree back by the corral. He could have hidden it in a more secure place, but thought it better not to go where the big loot was stored any more than necessary. Each trip to a pile of hidden loot put it at risk.

As he passed the graves of his men, he saw the mocking wood tombstone, "Hung Rustlers." Ben thought about putting it in front of the three graves over by the south canyon wall, but decided against it. He didn't want to leave any sign that he or his gang had been there. Going near the entrance to the cave he checked to see if there were any footprints in it. There were not. Then he walked around the canyon floor for awhile and saw where two men had camped, apparently waiting for him and his men. It must have been Colt and the Indian. Ben was glad he had waited. As he thought back, the delay in returning was mostly luck. He needed to recruit more men in Arizona; otherwise, he probably would have come to the canyon earlier, and walked right into an ambush. Ben finished with his inspection, and concluded that his secret was safe. Walking to get his horse he rode back to rejoin his men.

Ben told them that Bart Sanders was coming and their eyes went wide. They talked about little else in the days that followed. Sanders' telegram read: "BE THERE IN FIVE DAYS." The fifth day passed and nobody showed. Ben decided to send Buck into White Cloud again tomorrow. If Sanders didn't come soon, Ben would have to send someone to St. George to see if there was another telegram from

Bart. Ben began to have doubts whether the famous gunfighter would come to this little town in Utah, but he couldn't show those concerns to his men. He had to appear confident, and he did.

Buck came back the next day still with no news of Sanders. "Maybe he changed his mind, boss."

"He'll come," Ben said confidently.

The next day passed slowly and Ben spent a great deal of time outside alone. Whenever he was with the men he made it a point to look and act like he wasn't worried. Just before dark, Buck rode in proudly with a young man riding next to him. Ben walked outside on the porch followed by all of his men. Sanders rode the most beautiful black horse and the best looking saddle the men had ever laid eyes on. They had never seen so much inlaid silver.

"Mr. Sanders, you probably remember me; I'm Ben Caisson."

The gunfighter got down off his horse and walked slowly in the general direction of Ben. Bart looked at the other men first who had gathered outside. Some were on the porch and several were on the ground nearby. He made eye contact with each one and then walked up and shook Ben's hand.

"Name is Bart; good to see you again."

"Glad you made it. We were getting a little worried about you."

"Sorry I'm late. Got delayed by a young senorita down in Flagstaff."

The men laughed. Ben could tell they were impressed with Bart. He had an air of quiet confidence, not cockiness, just an aura that men noticed and respected. Sanders' brown eyes were dark and appeared hard as steel. Lefty felt a chill go up his spine when Bart looked at him. The gunfighter's gaze was like nothing he had ever experienced and it unnerved him.

"Nice horse you got there, Bart," Ben said.

The gunman turned to look at his horse. He was decidedly proud of him and the saddle as well. There wasn't a better horse in Arizona. If there were, he would have bought him. Bart had seen the horse in Santa Fe being ridden by a cowboy he had never met. The man wanted too much for the animal, but it was worth it to Bart. He made a lot of money in his business. Often ranchers hired him just to put a scare in somebody. He could make a good salary without firing a shot.

"Somebody's got a nice horse over there," Bart said, motioning toward a gray Arabian.

"That would be mine," Ben replied.

"Well, you got a fine animal, Mr. Caisson."

"Come on in, supper is about ready." Ben liked Bart noticing his horse.

It was a new experience for the men. Ben Caisson was well known as an outlaw leader, but not like Bart Sanders. The gunman was famous because he wielded life and death in his holster. It was that power the men respected, or perhaps feared. A gunfighter was a man willing to face another gunman in the middle of the street with only one walking away. A man had to be confident to take on a vocation of such deadly consequence. Whether they liked all of Bart's characteristics or not, they respected his willingness to stare calmly into the face of death.

Most men wouldn't draw against a man like Sanders; they knew better. Ben realized there was a possibility Tom Colt wouldn't either. Colt was a ranch cowhand who happened to be fast with a gun. He had killed a lot of rustlers, but he hadn't killed just to kill. While waiting on Bart to arrive, Ben had spent a lot of time figuring out a plan that would force Colt to go against his new gunslinger.

Late that night Ben took Bart out alone and explained his plan to him. Bart didn't care for part of it and let the gang leader know he would wait until he was needed. Ben agreed. He didn't really have an option; Bart Sanders could pretty much decide for himself. That night Ben let the men know his strategy, then they got out a bottle of whiskey and drank a toast to Tom Colt's death. The next morning, they packed up their gear and headed for Emmett Bailey's ranch. It would take them four or five days.

As Caisson's men rode with Bart Sanders, they couldn't help but look at him now and then. Each of the men felt a little more lethal. They were part of a gang that would be feared by any man they came across. This was an experience they would tell several times in the future to anyone who would listen. Each of the men reacted to the gunfighter a little differently, but each felt proud to be with him. His horse also attracted a lot of attention. Every cowboy loved a fine horse, and this was the best looking horseflesh any of them had ever seen.

When they camped several nights later, young Sammy led Ben away from the others and told him, "I've decided to leave the gang."

"What in the hell for?" Caisson nearly yelled at the young rider. He needed all the men he had and Sammy was good with a gun.

Sammy looked at the ground and said, "Well, Ben, it's kind of personal."

"Kind of personal my ass. You know our plans. I've got the fastest gun around in Bart Sanders riding with me, and we mean to kill a man. Now you're telling me you want to leave the gang, but won't tell me why. You better have a damn good reason. Maybe you were planning to go warn this Colt fellow."

"Oh hell, Ben, I wouldn't do that."

"And how do I know that?"

Sammy realized Ben wasn't going to let him ride away unless he told him, and so he did.

"For a half-breed squaw?" Caisson yelled. Ben glared at Sammy, and then walked disgustedly back to his men leaving the young man alone.

"What's the matter, boss?" Buck asked.

"That stupid kid wants to go get that squaw you guys saw last month. You and Lefty saw her too, didn't ya?"

Buck and Lefty both nodded. "She sure was purty," Buck said.

"Sammy was crazy over her," Lefty added. "He about left then."

Bart overheard the discussion and glanced at the young rider. He thought Sammy looked like a lovesick pup. "We don't need him," the gunslinger interjected. "If he doesn't want to be here, you're better off without him. Besides, I can handle Tom Colt."

Ben was impressed once again with the man's voice and his sense of control. He didn't want to go against Bart. The outlaw leader walked over and told the youngster he could go. Ben briefly tried to talk him out of it again, but Sammy wasn't listening anymore. The young rider mounted up and rode away.

Later that day they arrived at Butcher's Pass and split into two groups. The six men from Arizona would rustle a fair size herd of

Bailey's and head to the east. Ben told them it might take a day or two for Bailey's men to realize someone was taking his cattle. He cautioned Stanton to have one man hang back and watch their trail. When he saw Bailey and his men coming he could catch up with the rest, and then they could hightail it for the hills. When they were sure the posse wasn't following them, they were to work their way back to the hideout and wait for Ben and the others.

In the meantime, Ben and his group would camp close to the ranch and wait. Buck would find a place to spy on the ranch house and go back and get Caisson and the others when Bailey and his cowboys went after the herd. When the place was nearly vacated, the men with Caisson would go to the ranch. It was a good plan, thought Bart, but he didn't want any part of going to the house. Caisson and the five remaining men would take care of it.

In the morning the Arizona cowboys headed out. Jack Stanton was in charge. As they rode, Bob Stash pulled his horse alongside Jack's.

"Why go to so much trouble just to kill one man?" Bob asked.

"Kinda crazy, ain't it?"

"Sure is. We won't get the cattle, and there's no money in killing a man with no bounty on him."

"I know, it's crazy as hell, but Caisson paid us plenty. Come on, let's go find some cattle."

Most men they had worked for split the money up after the job was over. Caisson had paid in advance, and more than they had expected. Like the other men, Jack and Bob were pretty awestruck riding with Sanders. Bart had kept to himself most of the time, but especially at the campfire in the evening he would joke around. When they camped at Indian Waters, Bart had practiced his draw. No doubt that was partly to keep his skills at a razor edge, and partly to show off to the rest of the gang. Watching in amazement, they had never seen anything like it. The men talked later how they couldn't see his hand move. Jack didn't see how any man could be faster. Whoever Tom Colt was, Jack was sure he was a dead man.

Ben located a spot well off of Bailey's ranch, where it was unlikely they would be found by accident. Buck headed toward the ranch and found a place high up on the canyon wall where he could see the house and barn. He sat and watched. Everything seemed normal the first day.

The next morning started out just as slow, but in the afternoon Buck saw a cowboy ride in at full gallop. Moments later the ranch sprang to life. Cowboys were rushing around saddling their mounts. It was apparent to Buck that the time had come. An hour later he rode into Ben's camp.

"A rider came in hellbent for leather. That rancher and his men saddled up and left. It looks like they swallowed the bait."

"Did you see Colt and the Indian?" asked Ben.

"Yep, plus about a dozen others. If there's any men left on the ranch it couldn't be more than just a few."

"Okay, men, let's ride." Ben smiled as he climbed into the saddle; things were working out just like he had figured.

When they got within a mile of the house, Ben suggested to Bart that he stay in a grove of trees until they finished. The gang rode in at a normal gait and no one at the ranch took much notice until they were nearly there.

Margaret was in the house cleaning and Beth was working in the garden. Looking out the window Margaret saw several riders she didn't recognize. She went outside to find out what they wanted. Beth had heard the horses when they got close, but hadn't come out of the rows of sweet corn to see who it was.

Melinda had gone down to feed the chickens and gather eggs in the hen house. Then she went in the barn to play with her pet cougars for awhile before going back to the house. She had them out of the cage on a leash when she heard the riders approach. Walking to the barn door she opened it a crack, and saw six men ride up to the house. A dust cloud drifted slowly toward the barn when they stopped.

One of Emmett's cowboys had been outside the corral and saw the men ride up. He was walking toward the six men as they dismounted. Slim was an older cowboy and his eyes weren't as good as they used to be. When he got within fifty feet of them he realized who they were and went for his gun. Slim fired one shot before three bullets tore through him. Brad Lofton, a cousin of Emmett's, was the only other cowboy at the ranch. He had been inside the corral.

Hearing the gunfire, he came running with pistol in hand. As soon as Brad came around the corner one of the men shot him.

Melinda was horrified when Slim was hit. She almost ran outside to see if she could help him, but she stood frozen, unable to move, trying to figure out what to do. As she stood there, Brad was killed. Melinda backed away from the barn door and started to head toward the ladder that led up to the loft. Stopping to take the leashes off Ember and Flame, she called quietly for them to follow. Just before starting up the ladder she remembered the extra guns in the feed room that Tom and Mescal had brought in a couple of weeks ago. They were the guns from Matt Caisson and the three men. Melinda grabbed two of the holsters and scampered up the ladder as quickly as she could; the big cats followed. She went to the side of the loft where a large stack of hay would help hide her presence. The fragrance of alfalfa filled her nostrils. She strained to hear, but the only sound coming to her ears was her own breathing. Feeling her heart beating rapidly, she wondered if they meant to kill everyone there.

"Should I go down and try to protect Margaret and Beth?" she asked herself silently. "No, these men are killers; I wouldn't have a chance against them."

It was dark inside the barn with only two windows partially open. Ember brushed up against her just then, and Flame stood tense with the hair standing straight up on his neck. The big cats sensed her fear and were alert. She had taken care of them as cubs, now they were full-grown and had known nothing except her care and feeding.

Several minutes later Melinda heard footsteps outside the barn. Suddenly one of the big doors creaked. It was opened slowly at first, but then there were additional footsteps and both doors were opened wide. Shivers ran through Melinda's body, and her breathing grew more rapid. Flame had been tense earlier reacting to her fear, and now he sensed her increased nervousness, as well as the anxiety of the other cat. Without warning he let out the shrill cry of the cougar. The men who had stepped into the barn went quickly back out and closed the big doors.

Melinda heard someone yell, "What the hell you waitin for? Get in there and look for her."

She heard another voice reply, "Boss, I swear there's a cougar in there. I know that sound."

"Well, you got a gun, don't you? Shoot the damn thing," the first voice said.

Now they spoke more softly and Melinda couldn't make it out. Suddenly, she could hear the big door creak as it was slowly opened again. Next, there was the sound of footsteps coming through the doorway. Peeking out over the top of the hay, she saw one of the men below. Her heart was racing. What did these men want with her? Before long she could hear them opening doors to the various rooms downstairs and going through the stables. It was a few minutes later when she heard the thud of a boot on the ladder accompanied by the creak of wood and jingle of a spur. Again Flame let out his cry, much shriller and louder now. He was scared, but his teeth showed and he growled quietly, signaling he was ready for a fight.

Flame crept slowly along the wooden floor of the hayloft. He moved within ten feet of the ladder. Melinda could hear the man's boots and spurs climbing one rung at a time. The cat's body was low on the floor and his ears were laid back. His muscles were flexed and he was ready to pounce.

Melinda looked on in shock. This pet of hers had no experience at pursuing prey other than rats and mice. He had never shown any tendency to attack a human. Yet there he was, seemingly ready to fight. Surely he wouldn't, thought Melinda, not when he saw that it was a man.

Flame was reacting to Melinda's fear. An instinct deep within commanded him to protect the only family he had known. The man's hat showed first, and then a gun. Melinda was back in the shadows and could see the man's head. Flame remained crouched, motionless behind a small pile of loose hay. The man came up further so his whole chest was visible. That was when the cougar leapt, catching the lower part of the man's face in its jaws, its teeth clamping around the jawbones and mouth. The sound of bones breaking could be heard. The paws of the cat grabbed both sides of the man's head and the claws dug deep into his ears and scalp.

Only seconds earlier the man was the hunter. Knowing the cougar was in the loft he had tried to see the cat, but it had been too dark. He turned just in time to see the open mouth and large teeth attack him. His face was engulfed with the sharp spikes clamping down, crushing the bones. He let out a horrible scream partially muffled by the big cat's head. The man fell from the ladder to the ground below in utter terror, with the cat still firmly attached to his face. As they hit the ground the cat released its grip and went for his throat. The man managed to get out another quick scream before the cougar's teeth tore into his flesh. Instinct now guided this animal, and all animals know to go for the throat. The man's scream turned into a hissing rush of air passing through the gaping holes left in his flesh. He could feel the cat's breath on him, and the wetness of his own warm blood flowing down the skin on both sides of his throat.

The other men yelled in surprise and ran for the door. Hearing the ghastly cry of death, one turned and saw the plight of his companion. He raised his revolver and drew a bead on the deadly cat. A gun blast ended Flame's life. The loyal pet fell dead still on top of the dying rustler. The other men pulled the cat off just in time to see the stark terror on the face of their friend. His eyes were wide open and his jaw fully extended with some of the broken bones showing through the skin. He tried to talk but couldn't form any words. The man gasped his last breath and was dead.

Several minutes passed as Melinda waited, now more frightened than before. Her heart was pounding. The one remaining cougar, Ember, shivered beside her, not knowing what to do. A tear escaped Melinda's eyes as she realized Flame was dead. Maybe these intruders would go away since one of the men had been killed. She hoped, then she prayed. Suddenly, she could hear movement on the ladder again. Whoever it was must have removed his boots because he was quiet. Only the creak of wood from the rungs on the ladder announced his ascent.

Ember's body tensed and began to take the position of stalking. A low growl started from its throat. Melinda touched the animal and it ceased the noise. Another rung creaked and Melinda saw the top of a hat. She had one of the revolvers in her hand and now raised it and aimed at the hat. She focused on the sights of the gun rather than the target, just as Tom had taught her. The hat and the man under it were a blur as she focused on the front and rear sight. Now a head moved up under the hat; the sights were in alignment and she squeezed the trigger. The gun exploded in her hand and the man fell off the ladder making a loud thump below.

"Holy shit! She blew his head off," a man yelled.

"Go up and get her," another voice said.

"Shit no! You go, I'll cover you."

"Bullshit!"

Suddenly Ember let out a shrill cry even louder than Flame had before. It would have put fear into any man's heart, but was deathly frightening to those who had just seen the bloody face and throat of their dead companion. The cougar suddenly pounced on the hayloft floor near the ladder. It was scared out of its wits and let out another high-pitched yell. The men heard the cat land just above them, and then the horrible shrill cry. Melinda could hear the men run out the barn and close the doors.

Melinda didn't hesitate. Grabbing the guns she made her way quickly but quietly down the ladder. She rushed to the stall of the horse she loved. Melinda believed the stallion was her best chance to escape. If she could manage to get away from the ranch, she could ride to Jake's place where she hoped there would be enough cowboys to hold off these men.

As she saddled the big red stallion her hands shook, knowing the men might come through the door at any moment. Sensing her fear the big horse stepped anxiously while she was saddling him, slowing her task. The sounds of the cougar, the gunshots, and a nervous master made the horse skittish. She still wasn't finished when the door creaked. Peeking out of the stable Melinda gasped in fear as the door opened to reveal the silhouette of a man. The man showed no sign he had seen them in the dark of the stable area. Ember was in the hallway just outside the great stallion's stall. The cougar sensed Melinda's fear and shed its own. The big cat ran toward the door, lunging in great leaps. As it neared the entrance, once again it let out its horrendous shrill cry. Melinda heard footsteps running from the door.

Finally she had the big horse saddled and headed for the exit. The animal walked anxiously; it was clear to Melinda that Wildfire was ready to live up to his name. When they got to the door she directed the horse toward the narrow opening. With a burst of speed he exploded out of the barn, throwing the doors wide open. Melinda's heart was beating madly; she feared she would be shot at any moment. She leaned low over the neck of the horse and yelled at the stallion, "Run, Wildfire! Run!"

Melinda pointed him toward Jake's ranch and the big stallion galloped with majestic strides. Wildfire carried her effortlessly as he hurried away from the barn. Looking back Melinda saw that the men were only now getting on their horses. She had a sizeable head start and believed they had no hope of catching Wildfire; now if only Jake's men were at his ranch.

She had ridden for a mile when suddenly a rider on a black horse came out of the trees. It startled her at first, but then she decided it didn't matter. Wildfire was in the lead and would leave this black horse in the dust. On she rode, confident none of the horses could stay with Wildfire. Looking back later, she was shocked to see that the black horse seemed closer than before. "Surely not," she told herself. She bent down over the flowing red mane and yelled to the horse, "Run! Run like you never have before, Wildfire!"

The big red horse seemed to understand and lengthened its gait. The ground below sped by and the wind whipped through Melinda's hair. She squinted her eyes as they filled with water, stinging from the rushing air. After another mile she looked back and the big black horse was even closer. She could see the rippling muscles of its chest and hear the thunder of its hooves. It was a magnificent animal and appeared to be gaining on her with every stride. She looked again and saw the other horses were far behind, but she knew Wildfire could not outrun this black steed. Her body trembled with fear; she had thought she was safe and now she was vulnerable once more.

Melinda knew she had to decide what to do soon. At the rate the black horse was closing it wouldn't be long before it overtook her. She now realized they meant to take her. Otherwise, they would have shot at her as she rode from the ranch. It must be Caisson who had come to steal her away, his revenge for his brother's death. She would rather be dead. What could she do? Thoughts of killing herself with one of the revolvers entered her mind. Then it came to her. Why hadn't she thought of it before? She yelled out loud, "Fortress in the Sky."

Wildfire heard her yell and surged ahead straining every muscle to the limit. The fortress was in a canyon only a mile ahead. She would have enough time to get there, but would she have enough time to climb the wall before the man on the black horse arrived? If she could get all the way up to the fortress, she still had the guns and might be able to hold them off until help came. The red stallion sped on, its powerful muscles churning below her, its mane blowing in her face. Wildfire's tremendous surge after her yell had helped to hold the distance between them. When they reached the entrance of the canyon she encouraged him on; his race was almost finished. The fortress was just ahead.

Wildfire raced up the slope at breakneck speed. It should have slowed him down, but he labored all the more and in moments was at the split in the canyon wall. The stallion's big chest was heaving for want of air. Melinda dismounted and slapped the horse on the rump, sending him flying away. She ran through the split still clutching the guns and holsters. Going as quickly as she could, she had barely gotten up in the rocks when she heard the rider pull up. Melinda turned and aimed a gun at the opening, expecting him to come through the entrance, but he did not.

She resumed climbing, going as fast as she could. A minute later she heard the other horses ride up. On she climbed, short of breath, light-headed and her heart racing madly. Melinda could hear their voices below but couldn't tell what they were saying. In a few more minutes she was at the fortress and moved quickly to peer over the edge, looking down in the enclosure. Several men had come in through the split and were looking up. One of them spotted her and pointed in her direction. She pointed back, but with a gun in her hand and fired. The bullet kicked up dirt less than a foot away from the biggest man.

She didn't know it, but she had nearly shot Caisson. If she had hit him the siege would have been over. As the men rushed to take cover, Melinda saw a flash of yellow fur fly by them and scamper up the rocks. It was out of sight before any of the men could shoot. Ember climbed quickly like only a cat can. It snuggled up next to Melinda, making her feel more secure. She thought that surely these men would be hesitant to climb the rocks, having seen the hideous results of Flame's attack on the man in the barn. The man's shredded face and throat had been a ghastly sight.

Bart had been outside when the big cat came through the trees and ran in the opening. He had been shocked to see the cougar and drew his gun more as an involuntary defense action. The cat was moving so fast, he couldn't get a clear shot at it. Bart wanted no more to do with capturing the girl. He had seen her ride from the barn on the red horse, and when she came closer he could tell she had a fine animal. As she got parallel to the trees where he waited, Bart jumped on his big stallion and chased after her. He pursued her more to see if his treasured mount could outrun the big red horse. His black beauty had gained steadily, reaffirming his worth to Bart. When Sanders pulled up outside the split in the walls, he just dismounted and took his tired mount under the nearby trees. He probably could have shot her in the arm or leg and captured her for Caisson, but he felt like he had done enough just preventing her escape. As Caisson and the others rode up, Bart had second thoughts, wishing he had let her go.

Caisson couldn't believe it when the bullet struck so close to him. He was surprised that she could shoot so well. Things were bad enough having to climb up after her in the rocks, and now the cougar was up there with her. Caisson looked for the sun but couldn't see it in the enclosure. He could tell by the shadows on the canyon wall that he didn't have much time before dark. None of his men would climb up after her in the night with that beast ready to bite their throats.

"Come on, men," he yelled as he started up the stone wall. He knew he would have to lead them, subtly challenging their manhood. As he darted toward the first rock to begin the ascent a bullet ricocheted off the stone nearby. The other men quickly followed; one of them was grazed on the left arm by one of several bullets the girl sent their way. Up they went, moving from one spot to the next as quickly as they could. Caisson was hopeful there would only be a few places where she could get a good shot at them.

Now they were at a spot where they would have to cross a narrow ledge. The girl could see them easily from above. Caisson went first, running along a ledge that he would normally only cross cautiously. A blast sounded and rock particles hit his face. She had missed him by only inches.

"Damn, that woman can shoot," Ben exclaimed after he was safely across. He turned to his men and said softly to them so she couldn't hear, "Shoot at her to give each man cover, but don't hit her."

A volley of shots ricocheted off the rocks nearby, and Melinda backed away from the ledge. When she looked again, another series of shots followed. By the time she looked once more, they had all made it across. She wouldn't get another shot until they were nearly at the top. Loading her weapons in preparation, she was thankful she had brought two revolvers with gun belts. The belts had extra cartridges. As she moved behind the big flat rock, her heart raced and her mouth was dry. The cougar was beside her, breathing rapidly, seemingly every bit as scared as she was. They were cornered. She had hoped to hold them off longer. Someone would be riding to Jake's ranch by now to get help. Wanting to keep these men at bay until night set in, she believed they would not attack in the dark.

Several minutes later Melinda could hear them behind the rocks just below. She put both guns at the ready, one in each hand aimed at the opening. One of the men banged his gun on the rock wall. Listening intently she could hear their whispers, but couldn't ascertain what they were planning to do. One stuck his head around the corner and she pulled both triggers. The bullets made a zinging sound as they glanced off the rocks. The man had a bloody ear from a piece of lead that nearly took his life. She could hear them whispering once again.

Suddenly, all hell broke loose as men were firing their guns at her and the bullets were whistling over her head. She rolled back behind the rock on her left. Melinda knew the men were charging ahead, but there was so much lead coming her way that she was afraid to look. She had intended to shoot as many as she could, but the bullets whistling by caused her to seek cover.

Without warning Ember leapt from behind the rock and Melinda heard a man scream. The shooting stopped and she looked out to see the big cat attack the nearest man. The cougar's teeth sank deep into the man's shoulder and its claws dug firmly into the front of his body.

Melinda could see the stark terror on his face as he looked at the animal's head now entrenched in his flesh. The man retreated trying to free himself from the painful clutches. In his fright he forgot he was on the ledge, which opened up to the enclosure below. He stepped over the edge and both he and the cat plummeted down. The man screamed all the way, his cries ending only with the crash of their flesh and bones striking the earth.

Just then someone grabbed Melinda from behind. In the confusion, one of the men had slipped around the rock and surprised her. He held her arms down so she couldn't shoot. She was captured; it had happened so fast. Now she was their prisoner. Melinda wished she had not been afraid, but instead had fought valiantly and died in the process.

TWENTY- SEVEN

They had finally managed to capture Melinda. Lefty had slipped around and grabbed her. Now he and Buck held her as Ben looked at his prize. The outlaw leader concluded that any man worth his salt would come for her. This had been his plan and he decided it was still a good one—even though it had cost several lives to get her. Three men were dead, two by cougar and poor old Dub at the hands of this small woman. Ben thought she couldn't be much over five feet tall. He hadn't expected such a fight; losing so many men was astonishing.

Ben planned to kill Tom Colt come hell or high water. He wanted to see him die, and then with the hidden money he would enjoy the life of the rich. This beautiful woman would be his slave in a mansion somewhere outside the big city. Many things were possible in New Orleans. He watched the woman as they led her carefully down. She saw him looking at her and the look returned was one of hate. He felt certain that would change over time when she got to know him, and he lavished on her all that money could buy.

Bart Sanders was waiting for them outside the split in the canyon wall. He had retrieved her horse while they were climbing up after her. The two stallions stood side-by-side. As they approached, Ben could tell Bart admired the girl. It had cost Ben a lot of money to bring Sanders up from Arizona, but this was where the gunfighter would come into play. Even though Caisson was fast, he had heard the rumors about Colt outgunning Cooper and Simpson. Ben prided himself on being smart, knowing when to take easy pickings and knowing when to hire others to do the work.

"Hold her here for a minute," Ben told Lefty and Buck. The outlaw leader went back inside the area behind the split. He wrote a note instructing Tom Colt to come alone to the cabin on Clear Ridge if he wanted Melinda back alive. It was a long ways off, but the perfect spot. There was only one way up the ridge, or so everyone thought. Lefty had suggested Clear Ridge to Ben because he had found a way down the other side that no one else knew about. It would provide a perfect escape route from a posse. From the ridge it would be easy to tell if Colt came alone. Ben was sure the cards were his to play now that he had the girl.

While the outlaw leader was away writing the note, Bart Sanders looked down at the young woman. The sun, now low on the western horizon, reflected off her gleaming blond hair. "No wonder Tom Colt is in love with her," thought Bart. "Who wouldn't be?" The girl looked up at him; it was the first time they had made eye contact.

"That's a fine horse you got there, miss. What's his name?" Bart asked politely, smiling at the young woman.

"Give me a gun and I'll shoot that smile off your face," she replied defiantly. Melinda was in no mood for polite conversation with the man who ran her down. If not for him she would have made it safely away.

"I understand you're mad, miss." Bart saw there was no fear in her eyes. Not liking this part of Caisson's plan, he felt guilty about the role he had played in chasing her. Reluctant to give up attempting to engage her in conversation, after waiting a short while he tried again. "Your red stallion really is a fine horse."

She looked at his black horse, so similar to Emmett's pride and joy except for color. The black stallion was a little bigger and even better muscled. "Wildfire," she finally said. "I thought he could outrun any horse around here."

"Well, pretty lady, he probably can. This horse isn't from here."

Melinda heard a gentle voice containing no intimidation. She looked into his eyes and sensed for the first time that this man would not harm her. There was something in the way he talked and looked at her.

"Get her on the horse," Caisson said to Lefty and Buck as he returned.

After helping her on Wildfire, Lefty went to get on his horse. Ben was standing nearby and Lefty told him quietly, "She reminds me of that squaw Sammy went after."

"That half-breed is as pretty as this girl?" Ben whispered back in disbelief.

"She's small like her and damn good lookin."

"Hell, man, this is the prettiest woman I've ever seen."

"I sure ain't arguin that, she's the purtiest thing I seen too. All I'm sayin is that squaw is small and good lookin like this one. I'm tellin ya, she's got a body that many a cowboy would kill for."

"Well, they both do then," Ben replied. "I guess that explains why Sammy ran off like he did."

Bart Sanders watched Melinda sitting on the red stallion. The woman had fire in her eyes; she was a fighter. Bart didn't like kidnapping her. This was Caisson's play and his decision to make, but Sanders didn't care for it and decided he didn't care much for Caisson. If it weren't for the money, Bart would leave. Taking the girl was against his grain and he decided he had some thinking to do. He figured Caisson would want to keep the girl. Bart began to ponder whether he would allow that to happen.

First, Bart had to dispose of Tom Colt. Some of the men in Caisson's gang told him that Colt had to be fast to outdraw Cooper and Simpson. Sanders wasn't concerned. If Colt were really fast, he would have heard of him outside of Utah. Caisson had agreed to pay Bart handsomely, and already paid half up front. Sanders wanted to see the man who could attract such a woman and was worth so much money to kill.

Melinda's hands were bound in front of her and each ankle was tied to the stirrup. Caisson's men had been gentle with her; she had to give them that. Gentle or not, she was securely bound. There was nothing she could do but go with them. Having overheard Caisson talking to one of his men on the way down the canyon wall, she had figured out his plan. Melinda had heard of Bart Sanders, a gunslinger for hire—a killer. Even if Tom could outdraw him, there were four of them. She thought about the possibility of throwing herself off a cliff to protect Tom. Since her ankles were tied to the stirrups, the only way would be to run Wildfire off the edge. Finally, she decided it wouldn't do any good. Caisson would just proceed to the cabin and pretend she was alive. Tom wouldn't know if she were dead. She felt horrible inside, knowing she could be responsible for Tom's death. On the ride to the cabin she tried and tried to think of some way to help him, but couldn't come up with anything. Finally she wept, then she prayed; she prayed for a miracle. Melinda prayed with all her heart.

Beth had ridden to Jake's ranch. Four of Jake's men headed toward Emmett's place while one man went to catch up with the posse. He had ridden hard and found Tom and Mescal returning. Surprised to see them he asked what happened. Tom told him Mescal sensed something was wrong because they were too easy to follow. Jake's rider told them about Caisson coming to the ranch, Melinda escaping on Wildfire and how Beth had seen Melinda turn into Rocky Rim Canyon.

When Tom heard that he didn't hesitate, nor did Mescal. They rode their horses at full gallop to the Fortress in the Sky. By the time Tom and Mescal reached the split in the canyon wall below the fortress, the sun had set and it was getting dark. There was just enough light to see the tracks of horses and men. As Mescal studied the ground, also finding Melinda's footprints, Tom went behind the split in the rock and found Ember and the dead man. He also found the note. As he finished reading it, Mescal walked up and told him four men rode off with Melinda. Tom relayed what the note said.

"Me go with you. They no see."

"Not this time. We can't risk Melinda's life. I have to go alone."

Red and Sam arrived just then. They had first gone to the ranch house and then followed the tracks to the canyon. Tom walked out and showed them the note.

"Taking the cattle was a clever ruse," Tom said. "Caisson was after Melinda."

371

"Caisson has got to be the meanest, craziest sonofabitch I ever heard of," Sam said angrily. "Kidnapping a girl like Melinda is plumb loco; we'll round up a hundred men and go after them no good assholes."

"I'm going to have to go alone. You men can round a posse up if you want. By the time you get there, I'll have either killed them or be dead. You should probably wait for Emmett and his men. Mescal can help you track them down if they get by me. Hopefully someone can save Melinda. If not, I reckon she'd rather be dead than be taken as an outlaw's slave."

"Tom, you can't go there alone; that's crazy," Red argued. "You wouldn't have a chance. I'm bettin they'll ambush you as soon as you get close. Even if they don't, they have four guns. I know you're fast, but them ain't likely odds."

"You can't do it, Tom," Sam added. "The men will be back soon. We'll figure somethin out. Caisson, he's fast. I reckon his men are too."

"Caisson wouldn't give you a chance," Red concluded.

"Don't have any choice," Tom repeated. "I don't like the odds either, but he has Melinda. He wants me, not her. I have to go alone."

Tom started to walk to his horse when two more of Jake's men rode up from Emmett's ranch. They had stayed to be sure Emmett's wife, Margaret, was okay. She was nearly in hysterics and it had taken a few minutes to get her calmed down. Joe Carson, one of Jake's riders, told them Emmett's wife was scared but she was fine. Red filled them in on Melinda's situation.

"Melinda wasn't the only woman they took," Joe added. "The rustler called Sammy killed a good friend of mine over by Red Creek Canyon. He took his wife, Yellow Flower."

Mescal's eyes grew wide; he turned quickly to Joe. "Yellow Flower! She young and small, like Melinda?"

"Well, I reckon she is, not quite as short as Melinda, and real pretty."

The Indian had an intense look on his face. He asked hopefully, "She have scar, small one, below ear, here?" Mescal pointed just below and to the front of his right ear.

"She sure does."

"How you know Yellow Flower?" Mescal asked.

"Why, a fellow I know married her about two months ago. That's when I first met her. The local ranchers were all kinda upset on account she's a half-breed. No offense meant, Mescal. The guy that married her and I used to be pards. I was the best man at their wedding."

After a long silence, Tom walked over to his friend. "Who is Yellow Flower?"

Mescal looked at Tom, then looked away as moisture came to his eyes. "She my sister's child, only family I have. Thought she dead. All others dead." Mescal was pleased to discover she was alive, but fearful of what might happen to her. Putting those concerns aside, he remembered that he was sworn to protect Melinda. He turned to Tom.

"First we get Melinda, then get Yellow Flower."

"I have to go alone. You know that. They'll kill Melinda if someone goes with me. You go find Yellow Flower before that rustler gets away with her."

Mescal looked at his friend, then held out his hand. Rather than shaking hands, they grabbed each other's forearms and held firm. Mescal looked into his friend's eyes, knowing the peril he faced; the Indian said slowly, choosing his words carefully, speaking from the heart, "May your God protect you and Melinda." Mescal knew Tom's challenge was far greater than his, and that he might never see him alive again.

Mescal got directions to Yellow Flower's ranch. Before he rode away, Joe stepped forward. "Mescal, I've heard of that rustler, Sammy; he's really fast with a gun. We'll go with you."

The old Indian shook his head; this job was his to do. Mescal believed he had a better chance of slipping up on the rustler undetected if he went alone. Looking at Tom he nodded, and Tom returned the gesture. They rode away in separate directions. It would soon be too dark to ride and both would have to stop and camp, but first they could travel several hours in the dark while in familiar terrain.

It was a long way to Clear Ridge; Tom wasted no time getting back on the trail early in the morning. He didn't think Caisson would ambush him going in. Men like Caisson usually wanted to look a man in the eye before they killed him, or had him killed. Tom didn't expect to get an even break from the outlaw leader, but was counting on at least getting a crack at him. His goal was to get Melinda out safely, to trade his life for hers—then kill as many as he could. The one advantage he had was that Caisson didn't know who he really was.

As Tom rode he wondered if it was time for him to die. He had killed many men since coming to Utah. They had been outlaws and had robbed and killed innocent people; still they were men and he had killed them. If he was to save Melinda, more men would have to die and likely he with them. He tried not to think about the dream he had last night. The dark shadowy figure had visited him once again in his sleep. He had awakened in a cold sweat, once more thinking he had seen the face—still not remembering who it was. Tom checked his gun; it would be a long ride.

Red Creek Canyon was closer. Toward mid-morning Mescal picked up their tracks. The rustler had gone upstream in a creek, and later rode on hard rock. When a man kidnapped a girl, Mescal thought, he would be well advised to travel fast and hide his tracks so no man could follow. Apparently the rustler figured it was unlikely anyone would come after him to save a half-breed girl. Mescal rode as quickly as possible while reading the prints, and spotted them in the distance in the late afternoon. The man was riding at a fairly slow gait, leading Yellow Flower's horse.

Mescal thought he knew where they were heading, and took a short cut that should put him ahead of the two riders and directly on their route. Traveling over rough and rocky ground, Mescal pushed the Paint hard. When he got there he waited up in the rocks, meaning to ambush the rustler to ensure Yellow Flower's safe release. His concern was for his niece, not whether this rustler got a fair fight.

Time passed slowly for Mescal and he was becoming anxious. They should be there by now. He began to wonder if he had guessed their direction incorrectly. If he rode directly back toward their trail, it was likely that the rustler would spot him. But if he retraced his steps and went back to pick up their trail where he left off, it would become dark before he could find them. Knowing that when a man kidnaps a girl he usually has ill intent in mind, Mescal didn't want Yellow Flower to have to go through that experience. He decided he had no choice but to ride directly back on their suspected trail.

Sammy made camp early. It had been a long day's ride and he thought he had covered their tracks well. Wanting to get the chores done early, the young rustler planned to check out his new merchandise while there was still enough light. The first night he had started to take liberties with her. It had been a hasty and aggressive action and he had not taken the time to remove her clothing. She had fought him fiercely. They had been only ten miles from her ranch at the time, and Sammy thought lighting a campfire was too risky. He had decided to wait until tonight when he could see her body and take his time enjoying the prize.

While he made supper he glanced her way. The sun was setting on the horizon and the glow of light enhanced her natural beauty. Her arms and legs revealed muscle from hard work. She looked like a beautiful wildcat, which was exactly how she had fought him the night before. The young rustler wanted to see her naked and planned to leave her hands bound so she couldn't fight him off. Images of her unclothed body were flashing through his mind. He had paid little attention to other things around him, other than glancing at the girl, until suddenly he heard a horse approaching. Sammy had just taken supper off the fire when he noticed the sound and stepped back from the campfire.

Mescal had ridden around a bend and into view before he knew they were there. The only choice now was to ride up and let things evolve. He rode slowly, riding directly toward the young rustler. Mescal kept his hand on his right thigh, not far from his gun. The young rustler waited, and looked over at Yellow Flower once to see if she recognized him. If she did, it didn't show. The Indian rode up and stopped about twenty yards from the rustler. Sammy thought he was way too fast for some old Indian, and decided to find out what the old man wanted before he killed him. Mescal dismounted by throwing his right leg over the horse's neck and sliding off the horse. He walked forward, coming to within ten paces of the young man.

Having thought her uncle was dead, Yellow Flower was surprised when Mescal approached. Now she feared for him. When Sammy had come to their ranch he had goaded her husband. The gunman had told him he was there to take the young squaw for his woman and that he was going to enjoy peeling off her clothes. The taunting of her husband continued until he had finally gone for his gun; Sammy shot him down. She had been dreading this night knowing his thoughts from his glances. Now her uncle stood before the young gunman, ready to save her or die trying. She was afraid he would need help, but didn't know how she was going to provide it.

"What can I do for you?" Sammy asked.

"Let girl go."

Sammy wasn't about to let her go. He wasn't afraid of this gray haired old Indian, but was curious why he had come after her.

"Who are you and what is she to you?"

"Me Mescal; she my niece." The Indian kept a steady gaze at the young rustler.

Sammy knew then that he would have to kill him. It wasn't likely the Indian would let him ride out once the girl told him he had tried to rape her. Even though he hadn't succeeded, he had fondled her. Sammy decided to have some fun with the old Indian before he killed him.

"How'd you get a name like Mescal? Is it because you drink Mescal all the time, just another drunken Indian?"

Mescal was too smart to get angry, and now knew this man would not give up Yellow Flower. According to Jake's rider, this young rustler was fast with a gun. It seemed likely that Sammy would beat him to the draw. If he was hit, Mescal wanted to kill the rustler before he died. The wise old Indian looked for any edge he could find.

"No!" he replied, and now spoke with the voice of death he had often heard from his old chief. "Don't use real name. Rode with Geronimo, Chiricahua Apache. Mescal short for Mescalero. I Apache warrior. I come to get girl or kill you Apache way."

Sammy's face changed expression; the confident look was gone. The word Apache put fear in any White man, and Geronimo was the most feared Apache of all. This old man might know how to use that gun in his holster. If the Indian somehow got the best of him, a most frightful tortured death would follow. The young rustler recalled coming up on a homestead where the Apaches had tortured the family; it was the most horrible thing he had ever seen.

While he was reacting to the Indian's words, concentrating on the look in the Indian's eyes, the death in his voice, thinking about torture, he heard a loud scream from the girl and instinctively turned her way. Mescal turned too, but she was more in the old Indian's line of sight and he realized first that she did it as a distraction. Mescal didn't hesitate and went for his gun. Sammy's attention was diverted for only a fraction of a second longer, and out of the corner of his eye he saw the motion by Mescal. Sammy's mind ordered his hand to go for his gun, and he turned his head back toward the Indian as he drew. His gun was leveled when he heard a blast and pain tore through his midsection. Sammy pulled the trigger, his gun exploded and the Indian fell down.

"Good, I got him," Sammy said to himself. He looked at his stomach where he was shot. He fell to his knees. "Oh no, my stomach. Oh no," he said again. Sammy had never been shot before.

As the young rustler looked up, he saw the Indian was trying to get up. Sammy raised his gun, aimed it at the Indian's head and pulled the trigger, but nothing happened. It wasn't cocked. In his horror of being shot he had forgotten. Now he cocked the gun and brought it up again, aiming right at the Indian's head.

Mescal's revolver had flown backward and to the side when he was wounded in the leg. Now he was partially up and ready to make a dive for his weapon. The old Indian flung his body as the rustler's weapon exploded. The bullet hit him in the side. Mescal grabbed his revolver, trying to ignore the pain from two bullet wounds. As he began to bring up his gun to shoot the rustler, Mescal saw that he was too late.

Sammy had already cocked his gun and was ready to shoot Mescal again. Just then a flash of brown flew across Mescal's field of vision. It was Yellow Flower. She kicked the gun from Sammy's hand just as it discharged, causing the bullet to go astray. Her hands had been bound, but not her feet. She ran quickly to where the rustler's gun had landed and kicked it farther away.

Mescal held his gun on Sammy and got painfully to his feet. He had been shot in the upper thigh and to the left of his stomach. Pulling out his knife, Mescal motioned Yellow Flower closer so he could free her hands.

She smiled at the uncle she had thought dead and told him with concern in her voice, "You are losing much blood."

Going to the rustler's saddlebag, Yellow Flower tore the arm off a spare shirt and tied it around Mescal's leg to help stop the bleeding. Next, she retrieved the rustler's gun and gave it to her uncle. The old Indian asked her to gather up the horses, guns, utensils, food and water. He told her to take everything. Picking up the rope that the rustler had used to tie Yellow Flower's hands, Mescal bound the young man's hands and feet. He then doused the campfire with water, making sure it was completely out.

Yellow Flower was afraid of what Mescal might do if she told him Sammy had tried to rape her, and decided not to tell him. After getting everything ready, she brought all three horses to Mescal. As they climbed in the saddles, the young rustler got a puzzled look on his face.

"Aren't you gonna kill me?" Sammy asked.

Mescal thought for a second, then shook his head and started to ride away.

With all that he had done, Sammy wondered why the Indian would leave him alive. As soon as the girl told him about the attempted rape, Sammy knew the Indian would return and torture him.

After traveling for a short distance the Indian stopped, and rode back toward the young rustler. Mescal felt no pity for the man whose eyes were filled with fear. They were now out of Yellow Flower's earshot.

"You gut shot, sure die. Me see several men shot this way, much pain, scream much before die. I not help you die. You have no weapons, no horse, no matches for fire. No can run. Coyotes hungry, wolves hungry, mountain lions hungry, vultures and ants hungry. You die slow, long time think about animals. Think what part they eat first. Mebbe legs, mebbe stomach where blood is. Mebbe dead when they come, mebbe still alive."

The young man's eyes went wide as he realized the old Indian was right. The pain in his stomach was getting worse. He looked around him now expecting to see wolves lurking, ready to come and feast on his flesh. With his hands and feet bound, he felt like a piece of raw meat waiting to be eaten. Sammy realized he would die a torturous death, but not by the Indian. Mescal was almost out of hearing distance.

"Kill me!" Sammy yelled at the top of his lungs.

Mescal turned and looked at him, and then continued toward Yellow Flower. He and his niece rode away. Because of the wounds in his leg and side, Mescal wasn't at all sure he would live through the night either. They were a long way from help and he was becoming weaker. After they had traveled for an hour, the old Indian fell from the horse.

Yellow Flower knew a rancher that would help, but he lived several miles away. Quickly building a traverse out of small limbs found near a stream, she helped her uncle onto it. She led his horse, slowly dragging the traverse, with Mescal struggling to survive.

As he lay on the traverse the old Indian beamed with pride. His niece had kept her wits about her and helped him in the gunfight. She did not panic, but fought like a warrior. Later, when he had fallen from the horse, she knew what to do. Yellow Flower was strong in body and in heart, and would survive in this land. The old Indian was thankful he had been able to save her.

Growing rapidly weaker, Mescal suddenly realized he had not yet told Tom about Caisson's secret. If he died now no one would know. He called to Yellow Flower but his voice was weak and she did not hear him. Mescal called again, but still she did not hear. He reached for his revolver, planning to shoot it in the air to get her attention, but as his hand touched the gun he faded quickly and lost consciousness.

TWENTY- EIGHT

As Tom approached Clear Ridge he studied the trail to the rim above. It wound back and forth up the face of the wall making him a sitting duck to someone with a rifle. As he ascended he occasionally looked up, but had yet to see anyone. Nearing the top he heard the call of an eagle and turned toward the sound, but couldn't locate it. Looking out toward the west he was taken with the beauty. A huge cloud started at the horizon and reached far into the sky. It was majestic in size, and the sun behind it illuminated the less dense portions of the cloud so that it shone yellow and gold.

Hearing the eagle again, he spotted it this time hovering at eye level. The proud bird screeched out its call once more, sounding like a trumpet announcing Tom's arrival and sending him to battle. To Tom the beauty of nature represented the goodness in people who lived their lives helping others. They deserved to be protected from the dark side of man, from those who preyed on the innocent. Tom sensed that this was his destiny. He was here to free Melinda, and at the same time rid this world of the predators who waited for him. No man lives forever, and the concept of destiny suggests some men live their entire lives to carry out one supreme act so that others may live.

Finally he reached the rim. The cabin was a short distance away, having been built to take advantage of the view. There were five horses tied on the far side. Wildfire was among them. Tom stopped and tied Diamond to a tree. As he walked slowly toward the cabin, he noticed the doorway. The darkness within gave the door the appearance of a vertical lid to a coffin. Tom thought about calling out Melinda's name to be sure that she was inside and still alive, but decided it would serve no useful purpose. He was an easy target now whether she called back or not.

Walking up on the small porch, he peered in through the open door and could see Melinda across the room. A large man had his hand on her arm so she couldn't run. At least Tom now knew she was alive. He felt a sense of relief; Caisson had kept that part of the bargain. People often forget that thieves and murderers can have a sense of honor. It differs from the set of values most people follow, but it is still a code of honor.

There were only a few windows letting light in the cabin. Tom would be at a disadvantage until his eyes adjusted to the dimness. Stepping slowly through the door, he surveyed the situation, keeping his hand well away from his gun. There was a man on the far side, next to the big man who held Melinda's arm. The man's hat shielded his face from view, much like the recurring dream. As Tom moved into the cabin, the man raised his chin and the light revealed who he was. Seeing that it was someone from his past, Tom sensed it was the face from his dreams. Death seemed almost inevitable.

It took only a few moments for Tom to set that concern aside. His thoughts returned to the reason he was there. The only thing that was important to him was to get Melinda out safely. To him she represented the beauty of the world and innocence in its purest form. His actions were driven by that single objective. He thought not of his love for her, nor his desire to escape from this situation so that he could be with her. The objective was to get her out alive. Moving away from the door, Tom backed toward the other end of the cabin away from Melinda and the four men.

In his walk to the cabin he had gone through a transformation. It wasn't Tom Colt that stood before them; he was the gunman, the legend. There existed not a shred of concern for his own life. He was ready to accept the challenge from any man and die if necessary. What mattered now was carrying out his purpose, his destiny, with deadly precision. His thought processes and actions were now those of a gunfighter.

He spoke with the icy voice of a man who dealt out death, softly but with force. "Are you Caisson?" The big man's nod confirmed he was. "Well, I'm here. Now make good on your word and let her walk out."

Caisson smiled and appeared to be thinking over whether to let her go, not making any move to release her. Ben planned to keep her after Sanders killed this man. He also wanted to demonstrate to everyone present that he was in control here, not Tom Colt.

Tom gave the outlaw leader ample time to reply, and then spoke again. "If you don't let her go, I'll put a bullet through your heart before anybody has a chance to stop me."

Caisson's eyes flashed in anger. He almost blurted out a response but thought better of it; he had Sanders as his ace up the sleeve. It was better to keep his temper; he wanted Colt to be worried about Bart Sanders and have him as his first target, just in case. Caisson paused a few seconds more.

As Ben pondered the appropriate response, Bart Sanders had done his own thinking. There was something Caisson didn't know, and besides, Bart had decided on the ride there that Melinda was to be set free. He was not going to let Ben keep her when this was over. Bart also wouldn't allow the girl to stay in the cabin and risk a stray bullet. He had no fear of Caisson, but he did fear the man they now faced, four to one odds or not. Before this man walked in, Sanders thought his chances of surviving were very high, almost a sure thing, now he figured his chances were no better than fifty-fifty, and probably not that good. Bart responded before Ben did, and spoke in a serious tone.

"Caisson, a deal is a deal. Let the girl go or I'll kill you myself."

Ben turned and looked at Sanders in surprise and confusion. This was not the way any member of his gang talked to him. Caisson would have killed any of his other men who had dared say that, but this was Bart Sanders. Ben hesitated only a second more and then let go of the girl's arm. He motioned with his head for her to leave. As Melinda neared the door she stopped and turned toward the man she loved. Tom saw her pause but didn't look her way.

Tom told her in a steady voice, "The best thing you can do for me now is go out, get on Wildfire and ride away. That way I know you're safe and don't have to worry about you."

Melinda knew it was true, but was also aware she might never see him alive again. She looked at his eyes, a look he didn't return as he watched the four men. Tears streamed down her cheeks, and then she moved quickly out to the horse.

Caisson regained his composure, figuring Sanders was just soft on women. "Well, I've got to hand it to you, Colt. Not many men would have walked in here that way, even for their woman. I've got to respect you for that, but you shouldn't have killed my brother. Now we're gonna have to kill you." Ben paused for a few seconds, and then motioned toward the man on his right. "I'd like to introduce my new man, Bart Sanders. I suspect you've heard of him."

Tom said nothing and showed no reaction to the name. He had kept his attention on Bart ever since he walked into the cabin. Years earlier they had been on the same cattle drive to Kansas. Bart was young then, quick but still learning to handle a gun. The two of them practiced quick drawing together. A real friendship never developed; it was more like competition. They were both incredibly fast.

Bart Sanders chuckled, breaking the silence, and then said in his low distinctive voice, "So this is your Tom Colt. Well, gentlemen, I have a surprise for you. This man used to go by another name down in Texas." Bart paused, then let out a long breath and said, "How you doing, Ringo?"

Lefty and Buck's eyes went wide and both said loudly, "Ringo!"

The name reverberated through the small cabin and out to Melinda's shocked ears. Her hand flew to her mouth. "Can it be true?" she said out loud, but no one could hear her.

Lefty glanced at Buck who looked just as scared, and then he turned to Caisson. "Hell, Ben, we weren't figuring on goin against Johnny Ringo."

Again Lefty's voice was loud because he was nervous and it reached Melinda's ears. These men had thought they were in little danger with Bart Sanders here to kill Tom Colt, but this had become a game of life and death where their likelihood of coming out alive had taken a dramatic reduction.

Caisson's face didn't reveal the fear he felt, nor did his voice. "Shit, men, there's four of us and we have Bart Sanders. Find your courage, Lefty." The rebuke worked; Lefty and Buck, afraid or not, would not turn yellow. They stood with their boss.

Ringo's eyes never left Caisson and Sanders, but he also concentrated on the other men's gun hands with peripheral vision, something he had done several times before. He had to take Sanders first; Bart was terribly fast. Ringo knew there was a good chance they might shoot each other, especially if Sanders went for his gun first. The slightest edge or the slightest pause could make the difference. Ringo sensed he couldn't wait much longer. If there were movement toward a gun, he would not hesitate. If he was hit by anyone he wanted to keep his wits about him and kill Caisson, and then the others if he could before he died. Chances of getting out of this alive didn't seem promising.

Suddenly, Ringo had an idea. It would help ensure he could kill Caisson and his men, and he didn't think Sanders would go after Melinda. "Bart, you helped get Melinda out. You're welcome to leave if you've a mind to."

Ben, Lefty and Buck were alarmed; they hadn't realized these gunmen knew each other. Now they considered the possibility they might be friends. If Sanders left, they wouldn't have a chance against Ringo. They spent the next several moments like men waiting to hear their sentence from the jury. If Bart took him up on it, they were as good as dead. Somebody could start preparing their tombstones.

Bart gave it some thought; after all, this would be the greatest risk he had ever taken. He wasn't at all sure he would win, but if he did, if he could beat Ringo, he would become known as the fastest gun that ever lived. His name would transcend the legend of Ringo. Even Wild Bill Hickock had never killed another well-known gunman. Ringo had been faster than he was on the cattle drive, but that was many years ago. Bart had continued to practice; this was his livelihood. Ringo was older now, worked on a ranch and had a girl. Maybe he could take him now. These thoughts flashed through Bart's mind in a few seconds. "Reckon I can't do that. Already been paid, but appreciate the offer."

It would be soon; Ringo was sure of it. Because there were so many he decided to shoot for the chest. By not targeting the head, he knew there was a greater chance one of them might get off a shot after he was hit. But Ringo figured the chest provided the best opportunity of getting a bullet in each of them. His thoughts went completely to killing these men. The legend of the past was in full control of his mind and body.

Lefty wanted to leave but couldn't. He figured Ringo would take Sanders first and Caisson second because they were the fastest. Since Lefty was on the end farthest away from Sanders, he figured he would be Ringo's last target, maybe even if he drew first. Lefty noticed Ringo was looking at Sanders, clear over on the other side. He thought he might be able to sneak in a draw and shoot him first. That wasn't likely if Ringo made him the first target. The real question, Lefty thought, was whether Ringo would shoot him first if he saw him go for his gun. Lefty thought he wouldn't. He figured Ringo would go for Sanders because of his reputation, regardless of who drew first. That was his best chance of survival then. He had made his decision; now to make the move.

Ringo noticed the man on the far end was left-handed, and had just moved his body closer to the man next to him. It made it harder for Ringo to see his gun or gun hand. It is difficult to know how a man can sense that his opponent is about to draw. Possibly it is like when a person feels that someone is looking at them, and they turn and see someone was. There are times when a person senses a loved one is in danger, and then discover later that they were. Ringo sensed that someone was ready.

There was a motion from the man who had just shifted position; his left shoulder moved up slightly as he started to go for his gun. When it had just begun, the slightest movement upward, Ringo saw it. His response didn't require thought. With his body poised like a hair trigger, cocked and ready, his draw happened without hesitation, almost to the point of being simultaneous. Ringo's hand moved like lightning. The gunfight had begun.

Bart had been ready to draw; like Ringo he could sense when it was going to happen. To Bart this was between him and Ringo; the others didn't matter. Sanders had planned to make the first move; he was ready to draw and sensed it was time. But, as the signal went to his brain, somehow Ringo drew at the same time. There was no time to think at this point; these men had drawn and fired so many times in practice that everything was automatic.

For Bart things seemed to happen in slow motion when he was in a gunfight. He saw the look of death in Ringo's face and felt a sense of doom. Yet no man could beat his draw, Bart assured himself. Bart's hand reacted instantaneously to his thought—his gun jumped into his hand with a blur of speed. He nearly had it leveled when he saw the blast of fire from the barrel of Ringo's gun, and his chest took a tremendous blow. Bart had been almost ready to pull the trigger when the bullet struck him; his gun exploded hundredths of a second later. He could tell that Ringo was hit, but his eyes went to his own chest. The bullet had hit his sternum sending bone fragments tearing through his heart.

Caisson cleared leather just as a bullet caught him in the chest. Even though Buck was the third man, he was slower and never got his gun out of the holster before the fatal wound stopped his motion.

Lefty's plan had worked; he shot Ringo at the same time Buck took the gunman's third bullet. Lefty saw Ringo wince and his gun start to go down. He believed he had won. Having outgunned the legend he would become famous. These thoughts flashed through Lefty's mind in a fraction of a second. Lefty thumbed the hammer back to fire again.

Ringo felt the impact of Lefty's bullet. It had pulled his gun hand down. But Ringo regained his composure, aimed his gun with a flick of his wrist and fired his fourth shot. Lefty gasped in surprise. "Got him," Lefty blurted out, trying to proclaim victory even in death, blood spurting out of his heart.

Caisson was wounded, but the bullet missed his heart. He was bringing his gun back up to get a shot away. Ben saw Ringo turning back toward him; he fired at Ringo just before he took another bullet from the legend's gun, less well aimed now. The wound caused Caisson to drop his gun. He saw Ringo fall to the floor.

The sounds of shooting ceased. Melinda had heard many shots fired very close together. She couldn't count them all. She remembered when Tom had killed the three riders soon after she first met him. The three shots had sounded like one long shot. It was like that now, except there were more. It was all over in a few seconds. Gunsmoke rolled out of the cabin door. Earlier she had started to ride away, but had stopped and sat waiting on Wildfire. When she heard the name Ringo called out, she nearly went into shock.

Melinda had suspected he was a gunfighter and that Tom Colt wasn't his real name, but she never thought for a moment that he might be the legendary Ringo. It didn't matter, she loved him and that was all she cared about. If he was Johnny Ringo, then maybe he did have a chance. Maybe he could outgun all four. Melinda said a quick prayer and begged God to let him live.

There was movement at the door to the cabin. Melinda looked up and terror tore through her body. "Oh please, God, no!" she cried out.

Caisson stood in the doorway; he was wounded but still alive. Realizing Tom must be dead she let out a horrible blood-curdling scream that shocked even Ben Caisson. Melinda's hands flew to her chest, her body shook, and tears exploded from her eyes. It felt as though her entire insides were trying to empty through her tiny tear ducts. Filled with anger at Ben, she thought of nothing other than the desire to kill him. While still sitting on Wildfire, Melinda started to pull the rifle out of the scabbard. As she was retrieving the weapon, Caisson looked up and saw she meant to shoot him. In those few seconds he had to decide whether to go back in the cabin to get his gun. He might have time to get inside before she could fire. Ben thought about it for a second more as he watched her, but then walked forward and sat down on the step in front of the cabin.

Melinda cocked the lever and brought the weapon up to shoot Caisson. It wasn't until he sat down that she noticed he had no gun. Aiming the rifle at him she commanded her finger to pull the trigger, but it would not comply. Melinda didn't know what to do; her reason for living was gone. She climbed off the horse; thinking had abandoned her. Giving no thought to her own safety she walked slowly in Caisson's direction carrying the rifle. Standing in front of him, she leveled the weapon once more. Again she commanded her trigger finger to finish the evil man. This time he looked up at her, gave a half smile and looked down at the ground. He fumbled with something in his shirt pocket. She lowered the rifle unfired. She was still filled with hate for him.

Just then she heard footsteps inside the cabin. Someone else was alive and about to step through the doorway. Her mind went first to the possibility Tom had survived, but Caisson had walked out. If Tom had been alive Ben would have finished him. She would barely have time to pull the rifle back up and aim it at the dark doorway. Her mind told her she wouldn't let herself be captured.

It is said that many good people have died because they hesitate, for an evil man will not wait. In that short fraction of a second trying to be sure whether they should or should not shoot, the other person gains the advantage and kills them. Tom had told her this when he showed her how to use a gun, and it flashed through her mind as she leveled the rifle. But even as her finger sought the feel of the trigger she was thinking she had to be sure it wasn't Tom. Maybe he was shot but not dead; in her despair she grasped at the notion. Melinda knew inside that was asking too much, but she could not prevent her instinct to hesitate. It didn't matter that she might die there with Tom.

When she got the rifle up and targeted on the dark opening she saw the leg of someone just inside the door. Now the boot of a man stepped through the doorway. Melinda saw much blood, but couldn't yet tell who it was. She had no thought of running; nothing mattered at this point except to see if Tom might still be alive. Death could be seconds away, but it just didn't matter to her. If they were both to die like the famous story Romeo and Juliet, then so be it. She tightened her squeeze on the trigger with the rifle snug against her shoulder, and the gun sights targeted on the doorway. The man's torso came into the sights of her rifle. His arm was bloody and the gun in his hand pointed toward the ground. Just as she was about to pull the trigger his head passed out of the shadow of the doorway.

She blurted out in a whisper, "Oh my God!" Melinda's eyes swelled with tears until they hurt and her body began to shake. It was her beloved. Having heard her scream, he forced himself to get up and walk to the door. He saw that she was okay, though standing there in shock. He tried his best to smile at her, and then walked slowly to the step and sat beside Caisson.

Melinda stood there in disbelief. She had thought he was dead; now he was alive, though wounded. Her emotions tried to adjust to this turn of events. There on the step now sat the two men she most loved and hated. Less than a minute ago these men had tried to kill one another, and now they sat side-by-side. Caisson had pulled his cigarette makings from his shirt pocket and was trying to roll a smoke. Tom holstered his gun, took the makings and tried to help, but he was too shot up to complete the task. Melinda wiped the tears away, too confused to think. She just responded to the actions before her. Stepping forward she took the bag of tobacco and paper.

"I used to make these for Emmett," Melinda told them when she noticed the surprised looks on their faces.

"Thanks, miss!" Caisson said as he glanced up at her.

Tom watched her roll the cigarette with expert hands, and then he said softly, "Thought I told you to ride out."

She finished rolling the cigarette and gave it to Caisson, then took the matches and lit it for him. Brushing away more tears, she was still in a degree of shock and reacting now without thinking. "I started to, but then I just had to stay and see if you made it."

Melinda looked at their wounds. "Oh, you are both all bloody. Are there some bandages?"

Caisson had just taken a long drag on the cigarette, and motioned toward his horse as he exhaled. "There's some on that Arabian gray out yonder."

She ran to get them, and then came back. She paused for a second because they were both badly wounded, and Caisson sensed her predicament. "You go ahead and take care of your man. I'll be cashin in before long."

She didn't hesitate, and began to bandage Tom. He was bleeding from his right leg. There was a wound in his arm but it appeared minor. As she worked on bandaging Tom's leg, Caisson turned to look at him. The outlaw leader had been surprised when Ringo walked out and sat down beside him. Ben had thought for sure that the gunman took a bullet in the chest, but saw now that he was wrong. Things had happened so fast, and it had been hard to see because of the darkness and gunsmoke.

"He'll make it alright," Ben said. "Just stop that leg from bleeding and he'll be fine." He watched as she put the bandage on Ringo, and then he said to the young woman, "Your man is everything the legends say about him."

Caisson took a puff and blew it out, and then turned toward the gunman. "If I'd known it was you I was going up against, Ringo, I would have vamoosed a long time ago. I reckon I know why you changed your name though. Wanted to start life over. That's what I was gonna do too." After a long pause he added, "Funny how things work out." His breath was short and labored as he finished the last sentence.

Tom couldn't think of anything to say. He knew Caisson didn't have much time to live. He also knew he himself should recover. Tom figured he had just been lucky.

Ben Caisson took another puff; he knew his time had come. All that loot he had stored away would never be found. It was too well hidden and would serve no purpose. His dreams of those many years would all be for naught. Every second that passed put him that much closer to death. These were the last two people he would ever see.

"Funny how you forget your hate when you're about to die," he thought to himself. This man had killed his brother and now had killed him. But he was Johnny Ringo; Caisson couldn't help but feel a thrill sitting next to the legend.

"Damn, I wish I had known," he said out loud. He wished he could live so he could tell this story to everyone he met. What a tale to impress the ladies while he sat drinking and playing cards in New Orleans. Caisson spoke once more: "Ringo, are you gonna marry this girl?"

Melinda was shocked at the question and looked at the outlaw leader in disbelief. But then she recovered, and grew curious what the response would be. It caught Tom off guard as he was still dazed. He looked at Caisson, didn't give his answer much thought and just spoke honestly. "I reckon I am if she'll have me."

Then Caisson took another drag on the cigarette and asked Melinda, "Well, lovely lady, are you gonna marry him?"

Melinda had gone from despair to ecstasy in a matter of minutes, from thinking Tom was dead to marriage. "Oh yes, just as soon as he is well," she bubbled, the words understandable but run together in her rush to answer.

"Well, I reckon I'm gonna give you two a wedding present early."

Ben proceeded to tell Tom about the gold. Assuring him there was plenty, he disclosed the two places where the gold was hidden and how to find it. He used two spots and two methods, he explained, just in case one was found. Ben described in detail how to find the gold in the cave, but was still explaining how to find it in the second location when he paused for a few seconds.

His breathing became more difficult. With tears coming to his eyes, he looked at Melinda. Suddenly, his breathing became extremely labored; he tried to say something, but no sound came. He held his hands toward Tom and Melinda, and each took hold of one. Caisson squeezed their hands ever so slightly. Tears swelled in his eyes and one trickled down his cheek. His breathing stopped, and then he slumped over on the shoulder of the man who had killed him. Ben Caisson was dead.

TWENTY- NINE

Tom and Melinda sat on the porch, glad to be alive and free from the danger of Caisson and his men. They pondered the irony. Caisson had meant to kill Tom and kidnap Melinda, possibly causing her great harm physically and emotionally. Yet, in his dying moments he gave them a present they could not repay. Bart Sanders had been hired to kill Tom, yet he helped Melinda and even threatened to kill Caisson if he didn't let her leave.

Tom told her he believed there was always some honor among men, even outlaws. Melinda thought it showed there was a spark of good in all people. Suddenly Tom's leg had a sharp pain and he grimaced.

"The loss of blood is going to make you weak," Melinda said. "We need to get you home."

They had been talking about what had happened, but hadn't thought about what to do next. Getting to his feet, Tom walked to the doorway. As he looked inside it suddenly dawned on him there was a problem.

"Melinda, I have to take Bart's body away from here and bury him."

"But you can't do that. We have to get you home; you're bleeding."

"I know, but it doesn't matter. Bart's well known as a gunfighter. It wouldn't be good if people found out I shot him. It'll be hard enough explaining how all these other men were killed."

"You're right. I'm glad you thought about that. It just hadn't occurred to me."

"I'd kinda like to bury Bart anyway. He forced Ben to let you walk out. I feel like I owe him."

"I could hardly believe it when he said that to Caisson."

"Caught me by surprise too. Bart and I knew each other years ago."

Melinda had hated Caisson, and feared him, but in the final few minutes of his life he had been good to them, talking about their getting married, and his gift meant something.

"What about Ben? Shouldn't we take him too? He did give us that gold."

Tom looked at her surprised. "It'll be quite a chore just to bury Bart. Ben is big. Getting him on a horse will be a load. You'd have to do most of the digging and rock carrying."

"I can do it, and I'll help you get him on his horse. Kind of crazy isn't it, him wanting us to get married and giving us all that money?"

"I guess he wanted to do something good before he died. Being near death can change you."

Tom made the last statement deep in thought because he had been near death on two occasions. It was Melinda that saved him the last time, appearing at his bedside looking just like the angel at the mountain lake. Those experiences and the guidance of Josh had changed his life. Looking up he saw Melinda staring at him in anticipation. Tom knew she had heard Caisson call him Ringo. He had never opened up that part of his life to her. It was something he knew he would have to do if they were going to be married, but he wasn't quite ready.

"Well, you're right; we owe it to Ben to bury him," he said.

"I'll go get his horse."

Tom stepped inside and looked at the three dead men. The pools of blood made it a gruesome sight. He walked toward the place where he had fallen, and was surprised at the amount of blood on the floor there. When he stood in the exact spot he had fallen, he suddenly became lightheaded. He put his hand to his forehead, and images started flashing before him.

His mind began to replay falling to the floor and hitting his head. The next image he saw was a brilliant white light, and then a figure emerged and came rapidly toward him. It was a strong looking angel that carried a lance, which looked like a spear. The angel reached out with the lance and gently touched his chest. Then the images began to fade.

Tom shook his head, believing his mind was playing tricks on him. He thought perhaps that knock on the head when he fell was causing him to see things. Feeling dizzy, he took several steps toward the cabin wall and leaned against it. When he moved away from the place where he had fallen, all memory of the images left him.

As Tom's head cleared, all he remembered was that he had felt dizzy. Now, he heard Caisson's horse approaching and went outside to lift Ben's body. Melinda helped and they put him across the saddle. Ben was a big man and it took all of Tom's strength. Melinda walked back to get Bart's horse. As she brought the stallion in front of the cabin, Tom lifted Bart's body and carried it out to the porch. Even though Bart was more his size it was still a monumental task for Tom because of his wounds. Melinda helped him put the body on the horse.

Going back inside Tom got Caisson and Sanders' guns. He gave them to Melinda and asked her to put them in their saddlebags. For a few seconds he thought about torching the cabin to destroy the picture of what had occurred inside. Instead, he dragged one of the men to the spot where Bart had fallen to confuse anyone who tried to figure out what had happened. Tom went outside and sat on the front step to rest. Melinda came back and sat beside him.

"We have to come up with a story to explain why Ben and Bart aren't here," Tom said. "There's a lot of blood on the floor. I put one of the men where Bart was so they wouldn't be able to figure out there was a missing body. We could tell them I started to drag the bodies out to bury them, but then realized I couldn't do it."

"Since you were wounded you didn't have the strength to get them all the way out. We could also tell them Ben was shot but he got away."

"Yeah, that'll work." After a brief pause he added, "What about Bart?"

"I could tell them there had been a fourth man, but that he left before you got here. I could say that he hadn't wanted to be part of kidnapping a girl, argued with Caisson and walked out on him."

"And after I got here, you left the cabin and hid out in the trees until the shooting was over. You saw Ben ride away."

"Yes, and because I saw Ben ride off, at first I thought you had been killed," Melinda said, then sobbed and tears flowed as she recalled those terrible moments when she thought he was dead.

Tom hugged her and waited until she regained control. "I think that'll work," he concluded softly.

There was truth in the story, which made it more believable. Sanders did speak strongly to Caisson. Tom did wound Caisson and did shoot the other two. Caisson had walked out of the cabin. Much of the message was true, just not completely true. Before they left Tom went back into the cabin to get a shovel, and then walked over and got Wildfire and Diamond. Melinda left a note on the door saying she was safe and was taking Tom back to the ranch because he was wounded. She handed the reins of Ben's horse to Tom; she led Bart's black stallion.

Bart's horse had whinnied and stamped its front hoof when they put Bart's body on him. Tom was so light headed he had barely noticed. Melinda figured it was because of the strangeness of having his master's bloody body draped over the saddle.

They made their way down the face of the ridge and headed back toward the ranch, but took a different route than the posse would. Tom went to a patch of rocky ground he had noticed on the ride to Clear Ridge. Mescal had trouble tracking men earlier that year on similar rocky terrain. The tracking lessons the Indian had given Tom would help them now.

They took the four horses onto the rocky area. Tom took Caisson's body and carried him on his good shoulder back behind a large boulder. It was about twenty paces from the horses, a long distance to carry a big man. It would have been a struggle for Tom when he was healthy; it was miraculous he made it with two bullet wounds. He had to sit and rest before attempting to carry Bart's body.

Still lightheaded, he took Sanders off the saddle and began carrying him. Again the horse acted strangely, making snorting sounds and stamping his front hoof. Melinda held the reins tight and then took the horses up the trail about a hundred paces. She left them there and came back on foot. Walking away from the trail, she was able to stay on rocks much of the distance.

Tom had her take them forward because horses tend to make marks with their metal horseshoes. If there were numerous nicks in the rock, someone might get curious and find the nearby graves. Since the horses were only there long enough to unload the bodies, very few marks were made.

They buried the bodies and covered the graves with nearby stones. Even though tired and exhausted, Melinda said some words over them. She asked the Lord to be merciful and remember their good deeds. Tom used some branches with leaves to remove their tracks from around the graves as learned from Mescal. The mounds of stone were not visible from the trail, which was not well traveled. Tom thought it would be a long time before the graves were discovered. He doubted that anyone else would ever know who was buried there.

Tom and Melinda walked back toward the horses, staying on rocks most of the way, being careful not to leave footprints. On the way Melinda told him how Flame had attacked one of the men in the loft, and that Ember had done the same at the fortress. Tom remembered when he and Mescal had brought the two young cougars home to Melinda when they were tiny. He never imagined they might protect her someday.

As they got closer to the horses, she told him how she had escaped from the barn on Wildfire. She explained how she thought she would be safe on the swift red stallion and had planned to ride to Jake's ranch for help, but that Bart's black horse had outrun Wildfire. Tom stopped and looked at her dumbfounded. He asked in disbelief, "Outran Wildfire?"

Tom was tired and dazed, but reacted immediately to what she said. He knew that very few horses in the country could outrun the red stallion. Looking at the big black horse, Tom thought out loud, "Can it be?"

Walking slowly, Tom got close and held out his hand. The black stallion let out a whinny and stamped his front hoof. Tom petted the horse's neck. Melinda watched in amazement. She thought about asking but just observed for awhile. Finally she asked, "Do you know that horse?"

Tom nodded; he started to speak but stopped. He couldn't get the words out. He didn't let Melinda see the tear on his cheek. A quick hand removed the evidence. Looking at the sleek black coat of the magnificent animal, he was surprised he hadn't recognized him earlier. "Welcome back, Thunder."

Moments later he told Melinda that the black stallion was his horse years ago, but was stolen. Reminding Tom that he was still bleeding, she suggested they return to the ranch. As they got close they headed toward one of the remote canyons where Tom and Mescal kept their cattle. Tom put Thunder and Ben's horse in an enclosure where hay was stored. He knew the place well because of the detailed maps he had drawn. Far back in the enclosure there was a small pool of water from moisture that seeped out of the wall of the canyon. Tom put the saddles and saddlebags behind a large rock and covered them with a slicker from Ben's bedroll. A fence in front of the enclosure guarded the hay stored for the winter. The two horses would have plenty to eat. While closing the gate Tom told Melinda they would have to figure out later what to do with them. He thought perhaps Mescal could get the stallions in the morning, and was hopeful he would know where they could be kept out of sight.

They rode slowly because of his wounds, and it was dark when they approached Tom and Mescal's cabin. The moonlight allowed them to see Mescal's horse tied out front. They walked in to find an Indian girl asleep on Mescal's cot. It startled Tom at first, but then he saw his friend in the other bunk. The Indian girl woke as they entered.

"You must be Yellow Flower," Tom said.

"Yes! You are Tom Colt and Melinda?"

Melinda looked at Tom, puzzled. Tom was embarrassed and explained that in the excitement he had forgotten to mention the plight of Yellow Flower. He began to fill Melinda in on the story. After he had spoken only a few sentences, Melinda interrupted.

"Tom, we have to get you bandaged. You go ahead and tell me while we get started. Yellow Flower, could you help me?"

"Of course. What do you want me to do?"

"Why don't you get some water on the stove? I'll put in some more wood. It looks like we have plenty of bandages."

Tom told Melinda how Mescal had gone to save his niece at the same time he left to meet Caisson at Clear Ridge. After Yellow Flower came back with the water, Tom asked her to tell what happened when Mescal found her. She told how she was abducted, and then described the gunfight between Mescal and Sammy. Yellow Flower explained that when she had gotten to her friend's ranch, the owner had not been there. Borrowing some bandages and a wagon, she left a note for the rancher. She then took Mescal in the wagon to Emmett's ranch. When they arrived a few hours earlier no one was awake. She helped Mescal into the cabin, cleansed his wounds and put on new bandages. Yellow Flower told them he had lost a lot of blood, but she was sure her uncle would live.

Melinda and Yellow Flower cleaned Tom's wounds. He drank whiskey to ease the pain. Yellow Flower dug the bullet out of his leg, a task she had done several times before for her people. The pain was intense until she had the bullet out, and then they bandaged his leg. Tom's energy was spent and the whiskey he drank to dull the pain also dulled his senses. He tried to stay awake, but was asleep before they were done.

The two women went to the house to retrieve bedding. They would stay in the cabin for a few days until they knew the men were out of danger. While the men slept, Melinda and Yellow Flower went out on the porch. Melinda told her about Caisson coming to the ranch, the battle in the hayloft, the race to the fortress and her capture. She also told Yellow Flower about the gunfight at Clear Ridge. Melinda told her almost the whole story.

She and Tom had agreed they would tell Mescal. Melinda wanted the same close relationship with Yellow Flower. Having known her for only hours, Melinda already wanted to share the truth with her. The only things she held back were the gold and Tom's real identity. She didn't know if Tom would want either secret shared. Melinda then told Yellow Flower about Thunder and Caisson's horse, and Tom's hope to find a place for them until he could get a ranch.

Yellow Flower thought the rancher, where she got the wagon, would keep the stallions. Each of them briefly discussed experiences and got to know one another. Yellow Flower had been worried about the reception she might receive here, and was sure some wouldn't accept her. She was relieved that Melinda so openly welcomed her, and felt like part of the family already.

Melinda peeked inside at the clock and realized how late it was. "We must get to bed so we can tend to the men in the morning." They both went in and dropped off to sleep quickly.

In the morning Mescal woke around mid-morning and was weak from the loss of blood. Yellow flower fed him and enjoyed the closeness of caring for her uncle. Tom was still asleep at noon. Emmett, Jake and the posse arrived a little later and rode up to the cabin. Jake, Emmett and a few of the men dismounted.

Leaving Yellow Flower in the cabin to care for the two men, Melinda went out on the porch. She told Emmett and Jake that both Tom and Mescal were shot up pretty bad but would live. Melinda also briefly described Yellow Flower's rescue and the gunfight between Mescal and Sammy.

"We're sure glad you and Yellow Flower are okay," Jake said. "But we'd sure like to hear what happened up on Clear Ridge with Caisson and his men."

She proceeded and gave them the information as she and Tom had discussed. Jake, Emmett and the men listened eagerly to every word.

When she finished, Emmett asked, "Do you suppose there's any chance we could meet Yellow Flower? Most of us don't even know what she looks like."

"Yeah, we'd sure like to meet her if she could come out for a minute," Jake added.

Melinda stepped in quietly and asked her to come out. Being ill at ease in front of so many men, Yellow Flower walked out slowly. Jake and Emmett made it a point to shake hands with her. They had heard she was half Indian and half White, but all they cared about was that she was Mescal's niece. They wanted to make sure the men understood she was welcome on their ranches.

"Well, Joe told me you were pretty and he sure was right," Jake said.

Yellow Flower blushed and looked at Joe sitting on his horse looking sheepish. She replied, "My husband told me Joe had always been such a wonderful friend to him, and such an awful liar."

The men got a chuckle out of that and Joe stepped off of his horse, walked up and gave Yellow Flower a hug. She felt like they all accepted her. Jake asked if she would tell them, in her own words, what happened in the gunfight between Mescal and the man that abducted her. Yellow Flower described the standoff, and how Sammy had tried to taunt Mescal by making fun of his name. As best she could, she repeated the words Mescal had spoken about being an Apache warrior, and how she had screamed to distract Sammy. She left out the portion about Geronimo, having no idea if that part were true or if Mescal had made it up to scare Sammy. As she described the gun battle, the men all listened and relived it with her.

After she finished, Joe said, "Mescal was really brave. I told him Sammy was fast with a gun."

"Mescal was brave alright, but let's not forget how smart this little lady was, screaming like that," Jake said. "Miss, you probably saved Mescal's life."

"Thank you!" she said quietly as tears came to her eyes, and then she held up her hand to wave as she went back in the cabin.

After Yellow Flower went inside, Willie asked Melinda, "Could you tell us a little more about the other man you said was at Clear Ridge? The one that left, I been tryin to figure out for sure who he was."

Melinda had indicated earlier that she didn't know his identity, and now described his features as best she could. She told them again how he had words with Caisson and had walked out on the outlaw leader. Everyone believed her story, and some of the men mentioned Bart's name. They started talking among themselves about the gunfighter. Most thought it not surprising that a man like Sanders would question kidnapping a girl, and would be unafraid to argue with Caisson. Melinda could tell that they respected the famous gunman not so much because of what he had done, but because of his reputation.

One of the older cowboys, Gumpy, bow-legged and with a full wad of chewing tobacco, strutted in front of the other men. He spit on the ground for effect and then said, "Well, Miss Melinda, wur sure glad yur back with us, and Tom, Mescal and his niece too. I'm sure sorry though that I didn't get a chance to outgun that there Bart Sanders." The laughter that followed ended the conversation and Melinda took the opportunity to excuse herself.

Later that day Melinda asked Emmett if he would have someone take Yellow Flower to her ranch so she could see to her husband's burial and get her things. She explained that Yellow Flower would also need to talk to a couple of her neighbors about buying the ranch.

The next morning Willie and Yellow Flower headed out taking two wagons. They had to return the wagon Yellow Flower borrowed, plus they would need a wagon to bring her things back. Going first to her ranch they found no one there. There was a note inside the house from one of the neighbors that her husband's body had been taken to their place. Willie and Yellow Flower went there, and the neighbor and his wife were relieved that she was unharmed. They told her they had already made arrangements to have her husband buried the next day in the town cemetery, for which she was grateful.

Yellow Flower and Willie went on to return the wagon she had borrowed from the rancher. They arrived late in the evening and Yellow Flower briefly told the rancher, Cliff, what had happened. While Willie was in the barn looking after the horses, Yellow Flower took the opportunity to talk to Cliff in private.

"Cliff, could I talk to you about something that has to remain a secret?"

"Of course you can, Yellow Flower. Whatever it is, you have my word I won't tell anybody."

"It's about a couple of stallions. They used to belong to two of the rustlers Tom had the gunfight with. He has claimed them for his own and has hidden them in a canyon. Tom had planned for my uncle to go and get them, but Mescal is also recovering from wounds. Tom needs someone to take care of them for a year or so. He wants to use the stallions to start building a herd as soon as he gets his own place."

"Well, hell, that's not a problem. I'll take care of 'em."

"I've never seen the horses, but Melinda told me the black stallion is faster than Emmett's Wildfire. I told Tom you would probably look after them. I hope I didn't do wrong. Since the horses belonged to rustlers, there could be some danger. If you don't want to keep them I'll understand."

"Are you kidding? You've got a couple of stallions, and one of them can outrun Emmett's red. I'll keep them as long as Tom wants. Now you just quit frettin about it."

Yellow Flower gave him a hug while a few tears trickled down her cheek. "Thank you, Cliff. Thanks for being such a good neighbor and thanks for looking after the horses."

"The black is supposed to be better than Emmett's red, huh? How soon can I get 'em?"

"Well, actually the sooner the better. Tom doesn't want anyone else to see them."

"I'll go fetch 'em tomorrow then."

Yellow Flower got Tom's map out of the wagon. "This is a map of Emmett's ranch. You can see the 'X' where the stallions are. If anyone happens to see you taking the horses, show them this letter signed by Tom. It says he asked you to keep the stallions for him. I'll drop by later to get the map."

Yellow Flower and Willie stayed with Cliff that evening, and the next morning returned to Yellow Flower's ranch. She packed her belongings and then in the afternoon they attended her husband's funeral. Yellow Flower talked with several of the neighbors afterwards to see if any had an interest in buying her place. Fortunately, the family nearest to the ranch agreed to buy it. Since her husband had taken out a loan she didn't realize a great deal of money, but it would help her through the winter. Yellow Flower and Willie stayed at the ranch that night, with Willie staying in the barn.

The next morning was a sad and emotional departure for Yellow Flower. The many dreams she and her husband had shared were gone. She wept as they left and cried for many miles. Willie did his best to comfort her, but he didn't know much about consoling a woman. As they drew nearer to Emmett's place, she set the sadness aside. When the ranch house came into view, Yellow Flower thought about her new life. Melinda had told her before she left that she was to move into the ranch house with her.

While Willie and Yellow Flower were away, Melinda hitched up a wagon and went to get the saddles. She found the two horses grazing peacefully behind the haystack. The grass, hay and water were plentiful and the horses were content. After admiring the stallions, she loaded up the two saddles and saddlebags, and headed back to the ranch.

She returned at dusk while most of the men were still out. Those that were there were busy in the corral. No one seemed to take much notice as she halted the wagon in front of the cabin. Tom came out to bring the saddles inside and she carried the saddlebags. He put them up in the little attic. Tom told her they could stay there until he and Melinda got a place of their own.

THIRTY

It was several weeks before Tom and Mescal were well enough to contemplate making the long ride back for the gold. Tom had told his friend how Ben had made the gift in his dying breath. Mescal was glad to hear there was an additional place where Caisson had hidden the loot. The old Indian had left only four bags in the cave, disguising that the rest was gone.

Mescal didn't let on that he remembered the peanut-shaped rock where Tom said the rest was buried. The Indian had noticed it, but ruled out the possibility the money was underneath because it was too big to move. Preferring to keep what he had found a secret, he hoped there was a lot of gold hidden under the rock. While wanting Tom and Melinda to have enough for their ranch, he also now had Yellow Flower to think about.

Finally, after a month of healing, they decided it was time to go. Melinda was anxious because of the importance of the outcome to their future, and couldn't help but dream about a wedding and a new house. While the men were healing, she had created a drawing of what the house should look like. A week ago she and Tom decided that when they got a ranch they wanted Mescal and Yellow Flower to live with them. Melinda redid her drawing, adding size to the house. She wanted it to be plenty big for the four of them.

Tom and Mescal saddled up their mounts and loaded the supplies on a packhorse. Melinda and Yellow Flower saw them off, giving both of them hugs and waving goodbye. Enthusiasm was evident on Melinda's face as she watched the men ride away. She had grown close to Yellow Flower during the past month, but had not told her about the gold. Mescal had asked that they wait to make sure it actually existed.

"I feel like a little boy chasing after the rainbow, hoping there's a pot of gold," Tom said to Mescal after they left.

"Mebbe Caisson tell you big story, have last laugh."

"That would be a kick in the pants, wouldn't it? Get our hopes up, plan on buying a ranch, building a nice house, travel all the way down there and find nothing."

Mescal didn't say anything for awhile as they rode down the trail. Tom had become quiet, and Mescal could tell he was pondering the possibility there was no gold. The old Indian finally turned to his friend.

"Man not lie when dying. Gold there," Mescal said.

"Yeah, he wouldn't lie; not then." Moments later Tom gave the Indian a dirty look, realizing his friend was having fun at his expense. Mescal started laughing and after a few moments Tom joined him.

Several days later they had crossed the desert and set up camp at Indian Waters. Mescal was preparing supper. Tom was sitting in the water. Finding it difficult not to dream, he felt certain Melinda was having the same problem. He thought of her now in this wonderful setting. Someday he would have to bring her here and they could get in the pool together. After stepping out of the water, he sat on a rock to dry and let his mind drift back to Melinda. While continuing to daydream, he heard Mescal yell and realized he had spent too much time taking his bath and drying. When he returned to camp Mescal had the food ready and waiting.

"Me worry White man get lost, not find way back."

"Sorry I took so long. The water is just right. I guess time got away from me."

"Maybe someone else there. You find naked lady in water?"

"One came by but said she preferred Indians. Guess you're in luck."

"She in luck too."

Tom laughed. Mescal chuckled and ate, quite pleased with his own humor. When they were finished, the Indian sat and drank coffee with Tom before leaving to take his bath. While Mescal was gone Tom cleaned up the eating utensils and skillet, tidied up around the camp, and then sat and enjoyed the scenery. The sun was setting but not with spectacular colors this particular evening. His mind drifted in and out, first enjoying the surroundings and then dreaming about a ranch and cabin. He kept reminding himself every so often that they hadn't found any gold yet.

Tom and Mescal were up early the following morning, circled around White Cloud and then took the cutoff to the hideout. They arrived at Caisson's old hideout late that day. Nothing much had changed since they were last there. Tracks gave evidence that three men had stayed in the cabin for at least one night.

They decided to wait until morning to look for the gold because the sun was setting. Tom put the horses in the corral. Mescal tied string to some cans with rocks, and set them in key locations outside. If anyone was around, they wanted some warning. Both thought it wise to have someone on guard duty for the full night. Tom took the first shift. It was peaceful that evening.

Tom woke up to the smell of eggs, bacon, biscuits and coffee. Both ate hurriedly, eager to look for gold. Searching the cabin Tom found the mirror, and then the pole with the hook. He decided to go to the cave first because Ben had told him exactly how it was hidden. They found the cave without much trouble. Tom lit a torch and walked into the cave.

"It doesn't look like anybody has been in here," Tom said.

Mescal thought silently, "Indian no leave track."

"Here's the three areas Ben talked about. It looks just like he described."

"Where go now?"

"He said it was in the middle area. One with a lot of holes in the wall."

Finding the wall with all the holes, Tom lit a second torch and threw it in the largest one to locate the blind spot. The torch didn't go back far enough, so he used the pole to push it in further. Finally it illuminated the area to the side. Tom started moving a little quicker and Mescal could tell he was getting excited. Since the Indian already knew what to expect, he stayed calm and watched. Tom was having trouble getting the mirror aligned correctly but kept trying.

"It didn't sound that hard when Ben talked about doing this. Haven't seen anything so far. Sure hope he told the truth."

"Need more light? Mebbe get bigger torch."

"There they are." Tom saw some leather bags just as Mescal finished his statement.

His breathing grew rapid as he tried to hook the closest one. It wasn't long before he realized he had to reposition the mirror. He could see the bags, but when he tried to hook one he had to rotate the pole and then he couldn't see. Tom was getting impatient because he wanted to get a bag and make sure there was gold in it. There was no breeze in the cave and he began to sweat. Continuing to have difficulty trying to hook a bag, he had to reposition the mirror several times before he snagged one. As soon as he got the bag out of the hole, he undid the leather strip that bound it and grabbed a handful of gold coins.

Tom laughed and shook the coins in his hand, showing them to Mescal. He joyfully put them back in the bag and grabbed the pole. The second bag came much quicker now that the mirror was properly positioned. The third and fourth bag came in a hurry. Just as he started getting the hang of it, he couldn't see any more bags. The torch had burned low and he was unable to see clear back in the hole. Lighting another torch, he threw it in. Now he could see that there were no more bags there.

"Well, sure enough we found some gold, but I thought he was talking about more than this." After a pause Tom added, "I guess it's more than we had."

Mescal took the long pole and mirror, inspecting the hole as though he thought Tom might have overlooked a bag. After completing his effort he grunted and said in a dejected tone, "No more gold."

Sticking the torch in the other holes, Tom quickly surmised that was all there was in the cave. His expectations took a serious downturn. Four bags of gold were nice to have, but not enough for everything he was hoping to do. His mind started doing the math. Each bag felt like it weighed about five pounds; there were sixteen ounces in a pound, so there were approximately eighty ounces of gold per bag. That was a lot of gold and a lot of money, but ranches, cabins, cattle and horses cost a great deal. If there weren't any bags of gold under the rock, or only a few, their plans would have to be scaled down considerably. He sure didn't want to have to tell Melinda about the small pot of gold. Then he chastised himself; he should be happy with whatever they found. They would still be way ahead of where they were before Caisson had told them his secret. They could still start a ranch.

Tom had hopes of finding enough to help some of the ranchers whom Caisson had stolen from, as well as to buy a ranch. As Tom walked away from the cave he began mentally downgrading his plans. Going in search of the rock, he wanted to find it quick to answer the question of how much they would have and how much they could help others. He wanted to do both, get what Melinda had hoped for and help the other ranchers, but began wondering what choices they would have to make. Mescal could tell his friend was worried, but knew it wouldn't be long before they would find the rock and discover more gold.

Tom looked for the rock Caisson described as resembling a huge peanut. It was taking longer to find than he expected and he began to wonder if it existed. Mescal knew right where it was, but gave the impression he was also looking and trying to find it. For the most part he followed Tom, but eventually he sort of led his friend in the general direction. Tom finally spied it and his heart quickened.

"This must be it over here," Tom said.

"Big rock. How we move?"

Looking around the area Tom found the dead limb Caisson had described; he became hopeful again. Surely if both the rock and the limb were there then it must be true. He took a nearby smaller rock and put it close to the big rock. Using the limb for leverage he tried to roll the rock over on its side. It took his full weight and help from Mescal, but it finally rolled.

Tom was optimistic as he started shoveling, but after he had dug down two feet his face began to reveal concern. Standing up straight to relieve his back, he brushed the dirt from his clothes and sat down on the rock. He had perspired heavily and soil clung to his sweaty hands and arms.

"Thought I'd hit something by now," Tom said. "There's got to be something here if we can just find it."

"Mebbe deeper; me dig."

Caisson had been truthful about the cave, and Mescal knew it was likely there was gold here as well. He noticed the dirt was not packed. Somebody had buried something under the rock; he was sure of it.

Tom watched the removal of every shovelful. Mescal dug down another foot and widened the hole, still finding nothing. Tom relieved him and dug down another foot, widening it still more. The hole had become large and Tom's back was aching. He climbed out and sat on the rock next to Mescal.

"Well, what do you think?" Tom asked.

"Dirt not packed. Me think gold here, need dig more."

Mescal picked up the shovel, got back in the hole and dug a foot deeper. Noticing when the ground suddenly became harder, he stopped digging and got out to rest.

When Tom returned to the hole he put the point of the shovel in several places, but then stopped. He realized the dirt on the bottom of the hole was packed and had never been dug before. Tom climbed out and sat down dejected, nearly convinced there was no gold under the rock.

"It doesn't look good, my friend," Tom said.

"It here. Got to be here. Me dig more."

Mescal got back in and shook his head; he knew he was missing something. He tried digging in every square foot of the bottom. There was no unpacked earth. Turning slowly, he carefully studied the hole they had dug. He noticed that about three feet from the top some of the dirt on the side had fallen to the bottom of the hole, which was now five feet deep. At first it annoyed him because it was more dirt to be removed. Using the shovel he scooped out the dirt that had just fallen. When he did, more fell. Then it hit him. Mescal remembered how crafty Caisson had been in hiding the gold in the cave. Ben had put it in a side compartment, an indentation in the stone wall.

"That's it," the Indian said out loud.

"What's it?" Tom asked excitedly.

Mescal put the shovel aside and with his hands started taking more of the dirt out of the side, letting it fall into the bigger hole. Tom's heartbeat quickened as he watched Mescal's renewed efforts. The dirt was not packed and was coming out easily. The side hole went under the edge of a huge rock near the one shaped like a peanut. The bigger rock was four feet high and at least twelve feet across. After reaching in and removing dirt for nearly a minute, Mescal hit something. A big smile came across his face as he pulled out a leather bag covered with dirt. It was similar in size and appearance to the other four bags, perhaps five pounds in weight.

Tom yelled, "Whoopee! There it is." He anxiously opened the bag and sure enough it was full of coins. Tom grinned ear to ear. "It's gold alright. Now to see how much there is."

Mescal pulled out another bag, then another, and still another. It took them several minutes because it was far into the side hole. They took turns reaching in and extracting the bags, and then had to widen the hole to get the last few. When they were satisfied they had found them all, there were twenty-four bags on the ground plus the four they had found in the cave.

"If Caisson hadn't told us, nobody would have found this gold in a hundred years," Tom said.

"Caisson tricky. Hide gold good."

Tom was elated. All this gold would buy everything they wanted, with money left over. "We really should give some of this to Emmett and Jake, and some of the other ranchers who lost cattle to Caisson."

Mescal was not surprised and was glad he had already stored away the bags he found earlier in the cave. He was supportive of giving up some gold, but he didn't feel he nor Yellow Flower owed much to the White man, other than to their close friends Tom, Melinda, Emmett and Jake. With this much gold, Mescal knew they now had enough to do all the things Tom wanted, and still have some stored away for future use.

"Let's not waste any more time. It's still early; we can head back home," Tom suggested.

They put the dirt back in the side compartment and then shoveled the remaining soil into the larger hole. Using the limb they rolled the peanut-shaped rock back on top, and then carried the bags of gold to the cabin. It took two trips of each carrying a full load. Tom was ready to start putting them on the packhorse.

"First me go back, hide tracks at cave and rock," Mescal said. "Others mebbe know Caisson had gold. Mebbe someone figure out we find gold."

"Okay! While you're gone I'll get some food ready. We can eat before we leave."

Mescal went to the cave first. He was careful to give it the appearance that nothing had happened there. The cave was easy, but making the area around the rock look untouched took time. The old Indian was hot and tired when he finished, but was careful not to leave any footprints as he returned. He noticed there were quite a few tracks around the cabin. Mescal took some brush and smoothed out the dirt in front of the porch. When he was done he got something from his horse, and then went into the cabin. As he stepped through the door he saw that Tom had the meal sitting on the table next to the fireplace.

Suddenly, Tom stepped out of the back room with his hands in the air. A second man emerged with a gun pointed at Tom's back. It was Jeb, who had first told Mescal about Caisson's secret.

"Drop yur gunbelt, Injun," Jeb ordered.

Mescal complied, unbuckling his gunbelt and sliding it over to the end of the cabin where Jeb stood.

Jeb turned to Tom. "Sit down on the other side of that table where I can keep my eye on ya."

Tom walked over to the other side of the table and sat down. He could hardly believe their bad luck; they had found the pot of gold, only to have this rustler get the drop on them.

Jeb had spent the last month up on the canyon wall. He had left Utah just like he told Jake he would. Four weeks later, after hearing nearly all of Caisson's gang had been killed, he came back with his cousin, Casey. Jeb had sat waiting at the sentry point. He had watched three members of the gang come and then leave the next morning. They had not searched in the canyon and apparently knew nothing of the money. Jeb waited patiently at first, but almost gave up hope Caisson would come. At times he worried that Ben had already been there and taken all the money, which would make his wait futile. Jeb didn't think so and forced himself to be patient. Another week passed and it was beginning to look like he had wasted a lot of time for nothing. He finally decided he would wait one more week. Having made that decision, it was only three days later when Mescal and Tom showed up. He still had hope knowing the Indian was aware of the hidden money.

Jeb waited to see if they would conduct a search. Seeing them go to the cave he was elated when they carried several bags out, but could tell they were still searching. After Tom let out his holler, Jeb started making his way down the canyon wall. As he was climbing down, he saw Mescal head back to the cave. He crept up carefully to the cabin because he saw them put the string and cans out the evening before. Jeb slipped in and caught Tom off guard just as he finished preparing the food. Now he had captured the Indian; this was coming off even better than he hoped. Next he wanted to repay the Indian for the terror he had endured many weeks ago. Jeb started walking toward Mescal slowly with gun in hand.

"Well, Injun, it's my turn to do some scarin. You thought you had me licked, didn't you? Well, I fooled you, fooled everybody. Now I'm rich."

Jeb's eyes were open wide and his face had a wild look. He tried to grin and look confident, but his fear of Mescal was evident. Now he struggled to show that he was in control, something he needed after the incident at Death Rock. Jeb looked first at one then the other, rapidly back and forth.

"The only question about you two is how yur gonna die. How you wanna die, Injun?"

Mescal showed no fear as Jeb moved closer, and that made him angrier. The next time he stepped closer the Indian backed away. Mescal moved backward toward Tom, turning his back almost directly at his friend still seated at the table. That pleased Jeb; he wanted the Indian to feel fear like he had. Jeb pulled out his knife with his left hand and the Indian backed away again, but this time moving away from Tom and toward the door.

As Mescal got close to the door, Jeb ordered, "Hold it, Injun."

Mescal froze in his tracks and looked over at his friend. Tom saw and understood. He started to get up.

"Sit back down, Colt," Jeb ordered, but did not turn toward him. Tom was now half standing, and Jeb yelled, growing angry, "I said sit down or I'm gonna kill yur Injun friend."

Suddenly Tom dove across the table away from Mescal, turning the table over sideways with a loud crash. He hit the floor hard and Jeb turned and fired at Tom. The bullet hit the underside of the tabletop. Jeb hurried over to the end of the table, cocked his gun and pointed it at Tom's head.

Tom looked up to see the barrel of the gun pointed right at his forehead. A big grin erupted on the rustler's face as he started to pull the trigger. Suddenly, Jeb's head jerked to the side; the look on his face went blank as he fell over. Tom saw Mescal's tomahawk half buried in the side of Jeb's skull.

"Me lucky see track not ours when come back," said the Indian.

Tom breathed a sigh of relief and wondered how many times this man would save his life. He had seen the tomahawk tucked in the back of Mescal's pants when the Indian turned his back toward him. After Tom got to his feet they went outside and sat on the porch. Mescal went back in and brought out the plates of food. Tom hesitated, but knew he needed to eat. It was a meal slowly consumed.

After Mescal finished eating, he took the shovel and started digging a grave next to where the other rustlers had been buried. Tom helped him finish and they carried Jeb's body out and buried him, the tomahawk still protruding from his skull. It was a gruesome sight and Mescal did not want to remove it. After they completed the grave, Mescal did his best to remove the signs of a recent burial. In a week or two it would look like the other graves to anyone riding into the canyon. While Mescal was finishing up, Tom went inside and mopped up the blood and buried the rags behind the cabin.

As they carried the first few bags out, Mescal suggested they put some of the gold on Diamond and Paint and not all on the packhorse. He reasoned that if the packhorse ran off or was stolen, they would

413

still have some gold. They decided to put fourteen bags on the packhorse, and seven bags on each of their horses. On the packhorse they loaded the gold in two pairs of saddlebags, and then covered them with other supplies. Over it all they put a small tarp so it looked like an ordinary packhorse any traveler might have. Mescal hoped that Tom wouldn't notice the similarity to the two packhorses they had taken out earlier when he had found the gold in the cave. They broke camp and headed back toward the ranch.

THIRTY- ONE

Having so much gold made Tom and Mescal apprehensive. As long as no one knew about it they didn't have much reason to worry, but they worried anyway. The sudden and unexpected appearance of Jeb had heightened their awareness of the potential danger.

After they had traveled for several hours, Mescal stopped on the top of a hill and waited to see if anyone was trailing them. Later he stopped twice more, but no one came. That evening they camped near White Cloud where months before lightning had nearly hit them. They hid the twenty-eight leather bags on the ground under several dead limbs. Mescal tied two cans to the limbs, so they would make noise if anyone tried to take the gold during the night.

In the morning, the first thing Mescal did was walk close to the limbs to see if the bags were still there. When Tom woke he got up and stretched, then started to walk that way.

"Me look. Still there," Mescal said.

Tom smiled and sat down.

"You nervous; make me nervous," the old Indian said.

"Reckon it would be better if we'd get our minds on something else."

They stopped that evening at Indian Waters long enough to eat. Just before it was too dark to ride, Mescal led them a few miles away to sleep. Indian Waters was a popular place and they preferred to find a secluded spot where they wouldn't have to post guard. The next morning they returned to Indian Waters for breakfast, and then crossed the desert before the day grew hot.

That night they stayed at the site where Jeb and Jim had ridden up on them. It brought back images of Jeb in the bottom of the grave with the tomahawk still attached to his head. Neither spoke of him. He had sworn not to come back; he did and paid the price. They put the gold next to two large boulders at the edge of camp, and then piled their supplies over it.

A few days later, their long trip home was nearly complete. They were two days from the ranch and Tom was anxious to tell Melinda how much they had found. Mescal wanted to see Yellow Flower's eyes light up when he showed her the gold. It was late in the afternoon as they rode down the trail when four riders approached from the opposite direction. As the men drew close, Tom realized they were strangers. They had the appearance of drifters rather than cowboys and were well armed. As the four rode up they brought their horses to a halt.

"Howdy!" the one in front said. He was in his mid-thirties, which was several years older than two of the riders were but younger than the one on the right. "Do y'all know how to get to White Cloud?"

"As a matter of fact we just came from there," Tom replied in a friendly manner. He went on to tell them the route to follow, and described the desert they would have to travel through. Mescal kept his eyes on the men. He had his reasons for distrusting them.

"Do you live nearby?" the leader asked.

"No, up further north. We're heading back that way now. We work for Emmett Bailey." Tom could see the man's reaction to that piece of information.

"We heard there was a White man and an Indian that sorta look after that ranch. Heard they're known as the Gunman and the Tracker. People say they killed Bert Cooper. That wouldn't be you, would it?"

"I reckon that's us alright."

"Well I'll be darned." While the leader still smiled, it was now forced. The men with him looked ill at ease. "Word here of late is you even shot Ben Caisson, killed most of his gang."

"I wounded Ben alright, but he got away. A posse got his gang."

"Was hoping to get to meet you sometime. I have a spread up further north. I didn't lose any cattle to Caisson, but I figured my time was a comin." The leader had let his expression turn to a frown, but now he suddenly smiled again. "Well, sir, I want to thank you for getting rid of those rustlers."

"Appreciate the thanks, but suspect we just got lucky."

"Wish it was closer to supper time. We'd sure like to share a campfire with you, but we really need to be movin on." The leader pulled on the reins of his horse, turning it back toward the road.

"Yeah, we have to keep moving too," Tom replied. "Hope you have a good ride to White Cloud."

"Much obliged," the leader said and touched his hat.

As the four were riding by, Tom dismounted and checked the cinch on his horse, keeping Diamond between him and the riders. He glanced often in their direction as they rode away. Mescal watched Tom, ready to jump from his horse if he suddenly reacted. One of the men looked back a couple of times, but they never stopped. Tom took a drink from his canteen and then offered it to Mescal. When the men were out of rifle range he got back on his horse.

"He no rancher," Mescal said.

"No, I don't think so. Reckon the only cattle he sold had someone else's brand."

Mescal had wanted to kill the leader and his older friend on sight, but had resisted the temptation. He thought it best not to start anything when they had over a hundred pounds of gold. The future of Tom, Melinda and Yellow Flower would be ensured by the yellow coins in the saddlebags. Now he told Tom about these men.

After the four riders went over the top of a small hill and were out of sight, the leader pulled up. "Well, men, we all know their reputation for trackin and killin. They were responsible for buryin a lot of our friends. Do we let 'em just ride on, or do we circle back and ambush 'em?"

The three sat in their saddles for some time before one finally spoke. George was young and tall. His voice evidenced his reluctance. "It'd be right tricky tryin to ambush the Indian. People say he can see like a hawk."

The rider next to him, Bob, was the youngest. "Bert was a good friend of mine; I say we go back and get 'em."

The leader looked at the third man. "What do you think, Gibbs?"

Gibbs had been a rustler and outlaw for over twenty years. It was the only life he had ever known. He realized what he said could decide what came next, and he didn't want the responsibility. He spit out some tobacco juice. "I don't know what good killin 'em will do fur us. We're headin outta Utah anyway. That man, Colt, well, you saw him, cool as could be, never showed any fear. He'd be hard to shoot. It's true they killed some of our friends, just like you said, but George is right, that Indian wouldn't be easy to ambush. I reckon I'll do whatever you decide, Brock."

Tom and Mescal traveled on for an hour. The old Indian stopped at a high place on the road and walked over to a nearby ridge, waiting to see if they were being followed. Tom walked up beside him.

"What do you think?"

"If no gold, see if they follow. If no follow, ride to see if circle round." Mescal pointed to the left side of the trail. "Ride that way, see if come cross tracks, only way to circle round, then track them. But we have gold; take care of gold first."

"Is there a way to get around Butcher's Pass?"

Mescal nodded, and then pointed to the right. "Canyons, rough, slow. Not easy ambush there. If they follow, we see."

"Nobody would expect us to be going that way. Sounds good to me. How about you?"

The Indian nodded and led them off the trail. He rode where their tracks would be hard to follow. As it grew later in the day, he got off his horse and again walked to a rim where he could see well back on their trail. Sitting in the shadows he watched for nearly half an hour. The riders had not come and it was getting dark. The old Indian thought it would be safe to proceed now. The four men would not be able to follow their tracks in the rough and rocky ground at night.

Mescal led on; he wanted to be several miles farther away before it was too dark to ride. They went five miles more off the trail and made camp toward the back of a canyon. It would be nearly impossible for anyone to track them, and the only way they could be found was by blind luck. Even so, they set out the string and cans, and then took turns on guard duty the whole night.

Before his friend woke up the next morning, Mescal drew a rough outline of the canyons on the back of the map of Emmett's ranch that Tom carried in his saddlebag. He drew the major landmarks of the canyons Tom would have to travel through to get past Butcher's Pass. The old Indian thought sure Tom would be able to find his way back to the trail. When Tom woke up Mescal told him he wanted to see if Brock and his gang had doubled back to try and ambush them. He showed Tom the map and the landmarks. Mescal told him he thought he would be safe, as there was no grass in those canyons and no reason for anybody to be there. Before leaving, the Indian gave his saddlebag of gold to Tom to put on the packhorse.

Tom headed out alone and started working his way around the hills and canyons. The terrain was rough and rocky. It was much slower going and would add at least a day or two to the travel. As the sun set Tom rode back to a ridge and watched until nearly dark to be sure that he wasn't followed, just as Mescal had the night before. He camped in another remote canyon where it would be safe to build a fire.

He was about ready to turn in for the night when there was a noise in the surrounding darkness. It sounded like something moving in the trees. His hand went to his gun and he moved next to a nearby boulder and waited. Again he heard the sound, and then suddenly there was the rustle of many feet on the ground. Tom looked out to see eyes glowing in the dark. It was an eerie sight with all those pairs of shining eyes just outside the circle of light provided by the campfire. Man seldom traveled these canyons and the coyotes were curious about their visitor. After a few minutes the animals departed into the night.

While Tom headed back into the canyons, Mescal retraced his tracks and waited in the rocks by the trail to see if the four riders returned. He waited there until noon, and then rode past the trail. Several minutes later, he came across their tracks where they had circled around. After following them halfway to Butcher's Pass, he felt certain that was their destination. Leaving their trail he took a different route and located their tracks again about a mile from the pass. He hobbled his horse near grass and water, planning to slip stealthily into the pass while the four men slept.

The riders had been waiting in the rocks since early in the afternoon. Brock had expected to see the Gunman and the Tracker that evening or early the next morning. It was getting dark and there had been no sign of them.

"Think it'd be alright if we start a fire?" Gibbs asked Brock.

"Better not. I reckon that Indian is smart enough to know this is where he'd get ambushed if one was going to happen. He might ride ahead and check. We'll have to make cold camp tonight."

Brock walked down to the horses to get some chewing tobacco. When he came back, Bob was sitting on a rock high in the pass smoking a cigarette. It was dark and the tip of the cigarette was bright, especially when he inhaled.

"Why don't you build a fire and send a smoke signal to the Indian that we're here?" Brock asked sarcastically.

Bob looked at him questioningly. Brock shook his head and added in a disgusted voice, "If you're gonna smoke do it down below where they can't see the glow of that cigarette."

Later, as they sat in the dark, the oldest rider, Gibbs, said, "You know, they just might try to make it through tonight while it's dark, especially if they're worried about an ambush."

"Yur right," Brock replied. "I'll take the first watch."

It was darker than usual that night. When the quarter moon went behind a cloud it was nearly pitch black. Brock listened intently. Once he thought someone was out there, but then he heard the bark of a coyote nearby. Brock was glad when his watch was over and it was time to wake Gibbs. The leader was tired and quickly went to sleep.

After eating cold food for breakfast, they took their places in the rocks and waited. Later, as the sun rose high overhead, it became hotter. By late morning the two young riders, George and Bob, were uncomfortable and impatient. Bob went down to get some food and check on the horses. The rest waited in the rocks.

Gibbs was upset when Bob hadn't returned after what seemed like half an hour. The sun was bearing down and the rocks were increasingly hot. Gibbs figured the youngster was probably sitting down in the shade. Just as he was about to go after him, he heard Brock tell George, "Go see what the hell he's doing."

Gibbs smiled. Brock could sure get angry. He remembered when Brock had killed one of his men for kissing a whore down in Arizona. It was a girl the leader was particularly fond of, and he had told his men to stay away from her. The young rider had been drunk and the girl kept flirting with him until the young rustler kissed her. Gibbs didn't blame the youngster at all, but Brock had been incensed and shot him. He had a mean streak. Gibbs knew to stay out of his way when he was mad.

After thirty more minutes the sweat was rolling off of Gibbs. George hadn't returned either. Gibbs went over to Brock; the leader was almost beside himself with anger.

"Never should've taken on those no account young shithead dummies," fumed Brock.

"I'll go see what's keepin 'em," Gibbs replied.

"We got two men comin who sposed to be the most dangerous damned gunmen around and those two dumb shits are sleeping under a shade tree."

"I'll find 'em, boss, and kick their asses all the way back up here."

Tom continued to make his way through the labyrinth of canyons. After crossing a small stream he came across tracks. It looked to him like at least six to eight horses. They had come in from another canyon, but were headed in the same direction he was. The hoofprints revealed that the horses had horseshoes, which meant the riders were probably not Indians. After following them for a short distance, he came upon a pile of horse droppings. Based on the softness, he could tell it was less than a day old.

As Tom continued he started wondering whether he should backtrack. There were four men that could be behind him and six to eight men ahead of him. One problem with going back was that Mescal would be expecting him north of Butcher's Pass. The Indian wouldn't know where he was or what had happened to him. As Tom pondered whether to turn back, the tracks of the riders headed in a different direction from the route Mescal had drawn for him. Tom was greatly relieved, but still didn't like riding into no-man's-land with a hundred pounds of gold when a bunch of unknown riders were in the same area. Tom continued in the direction Mescal had laid out. He took comfort knowing that if the map were reasonably accurate, he should make it back to the main trail before nightfall.

Unseen by Tom, a man in the rocks high on a ridge tried to make out who the lone rider was. The man, named Jesse, went down below and described him to Jack Stanton. Jack turned to Casey who had also heard the description. Jack knew Casey was slow mentally.

"That him," Casey said, nodding his head while his face twitched.

"Jesse, did you see anything of the Indian?" Jack asked.

"No, but he's got a packhorse just like Casey said."

"It got be him," Casey proclaimed, still looking nervous.

Casey was Jeb's cousin and had been with him on the canyon wall waiting for Caisson. Jeb had told Casey to stay put while he went down to get the drop on Colt and the Indian. Later Casey saw Jeb's body carried out and buried. He nearly went crazy not knowing what to do, and finally went back to White Cloud because he didn't know where else to go. With Jeb gone he had no family, and it would be hard for him to make it on his own.

Stanton and his gang had stayed for a long time at the hideout. They waited on Caisson but he never came back, nor did any of the men that had gone with Ben to Emmett Bailey's ranch. Jack had almost decided to move on, but before leaving he wanted to check one last time. He sent one of his men, Bickford, to White Cloud to see if there was any word on Ben.

When Bickford went to the saloon he met three men who had ridden with Caisson earlier. They told him about going to the hideout and finding the cabin all shot up and thirteen graves out back with a tombstone that read "Hung Rustlers." Since then they had been hanging around White Cloud hoping somebody from the gang would show up. After talking with Bickford, they all decided to head back to the new hideout.

They were just getting on their horses to leave when Casey rode in. Casey recognized one of the men as a friend of Jeb's and told them what had happened—Tom Colt and the Indian had killed Jeb and taken Caisson's gold. The men had known nothing about the gold, but they all believed Casey's story. They rode back to tell Stanton and the others at the hideout.

Jack had been excited at the news, and assured Casey that he'd get an equal share. The gang now included Jack Stanton, his five men, Casey and the three men who used to ride with Caisson. Jack was the leader. They had ridden hard to get ahead of Colt and the Indian. One of the men knew that five of Caisson's riders had been ambushed and hung in Butcher's Pass by Colt and the ranchers. They figured the Gunman and the Tracker would be extra careful there, so they planned to ambush them north of the pass.

Stanton left one of Caisson's men on the trail that could identify Colt, along with one of his Arizona cowboys. When they spotted him they were to ride ahead and let Stanton know. Jack now figured Colt must be avoiding the pass and had slipped around the sentries. Stanton was concerned because he didn't know where the Indian was, but not concerned enough to prevent him from going after the gold. The outlaw leader sent one of his men to get the two sentries. Jack and the rest started after Colt.

Not knowing he was being followed, Tom proceeded at a steady gait. An hour later he came across more tracks. These hoofprints were unshod; he couldn't determine the number for sure, but could tell there were many horses, possibly more than twenty. Fortunately the tracks were crossing his trail, and not going in the same direction he was. Tom continued on his journey at a faster pace than before.

Twenty minutes after Gibbs had gone down to check on Bob and George, Brock still hadn't heard from any of his men. He vacillated between being angry and worrying about what had happened to them. Finally he decided it didn't make sense to wait in the rocks any longer. If Colt and the Indian were coming they would have been there by now. They either didn't stay on the trail or had slipped past them in the night. The leader fumed even more, blaming the youngsters for being asleep when they went through. Climbing down out of the rocks he headed to where they had left the horses.

Coming within sight of the grove of trees where the horses were supposed to be, he saw his three riders instead. Their hands were tied behind them and there was a short rope with a noose around each of their necks tied to the tree limb above. Bob, George and Gibbs were each standing on a rock, balanced on yet another rock. They all had gags in their mouths. The rocks were round and small, less than a foot in diameter, and they had to keep their balance because the rope had very little slack. If the top rock fell off they would hang.

Brock felt certain Tom Colt and the Indian were in the boulders nearby. They must have slipped in during the night and taken the men one at a time as they came down. Brock crouched behind a boulder and looked all around. His forehead began to perspire heavily. The three men who rode with him looked terrified. They saw Brock but were unable to say anything because of the gags.

Brock left them and went quickly back to the rocks where they had sat earlier waiting for their prey. He would need the canteen of water and rifle he had seen Gibbs leave there. When he reached Gibbs' perch, the water and rifle were gone. In that short amount of time they had taken it. Even more fearful now he ran from rock to rock, crouching behind each one. The sun was high overhead. Sweat rolled off of Brock's face and his shirt soaked through. Every time he saw a shadow he pointed his gun, thinking it might be them.

For the next hour Brock searched for his horse, but spent most of the time hiding behind boulders. He was growing frantic from the strain of expecting to see them at every turn. Losing track of where he was, he suddenly realized that he had gone in a circle. His men were just ahead of him still hanging from the tree. The two young men had lost their balance. Apparently the tall rider, George, had slipped off his rock just a little while ago. He was still kicking, slowly spinning round one way and then back the other. The youngster, Bob, was already hanging limply, dead.

Gibbs saw Brock and cried out a muffled plea for help. As he did his body shifted to the right and he nearly fell off the rock. Slowly he managed to regain his balance. His legs were tired and his body felt like lead pulling his throat into the rope. Gibbs held his head at an angle straining against the rope, gasping for breath.

Brock considered going to help him, but decided against it. Surely Colt and the Indian were waiting, just waiting for him to make that attempt. He wanted to help Gibbs. The man had been his partner for many years and they had been through a lot together, but Brock was sure it was a trap. His head hurt, he could feel the pounding of blood in his temple and his thoughts raced. While Brock watched, George stopped kicking.

Brock abandoned Gibbs and continued climbing through the rocks of the pass, hoping to find the horses. While the sun continued beating down he kept moving. Finally, thirsty and half-crazy with fear, he saw his horse. It was eating grass under a tree, only thirty paces from where he stood. The horse wasn't tied. It must have wandered there. Brock looked all around and saw no sign of Colt or the Indian. He grinned nervously; it looked like he had outsmarted them and was going to make it. Brock thought about calling out to the horse, but decided that was too risky. It was better not to make any sound, run to the horse and ride hellbent. Looking all around once more, he made a dash for the horse, running as fast as he could.

He was almost there when he heard a swoosh of air and a thud. Pain tore through his left leg and he fell to the ground. Seeing the Indian he aimed his gun and fired, but the Indian had moved behind a rock just in time. As Brock sat on the ground he fired again and again, his mind in a state of panic. Getting painfully to his feet, he took another step toward the horse. Again he heard the swoosh of air; an arrow hit his other leg and he fell cringing in pain. He fired another shot, but the Indian had disappeared behind another rock. Brock checked quickly and saw that he was down to two bullets in his gun.

"He's tryin to get me to shoot all of 'em. I'll fool him," Brock said nervously to himself as he set to loading his gun with the shells in his gun belt.

Sweat rolled from his forehead and blurred his eyes. His hands shook with fear and he dropped several bullets as he was trying to load his revolver. Finally, just as he put in the final bullet, there was another swoosh of air and an arrow pierced his right arm. His gun fell from his hand and in desperation he got up and tried to walk the last several steps to his horse. When he was nearly close enough to grab the reins, a rock hit the horse and it ran off.

425

Brock stood there, barely able to move. Turning around, he saw the Indian walking toward him carrying a rifle. The outlaw leader now knew he would die; he began to fear the type of death that awaited him. The revolver he dropped earlier was six feet in front of him on the ground. His mind told him he should make a leap for the gun; at least that way the Indian would have to shoot him, and he could die a quick death. But he stood there, afraid to move. "Go for the gun, you dumb sonofabitch," he cursed himself silently. But he didn't move, unable to force death upon himself. The Indian walked up slowly and picked up the gun. Brock looked helpless, arrows protruding out of one arm and both legs.

Mescal looked at Brock. This was the proud leader of an outlaw gang, a man who had mercilessly killed many and ordered others to kill more. He pretended to be strong, but when his life was at risk he was a coward. The outlaw was trembling, afraid, and unable to move. Mescal did not feel sorry for him. If he let Brock live, the outlaw leader would kill others. The old Indian knew what must be done; this man must die. Mescal tied Brock's hands and then retrieved his horse. He put the outlaw on the horse, draping him over the saddle, and tied his arms to his legs underneath the animal. Mescal got on Gibbs' horse, and led Brock away from Butcher's Pass.

Tom was still making his way through the rough canyons. He pushed the horses harder, trying to get back to the main trail before nightfall, and hoping Mescal would be waiting for him. Suddenly, he heard a sound from behind like a rock had fallen. Riding up to the next high point, he dismounted and climbed quickly to the ridge and looked back. He could see several men on horseback that appeared to be following him. Tom didn't take time to count, but could tell there were at least half a dozen. They were probably the men whose tracks he had seen earlier. He went quickly back, climbed on Diamond, grabbed the reins of the packhorse and got back on the trail. He hurried, but tried to do so without making much noise. Tom didn't want the men to hear him. It was possible they were just going in the same direction and not following him. If they were following him, he didn't want them to know he had seen them.

The sun was low on the horizon when Tom got back to the main trail and discovered Mescal was not there. He decided to head toward Butcher's Pass. Tom rode at a brisk pace, reaching the pass just before nightfall. If the riders were following him, he thought it doubtful they would try to take him at night. He found the three men hanging from the tree. It was not difficult to decipher what had happened. Tom thought about burying them, but had to go up into the rocks to watch for the riders.

Mescal rode out into the desert leading Brock's horse. When he got to the middle there was nothing but sand and cactus. Far away from any known trails, he got the outlaw leader off his horse.

"You can't leave me here. You just can't," Brock said almost in a whimper. His mouth and throat were dry.

"Do you remember old Indian you shot, left for dead in desert, Arizona, years ago?" The outlaw had a puzzled look on his face. Mescal continued, "Gibbs wanted shoot him; you said 'no, let him suffer.' Do you remember that Indian?"

Brock looked at Mescal and for the first time realized he was that old Indian in the desert. "Damn the luck," he said out loud. He realized he was doomed to a similar fate. "Should have let Gibbs shoot you, you filthy red bastard."

After climbing on his mount, Mescal looked at him and shook his head. As the outlaw leader sat pitifully in the sand, the old Indian rode away leading Brock's horse.

THIRTY-TWO

It was growing dark as Tom sat hidden in the rocks. He could see seven men in the distance riding toward the pass. While still a mile away they pulled off the road, apparently to make camp. Tom considered trying to sneak away in the night, but knew that if he were caught out in the open he wouldn't have a chance. It was possible these men weren't following him, though he suspected they were. Figuring his best bet was to stay put, he hoped Mescal would return in time.

Realizing they might try to sneak in during the night Tom decided to make a false camp, much like Mescal did at Caisson's hideout. First he made a campfire near the tree where the three men were hanging. He cut one of them down and sat him against a rock. Laying the other two on bedrolls, he placed hats on all of their heads as though they were asleep. Before leaving, he took two cans with string and set alarms so he would hear the noise if anyone came close during the night. After adding more wood to the campfire, making it look like the "camp" was all settled in for the night, he slipped up into the rocks and went to sleep.

In the morning Tom was up before sunrise. Finding a place amongst large boulders, he buried the bags of gold. He then put three small rocks over them, with a fourth larger rock sitting on the three.

Tom didn't want the gold to fall into the hands of these men, and hoped Mescal would be able to find it.

An hour after sunrise he saw the riders approaching at a leisurely pace. There were now ten of them. He began hoping they were not following him and would ride on through. When they got to the edge of the pass they rode quickly to the side, got off their horses and took cover. Tom was outnumbered and knew his chances for survival were not good in such a one-sided fight.

Getting on Diamond, Tom led the packhorse and retreated back to the side of a tall stone canyon wall. There was a steep incline leading up to several large boulders by the wall he could use as cover. He had noticed it earlier and thought it was the perfect little fort for someone fighting against greater odds. The attackers couldn't encircle him because of the high canyon wall behind him. The wall went straight up fifty feet, where an overhang jutted out, and then went back up at an angle. Even if the men got on the rim above, they couldn't shoot at him from there because of the overhang. The attackers could make Tom's life miserable from the half circle in front, but the last thirty yards would be treacherous for them. It was an uphill slope to where he had cover from rocks, and they would be out in the open.

Tom placed in front of him both the weapon Jake had given him and the Winchester. Next to the rifles he laid the three revolvers and gunbelts from the hanged men. There was plenty of extra ammunition on the packhorse; he wouldn't run out anytime soon. Tom readied the long distance weapon, hoping to hit several men while they were still distant. The present from Jake gave him the initial advantage and a chance to cut down the numbers.

The riders started moving forward, going from rock to rock. Tom took several shots, but missed because the men were far away and moving. He finally tried anticipating their path and shooting in front of them. One man was hit hard in the chest, fell backward and did not move. That was followed by several minutes of rifle fire directed at Tom. Most of the bullets missed badly, but a few struck the rock he was behind. He tried many more shots over the next few hours, but failed to hit any more of the men with the long distance weapon. It slowed their progress, as they were concerned about the rifle's capability.

It was now mid-morning and Tom was out of cartridges for the long distance weapon. It was just as well because the men had moved within normal rifle range. Taking aim with the Winchester, he tried downing one of them with it. Tom knew he had to be more careful now because their weapons were just as effective. After several attempts, he managed to shoot another attacker as he rushed forward. The remaining men began sending more lead his way and moving forward more cautiously. Tom took a shot now and then to remind them of the danger and to slow their progress. Each shot he fired was done quickly and from a different place behind the rocks. He knew from past experience if a man comes up in the same spot, someone could target that particular place and wait for the man's head to appear.

Another stressful hour passed as the men moved in little-by-little. They had finally closed to within fifty yards. Suddenly, bullets were hitting the rocks all around Tom. He looked out to see several men rushing forward. Tom took a quick shot with the rifle but missed. He heard a bullet go right past his ear. Half a minute later a hail of bullets was again unleashed while men hurried to the boulders below. Now all of the men were in the rocks only thirty yards away.

There was no cover for the attackers in the remaining distance. Tom thought it was clear what tactic they would use. All would charge at the same time with guns blazing. The advantage they had in numbers almost assured he would be hit when he tried to return fire. He might get a few, but with so many they were sure to get him.

Tom looked up to see the sun getting higher overhead. He had managed to hold them off until almost noon, but Mescal was nowhere to be seen. Hopefully he hadn't been killed, and would be able to find the gold hidden under the four rocks. Setting the Winchester aside, Tom made sure the revolvers were fully loaded. It was only a matter of time until they charged. He decided to wait until they were halfway before he shot back. Planning to step out just far enough to fan his gun, he hoped to still be alive to draw and fire the second revolver. Firing only one gun at a time would require less of his body to be exposed as a target. Most of his body would be protected by the rock. Because of his proficiency with fanning the weapon, he thought he could hit several before he was killed.

It was hot and Tom was perspiring heavily. He wasn't sure whether it was the heat or the imminent battle. All at once the men started yelling and came out of the rocks firing. Their sheer numbers and firepower had bullets ricocheting everywhere near Tom. A quick peek revealed they would be halfway within a few seconds. Tom readied himself to take a half step to the right and take as many with him as he could. Suddenly, the sound of a different gun could be heard.

Tom peered around the boulder to see bullets striking the ground in front of the men. One of them threw up his hands and fell dead. Tom glanced up, but couldn't see the top of the ridge because he was so close to the wall. He looked around the boulder again and saw that the attackers had stopped charging forward. They were shooting at the top of the ridge. The rifle fire from above stopped just as suddenly as it had started. Realizing what that meant Tom stepped halfway from behind the rock and fanned the first revolver quickly, then ducked back behind the rock. Almost as soon as he stopped, the rifle opened up on them again from above. Tom waited a few seconds then stepped out and emptied the second revolver, fanning the weapon rapidly, pointing at anything standing. Moments later all the shooting stopped.

It had taken the gang of ten men four hours to move close enough to make their charge, and they had lost only two men during that lengthy time. After they started up the slope and the rifle opened up on them, followed by the rapid fire from Tom's revolvers, it was all over in a matter of seconds. The outlaws were lying on the ground. Tom walked cautiously away from the wall, realizing one of the men could still be alive. He checked them all; they were dead.

Only then did he turn and look up to see Mescal standing with a rifle, keeping an eye on the outlaws below. Tom took his right hand and touched the tip of his hat with the gun barrel as a form of salute. Mescal raised the rifle high in the air with one arm.

It took Mescal a while to join him. He had a long walk back to his horse, and then had to ride nearly a mile around to get back to the pass.

"You thought it time to die?" asked the old Indian.

"I'd have to say it got a bit worrisome. That was pretty good timing on your part."

"Been there long time. Wait for men to come out of rocks. They were many. In rocks, hard to shoot. When rush, easy targets."

"It was smart to wait."

After retrieving their horses, they loaded the bodies and took them where the four rustlers had been buried several months ago. They dug shallow graves for the ten men who attacked Tom, and the three that had been hanging in the tree. The task took several hours. The old tombstone that had read "Hung Rustlers" was nowhere to be found. Tom took the packhorse over to the four rocks and dug up the gold.

Before going to the ranch, they went to the "Fortress in the Sky." Mescal wanted to bury four of the bags there for Yellow Flower. He explained that she would need it after he was gone. Tom helped him. Mescal deserved a lot more gold than that, and it was easy to understand his concern because he was much older than his young niece. The old Indian buried it next to the canyon wall in the clearing behind the split in the rock. On the canyon wall, right at ground level, Mescal used his knife to scratch the symbol of the sun the size of a silver dollar. Regardless how much time passed, Yellow Flower would be able to find the gold. The old Indian then piled several small rocks in front of the symbol so it couldn't be seen easily.

Mescal removed their tracks before they left. Tom couldn't help but notice the smile on the old Indian's face, knowing he had taken care of his niece's future. Mescal was indeed pleased about that, but he was also smiling because he had been able to set aside more of the gold. He knew Tom would be generous, as would Melinda. Mescal didn't want Tom to have as much to give away. It wasn't that Mescal was greedy, he just didn't feel as much kinship to the White Man as Tom and Melinda.

By the time they arrived at the ranch it was dark and they rode straight to the barn. There was no one inside so they closed the door, lit a lantern and hid the gold in the corner of the feed room. The old Indian thought about Bert Cooper's gold, that he and Emmett had buried when Tom first arrived at the ranch. It was only ten feet away under a barrel. Neither Mescal nor Emmett had told him about it. Emmett wanted to save it as a wedding present for Tom and Melinda.

Mescal began unsaddling the many horses of the rustlers and putting them in the corral. Meanwhile, Tom went to the ranch house and tapped lightly on Melinda's window. She and Yellow Flower woke up startled, but soon saw that it was Tom. They slipped outside and went to the cabin. The women began preparing something to eat while Tom went to help Mescal finish with the horses.

The men washed up and then ate. They talked about Indian Waters and the trip in general, but said nothing about what they had found or the men they had met on the way back. Tom and Mescal had decided not to mention the outlaws until much later so as not to spoil the evening. Melinda was anxious to hear how much gold there was, but so far neither man had said anything about it. She could tell they had found something because they were both in good spirits.

"Well, I reckon it's about time to go to sleep," Tom said yawning.

"Me tired," the old Indian added and walked toward his bed.

As Tom got up, Melinda stepped in front of him, put her hands on his chest and looked him straight in the eyes. "Okay, now it's time you told me."

Yellow Flower had no idea what this was about. She could tell the men were acting a little unusual and were very happy about something, but had thought they were just glad to be home. "Is there something I don't know?"

Tom and Mescal laughed. "You girls stay here; we'll be right back," Tom said.

Melinda decided to wait and not tell Yellow Flower just yet. The Indian girl was patient, asking with her eyes but not saying a word. In a few minutes the men came back. Each was carrying a saddlebag. They both smiled as they pulled out a total of eight leather bags. Yellow Flower's eyes sparkled when Mescal opened one of the bags revealing the contents. Her uncle reveled in her amazement.

"Come on, you old Indian," Tom said as he headed for the door. Looking back at the girls he added, "Be right back."

"There's more?" Melinda's heart leaped. While the men were gone, she revealed to Yellow Flower the story of Caisson telling them about the gold in his dying breath, and how they had wanted to be sure there really was some before they told her. Soon Tom and

Mescal came back and pulled eight more bags of gold out of the saddlebags. Melinda was ecstatic.

"Surely with all this gold we can buy our ranch and build our house," Melinda said hopefully.

"We sure can," Tom replied. Melinda gave him a long hug, then hugged Mescal and finally Yellow Flower. Suddenly, Tom and Mescal turned and headed for the door again.

"There's still more?" Melinda nearly yelled.

Tom put his finger to his lips and out the door they went. While they were gone, Melinda told Yellow Flower they planned to build a big house so she and Mescal could live with them, and then she showed her the drawing she had made. They were still looking at it and were in a joyous state when the men returned the third time. They brought in eight more bags and put them on the table.

"This is all of it; you women will just have to be happy with what it will buy," Tom said.

The two girls grabbed each other's hands and danced around the room. After they finished their celebration, including a drink of whiskey by each, they pried up a few floorboards and hid the gold underneath the floor toward the middle of the cabin. They put the boards back down and laid a rug over the area. Tom told Melinda he thought they should share some of it with the ranchers who had lost cattle to Caisson; after all, he reasoned, some of it was really their money. Melinda readily agreed, but asked if there would be enough for their ranch and cabin. Tom assured her there was plenty. All four of them talked a great deal that night and it was late when they finally went to sleep.

The next morning Tom told Emmett about the gold, but not how much. He used the story that he and Mescal had decided on the night before. Mescal had first realized the need to alter the truth. Since Tom didn't want to tell anyone about Caisson dying, they needed a story to explain how they found the gold. Mescal suggested telling them that he had noticed some suspicious tracks earlier when they had waited on Caisson, and they had gone back to check it out.

Tom agreed they would believe it because Mescal was such a good tracker. After explaining to Emmett that there had been a lot of footprints around a particular rock, he described how they used the limb to move the peanut-shaped stone. Tom didn't say a word about the cave. For some reason Mescal hadn't wanted that part revealed.

"We replaced the stone and covered our tracks so Caisson wouldn't have any idea who found his gold," Tom concluded.

"He spent all those years rustling, and now that he's done he doesn't have anything to show for it. Serves him right if you ask me," Emmett said.

"I agree, but that's why we have to do this kind of secretly. We don't want Caisson finding out it was us that found his gold."

"Good thinking, Tom," replied Emmett.

Emmett sent a rider over to get Jake without telling him what it was about. Late that afternoon Tom told Jake the same story he had told Emmett earlier, still not mentioning to either rancher how much gold there was. Emmett wasn't bored and listened to every detail for the second time. Tom and Mescal took them in the cabin, removed the floorboards and started retrieving the gold. The ranchers stood dumbfounded as they watched twenty-four bags being lifted out. Tom told them that he and Mescal discussed it and thought both of the ranchers should get enough to cover any losses to Caisson. Tom added he hoped there was enough that they could give some of it to the other ranchers who had lost cattle to the rustler. Finally, he told them they also wanted to give some money to the families of the men who had been killed in the shootout at Caisson's hideout.

"Tom, you sure don't need to do all that, but I reckon nobody will argue with you," Emmett said. "There's plenty enough here to do everything you mentioned and still get a ranch like you been wantin."

Jake shook hands with Tom, and then with Mescal. He finally said, "Well, damned if I ain't speechless; that's a darn fine thing to do."

The two ranchers went outside and talked for awhile. They decided that Tom and Mescal should keep eighteen bags of gold. Emmett knew of Tom and Melinda's dreams to buy a ranch and build a house. He had seen the drawings Melinda had made one day when she and Yellow Flower had gone for a ride.

"They don't need that much, but I wouldn't feel right giving them any less," Emmett said.

"Six bags will cover everything else," Jake agreed.

Emmett told Jake about Tom's concern of keeping the gold a secret so Caisson wouldn't find out and come back for revenge. Jake suggested that they take the gold to other towns over the course of a year, cashing in no more than one bag at a time. He could take part of them and Emmett the rest. They would wait at least half a year to start giving some of it to the other ranchers, explaining that some of their cattle had been found and this money had been sent for them.

"We can work the rest of the details out later, but I'd be willin to bet Sheriff Hodges will work with us if we give him a small fee," Jake said. "That'll make it seem all legal like and he would agree not to say where the money really came from."

"Hard to believe, isn't it?" Emmett asked as they walked to Jake's horse.

"It sure is. How'd you find a man like that?"

"Don't want to forget Mescal; he's part of this too," added Emmett.

"Right you are, the Gunman and the Tracker."

"I reckon we have Melinda to thank; she saved both their lives."

Jake stepped up on his horse and rode away, still shaking his head. Emmett looked up at the sky, almost as much in disbelief as his old friend. Emmett went inside and gave them the news of eighteen bags for their own purposes, and then he went toward the house so they could celebrate. When he got to the porch, Emmett looked back at Tom and Mescal's cabin and said out loud, "Guess we're gonna have some good years round this here part of Utah."

All four in the cabin were delighted with the news of eighteen bags of gold. That night Melinda, Tom and Mescal studied the maps of the canyons and each came up with a different spot for the house. They joyously argued for the one they selected. Yellow Flower hadn't seen enough of the canyons to have a favorite place. Finally they decided to ride together to each of the locations and try to decide tomorrow. Then they studied Melinda's drawing and began to add details both to the house and the other buildings they would need. As the night wore on their eyes grew tired and the whiskey made them sleepy. They all decided to get some rest so they could start their search in the morning.

One thing they all agreed on was that at noon they would picnic at Melinda's favorite spot. Mescal smiled; little would the others know when they ate tomorrow, even more gold was stored so very few feet away. He waited a few years before telling Tom there was more gold in the cave. Mescal didn't reveal how many bags there were and Tom never found out. They used a few bags later on, but much remained even after they had all left this Earth. It remains there to this day hidden in the little cave at the "Fortress in the Sky."